I0636521

Geneva's Promise

Payton Lee
Author-Publisher
For information Address:
Payton Lee Author/Publisher
14122 Hunters Grove Drive
Orlando FL 32828
www.paytonlee.com

Contact Payton Lee at
Email: pyoung8@cfl.rr.com

Ebook authorized for free download only by Payton Lee.

ISBN: 978-0-6151-8160-8

Geneva's Promise

'Way out in the land of the setting sun,
Where the wind blows wild and free,
There's a lovely spot, just the only one
That means home sweet home to me.

If you follow the old Kit Carson trail,
Until desert meets the hills,
Oh you certainly will agree with me,
It's the place of a thousand thrills.

Chorus
Home, means Nevada, Home, means the hills,
Home, means the sage and the pines.
Out by the Truckee's silvery rills,
Out where the sun always shines,
There is the land that I love the best,
Fairer than all I can see.
Right in the heart of the golden west
Home, means Nevada to me.

Whenever the sun at the close of day,
Colors all the western sky,
Oh my heart returns to the desert grey
And the mountains tow'ring high.
Where the moon beams play in shadowed glen,
With the spotted fawn and doe,
All the live long night until morning light,
Is the loveliest place I know.

Chorus
Home, means Nevada, Home, means the hills,
Home, means the sage and the pines.
Out by the Truckee's silvery rills,
Out where the sun always shines,
there is the land that I love the best,
Fairer than all I can see.
Right in the heart of the golden west
Home, means Nevada to me.

Payton Lee

Dedication

I wish to dedicate this book to you the reader. It is for you I write. Please enjoy the movies of my mind. Please take a moment and drop us a line to let me know if you enjoyed the story.

Thank you,

Payton Lee

Geneva's Promise

Chapter 1

Christmas Eve 1879
Geneva's Hope Ranch

Almost everyone in Geneva's Hope Ranch house was cocooned in their rooms and tucked away in their warm beds. The fireplaces were blazing throughout the house warming its inhabitants as the blowing storm continued an onslaught bringing a heavy snow, but a welcomed White Christmas.

One silvery shadow sauntered from her room on the second floor and into the hallway. Breena walked quietly on slipper feet down the steps. She was careful not to make any noise and disturb anyone in the West Wing. Fortunately all the oil lamps in the halls were on low flame allowing a subtle light. Breena tightened her white eyelet cotton robe at her waist with its white satin ribbon. As she passed the door to the white room of Geneva's Hope Ranch she smiled. Breena really liked Ayden's British wife, Paige. She thought about Ayden and Paige snuggling together in their bed. Breena remembered holding Jared and then Aurora Blue this morning, but just for a moment because big old bear Ryan McGillinen would give up his baby girl for only a moment at a time.

Breena walked into the kitchen from the back stair entrance. She thought she would fix herself a cup of hot chocolate and that might help her sleep.

"You can't sleep either?" a shadow sitting in the small dining room off the kitchen questioned.

Breena jumped almost a foot high with the voice. "Dwayne? Is that you?" Breena queried hesitantly. Her heart was still racing at twice its normal speed from the fright.

"Yes, Breena," Dwayne teased with a chuckle. "It is I."

"It is me," Breena corrected.

"Good grief, you're not going to start correcting my English again like you did in grade school, are you?" Dwayne grumped. He bent over his cup of hot coffee and inhaled the aroma.

"Some habits are hard to break," Breena giggled. She felt like a schoolgirl again. Her mind flashed back to ten years ago. The twelve year old kid with a big crush on the fourteen year old, Dwayne McGillinen. Oh those were tough years. Dwayne was so good looking and all the pretty girls and some older girls in class seemed to keep his attention. Little Breena, orphan and ward of Brian Duffey, scraggly and plain looking, didn't have a chance to capture the handsome Dwayne McGillinen's attention.

"You just used that to get my attention," Dwayne laughed. "Is that what you're trying to do?"

"No, I'm not!" Breena stated indignantly. In truth it was an old habit. Lord, she still had that childhood crush. Breena bit her lower lip.

"Then why are you biting your lower lip?" Dwayne teased. "When you don't tell the truth you bite your lower lip."

"I do not!" Breena shouted defensively.

"Lord, I love it when you get rattled," Dwayne laughed heartily. "Do you want a cup of coffee?"

Breena grabbed at the opportunity to change the subject. Being around Dwayne always unnerved her, but he was like an addiction. It would be an addiction she would break. Her mind was made up and she would tell her Uncle Brian tomorrow. "Actually I came downstairs to get some hot chocolate."

"That sounds great," Dwayne stated. "Would you mind making enough for me?"

"Why didn't you make some instead of coffee?" Breena chortled. She walked to the cupboard that Aumond kept the chocolate powder.

"Coffee is a man's drink. Chocolate is a drink women make," Dwayne teased knowing exactly what kind of result he would get from Breena. He loved teasing her and did love teasing her since he first met her when she came to live in Ely with her Uncle Brian after her parents died. There was something special between them. Neither knew what it was, but there definitely was something special between them.

"Is that a fact?" Breena bristled. "If hot chocolate is a woman's drink why on earth do you want some, Dwayne McGillinen?"

"I said it was a woman's drink to make," Dwayne corrected cheekily.

"Dwayne that is a very sexist remark!" Breena exclaimed angrily. "Nevada recognizes the importance of women. Why can't you?"

"Oh but I find women very important," Dwayne contradicted. "Very important indeed." He rose from his chair and walked toward Breena.

She held her breath. Would he kiss her? He kissed her several times before. Once when he was sixteen and he found her trying to catch fish in the pond. He showed her how to cast the baited line. While he was showing her to cast she turned to look up into those dreamy gray eyes. Their lips were so close. Dwayne bent down to kiss her. *Oh that first kiss!* Breena remembered her knees shaking. She couldn't and didn't want to breathe.

"Are you sleeping?" Dwayne's voice interjected into her thoughts.

Dwayne had walked past her to the cold box and pulled out a tin of milk. He now stood next to Breena and handed her the milk.

Reality broke into Breena's daydream like a hard slap across the face. What was she thinking? She was a grown woman about to start her own life. That crush on Dwayne was for a child. She wasn't a child anymore. With defensive sarcasm Breena answered, "No, I'm not sleeping. I can't sleep. That's the reason I came down for some hot chocolate you dolt!" Breena poured the milk into a saucepan she placed on the stove. Aumond always kept a low fire in the black iron stove at night. "Just what did you mean by that remark about your finding women very important?"

A wicked smile crossed over Dwayne's lips. Breena was so beautiful and so much fun when he tweaked her nose. "Aw gee Breena, a man needs that warm body at night to cuddle up to. After a hard day working a man needs to come home to a fine meal and roll in the hay," Dwayne snickered. "We just saw this morning what fine babies a woman makes for a man. And a man has a lot of fun making those babies."

Breena reacted with the passion Dwayne expected. She had just washed her hands and threw the wet cloth at Dwayne with force. "You bigot!" Breena screamed.

"Shhh," Dwayne laughed holding his finger over his lips. "You'll wake the babies!"

Breena realized she was loud and blushed crimson.

"Lord Breena," Dwayne continued laughing, "you are so easy to rile."

"Why do you do this?" Breena breathed out in exasperation while adding the chocolate powder to the warming milk.

"Probably because you're so beautiful when you get upset," Dwayne replied seriously. "Your eyes just light up and sparkle when you get angry."

Breena's mouth dropped. *Did he say beautiful?* "You think I'm beautiful?"

"Only when you get angry," Dwayne teased once more. He grabbed the spoon from her hand and started stirring the warming chocolate milk. Suddenly he was nervous. How could he explain how he felt when he and Breena were together? He was different around Breena. She was the brain of the class during their Ely school years. She was the real smart one. The other girls made him feel superior. They pawed at him, cooed for him, and told him how wonderful and handsome he was. Breena challenged his mind consistently. She made him feel inferior or humbled him at best. He had to concentrate on his spoken language or Breena would catch his error and correct him. If Dwayne made a statement about history or current events, Breena would always be correcting him or adding more fact than he ever imagined. All through school Breena made him feel inadequate, but he countered by remarking with barbs he knew would get Breena's goat, or so to speak.

"I sometimes wondered if you said all those obscure remarks to purposely make me angry," Breena giggled. "I don't recall anyone but you able to get under my skin."

"I'm special that way," Dwayne responded shooting Breena a broad white-toothed smile.

Breena bent her head to concentrate on pouring the hot chocolate into the cups she had taken from the cupboard. "You are special, Dwayne," Breena whispered.

"What was that?" Dwayne asked looking up. He had just sat down at the table. He wanted Breena to serve him the hot chocolate. He didn't even understand why he did the things he did. He only knew Breena's admiration was important to him. Life would be easier if Breena were like the other girls that cow toed to his every whim. Fact is, Breena didn't, and he felt like he always had to work hard to get her attention.

Breena sat down next to him with her cup of hot chocolate.

"Where's mine?" Dwayne questioned.

"On the work counter," Breena grinned mischievously. She wasn't about to serve any man hand and foot. Nope, not Breena! She wouldn't do that even if it were Dwayne McGillinen expecting it.

"If you ain't the most cantankerous stubborn woman I know," Dwayne grumbled rising once more from the table to retrieve his hot chocolate. He knew arguing with Breena was an exercise in futility.

"If you aren't the most cantankerous stubborn woman I know," Breena corrected automatically. Old habits were indeed hard to break.

"Excuse me?" Dwayne grouched returning to the table with his hot chocolate.

"There is no such word as ain't. The correct English is the contraction aren't or the two words are not," Breena said without thinking and sipping her chocolate.

"Do you think it would be possible in our lifetimes to have one conversation without correcting me?" Dwayne grumbled taking his seat at the table.

"Can we have a conversation once in our lifetime without you teasing me. Without you trying to rile me?" Breena returned.

"Do you always have to answer a question with a question?" Dwayne grumped.

"Do you?" Breena shot back.

Dwayne rolled his eyes and leaned back against the chair. He raised his arms up and placed his hands behind his head. "You make real good chocolate."

Breena looked at Dwayne and was about to correct his English once more when she realized his shirt was unbuttoned and she stared into his broad expanse of muscular chest. A hard lump formed in her throat. Dwayne McGillinen had the body of a Greek God. Or at least his body looked like the pictures she had seen of the marbled statues. Instead of correcting his grammar Breena queried, "Why aren't you sleeping Dwayne?"

Dwayne stopped leaning on the chair and put his forearms on the table. Dwayne cupped the mug of chocolate with his hands. "I guess I'm excited over the birth of Jared and Aurora Blue. I can't seem to stop thinking about them. What a wonderful creation from love."

"Aurora Blue is beautiful. I still can't get over how much little Jared looks like Ryan," Breena agreed softly.

"Yeah, Braden is going to have fun with that little one," Dwayne mused thoughtfully.

"Little Garrett looks just like Bennett," Breena added. "It's amazing how blood lines show through."

"More of the McGillinen blood line I hope," Dwayne responded with a chuckle.

"The McGillinen's are a pretty tough bloodline," Breena giggled. "I can't believe all the changes here since I went off to school."

"Well you've changed sort of," Dwayne clucked wickedly. "You've filled out real well. You've become a fine little filly."

"Does everything equate to horseflesh with you?" Breena questioned sarcastically. "What I meant is, when I left there were three bachelor McGillinen brothers and a sister. I would have never believed to come back and find Kerry married to a British Lord. Kerry is a mother of two babies and a young boy in just two short years. Your brother Ryan, the real bachelor of the family gets married and is madly in love with his wife and new baby girl. Then the intelligent brother finds a British heiress and they are expecting. To top off the cake, my uncle marries your aunt."

"What do you mean intelligent brother?" Dwayne groused picking up on only the one statement. "Just where do you classify me?"

"You're the irritating Casanova," Breena chuckled.

Dwayne's eyebrow arched. "Irritating? Me irritating? What the Hell is Casanova?"

"Shhh, you'll wake the babies," Breena whispered repeating Dwayne's very same words.

Dwayne sat back and repeated softly, "Sorry! What the Hell do you mean irritating and what is Casanova?"

"Casanova was a world famous lover of the last century. Don't you know anything?" Breena teased.

"And you call me irritating? Isn't that the pot calling the kettle black?" Dwayne growled. "I'm no great lover."

"That's not what Lisa, Deborah, Suzanne, or Lilly think," Breena oozed out. Again she simply was not thinking. It was hard to think correctly with Dwayne about. Especially when she couldn't take her eyes off of his expansive chest.

"Jealous are you?" Dwayne queried. His eyes twinkled with delight. Now he had the aloof and aristocratic Breena Hodges painted into a corner.

Dwayne caught her by surprise. How right could a man be? What could she say? The truth of the matter is she was jealous. She did the only thing a woman would do and she hated herself for it. She lied, "I am not! I merely stated what everyone thinks about you."

"Oh yeah? Just exactly who is everyone?" Dwayne countered immediately. He leaned closer to stare at Breena. "Besides, you're lying again."

"I am not!"

"Yes you are!" Dwayne chuckled. "You're biting your lower lip. You always bite your lower lip when you lie."

Breena put down her mug and put her hands on her hips, "Just how did you figure that out, Mr. Dwayne McGillinen?"

"When we were little and we got caught sneaking into Auntie Alyson's kitchen to get a piece of fresh baked cookie. You didn't want me to get in trouble so you told Auntie Alyson you had asked me to get you a cookie. That was a lie. I had talked you into coming in with me to get them. When you were telling Auntie Alyson your story you kept biting your lower lip. Ever since then I've noticed that when you aren't telling the truth. You bite your lower lip."

"Well that's something I'll have to be more careful about," Breena replied testily.

"You can try, but you can't help it," Ryan laughed.

"Oh and you think you are all so perfect do you?" Breena chirped. "Well Mr. Wonderful, your eyebrow twitches when you lie!"

"It does not," Dwayne squeaked touching his brow.

Breena cracked open a huge smile, "No it doesn't, but I got you good! Didn't I?"

"Breena, you are a woman and a half," Dwayne laughed.

"Does that mean you think I'm fat, or does that mean you finally think of me as a woman?" Breena queried.

"For the first time in my life I have finally heard you ask a stupid question," Dwayne needled.

Immediately Breena's hackles went up. "What do you mean stupid question?"

"That is a stupid question," Dwayne replied seriously. "You don't think for one minute you are fat and even if you were, do you think any male in his right mind would tell you that? So obviously there is no need for that question. You are a full grown tantalizing woman!"

"I must be losing brain power because I'm in your company," Breena quipped. She was suddenly in a wonderful mood to discover not only did Dwayne consider her a woman, but a tantalizing woman.

"And you tell me I'm the irritating one," Dwayne snapped angrily. Why did Breena upset him so much? She was the only woman who ever got under his skin. She was the only woman whose opinions mattered to him other than his aunties and Morning Song. Boy, was Breena suddenly a woman. He couldn't help but focus on those luscious globes of femininity. Their form was perfect under that lacy eyelet cotton robe. He felt his body begin to warm.

Breena sipped her chocolate. "I'm sorry Dwayne. That was completely uncalled for. This is Christmas Eve. It is a time for sharing love. I feel so fortunate I was able to be here with your family to share in the births of Jared and Aurora Blue. I don't want to appear ungrateful."

"You are ungrateful. You little brat," Dwayne chuckled. "This is your family too! You became part of the family when your Uncle Brian married my Auntie Alyson."

"Does that make us second cousins?" Breena quizzed playfully.

"Probably, but I prefer kissing cousins," Dwayne replied huskily. "Do you remember our first kiss?"

Breena blushed crimson. She had been thinking about it only a few minutes ago. "Yes I do. You were sixteen and I was fourteen. You were teaching me to cast my fish line."

"It was nice wasn't it?" Dwayne said in memory. "You always were a quick learner." Dwayne was starting to get warmer. His mind couldn't seem to stop thinking about taking Breena into his bed. He had to change the subject. "So what do you think about all my family getting married and having babies?" Oops that was the wrong thing to say. He started thinking about making babies himself. He wondered what his and Breena's baby would look like.

Breena felt herself starting to warm. She began thinking about marriage and babies and making babies. What she had read about procreation, those naughty little books she really wasn't supposed to read, seemed very interesting. "I adore Kerry's Braden. He seems so different from what I thought a British Lord would be like. Who wouldn't love Bennett, Garrett, and now Jared? I don't think I was ever going to stop laughing when I saw Ayden holding up the Christmas tree while Braden rescued his sticky little Garrett. Was he a mess?"

"That was so funny. I still laugh thinking about it," Dwayne chuckled. "When Kerry came in scolding Braden for scaring Little Twenty Hands and he handed Garrett to her...."

"Kerry's face was priceless!" Breena laughed with Dwayne. "Paige and Morning Song really gave Garrett his perfect name. Little Twenty Hands!"

"Yeah, and who would believe that big old burly Ryan would turn into one great big mush?" Dwayne added thoughtfully. "I still can't get over how much he loves Twiggy."

"It is amazing to see big Ryan hold his tiny little girl," Breena said thoughtfully. "I would never have believed that big tough burly man could be so gentle."

"Little Aurora Blue surely is pretty ain't she?" Dwayne caught himself quickly, "I mean isn't she?"

"Yes," Breena agreed. "Tell me Dwayne, what do you think of Ayden's wife Paige?"

"Now there is one very beautiful woman," Dwayne sighed. "Who would believe that dish would fall for someone like Ayden? All brains and few looks."

"Ayden is a very handsome man," Breena grouched. Dwayne had touched a raw nerve. She was simple. She wasn't beautiful by any means, but she had a large crush on the handsome Dwayne McGillinen. "Besides, why wouldn't someone who is beautiful fall in love with someone that is smart. And Paige is very smart even being beautiful. She invented the child corral, and the cat carrier, and she designed the walker for little twenty hands. I've talked with Paige. She is very smart. We had a lot of interesting conversations. Do you know Paige is helping Ayden build aqueducts to irrigate farmland on his estate? Did you know she is cataloging all of the priceless heirlooms of the Stuart Estates? Paige had been to see the Acropolis, the Vatican, and the Kremlin. She has visited Stonehenge. Paige has been just about everywhere and knows so much. Paige admires Ayden's intelligence...."

"Whoa!!!!!" Dwayne protested lifting his hands palms out. "I'm sorry I said it! I love Paige's intelligence. I'm glad my brother found an equal."

"Superior!"

"Fine, superior then," Dwayne conceded quickly.

They were both silent for a few minutes.

Breena was furious with herself. Why did she always make a fool out of herself when she was around Dwayne? When Breena was around everyone else she was generally shy, reserved, and in control of her emotions. She could never maintain that decorum when she was near Dwayne.

Dwayne sat sulking as well. It seemed he always put his foot in his mouth when he was around Breena. He either got tongue tied or always managed to say the wrong thing and even though he didn't understand why, it was important to him to impress Breena.

They finished their chocolate drinks in silence.

"I suppose we'd better go to bed," Breena volunteered breaking the silence. "I'll just wash these cups and pan." Breena rose from the table taking the cups and walking to the sink with the pump.

Dwayne picked up the pan and brought it to the sink. He primed the pump and began pumping until the water flowed. "The water is pretty cold. I'll wash and you dry."

Breena nodded her head and took the flannel towel to dry the first mug after Dwayne had washed it. "It really has been a terrific day hasn't it?"

"Yeah it really has," Dwayne agreed.

"The birth of your nephew and niece was truly a wonderful Christmas gift," Breena said in conversation.

"The best," Dwayne replied. He couldn't help his mouth blurting out for no known reason, "Do you ever think about having babies?"

Breena almost dropped the second cup. She gathered her wits and replied as stoically as possible, "Yes, I've thought about having babies. I just don't think that will ever happen for me."

"Why not?" Dwayne questioned. He stopped scrubbing the pan to look at Breena.

"I'm not exactly the marrying kind you know," Breena said ruefully. "You know I'm stubborn, leaning toward suffragette attitudes, and Heaven knows a man doesn't like a woman smarter than he is. Besides I'm really not pretty enough to get married."

"You're real pretty Breena," Dwayne contradicted offering her a big smile. "Didn't you just tell me that Paige is smarter than Ayden? I guess that means some men like their women smart."

"You really think I'm pretty?" Breena gulped.

"Yeah, real pretty and real smart," Dwayne answered. His eyes' focused on her breasts again and he felt that warming overcome him again. He quickly turned back to the pot and cleaning it.

Breena felt herself warm up inside again. She thought she had better change the subject before she said something stupid once more. "It's almost Christmas. Tell me Dwayne what is there to give a McGillinen for Christmas? You and your family seem to have everything including anything money can buy?"

"You thinking about giving me a Christmas present?" Dwayne teased. "It would be a little difficult to go shopping."

"Stop it!" Breena giggled hitting Dwayne with they damp flannel cloth. "What would anyone be able to give you for Christmas anyway?"

Dwayne handed the pan to Breena. "There is something I really want for Christmas."

Breena dried the pan and put it on the stovetop. "What is that?"

"I want you for Christmas," Dwayne said quickly before he lost his courage to say it. He pulled Breena into his arms and planted a long deep kiss on Breena's lips. Dwayne's one hand found the crook of Breena's back and pushed her into his muscular frame. His other hand slid into the white eyelet robe past the silky nightdress to grasp the soft breast. His allowed his thumb to play with Breena's hardened teat while kissing her passionately.

Breena turned into jelly. If there were any logical or reasoning thoughts in her head they were quickly lost. Breena's body warmed, swirled, tingled, and filled with strange urging animal sensations. Dwayne's powerful embrace pushed her deeper into his form. She felt a hardness pushing on her belly that she realized was Dwayne's manhood. Breena's heart began racing. Her body wanted to feel his. Breena had forgotten about Dwayne's open shirt until her hands searched and found that strong muscular chest. Delicately Breena touched his warm flesh wanting him. Inhaling him.

"Oh my God," Dwayne uttered in agony. "Breena, I want you. I need you."

"Merry Christmas!" Breena replied breathlessly.

Chapter 2

Dwayne scooped Breena up into his arms. He carried her out of the kitchen and into the hall. He didn't release her lips but continued his onslaught. Taking Breena is something he had wanted to do since he first kissed her eight years ago. He hadn't stopped thinking about her since she left for college in the east. He had wanted to see her when he heard she came back, but with everything that happened to Kerry and then Ryan courting Twiggy. He just never seemed to get the time to visit Breena in Ely.

Breena draped her arm over Dwayne's powerful shoulder. She continued tongue delving and dueling with Dwayne's tongue as he mounted the steps. Breena felt Dwayne take the steps two at a time. They both felt an unspoken urgency. Breena knew if either of them thought about what was about to happen they would change their minds.

Personally this had been Breena's hope and desire. She always wanted Dwayne to want her in the way of a woman and now her dream was coming true. Breena was as wrapped up in the moment as Dwayne. Her breathing was becoming more and more shallow. A warmth and fire was raging inside her.

Dwayne literally ran down the hall with Breena in his arms. He took her to Ayden's room. It was separate from his and Ryan's old room. Braden had taken over Ryan's old room to allow Kerry a night of rest after delivering Jared. Dwayne could barely breathe when he opened the door to the room and still held Breena tightly. His foot shut the door once they were inside. Carefully he laid Breena upon the bed. He removed his shirt and unbuttoned his jeans still kissing Breena. Fortunately he was wearing slipper moccasins and had jettisoned them when he entered the room.

Breena felt Dwayne's naked body next to hers. She had to feel all of him. Her hands began to roam freely over every bump, hill, and dale that belonged to Dwayne's muscular being.

Dwayne groaned in agony. He was fired and ready. His hand deftly untied Breena's sash and with gentle pushes and tugs removed it sending it flying through the air overhead and gently falling to the floor. Dwayne untied the shoulder ribbons on Breena's silken nightgown. His mouth followed his hands down to treasure a soft breast. With a little more wiggling and pulling Dwayne removed Breena's nightgown. That sailed through the air to join the robe upon the floor. There was nothing between them now. His free hand explored the soft silky body he had only guessed remained hidden beneath Breena's severe Victorian clothing. Her body was everything he dreamed it would be.

Breena arched her back when Dwayne took her breast in his mouth. His hand explored her body and every touch left a branding of fire. Then his hand was between her legs probing and finding the hot wet femininity he had created. Breena felt Dwayne laid her upon her back and carefully mounted her keeping his weight on his forearms. His mouth found her mouth, earlobe, neck, and throat. Breena was nearly giddy. She felt his soft satiny tip enter her womanhood. It felt wonderful. She felt warm and tingly. Dwayne was filling her need. Slowly and methodically Dwayne teased her womanhood be entering and withdrawing rhythmically. Breena could take no more she arched her pelvis into the heat and cried out when she felt a sharp tearing pain.

"God Breena, I'm so sorry," Dwayne wailed quietly. "I'm so sorry Breena." He stopped completely disregarding the mounting need and agony he felt. Dwayne had never known a virgin before. This was his first experience with a virgin and it was his Breena. He had deflowered his Breena. He wasn't certain what to do.

The fire they both had blazing gave them the answer. Breena no longer hurt and needed fulfillment. She arched hard into Dwayne.

Dwayne felt the warmth Breena released and felt her muscles contract in spasms around his manhood. This drove him to the edge. He lost control and rammed his need home right into Breena's cone of womanhood. A quiet roar erupted from his lips and he spasmodically released his seeds into his Breena. It was then he realized he hadn't taken any precautions. He always used a Dutch rubber for protection from disease and pregnancy. He smiled. It didn't matter now. Breena was his and only his. He feared no disease. Breena was a virgin and as for a baby? Hadn't he just pictured their baby in his mind? Dwayne was euphoric. Slowly he rolled on his back keeping Breena in his arms. He couldn't stop kissing her. His lips caressed her forehead, her brows, her eyes, her nose, her lips, and her throat. "Thank you Breena. Thank you Breena."

"Merry Christmas," Breena breathed sensually. "Is it always like this?"

"It's never been like this," Dwayne responded. "It's never been this wonderful. God Breena, you're wonderful. Wonderful! Wonderful!"

Breena snuggled into Dwayne's chest. Her fingers walked delicately across his massive chest. "You really mean that? You've never felt like this."

Dwayne took Breena's wandering hand. He pressed her knuckles to his lips. "Breena, I really mean that. Thank you for my Christmas Present."

Breena felt pretty good herself. She was really comfortable in Dwayne's arm. She seemed to fit perfectly there and belong there.

They held each other tightly for several minutes. Each one was enjoying the pleasure of the other, scent, body, and satisfaction.

"Breena?"

"Hmmm?"

"Want another go?"

"Hmmm."

"Is that a yes?" Dwayne asked huskily.

"A Christmas Present is a Christmas Present," Breena responded and nuzzled Dwayne's chest.

"Lord God above. Thank you!" Dwayne exclaimed. "Let's play stallion and filly."

"What?" Breena asked furrowing her brows. "Is this everything in horseflesh terms again?"

"Yes," Dwayne breathed erratically. "Oh yes!"

"Mmmm," Breena agreed. Dwayne was already bringing her to a high fever once more.

It was nearly four o'clock Christmas morning when both Breena and Dwayne slipped off into exhausted sleep.

Dwayne woke up and stared at the sleeping Breena. "Thank you God," he breathed gratefully. "This wasn't a wonderful dream." He realized he'd better leave Breena's room before anyone came to wake her or him for that matter. He grabbed his pants and put them on quickly. He picked up his moccasins and shirt. Stealthily he left her room, but first he brushed her lips with a gentle kiss. "Thank you, Breena."

Breena rolled to her side and slept. She was dreaming and they were wonderful dreams. She was dreaming about her and Dwayne.

Dwayne bathed and changed into his comfortable jeans and flannel shirt. He wore his favorite boots. After looking at himself in the mirror several times he noted he couldn't take the smile off his face. *Damn, last night was the best ever!* Dwayne walked past Ayden's old room and chuckled, "the best ever, Breena."

Breena started to wake when she heard her door close. A smile crossed her face. She felt positively wonderful. Dwayne really loved her. All her dreams had wonderfully and marvelously come true. Breena reveled in her new feelings. Last night had been absolutely fabulous.

Breena rose from her bed and realized a bath was an absolute necessity. "Merry Christmas Dwayne," she whispered to the sun peeking through her window.

Dwayne walked into the great room of Geneva's Hope Ranch to see Braden carrying his sister into the room. Ryan carrying Twiggy and Aurora Blue followed Braden. Little Twenty Hands was lovingly placed into the child corral Paige had designed. Dwayne watched Bennett run to the Christmas tree and start tearing into packages to see which ones were his. Dwayne chuckled remembering his own young Christmas times.

Morning Song, Grady, Small Bird, Willow, Corey, and Edward were already in the parlor.

Dwayne entered with a big grin on his face.

"What are you grinning for?" Grady asked his youngest son.

"Let's just say I got a great Christmas present last night and leave it at that," Dwayne answered cheerily.

"Well glad to hear it," Grady ignored. "Why don't you fetch Alyson, Duffey, and Breena?"

"Sure Pa!" Dwayne responded too quickly.

Grady raised his brow. "What got into that one?" he asked Morning Song.

"I'm certain we do not wish to know," she replied. "Will you fetch Paige and Ayden?"

Dwayne recognized his spirit was soaring and he was amazing light on his feet. How could he explain how happy he was? Why having Breena last night would lead him to this euphoria even he didn't understand. He ran up the stairs to bring Breena downstairs for the family celebration. "Family," Dwayne whispered. "Breena you're my family." He saw Breena, Auntie Alyson, and Uncle Brian walking toward the front stairs. "Wait up!" he shouted merrily.

Breena turned immediately to his voice. A bright smile lit up her face.

"Pa sent me to fetch you," Dwayne beamed taking Breena's hand. "The McGillinen Christmas is about to begin."

"The McGillinen Christmas?" Duffey chortled. "As opposed to our Lord's Christmas?"

"I know where Peanut gets her talents," Dwayne responded glibly staring at Breena. "Don't worry, we let the Lord come by too!"

"Just why and when did you start calling our Breena, Peanut?" Alyson Duffey asked Dwayne sharply.

"I'd like to know that myself," Breena clucked. She attempted to pull her arm away from Dwayne, but his hold was firm and strong.

"Breena has a hard tough shell on the outside, but a delectable soft and tasty inside," Dwayne answered quickly. It was obvious he had thought about this for some time. "I've known for years, but last night over a cup of hot chocolate confirmed my belief."

Breena flushed. She hoped and prayed Auntie Alyson and Uncle Brian couldn't figure out what Dwayne really meant. She wasn't ashamed of what they had done. She was a modern woman. Breena was aware of strict and rigid society standards her uncle and most of the kind people in Ely maintained. She admitted last night Dwayne was more to her than a crush. She really loved Dwayne McGillinen. That's all that mattered to her. She wished Dwayne would love her, but if he didn't she could only ask for one major wish in her lifetime and he gave her that last night.

"Hah, an excellent analogy my boy," Brian Duffey chuckled as they rounded the corner to enter the great parlor room.

The sights, sounds, and smells of the McGillinen Christmas once more accosted Breena. The walls had boughs of pine branches decorated with holly. Cinnamon scented candles lit the parlor with a warm glow. The fireplace was blazing with several stacked Yule logs. From the kitchen Breena inhaled the scents of hot-spiced apple cider wafted to tempt her taste buds. The large Christmas tree in the corner had been repaired and looked lovely as long thin tapered candles sparkled and reflected light to the exquisite imported hand blown glass ornaments. Crocheted stars, bells, and trees accented the tree branches. Candy sticks adorned the tree with cranberry and popcorn garlands.

Breena looked around the parlor quickly and gulped a breath of relief to find Twenty Hands secured in the child corral. Paige's servant Veronica was playing with Garrett. A warm emotion overwhelmed Breena when she looked at Twiggy and Kerry still dressed in their robes doted on by their husbands. In their arms were their brand new babies, Aurora Blue and Jared. Suddenly her biological clock struck twelve. Suddenly she wanted her own baby.

"Breena? Do you want a cup of apple cider?" Dwayne broke into her thoughts.

"Yes Dwayne, I'd love one," Breena replied quietly.

She was a little too quiet for Dwayne. He could do something about that. "Great, go get one for me too."

Breena turned and gave a squinted glare to Dwayne that could have melted glass.

It didn't bother Dwayne one bit. He laughed, "Hey, I was only kidding. I'll get one for you now."

Breena's attention was again focused on Ryan. The big bear brother. He had been talking to Twiggy. Breena watched as the big bear took his baby daughter. He was a sight indeed, that massive giant holding the tiny Aurora. Breena held back a laugh while watching the mountain of a man talk to the little new born. Then Breena watched as the English Lord Braden Wessex dressed in western style jeans and flannel shirt take his new son, Jared. Breena watched Bennett dig into packages under the tree. Jerica and Joshua, Twiggy's little sister and brother, soon joined Bennett. A second later Willow ran to the tree to join her friends and cousin. Tears threatened to spill over as Breena choked back emotions. Her Uncle Brian had always made Christmas special for her, but never had Breena shared such a large family Christmas. "This is what Christmas is all about," Breena whispered to herself.

"Yep! It certainly is," Dwayne agreed handing her a large mug of apple cider. "I really enjoyed the McGillinen Christmas as a boy, but every year it seems to get better and better. With the family growing I mean. Christmas is all about family."

"I think I agree with you," Breena beamed.

"I hope the world doesn't end," Dwayne chuckled. "You, Breena Hodges agree with me? What can I hope I've said?"

"This is the McGillinen Christmas you invite the Lord to attend," Breena said softly. "I do believe this is the best Christmas I've ever been a part of."

Dwayne tucked Breena under his arm's embrace and sipped some of the hot cider. "I hope last night was a part of your wonderful Christmas. It sure was one of the best presents I ever got," Dwayne informed gratefully. "Thank you, Breena."

Once more Breena flushed in embarrassment. "Dwayne, someone might hear."

"I wish I could shout it on the mountain tops," Dwayne teased.

Breena looked at Dwayne in horror, "You wouldn't?"

"Nope, I understand a woman's need for privacy in these matters," Dwayne whispered with a wicked wink. "I want to crow, but I won't dear Peanut."

Breena and Dwayne sat down together on the little loveseat. They watched in joy as Grady handed the children their presents. The excitement was contagious. Soon the children were off to get Marseille Aumond's French Vanilla hot chocolate with a stick of cinnamon for flavor. Even Garrett was allowed a candy stick from the tree. He managed to get the goo all over his face once more. Next the women and men of the McGillinen family exchanged gifts. Paige was the center of attention with all her gifts. Ayden had gone all out and obviously enjoyed shopping. It appeared that everyone else had shared the same eagerness to smother Paige. Breena giggled every time Paige opened another present that was duplicated.

Kerry bubbled, "We still don't know if you are carrying a boy or girl so Braden and I bought two baby dresses, one in pink and one in blue."

"Thank you," Paige said graciously. "I'm certain one or all of us will get use from them. Even if you only get blue, your lordship."

"You see Kerry," Braden groused. "Even our new sister in law feels sorry for me. Even Paige wants you to give me a baby girl."

Kerry smacked Braden's arm. "This is Christmas. A very special Christmas that brought us a healthy baby, Jared."

"I am very grateful," Braden continued. "Just jealous."

Kerry tsked, "Give me back our son!"

"Nope," Braden chided. "You gave him to me and you can't take him back."

"You're hopeless," Twiggy snickered at her brother in law.

The McGillinen husbands then gave their wives their special Christmas gifts. Everyone ahhed and oohhed as each wife opened their jewels. Grady quietly gave Morning Song several boxes that contained a diamond bracelet, a diamond necklace, and a pair of diamond earrings. He also gave her diamond-studded combs. "Diamonds are forever my love," Grady said kissing his loving wife.

The McGillinen men received their gifts with the same excitement. Grady received a collection of Mark Twain's writings. Ayden received a new riding outfit for England and a book on Roman Aqueducts. Braden received a new Stetson, jeans, chaps, and custom tooled boots with scenes of Geneva's Hope ranchlands. Dwayne was given new clothes including a fancy looking city suit that Ryan started harassing him about immediately. It was a fine English cut suit that Paige had selected for him from a British Tailor. Everyone got something. Alyson was given lacy nightgowns, gold bracelets, necklaces, and earrings from Brian Duffey. Even Breena was given a set of medical books from Uncle Duffey that little Bennett started looking at until he came across sketches of the female reproductive organs. Braden pulled the book from his hand immediately and handed him another from the set. Auntie Alyson gave Breena two new silken peignoir sets in white and soft yellow.

Dwayne walked across to the tree and reached way behind it. He pulled out a small box wrapped in simple brown paper. There was no name on it.

"I can hardly wait to find out who gets that one," Grady noticed. "There was no name on it. I figured it must be special."

"It is Pa," Dwayne acknowledged. He walked to Breena and handed it to her. "It's from me. I hope you like it. I asked Ayden to buy it for you in England."

"But how did you know I would even be here?" a surprised Breena questioned taking the package.

"When Auntie Alyson married Uncle Duffey we knew you would be here at the McGillinen Christmas," Dwayne explained. "I hope you like it. You were always special to me Breena. You've always made me question my thoughts and assisted in driving me to learn more all through matriculation. Even if it was just to prove you wrong. Which I never could."

"Dwayne," Breena choked. "I don't know what to say."

"You don't have to say anything," Dwayne ordered. "Just open the dang thing!"

Breena slowly untied the string and then carefully opened the brown paper.

"Damn! Open the dang thing would you?" Dwayne grouched impatiently

"Watch your language Dwayne Sean McGillinen," Auntie Alyson scolded. "You're not to old to get your mouth washed out with lye soap!"

Payton Lee

Dwayne looked at Breena sheepishly, "Please open it." How many times had he heard those words from his Auntie Alyson, yet he still didn't learn from her warnings? He remembered how many times he had eaten soap as a child.

Breena's eyes opened wide in wonder as she removed an elegantly carved and gilded music box. Carefully as if it were made of the finest porcelain she opened it. The music box began playing a Brahms tune. It was the Brahms lullaby. Inside Breena found a delicate gold chain. On the chain was a small heart pendant. The heart had a diamond in the center.

Just at the moment Breena thought she would flood the room with tears of joy everyone's attention was pulled to an old Sosoni holy man, Tells the Truth.

Dwayne asked quietly, "Do you like it Breena?"

"No, I don't like it," Breena replied trying to keep her voice as low as possible and waited a dramatic minute for Dwayne's face to fall with rejection. "I love it Dwayne Sean McGillinen. Why?"

Dwayne's face rebounded in happiness, "You're special to my heart. I want you to remember me every time you wear it. Do you want to put it on?"

Breena nodded. She wiped a tear from the corner of her eye. "You're special to me too! I'll always wear your heart."

Dwayne picked up the pendant and as Breena picked up her hair for the pendant, he placed it around her neck and closed the clasp. "Does this mean we're a special couple now?"

"Does it?" Breena returned

Dwayne was about to respond when the conversation topic grabbed his attention.

"It is the same on the day my Kerry was born," Grady gulped. "Tells the Truth came and told me not to mourn the death of my wife Ashley. He then told me some futures of my children. All have come to pass with the exception of Dwayne."

"I heard about Ayden, Ryan, and Kerry," Dwayne declared. "I heard nothing about me."

"It was to be kept a secret until the day I would return and tell the future of the next generation," Tells the Truth said quietly as he sipped the hot chocolate. "This is good to drink. My favorite."

"What is my future?" Dwayne asked inquisitively.

"You will go and work for the people with the Great White Father," Tells the Truth said. "Your woman precedes you."

"He's going to Massachusetts to complete his education," Grady stated. "That is very close to Washington City and the President."

"Who is going to handle the paper work for Geneva's Hope?" Ayden inquired.

"Braden has been handling that for sometime," Grady answered. "Morning Song and I have built a smaller house with the people and will retire there. Geneva's Hope now belongs to Kerry Wessex and her family."

"As it will be," Tells the Truth agreed and turned to speak to Kerry. "Your new son is of the land like Ryan." Tells the Truth then spoke to Ryan. "Your daughter will be a true arrow of justice. United with her mate a protection will cloak the people. She will work for and protect the people during a trying time and shall keep her heritage strong. She will have great puha in her old age."

Twiggy knowing the power of puha from her adopted father, Blue Pool, bent her head in prayer to Tam Apo. This was a great gift.

"You each will have many more children," Tells the Truth stated calmly. I will write down all the legacies on paper to give you upon my walking the spirit trails."

Ayden had stood in awe. Truly the puha of the Sosoni' was powerful.

Tells the Truth put down his cup and lifting the buffalo robe walked to Paige. He placed his hand upon her abdomen.

The baby started kicking powerfully as soon as Tells the Truth placed his hand upon Paige.

"Oh my God," Paige grimaced with the violence of the movement. There was no fear of this man present. Normally Paige would never let a strange man touch her so intimately.

"In you are the holy ones," Tells the Truth prophesied. "The truth givers of history." With that statement Tells the Truth rose to leave. "Come Tracker, it is time to go home and leave these people celebrate their holy day."

Tells the Truth left with Tracker as quickly and as silently as he had arrived.

Breena grabbed Dwayne's hand, "What did your father mean when he said you are going to Massachusetts?"

"I've been accepted into Harvard, Peanut," Dwayne answered. "I'm entering the spring semester. If I work hard I'll finish in less than four years. I intend to be the McGillinen solicitor. Maybe I'll join your Uncle Duffey's firm. What do you think?"

Breena fingered her heart pendant. "I'm very happy for you, Dwayne. And I am envious. I wanted to obtain that very same education but Harvard won't accept women."

"I'm sorry, Peanut," Dwayne replied soothingly. "You may not have the sheepskin, but from what I've seen with the education you brought back with you, you could put the judges on the U.S. Supreme Court to shame."

"I am happy for you," Breena restated. "Really I am."

"Will you wait for me?" Dwayne asked quietly. "We are a couple now."

Breena opened her mouth to tell Dwayne her plans when Geoffrey and Edward announced that Christmas Dinner was now served.

Dwayne assisted Breena to rise and walked her to the dining room. He seated her next to him on the left side. Throughout the meal he used his right hand only and kept his left hand on Breena's knee.

Braden's keen eye noticed Dwayne's gesture. He mentioned his observance to Ryan. The two new fathers were sitting together. It was the only time they allowed the respective governesses to hold their new babies. "Do you think we'll have another wedding here soon?"

"Not if Breena is as smart as I think she is," Ryan teased. "No woman in her right mind would want to marry Dwayne."

Ayden sitting across the table heard his brother and said, "Funny, that's the same thing I told Paige. I couldn't imagine a woman in her right mind would marry you."

Chapter 3

"Thank the Good Lord this Christmas Day you were wrong," Ryan growled with good humor.

Paige leaned into Ayden's side. "What are you men talking about?"

"We were just noting that our baby brother Dwayne seems to have a soft spot for Breena Hodges," Ayden whispered to Paige.

"Yes I've noticed. They will make a smashing couple. I do so like Breena. She's so intelligent," Paige elaborated. "Do you think he's asked her to form a merger yet?"

"That's marriage! Silly Goose," Ayden corrected. "No, not yet. She just came back from college and Dwayne's about to go. You can't have a wife and concentrate on studies. There are a lot of miles that will be between them."

"Who says you can't have a wife and study?" Paige asked indignantly.

"Whoa!!" Ayden exclaimed. "I only mean I can't see little lover boy Dwayne concentrating on his studies with a wife to care for."

"If he's such a lover boy then maybe he needs a wife to keep him in line," Paige argued logically.

"You have a point," Ayden conceded. "I think Dwayne wants to prove himself to Breena first."

"Prove himself?" Paige queried.

"Since we were kids Dwayne was outgunned by Breena in the smarts department," Ayden shared. "Sometimes I think his pursuit of Harvard was a one upmanship to prove he was equal to Breena."

"Do you think you will ever equal me?" Paige teased.

"I doubt that sincerely," Ayden snorted. "I do intend to take advantage of your smart department every way possible."

After the pie was served Breena thought her body would blow up. She could never remember eating so much. It certainly didn't help when Dwayne kept putting food on her plate.

"Do you want to go for a ride?" Dwayne asked hopefully. He wanted to take Breena away from the crowd and talk to her by himself. When they were kids they would ride and talk, just the two of them.

"I feel a great need for some exercise," Breena confessed. "I would love to go for a ride. I hope I don't break the horse's back. I must have gained twenty pounds."

"You can only stuff ten pounds into a hundred twenty pound turkey," Dwayne said jokingly. "I promise you if any one would break the horse's back it would be me. Patches would be furious with me."

"I guess that means you can stuff twenty pounds into a hundred and eighty pound turkey," Breena teased back. She placed her napkin on the table and rose from her chair. "Give me a few minutes to change into some riding clothes."

"I'll be in the parlor waiting," Dwayne answered rising to move Breena's chair out so she could leave the table. "If I hurry I'll be able to hold Aurora before big brother comes back from the library with Pa. He had to leave Aurora for a few minutes so Twiggy could feed her. She's hungry for such a little thing."

Breena smiled at Dwayne and left for her room. Fortunately she had brought her woolen pants skirt to wear for riding. She had also brought her bulky hand knit sweater she had made and her short sheepskin range jacket. Breena put on a woolen cap and covered that with her Stetson. She changed into her hand tooled leather boots and slipped on her squirrel fur lined leather gloves. When Breena walked into the parlor she could swear she saw a large white glow surround Dwayne, who was holding Aurora Blue. He was talking to the sleeping newborn and to Breena's surprise, Dwayne appeared to be rocking Aurora with his arms, just like a woman does instinctively when holding a baby.

The spell was broken when Dwayne looked up and saw Breena. "Ready to Ride, Peanut?"

Kerry and Twiggy looked at each other and mouthed, "Peanut?" Paige nodded approvingly at the women and winked. Paige tossed her head toward Breena and Dwayne who was rapidly moving toward Breena. Paige opened her hand and tugged at her wedding band.

Kerry and Twiggy dropped their mouths.

"Our Dwayne marrying the girl next door," Kerry giggled. "How sweet!"

"Can I hold Aurora a moment?" Paige queried Twiggy. "It seems Dwayne seems to think I should."

"Only for a minute," Twiggy answered. "This will be my only chance to hold my baby before her daddy takes custody once more."

Dwayne didn't hear any of his sister in law's remarks. He absentmindedly handed Aurora Blue to Paige and only saw and heard Breena. Briskly he walked to Breena's side and took her arm nearly yanking her out of the room.

Breena straining to fight Dwayne's strong pull turned back and waved to the women.

The sister in laws waved back. The three were wearing large grins.

Dwayne opened the front door and took the immediate slap of the icy cold fingers of Nevada's winter. Still holding her hand they walked to the barn. It was too cold to waste their warmth talking before they were alone.

Once in the barn Dwayne pulled Breena into his frame and planted a long sensual kiss on her.

"Dwayne," Breena uttered returning her lips to his.

"Damn Breena," Dwayne croaked out. "I never had a night like last night. Thank you Peanut." He stole several more kisses until a familiar horse whinny and soft nudge from a horse muzzle reminded him why he came to the barn in the first place. "Okay Patches, we'll go for a ride. Let me saddle Lady Anne for Peanut."

Patches shook his head in approval and followed with his snicker.

"Dwayne," Breena addressed while grabbing a saddle blanket for Lady Anne. "Are you always going to call me Peanut from now on?"

"Yeah, I think so," Dwayne grinned. "It fits you so perfectly."

In a few minutes Dwayne had saddled Lady Anne and Patches, his pinto mustang. Lady Anne was the alpha horse of Geneva's Hope Barn ponies and was the most evenly tempered.   Soon they were high on a hill overlooking the ranch and the splendor of Steptoe Valley.

"It is incredibly beautiful," Breena sighed. "I know I say that every time we ride on Geneva's lands, but it really is incredibly beautiful."

"I love this land," Dwayne said automatically. "It's funny though. I feel this isn't where I'm going to settle down. This isn't where my future lies."

"Where do you think you'll end up?" Breena queried. It was funny. She felt the same way. She loved Nevada, but somehow she knew she wouldn't live here. This would be a special place to visit.

"I don't really know, but I hope it isn't England like Ayden chose," Dwayne chuckled. "That is one Hell of a commute to Nevada."

"Maybe it will be Massachusetts," Breena suggested. "You'll be going there in the spring."

"I want to talk to you about that Peanut," Dwayne said seriously.

Breena leaned over and started scratching Lady Anne's neck. She had ridden Lady Anne before and knew the horse liked that particular spot scratched. "Go ahead, we're alone."

"Yeah that's the first thing I want to take care of," Dwayne replied impishly. He braced his legs straight against Patches' ribs to stand on the stirrups. He cupped his hand over his mouth and shouted. "I love Breena Hodges! Last night I had the best Christmas Present ever. Peanut belongs to me!"

Breena felt her face and entire body flush with excitement and fear at the same time. "Dwayne Sean McGillinen, are you crazy? Someone could hear you!"

"Up here?" Dwayne laughed. "I had to tell the world about us. Peanut, wait for me!"

In the ranch house Victoria's ears perked. Amore meowed, and Morning Song craned her neck looking through the window to see little black dots on the hill above. She shook her head.

"What is it my love?" Grady queried.

"I'm not certain. I just find it strange to see the two little playmates up on the hill and one of them is shouting to the wind," Morning Song shared.

"Two little playmates?" Grady queried raising a questioning brow. He glanced about the room and mentally counted his grandchildren. They were all there.

"Since they were little, Dwayne and Breena have shared something special between them," Morning Song stated. "Perhaps the two have just discovered that fact."

"Wait for you to do what?" Breena asked with curiosity.

"Damn it Peanut, you know what I mean," Dwayne growled.

"The Hell I do!" Breena snarled back. "Wait for you to do what?"

"Wait for me to come back from Harvard," Dwayne sighed testily. "You're my girl now."

"I'm not a girl!" Breena quipped in her old habit. "After last night you should have noticed that I am a full fledged woman."

"Yes you are that," Dwayne agreed quickly. "You know what I mean. You're my woman. I'm asking you to wait for me."

It suddenly hit Breena exactly what Dwayne meant. It was his extremely awkward way of proposing an engagement.

"I can't wait for you in Ely,:" Breena replied.

Dwayne gulped hard. "Is there someone else? Someone you met at school?"

Breena laughed, "I can't wait for you in Ely because I'm moving to Washington City. I made my decision and obligated myself right after Thanksgiving. Don't say anything to anyone yet. I haven't even told Uncle Brian and Auntie Alyson."

"That's great!" Dwayne bubbled. "We'll be almost as close as Ely and Geneva's Hope. I'll get to see you on holidays. Where will you be staying?"

"I'm going to take back Hyacinth House," Breena explained. "It is my inheritance and my legal property now that I'm past twenty one. A Senator had rented it from Uncle Brian and now he's retiring in Illinois. The house will be empty and I'm reclaiming my heritage."

"What obligation have you taken?" Dwayne asked warily.

"After Thanksgiving I happened to meet Senator John Percival Jones. He was visiting Ely as part of his campaign trail. He was sitting at a table listening to a discussion I was having with Matthew Bronson, one of Uncle Brian's junior partners."

"Why were you having dinner with Matthew?" Dwayne queried jealously.

"Matthew and I often enjoyed dinner together, especially after Uncle Brian married Auntie Alyson," Breena bristled.

"Well you aren't going to have dinner with Mr. Matthew Bronson anymore, " Dwayne snarled. "I won't have it!"

"I beg your pardon," Breena sneered. "You will not ever tell me who I can and cannot have dinner with."

"Did Matthew propose to you?" Dwayne growled. "Is his interest in you other than law?"

"You mean like your interest in me?" Breena snapped angrily.

As usual Breena cut Dwayne to the quick. He immediately felt stupid and guilty. "That's different. I love you Peanut."

"Do you think it is impossible for anyone else to have feelings for me?" Breena spiked back. She didn't believe any man was interested in her but she wouldn't let Dwayne think that.

"Does lily livered Bronson have feelings for you?" Dwayne demanded in question.

"Maybe," Breena stretched her neck jutting out her chin.

"Maybe not," Dwayne laughed. "You're lying. You're biting your lip again."

"Well maybe not," Breena laughed with Dwayne. "Do you want to hear my news or don't you?"

"Yes I do want to hear your news," Dwayne chortled. He rested his hand on Patches' withers.

"Senator Jones was impressed with my knowledge of law and the political arena," Breena shared gleefully. "He's asked me to be his secretary in Congress."

"Wow, a large inheritance and a job with a senator," Dwayne smiled broadly. "This is fabulous. We can see each other while I get my lawyer's shingle. You will see me won't you?"

"Maybe," Breena jutted out her chin once more. "But you won't tell me who I can have dinner with."

"Just make sure I never have to shoot your dinner partner in a jealous rage," Dwayne teased. "You're mine Peanut. I branded you last night."

"There you go again with that horseflesh analogy again," Breena said with exasperation.

"Are you going to tell me you didn't like stallion and filly?" Dwayne teased.

"I didn't say that," Breena admitted honestly. She did enjoy last night.

"Can we have one more night," Dwayne asked hopefully. "It still is Christmas."

"Yes," Breena replied in one word. She picked up the reins for Lady Anne and gently pushed the horse's ribs with her knees. Lady Anne knew it was time to go back to her herd in the barn.

Patches and Dwayne followed dutifully. Dwayne was hard and in agony on the ride back to the ranch. He barely made it through supper. All Dwayne could think about was having Breena in his arms for the night once more. To everyone's surprise he excused himself early in the evening.

"You sick son?" Grady questioned worriedly. It was usually Dwayne that tucked everyone else into bed.

"No Pa," Dwayne answered quickly with a yawn. "Christmas is a long day. The ride seemed to tire me the most. Maybe it was all the food I ate."

Ryan, Braden, and Ayden didn't even seem to notice. They were busy teasing each other about their new babies. Brandy after brandy was consumed in toasts to their wives, children, and best Christmas ever.

Kerry, Twiggy, and Paige were already in bed sleeping. They were genuinely tired out from Christmas Day. Even though Ryan would breast feed Aurora Blue if he could, he couldn't. The women tried to get as much rest between feeding as they could. Paige was big, huge, and uncomfortable. She was plain tired.

Breena remained downstairs with Auntie Alyson, Uncle Brian, and Morning Song. She watched Dwayne over their shoulders as he gestured towards the upstairs. She watched Dwayne disappear in the hall. Breena couldn't help herself. Those wonderful memories from last night's love making started swamping her body with sensations she longed for. Breena started yawning.

"Are you tired dear?" Alyson questioned.

"No, I'm fine," Breena lied. She started biting her lower lip.

"Why don't you go to bed?" Brian suggested. "And don't tell us you're not tired. You bit your lower lip when you answered Auntie. You can't lie to me, Breena."

"I am a little tired," Breena admitted half-heartedly. *Just how many people knew about this lip biting habit of hers when she fibbed?* "This has been a most wonderful Christmas and it has been a long day."

"Run along dear," Alyson excused. "Stay abed later tomorrow if you wish. I don't think Uncle Brian and I will return to Ely until late morning."

"Thank you Auntie Alyson," Breena acknowledged gratefully. She had an excuse to snuggle in bed with Dwayne a little longer. She couldn't believe her own mind. She was contemplating acting like a wanton woman. She was a soiled dove. She was also feeling the most contented in her entire life and more importantly; she was sharing it with Dwayne.

Dwayne was undressed and waiting for Breena in her bed. He closed his eyes anticipating her walking through the door. Would he ever get that smile off his face? He hoped not. Breena was his. A soft light cast a sliver of amber hue on the bedspread announcing the entrance of his Breena. "Hi Peanut," he whispered invitingly.

"Dwayne?" Breena queried squinting her eyes in adjustment for the darkness.

"Right here in bed waiting for you Peanut," Dwayne invited sensually. "Let me put my arms around the best Christmas present yet."

"Shhh," Breena warned. "Some people are still awake. Someone might hear you."

"Do you need any help undressing?" Dwayne whispered. "I'll turn on a light and help."

"I've managed to dress and undress myself for several years now," Breena quipped softly. "I think I'll manage alright."

"I'm trying to be a gentleman, that's all," Dwayne chirped.

"You are no gentleman," Breena teased. "No unwed gentleman waits in an unwed lady's boudoir."

"This gentleman waits for his lady," Dwayne retorted. "It's only a matter of time for us to make it permanent."

"Make it permanent?" Breena questioned hopefully. After many years without a glitch, this night she couldn't seem to unlace her corset. "Damn!"

Dwayne jumped from bed and lit the small kerosene lamp next to the bed. He saw Breena struggling with her corset laces.

"Let me do that," Dwayne volunteered. He walked in his full glory to Breena's side and quickly released the knots in the laces. His long fingers quickly undid the laces and with a small movement of his hand removed her corset. "I hate these things. I liked the soft silky nightgown you wore last night much better. His hands had already removed her drawers and were removing her chemise before she could get out a response.

"What do you mean you hate these things?" Breena mumbled. "How much experience have you had removing female underclothes?" By the time she had finished her questions she was in the buff.

"Peanut, shut up," Dwayne ordered and placed his lips over hers to silence Breena.

In moments there was no more talking and no more thinking. In moments there were only wonderful feelings and sensations. Dwayne edged Breena slowly to the bed.

Once they were in the bed, she was his. Breena was his totally and completely. *God, life could be wonderful.*

The sun had been over the horizon for two hours before Dwayne and Breena stirred from their bed.

"Peanut?"

"Hmmm?"

"Want another go?"

"Actually I want a nice hot bath," Breena replied glibly. Would these wonderful feelings stay with her forever?

"First another go," Dwayne whispered. "Then the bath." One move and Dwayne had Breena completely lost once more.

When Breena had recovered substantially she watched as Dwayne dressed only in his natural glory prepare the hot water for her bath. A few minutes later he picked her up from bed and placed her gently in the sudsy bathtub. To her surprise, Dwayne followed her in.

Dwayne picked Breena up and put her on his lap. He grabbed a tin and soaked her hair after several cupfuls. He took a scented bar of soap and washed her hair.

Breena closed her eyes while enjoying Dwayne's gentle ministrations during bathing. *Lord, I could get used to this.* "If you ever need a position, you are hired."

"That position is exactly what I'm interviewing for," Dwayne quipped.

The calm was interrupted by a knock on the door.

"Breena, are you up?"

God, she couldn't get caught. *Quick thinking! Quick thinking!* "I'm taking a bath Auntie Alyson. I'll be downstairs in a few minutes."

Chapter 4

"I won't hear of it!" Brian roared angrily. "You will not travel to Washington City alone."

"I'll be fine Uncle Brian," Breena said quietly. "I went to school in the East."

"You were accompanied by your Uncle or a companion," Alyson reminded. "I agree with your Uncle Brian. You may be a woman of twenty two, but you will not travel alone."

"I will arrange for tickets at the railhead in Salt Lake City today," Brian stated firmly. "We'll take the stagecoach to Salt Lake City and then the train to Washington City."

"We?" Breena questioned.

"Your Auntie and me," Brian replied strongly placing a fist down upon the armchair decisively. "We've discussed it and agreed upon our course of action."

Alyson rose from the divan and placed a gentle hand on Breena's shoulder. "It won't be bad darling. I know we are too old people to have as companion's, but I do so want to visit Audrey."

"You and Uncle Brian aren't old," Breena disputed grasping Auntie Alyson's gentle hand. "I'd love to have you as company. I don't want you to worry or be a burden. You two have a new wonderful life ahead of you. You need not worry about me."

"It's my right to worry about you until I draw my last breath," Brian countered. "Don't even try to take that away from me, Breena Hodges."

"Yes sir," Breena saluted. "I love you too!" Breena walked to Brian Duffey and cuddled on his lap as she had done when she was a little girl.

"That's my girl," Brian remarked kissing the crown of Breena's hair. "You will always be my little girl."

Alyson smiled broadly. "We leave on Ely's Stagecoach in the morning. I've already sent a telegram to Audrey Astor. She will meet us in Washington City upon our arrival."

"Once we get you settled," Brian informed. "Alyson and I will go to Boston with Audrey. We want to see her new grandchild and visit with her and her family."

"So you see Breena, you are only one of the reasons we will be accompanying you," Alyson assuaged. "I also want to talk to Audrey about letting Dwayne stay with her while he attends Harvard."

Breena went rigid at the mention of Dwayne's name. Those warm wonderful feelings she had only a few weeks ago came rushing back. Her face flushed. It took great concentration to ask calmly, "When will Dwayne leave for Harvard?"

"Oh he'll start classes in the spring dear," Alyson responded. "He'll leave Geneva's Hope in March and start classes in April. He plans to take summer courses to catch up. "

Brian squeezed Breena in the same manner he used to do when she was a little girl, "The lovely ladies of Ely won't be seeing their dandy for sometime to come."

"Do you think they'll survive?" Breena breathed tersely.

"They'll find some other dandies," Brian chuckled. "The first thing I'm going to do when we get to Hyacinth House is to hire a bodyguard for you. I want you safe from all the dandies. There will be no dandy to break my little girl's heart."

"Dandies aren't really interested in the likes of me," Breena stated dejectedly. If only Uncle Brian knew one dandy had already taken her heart and body. It had been several weeks and Dwayne hadn't tried to contact her once. The fact there were several storms that had made the road from Geneva's Hope to Ely impassable didn't register with logic in Breena's emotional state. She felt used by Dwayne. The truth in her heart was she was furious for having become the male play toy or possession she had promised herself she would never become. To make matters worse, Breena still thought about all those wonderful feelings she shared with Dwayne. Breena thought about those feelings and Dwayne everyday. Breena rose from her Uncle's lap and started toward her room to finish her packing.

"Breena," Brian addressed.

"Yes?"

"A lot of dandies would be interested in you," Brian said firmly. "You look like your mother and are just as beautiful."

"You say that because mother was your sister," Breena replied. She felt her uncle's love as a father's love in every way.

"I'm not your mother's sister," Alyson charged. "I think you're very beautiful Breena in mind, body, and soul."

Breena forced a small smile and told her small family lovingly, "Thank you. I don't believe a word of it, but thank you." With that statement Breena left the parlor.

The trip to Washington City was uneventful. The stagecoach ride to Salt Lake City railhead was freezing cold even with the heavy buffalo robes they used to protect themselves from the elements. The traveler's good fortune was the fact there were not any snowstorms to interfere with the ten-day trip. They arrived at the Baltimore & Ohio Railway Station mid morning.

Audrey Astor had come down from Boston the night before and was waiting for their arrival. The eldest of the Stuart sisters greeted Alyson with an embrace and kiss, "Welcome to the East, Alyson. It has been nearly a decade since you have graced us with your presence."

"Our family is growing, Audrey," Alyson responding still hugging her elder sister. "You didn't think I would miss seeing your new grandson did you?"

"Matthew is an absolute angel," Audrey bragged. "He's trying to walk. We put him in one of those walker things Paige McGillinen had made for us. How is Paige?"

"She's big and big," Alyson laughed. "The tiny little thing looks like she would burst any day the last time we saw her."

"When did you see her last?" Audrey asked taking Alyson's hand and leading her to the waiting carriage.

"We celebrated Christmas at Geneva's Hope," Alyson answered. She turned to Breena. "Come along dear. Let your uncle and the porters worry about our luggage."

"Yes Auntie Alyson," Breena obeyed.

The women waited in the enclosed carriage until Brian Duffey and the porters had loaded the wagon with the entire Duffey family luggage. Breena of course had the most since she would be staying in Washington City.

At last Duffey climbed into the carriage and sat next to Breena.

The carriage gave the women a jolt as it moved forward.

"Where are we going?" Audrey questioned. "I'm staying at the DuPont Hotel on Massachusetts Avenue near the circle.

"I asked your driver to take us directly to Hyacinth House. It's bit further than your hotel," Brian answered. "I hope you don't mind."

"Mind? Of course I don't mind," Audrey replied reaching across the carriage to give Breena's hand a squeeze. "I've been dying to see this Hodges Hyacinth House ever since Alyson wired me our little Breena would be living there. And working with one of our country's Senators. How exciting, Breena!"

"Yes our Breena impressed Senator Jones when they met in Ely after his election," Brian bragged. "He hired her on the spot to assist as a personal secretary."

"Our Breena's expertise in law is dumbfounding," Alyson added with pride. "She is a chip off the old block."

"I have to admit I'm rather excited about all of it," Breena confessed. It had helped her get through those lonely nights remembering being in Dwayne's arms. She concentrated on her future and her new career. It didn't stop the hurt of not seeing Dwayne again, but it gave her hope for happiness in her life.

The carriage pulled in front of a Greek revival style home built before the Civil War.

"Do you have the key?" Brian asked Breena after the carriage came to a stop.

"Right here," Breena replied holding the key in her gloved fingers.

"What a quaint little town home," Audrey described.

"It was my home as a little child," Breena commented nostalgically. "I remember sitting on the front porch with my mother."

"I remember the first time I saw you," Brian Duffey reminisced. "You were a month old and your Mama had you in her arms. She was rocking you on that very chair. Your Father was kneeling next to her and playing with your little hand. They both loved you so very much." A tear threatened to fall from Duffey's eye.

Alyson took his hand and squeezed it. "You love Breena as deeply. We know that."

Duffey looked at his bride and smiled appreciatively. They followed Breena to open the door.

"I hope you like it Auntie Audrey and Auntie Alyson," Breena shared while opening the locked door. "I know it's a lot smaller than what you are used to, but it's full of warmth and coziness."

"Of course we'll love it," Audrey consoled. "This is your family home and you are part of our family. That makes it our home to share."

"Do you think the Senator and his wife changed anything dear?" Alyson queried stepping in behind Breena who walked into the parlor.

"It looks like they did," Breena said glancing around the room and down the hall into the kitchen. "They seemed to have changed the wall paper and furniture. It doesn't look like they remodeled the house itself."

"Do you remember what color this room used to be?" Duffey asked his niece. He wanted to know if she still had those memories. Her parents had died in that railroad accident when she was only eight years old.

"Oh yes Uncle Brian. Mama's favorite color was deep blue. The walls were deep blue. All the furniture had a deep blue flower pattern," Breena replied removing the white sheets covering the current furniture. "I remember it well."

"Did the Senator want this furniture shipped to him?" Audrey queried. She was removing some of the sheets covering furniture. "Surely you will want to redecorate."

"The Senator sent me the forwarding address and money for movers in a post," Brian replied. "I wrote him back to let him know we would forward it as soon as Breena was settled in."

"Uh Oh!" Alyson chuckled. "I see that gleam in your eye Audrey!"

"As if you aren't thinking the exact same thing," Audrey returned laughing.

"I should have guessed," Brian piped in.

Breena was at a total loss. "What?"

"I think I will be staying in Washington City with my sister, her husband, and my niece for a while," Audrey giggled. "I'll send Henry a note and let him know I'll be staying here a little longer. You won't mind if I move in from the hotel, Breena?"

"Of course not. You are more than welcome to stay with me here," Breena offered. "Of course I haven't a staff as of yet."

"But of course you do dear," Audrey corrected. "We'll use my Thomas and Lily until you hire a staff. They are waiting for me at the hotel. We'll be just fine."

"I appreciate you volunteering, but that isn't necessary. I can cook and clean myself," Breena informed politely. She didn't want Audrey to feel obligated in any way.

"Nonsense!" Audrey declared. "Alyson, you, and I will be far to busy restoring Hyacinth House."

"What?" Breena questioned.

"I find it easier to be in the house when I restore," Audrey stated. "Don't you agree Alyson?"

"Absolutely!" Alyson agreed. "This will be ever so much fun. I haven't decorated since …"

"You married Brian and started redecorating his townhouse in Ely," Audrey chided.

"And you redecorated Robert and Eloise's town home last year," Alyson reminded.

"I simply must redo a home at least once a year," Audrey laughed.

"I knew that is what the two of you were plotting," Brian chortled.

Breena sat on the large divan. She really wanted some time alone, but one couldn't say no to Alyson and Audrey Stuart. She sat silently for a while listening to the two sisters start to plan the shopping trips. Breena slowly began to smile. It would really be fun to restore Hyacinth House to the memory she had as a child.

Alyson pulled Breena into the conversation with Audrey, "Stop daydreaming child! You must share with us every one of your childhood memories."

"I'll start a fire," Duffey puffed billowing steam from his mouth. "I'm certain you hadn't noticed, but it is so cold in this room you can see your breath."

"Thank you darling," Alyson responded. "You are right. We didn't even notice."

"I hope there are some cords out in the back," Duffey grumbled. He never liked being cold.

Just as Duffey walked toward the hall a large black figure cast its shadow on the floor. Duffey reached inside his pocket for his Derringer but realized he had packed it and had not taken it out this morning.

A large Negro appeared in the doorframe. He was tall and built well, but looked frail and half starved. White curly hair topped his head and he had deep brown eyes that showed a lot of sorrow. "Would you be Massah Duffey, suh?"

Duffey took one step back to look up at the tall man. He no longer felt any fear, but looked to see the women and make certain they were not afraid. The women were still talking and hadn't even noticed the Negro's entrance. "I am Brian Duffey. You are?"

"I'm Abel Thornton suh," he answered. "Me and my Missus worked for the Senator. We was hoping you might hire us."

"The Senator didn't take you back with him?" Duffey queried.

"No suh," Abel said dejectedly. "The Senator said he couldn't take no black folk back with him to his fine neighborhood."

"We'll think about it," Duffey evaded. If the Senator didn't take them with him, maybe they weren't good servants. "Is there a cord in the back of the house? I need to start some fires in the house."

"Yassuh, I'll get it for you suh," Abel volunteered.

"I'll come with you. You look half starved and ready to fall over," Duffey noted. Together they walked through the kitchen. The kitchen was full of unused foodstuffs. "Why didn't you and your wife eat some of this food?"

"That would be stealing suh," Abel answered walking to open the door. "This foodstuff belongs to the Massah."

"But you look starved," Duffey insisted. "That's a great waste of food in there."

"My family done all right until you come, Massah," Abel replied. He bent over and picked up several cords of wood. "We need the work, Massah. My Aida and Mattie have no where else to go."

"The Senator and his wife moved back to Illinois three months ago," Brian observed. "He said someone would watch the house. I guess it was you. Where have you been living and how have you been surviving?"

"We stayed in the servant house there," Abel pointed to a run down cottage next to the livery and stable. "My Aida was able to get washing and ironing from some of the Congressmen every now and then. That managed to buy us some tripe from the butcher and beans from the dry goods store. We hope you don't mind we stayed in the cottage. We had no where to go."

"Of course I don't mind. Let's get the fires going in the house and then bring me your Aida and Mattie to meet," Brian suggested. He felt so sorry for the half starved old man. If nothing else he would make sure the Thornton family would get a hot meal today.

When Brian walked into the parlor he noticed Audrey was missing. "Where did Audrey go off?"

"She went to the carriage driver to give him instructions," Alyson answered. "We checked the kitchen and although there are plenty of foodstuffs, we don't know how old it is. Audrey is bringing Thomas and Lily with orders to bring some of her clothes, some food for several meals, and other necessities."

"I'll help get some wood and start lighting the fireplaces, Uncle Brian," Breena volunteered.

The words were no sooner uttered than a large black man appeared from the kitchen. "I's started the stove."

"Who are you?" Breena queried with a start. She covered her heart with hand automatically.

"I am Abel Thornton, Ma'am," Abel said softly. "My family be servants to the Senator."

"Why didn't you accompany the Senator to Illinois?" Breena wondered out loud.

"The Senator and Missus told us they couldn't take black folk to their fine neighborhood in Illinois," Abel replied with no emotion. "No black folk, not even servants."

"Unfortunately that is true," Audrey agreed walking back into the parlor. She had returned from giving the driver instructions and heard Abel's introduction. "We supposedly fought the Civil War to free slaves, but in reality their lot has not changed. The prejudice is still strong, maybe stronger than ever."

"We fought the Civil War on Federal power versus State power. Nothing more. Nothing less," Breena seethed. There were so many people who sacrificed their lives in this noble cause. They didn't realize their noble cause was not the reason for the war. The real reason was political power and industrial greed wanting natural resources. That is what all wars are really about."

"Exactly my feelings," Audrey agreed. "Which leaves this poor man and his family without work, a place to live, and food to eat. Did the Senator leave you any money to survive?"

"Yes ma'am," Abel replied. "The Senator done give me two weeks full pay when he left."

"Two weeks?" Alyson gasped. "This house has been empty for three months! What did you eat? Where did you stay?"

"My Aida got some washing and ironing from some Congressman, and we stayed in the cottage behind the house," Abel shared with the women.

"Brian, you write to that Senator of yours and tell him what a bastard he is!" Alyson said far too calmly. "Leaving this poor family all alone and not telling anyone!"

Breena dropped the wood cord she brought in when she heard Auntie Alyson use a swear word. "Auntie Alyson?"

"I'm sorry dear," Alyson apologized. "A bastard is a bastard. That Senator is a bastard."

"Some people still look upon the Negroes as sub life," Audrey added shaking her head in disapproval.

"I will write. You will be guaranteed on that point," Brian stated. He turned to Abel. "Before we light the rest of the fireplaces in the house, you fetch Aida and Mattie."

"Yes indeed," Alyson agreed. "If they look as half starved as you do, then we need to get everyone here some hot food." She shooed Abel along and went into the kitchen rolling up her sleeves. As long as the cook stove was lit she would go through the foodstuffs and find some salvageable dry goods and start a hot soup. She was in her glory. Alyson felt needed and more than capable of starting this household off right.

Audrey joined her in the kitchen. "This is so fabulous. I haven't helped cook anything since my children were babies. Thomas and Lily will let me know if Abel and Aida will be good servants. We'll find work for them."

"If Thomas approves of them, why not let them stay here with Breena?" Alyson queried.

"You're right, if they are good servants they know this home better than anyone," Audrey agreed.

Breena and Duffey brought in more wood to take upstairs to the bedrooms. "When I get the fires going upstairs I'll come down and help."

"Of course dear," Alyson and Audrey said in unison.

The two women set about creating a nice hot meal. The two women were happy and having a lot of fun doing everything together.

Chapter 5

"Here's the list of everything we need," Grady said to Dwayne handing him a handwritten note. "Are you sure you want to go into town?"

"Yeah Pa," Dwayne answered stuffing the note in his jacket. These storms locking us up in here have kind of made me a little stir crazy."

"Another storm could come and we'd be snowed in again, but this time you'd be snowed in at Ely," Grady commented.

"Yeah, but I'd be snowed in somewhere else," Dwayne offered.

"Still, you and old George take care," Grady told his son. He walked with Dwayne to the door.

Dwayne mounted Patches and followed George driving the buckboard.

Arriving in Ely a set of blue eyes watched carefully as the two came into to town and headed toward the Crawford Mercantile.

"At last he's come to town!" Deborah Wheeler breathed. "Now we've got him before it's too late!"

"I'll be right back," Dwayne told George when the old man came to a stop in front of the Mercantile. He handed the McGillinen list to George. "I want to visit Auntie Alyson and Uncle Duffey."

George waved his hand in understanding and took the note into the store with him.

Deborah quickly put on her long coat and boots. She wrapped a muffler around her head and neck. When she walked out the door she put on her woolen gloves.

"Where are you going?" Margaret Wheeler questioned her daughter. "Your father will be home any minute. He went to the newspaper to get word on the election."

"I want to go out for a minute. That's all," Deborah replied.

"It's freezing cold outside!" Margaret declared. "Why on earth you want to take a walk now is beyond me."

"Someone came into town that I have to see," Deborah stated walking out the door. She would see him. She had been waiting two months for this meeting.

"I hope it's not that Tim Miller," Margaret said under her breath. "That no account excuse for a man child."

Deborah hurried to the Crawford store.

Bert Kepler, Brian Duffey's butler, answered the knock on the town home door. He opened it to Dwayne McGillinen. "Yes sir. May I help you?"

"I was wondering if Breena was here," Dwayne said. "I went to the law office and it appears to be closed."

"Yes sir it is closed," Bert replied stoically. "Mr. Duffey, Mrs. Duffey, and Breena have left for Washington City. I received a wire that they will be there until spring."

Dwayne felt his heart stop. "They've left already?"

"They left for Washington City right after New Year's Day. Before the storms came sir," Bert offered.

"Breena said she was leaving for Washington City, but I didn't know it would be this soon," Dwayne commented dejectedly. "Did they leave an address?"

"Yes sir. If you come in, I'll fetch it for you," Bert offered. "Now that his employer was family to the McGillinen's he felt it would be alright for him to give Dwayne the address.

Dwayne followed Bert into Duffey's study. He waited patiently while Bert scribed the Washington City address on a piece of paper. Dwayne looked at the address when Bert handed it to him. "1202 Massachusetts Avenue. Thanks!" Dwayne returned to the cold and rode Patches back to the Crawford store.

Deborah was inside waiting for him. "Dwayne!"

"Debbie? What are you doing outside in this cold?" Dwayne questioned. He never cared very much for Debbie Wheeler, but he was always polite.

"I came to talk to you," Deborah answered. "Do call me Deborah. I've never cared for that short name."

"Sorry Deborah," Dwayne responded lamely. "What do you want to talk to me about?"

"I'm with child, Dwayne," Deborah announced.

"Is that for a congratulations?" Dwayne queried. He wondered why Deborah would want to give him that bit of information.

"I'm naming you the father," Deborah said triumphantly.

"What the Sam Hill for? You know I'm not the father," Dwayne almost shouted. He was furious. What was Deborah trying to do?

"You slept with me," Deborah hissed. "Did I mean so little?"

"I was drunk and that was a year ago," Dwayne gritted through his teeth. "Seems to me that's a mighty long pregnancy. And you weren't a virgin!"

"What does anything matter other than the fact I say you're the father!" Deborah declared.

"I'll deny it!"

"Go ahead. Some will believe you and some will believe me, but there will always be a question and your reputation would be ruined," Deborah sniped nastily.

"What do you want from me Deborah?" Dwayne snarled angrily.

"I might want marriage. I might want money," Deborah replied smoothing her coat over her abdomen. "If I married you I would have both, but we wouldn't be happy together would we? So I give you an out. Give me money!"

"How much money do you want?" Dwayne demanded.

"I was thinking about $100,000. That would give me a good start," Deborah answered coquettishly.

"It would give you and Tim Miller a great start. Is he the father?" Dwayne asked. This plan was beginning to make sense to Dwayne.

"With the McGillinen millions, you wouldn't even miss that coin," Deborah needled sarcastically. She had always been jealous of the McGillinen family. Her father was a poor laborer. He worked in the mines until his health failed. Now he earned even less money being a helper in the Ely City newspaper. The McGillinen's had what she wanted. Tim Miller gave her promises and it was Tim that came up with this plan when they discovered she was pregnant. Losing her reputation was a small price to pay for obtaining some of the McGillinen fortune. She and Tim would move to California and buy land there. Tim had told her there was a future to be made in California. All they needed was a little monetary help.

"What if I say no!" Dwayne uttered belligerently. He hated the idea of being blackmailed. The McGillinens weren't saints, but they all took pride in their good name.

"Then I'll start telling everyone and my father I'm carrying your child," Deborah replied cocking her head spitefully. "Your uncle isn't the only lawyer in town and I understand Brian Duffey isn't in town. Do you really want Matthew Bronson to represent you? He's not that good you know. He always used Breena Hodges to help him out with cases."

Dwayne was really furious now. Breena and Matthew were seen together a lot. "I won't be blackmailed, Deborah."

"Very well," Deborah replied. At that inopportune moment, Harriet Hampton Weiss walked into the store. Harriet was the town gossip and was even more pompous now that she had remarried a miner who struck it rich. "Dwayne, you can't mean it! You can't just throw me away! I'm carrying our baby!" Deborah shouted drawing the attention of everyone in the store. Deborah continued the dramatics by running out of the store into the street. When she was out of sight of her audience she smugly tightened her muffler and walked home.

"What the devil was that all about?" George asked Dwayne.

Harriet Hampton Weiss pretended to ignore Deborah Wheeler and went to Joseph Crawford. "I need to buy that bolt of satin after all. Mr. Weiss and I will be visiting the East in spring and I'll need several new gowns." Secretly she couldn't wait to get home and tell her husband that the McGillinen's would be facing a shotgun wedding. Oh this was fantastic news. The high and mighty McGillinens, the Indian lovers, the pure family was about to get their precious name soiled.

"Deborah thinks she can blackmail the McGillinen family by using my name in a paternity suit," Dwayne told old George.

"Are you the father?" George asked.

"How is that possible, George?" Dwayne queried. "I've been with my brothers and up at the ranch for four full months. I haven't even been to town in that time. Is she even showing yet? It's impossible for me to be the father even if I had been stupid enough to bed her."

"What does she want then?" George asked bluntly.

"She wants money. Deborah wants $100,000," Dwayne said sharply.

"Whoopee! That's some grubstake," George grumbled. "I think we'd better get back to the ranch and talk to Grady. That's old Harriet. The entire town of Ely will know about this by tomorrow."

"That's Deborah's plan. If I give her the money she will disappear."

"She'll disappear and everyone will think you killed her or still believe you bought your way out of it," George surmised. "Either way you look bad."

"That's why I can't give her the money," Dwayne agreed. "I need to talk to Pa about this."

Harriet left the store and Joseph walked up to Dwayne. "There goes the Ely telegraph. I don't believe the girl, Dwayne. A lot of people won't."

"Yeah, but when she threatened me she said, some will believe you and some will believe me," Dwayne sighed removing his hat and rubbing his gloved hands over his hair. "I can't let her get away with this. I can't." Dwayne was thinking about Breena. He couldn't have her believe anything bad about him. He didn't want to ask her to marry him if she had any doubt about him. He wished she were there to talk to her. He always felt better when they talked about things, even if they did argue once and awhile. "Let's go home. I want to talk to Pa."

There was an urgency to return to Geneva's Hope. Dwayne was upset and anxious to talk to his father. His father had an answer for everything. His father could help him. Dwayne felt very alone and helpless. "Breena why aren't you here to give me answers, or at least get me mad. Then I wouldn't be so scared."

"What'd you say boy?" George asked.

"Just muttering to myself," Dwayne grumped.

"Don't worry none boy," George comforted. "Grady will handle that little she devil."

"That's part of the problem, George," Dwayne grouched. "I'm a man and I am supposed to handle my own problems, but here I am running to my Pa."

"Son, there ain't no shame asking family to help when you can't think straight," George responded in great wisdom. "You have to give value to men like your Pa that have lived through a lot more things than you have. An older man is a wiser man. Besides you've got Morning Song. She's a right smart woman and would know how another woman thinks. Ain't no shame in that boy!"

"Isn't," Dwayne laughed. "Breena would correct your grammar. It's *isn't any shame.* You're right George. Thanks."

"You're might fond of that little Breena gal, aren't ya?"

"Yeah George, I am might fond of her," Dwayne chuckled. "I don't want her to think bad of me."

"I may be an old man, but let me tell you that if you and a woman are really in love, that woman would stand by your side," George shared. "I wouldn't worry too much about that little Breena gal. She's got a fine head on her shoulders. Right smart little gal."

"Breena is really smart," Dwayne agreed. "She's off in Washington City already."

"What's the little gal doing there?" George asked in with surprise. "Seems to me it might be a bit difficult to court the little gal all the way in Washington and you in Nevada."

"A senator hired her as his secretary assistant," Dwayne shared. "I'll be going to Massachusetts in the spring so I'll be closer, but I can't court her until I get my sheepskin. I want to prove to her I'm worthy of her. Getting that lawyer shingle from Harvard will show I'm equal to her."

"Why do you have to prove to her you're worthy?" George asked without expecting an answer. "Seems to me that if a man and woman love each other it don't matter about smarts."

"It matters to me," Dwayne groused. "It matters to me a lot."

"Well boy, you best expect a whole lot of problems to interfere. It appears to me you just might lose out on that little gal if you let your fathead get in the way," George chuckled.

"Thanks a lot, George," Dwayne complained. "You made me feel all warm and cozy."

"No problem," George laughed and clucked at the horses to make them pick up their gait. They could see Geneva's Hope ranch house and George knew the horses were cold, tired, and hungry. The horses were as anxious to get back home as the two men.

Grady walked out of the ranch to greet them. He had put on his jacket and gloves when he saw them coming up the trail. It was a little earlier than he had expected. His large welcoming smile drooped when he saw Dwayne walking toward him. He knew his sons well enough to know there was a problem. "What is it Dwayne? What happened?"

"It's Deborah Wheeler, Pa," Dwayne told his father without hesitation. "She's going to tell everyone in town I'm the father of the baby she's expecting."

"Are you?" Grady asked his son grabbing him by the arms and looking directly into his eyes.

"No," Dwayne answered returning his father's stare. "Deborah is only saying this because she wants $100,000 from me."

"Come inside son," Grady invited. "We'll go to the study and talk about this over a glass of brandy. I want Morning Song there with us." When Grady walked into the house, Morning Song was waiting for him. It seemed to be uncanny how she knew when Grady needed her. "I need you in my study love."

The three walked into the study and Grady closed the door. "Take a seat love," Grady offered Morning Song and then walked to the bar to pour two large glasses of brandy. Grady offered one to Dwayne and then sat down in his large leather chair behind his massive desk. "Tell us what happened son."

"Deborah was waiting for me at the mercantile. She must have seen George and me come into town," Dwayne began.

"Waiting for you?" Morning Song asked.

"I went to visit Auntie Alyson and Uncle Duffey to see how they were doing," Dwayne answered. "They weren't there."

"You went to see Breena and she wasn't there," Morning Song corrected. "Tell us the truth Dwayne."

"Okay, I went to see Breena. She wasn't there. They all went to Washington City for Breena's new employment," Dwayne answered. "I didn't know they would leave this soon. How did you know Morning Song? I mean how did you know I went to see Breena and not Auntie Alyson?"

"You always raise your hand and scratch your chin when you don't tell us the truth," Morning Song enlightened. "What happened then?"

"Deborah came in to tell me she was carrying a child and that she would name me father if I didn't pay her $100,000," Dwayne told his stepmother.

"Are you the father?" Morning Song queried repeating Grady's question.

"No! I am definitely not the father!" Dwayne decreed loudly.

"Did you ever sleep with her?" Morning Song pursued.

"Yes, I did. It was over a year ago. I was drunk," Dwayne confessed.

"I believe you," Morning Song assured and looked to Grady. "Your son is telling us the truth."

"I know love," Grady agreed. "The boy didn't scratch his chin."

"She wants money Pa, and I don't want to give it to her," Dwayne stated. "If I do, she and the real father will disappear and I'll look like a rogue that uses his family name and money to get out of trouble. I can imagine other people seeing I'm an easy target for blackmail."

"Your son is right," Morning Song suggested. "What do we do?"

"What's going on in here?" Braden asked entering the library. "I heard Dwayne shout."

"A small family matter," Grady said simply. He then explained the situation to Braden Wessex, his son in law.

"There's no doubt Dwayne shouldn't pay the blackmail," Braden concurred. "We need to take this to court. How many months enceinte is she?"

"She's not showing at all so I believe she would be about three or four months at the most," Dwayne replied.

"Have you slept with her?" Braden asked pouring himself a brandy.

"Damn! I am sick of that question," Dwayne complained.

"Yes he did," Morning Song answered for him. "It was almost a year ago."

"Bloody Hell! That is a long pregnancy," Braden laughed. "The only mammal pregnancy I know is that long belongs to an elephant."

"That's pretty much what I told Deborah," Dwayne chuckled a little. It felt good to chuckle at a little humor.

"This Deborah needs to be taken to court to prove paternity," Braden suggested. "You can't be the father. You've been in my sight for the past four months and haven't even ventured into Ely until Christmas time. Unless..?"

"Don't even go there, Brit!" Dwayne yelled. "I went to get presents from the mercantile. I was in and out in a day. I went with Ryan and Ayden and you know how strict they are about fooling around."

Payton Lee

"You're right!" Ayden agreed walking in on the family meeting. "I am strict about fooling around. Especially about you fooling around, my dandy little brother. What's going on in here?"

"Have a seat and a brandy," Braden offered. He went to Grady's bar to pour himself another brand and a snifter for Ayden. "Where's Paige?"

"Right here!" Paige answered waddling into the study. "Is this a family meeting?"

"If it is, why wasn't I included?" Kerry queried walking into the room with Jared in her arms. "Here Papa, it's your turn to hold Little Moose. He's sleeping."

Braden was over to Kerry in a shot and took Jared from her arms.

Ayden had walked Paige to a comfortable chair and helped her to sit.

"What's going on here?" Kerry queried walking over to the bar and pouring herself a Brandy. "Don't look at me like that, Pa! This will help Jared sleep the night. He's already two months old. Tell me what's going on here."

Grady explained the story once again. He included all details so Dwayne wouldn't be asked again.

"That Bitch!" Kerry growled. "I may have to go into Ely and have a talk with her."

"I don't think that will do any good," Dwayne complained. "You see the way she set it up, it wouldn't even matter if I were the father."

"She wants the money. Deborah doesn't want you. Not really," Paige offered. "Yet I see you cannot pay the blackmail. It would open too many doors left closed. It would actually put us all in danger to become victims of blackmail."

"Told you she was smart," Ayden bragged gently brushing a kiss on Paige's brow.

"There must be something we can do," Braden said quietly as he rocked Jared.

"I've got a plan," Grady announced. "It will take a month or two. I'll send a wire in town tomorrow. We also will need Ryan to make this work when the time comes."

"What is it?" everyone asked at once.

Chapter 6

"No! No! The cradle goes over there," Breena ordered the deliveryman. Refurbishing her childhood home was laborious even though Audrey and Alyson did most of the work. Breena was put in charge of redoing her childhood nursery. Breena had selected the white stars on the blue background when on a shopping trip with Audrey and Alyson they stopped at a mercantile and found it. The fabric amazingly had been exactly as Breena remembered as a child. They also found the blue stars on the white background her mother had chosen for sheets. Breena was beside herself with happiness this past month. Audrey and Alyson had completely refurbished Hyacinth House nearly to the exact house it had been when Breena was a toddler.

Even against Breena's wishes, Alyson and Audrey paid for nearly the entire cost of refurbishment. They told her they hadn't this much fun in a long time, and it was special for the two of them to work together as sisters even for such a short time.

"Breena," Alyson called up to the nursery from the first floor. "We're about to leave."

"I'll be right there!" Breena responded. She turned to leave the nursery and ran down the stairs. Facing her Auntie Alyson she said sadly, "Must you really leave? I'm going to miss you very much!"

"We'll miss you too dear, but Henry is insistent on Audrey returning home now that she's finished Hyacinth House, Alyson replied. "I do want to see little Matthew before your Uncle Brian and I return to Ely."

"I love you so very much," Breena cried and hugged her Auntie Alyson. She walked to Audrey and hugged her. With a strong sob, Breena said, "I will miss you most dearly."

Henry Astor walked to Breena and gave her a fatherly hug. "I promise you I will take good care of your funds and invest them wisely for you. Thank you for your trust."

"I know you will," Breena sniffed wiping her tears. "I trust you completely."

"You know if you ever need us," Henry said lovingly. "You just need send us a note on Beacon Hill and we will be right here for you."

Breena left Henry's arms and went into her Uncle Brian's waiting open arms.

"You be a good girl for me," Brian admonished with love. "If you get bothered by anyone or anything, you let me know and I'll come back from Ely to take care of it."

"Uncle Brian, I simply do not know how I will adjust to my new life without you near," Breena sobbed. "I love you, Uncle Brian."

"You're all grown up now, Breena," Uncle Brian soothed. "Although I would prefer you stay in my nest. A bird must learn to fly. Just remember my love will be near you every minute of every day."

"The carriages are ready, madam," Thomas announced when he returned to the parlor.

Still remaining in Uncle Brian's arms, Breena gave Thomas appreciation, "Thank you for all your assistance, Thomas."

"No thanks," Thomas bowed politely. "Your Abel is a very capable houseman. He and his family will serve you well. Of that I have no doubt."

"We still appreciate your guidance and advice," Brian concurred. "With your approval, I feel a little bit more comfortable leaving my Breena here."

"Of course sir," Thomas responded and bowed slightly. "Now, the carriages."

Breena walked outside still in Uncle Brian's arms.

Brian Duffey was the last to enter the carriage. When he released Breena he whispered, "Remember, you are the daughter of my heart. If you ever need me you must promise to send for me. Promise?"

Breena nodded her head and held back the tears threatening to flood her cheeks and freeze upon them in the bitter cold.

"Good! Run along into the house before you catch a cold," Brian shooed pushing her off toward the door. "I love you!"

Breena ran into the house and to the window. She pushed aside the heavy drapes and watched the carriages disappear down the road. They were heading toward the rail station. "I love you Uncle Brian. I'll miss you."

On the first night alone in the house the silence was nearly deafening. Breena did not sleep well at all. Mattie woke her up gently and had prepared a hot bath. Breena needed to dress for work.

Breena had made it to work in plenty of time. Everyday she reported to Senator Jones offices in the Capitol. Everyday she worked with his secretary and prepared his schedule and reports. Her knowledge of law was greatly admired by the Senator and his secretary. Already the Senator and his wife had invited Breena and her family to dinner and parties. The Senator's wife was impressed that Breena was related to an Astor even if it was distant cousin. Although the Senator was impressed with Breena's knowledge and capability, he was also impressed with her family status and wealth.

"Good morning, Madam," Senator Jones greeted. "I have a surprise for you. Mrs. Jones bought this for you last night knowing your family left for Boston yesterday."

A congressional page came in carrying a wicker box and gave it to Breena.

"What is it?" Breena queried taking the box. It was heavy and then she heard soft whimpering. Carefully she put the box down and opened it. Inside was an adorable brown and white spotted puppy. It was a spaniel. "Oooh! It's adorable!"

Breena squealed with delight. She picked it up speaking to it, "Are you a girl or a boy?"

"The pup is a girl," Senator Jones chuckled stroking his long white beard. "Do you like her?"

"Like her?" Breena repeated snuggling the puppy with her arms. "I love her!"

"Mrs. Jones thought you might get a little lonely in your town house. I'll be happy to let her know how pleased you are," Senator Jones said showing a soft side he often tried to keep hidden. "Let us know what name you give her."

"I've always thought that if I ever did have a pet, its name would be Justice," Breena said holding the puppy. "But I think this one will be called Liberty."

"Great name," Senator Jones approved. "Take Liberty home and take a week off to settle in with her. We're closing our office for two weeks. I have to be in New York for special meetings. You enjoy this time with your Liberty."

"We have everything in order," Samson Miles, the Senator's secretary, shared. "Madam Hodges was efficient as usual. Your briefs are prepared for today's session."

"You see?" Senator Jones smiled graciously. "I knew they would be. Run along home, Breena."

"Thank you Senator Jones," Breena appreciated. "Thank Mrs. Jones. I shall take good care of Liberty."

The Senator grinned and walked into his office. Samson followed him.

Breena put Liberty back into the wicker basket and grabbed her coat from the hook. In moments she was dressed for the cold February weather and carrying Liberty out the door. She hailed one of the cabs that were always waiting outside the Capitol building. Soon she was paying the cabby and entering Hyacinth House.

Abel heard the carriage and opened the door. "Welcome Madam. Is anything a miss?"

"No Abel," Breena answered walking briskly past her houseman to put the wicker basket on the divan. "The Senator will be out of town so he gave me the time off to acquaint our Liberty with Hyacinth House." Breena opened the wicker basket. A tiny puppy head peered behind two paws.

"Lordy!" Abel declared. "That little pup is cute as a button."

"She's ours Abel," Breena breathed out happily. "She belongs to us."

"We'll take good care of her," Abel promised. "I'll fetch Aida and Mattie. That little pu0p will sho make 'em happy." He left the room.

Aida came into the room carrying a small piece of cooked chicken meat. "Lordy, that is sho one cute pup," she cried handing the piece of meat to Breena. "We'll take good care of her."

"Thank you Aida," Breena replied taking the meat from Aida and giving it to the pup.

"You think that little pup would like some cream?" Mattie asked holding a small bowl.

Liberty yapped an acceptance while wagging her tail.

"I do believe Liberty would like some cream," Breena laughed putting the pup on the floor.

Liberty ran immediately to Mattie who placed the bowl in front of the pup. Liberty lapped up the cream in no time. She then yapped some more and ran back to Breena.

That night Breena went to bed and didn't feel alone anymore. Liberty jumped on the bed and went to sleep curled up by Breena's feet. For the next two weeks Breena and Liberty kept each other company. A strong bond formed between them.

"Who could that be?" Breena asked her little shadow, Liberty. Abel was in the kitchen with Aida so she rose from the divan to answer the door. In front of her stood a tall handsome middle-aged man about forty-five years old. His sideburns were graying but his hair was still black. The man was tall, well built and dressed in black. "May I help you?"

"Ya don't recognize me do ya lass?" the man replied with a slight brogue accent. "Ya see me every Sunday at morning mass. I'm the one in the white robes holding the sacraments and bestowing the blessings."

"Father?"

"Aye, that would be me lass," the priest chuckled. "I'm Father Michael O'Casey, the parish priest of Saint Jerome."

"You're right," Breena laughed. "I didn't recognize you. I guess I keep my head bowed too much!"

"Tis not a bad thing to do afore the Lord, but we would like ya to raise that head and talk to me if ya will," Michael teased. "We found out from other parishioners you'd be new to the area. We thought we'd invite ya to become a permanent member of our parish."

"Please Father Michael," Breena invited. "Come in and warm yourself. I'd be pleased to talk with you."

"Thank you," Father Michael responded entering the parlor and removing his large woolen topcoat. "Tis a bit nippy out today. Soon the cherry blossoms will accost our senses and the renewal of Spring will be upon us. Until that time however, a warm home and hot drink would be most inviting." When he entered the parlor a brown and white spotted puppy ran up to him and sniffed at his trouser leg.

"This is Liberty, Father Michael," Breena introduced. "She's my little dog."

"Well if you aren't the cutest little pup I've met since County Fermanagh," Michael said scratching the pup behind her ears.

Liberty rolled over to let Michael O'Casey scratch her belly.

"I'll ask Aida to make some hot chocolate for us. Or would you prefer tea?" Breena queried walking toward the kitchen.

"I'd prefer a cup of hot chocolate," Michael answered grinning broadly. He took a seat on the large divan and Liberty jumped up on his lap. "Well there Liberty, if you aren't the sweetest little thing." Michael said to the pup while scratching her head. "Tell me all about your mistress."

Liberty replied, "Yap, yap, yap."

"Oh I See!" Michael answered humorously. "Your mistress is Breena Hodges. She is the widowed niece of Brian Duffey who lives in some place out in the West, right?"

"Where did you hear all that?" Breena questioned with surprise returning to the parlor. She was especially surprised to hear the widowed part.

"This is what I've heard in the Parish," Father O'Casey grinned mischievously. "Is any of the gossip true?"

Breena liked the priest right off. "Most of it."

"Ah tis true of all gossip. It never is all-true. Only most of it is true," Michael chuckled. "So tell me about you lass."

"Why would you be interested in this dull person?" Breena teased.

"I have a passion for learning about my parishioners," Michael teased in return. "It makes the gossip more interesting if I know the truth, and it makes me a better priest. I find I can help every now and then if I know my parishioners."

"In that case," Breena smiled broadly with reply. Liberty jumped to her lap. "My name is Breena Hodges. I am the niece of Brian Duffey. I lived most of my life with my Uncle Brian in Ely, Nevada. We moved there to start his law firm shortly after my parents died in a train accident."

"How old were you?" Michael asked sincerely interested.

"I was eight years old," Breena responded nostalgically. "I had eight wonderful loving years with my parents before I lost them. Uncle Brian has been a wonderful father to me for the rest of my fourteen years."

"You haven't spoken about an auntie," Michael noticed "During the past six Sunday masses I saw two older men with older women entering, sitting, and leaving with you."

"My but we are observant," Breena laughed scratching Liberty on her tummy. "My Uncle married only this year to a wonderful woman from Ely, Nevada. Her name is Alyson. She is my auntie now. The other couple was Henry and Audrey Astor. Audrey Astor is Auntie Alyson's sister."

"How! The Astors indeed!" Michael marveled.

"Not quite," Breena giggled. "Uncle Henry is a distant cousin of the New York Astors, but a very wealthy self made man. He is nearly equal in bank drafts to the New York Astors. They even have holdings in England that belonged to the British noble family of Stuarts. You see, Audrey and Alyson are sisters and descendents of the English Stuart bloodline."

"I came to meet the lovely little girl who visits mass on Sunday," Michael guffawed. "I end up begging the child to become a member of my poor parish. It truly wouldn't hurt to have the Astor's name bandied about. It might bring in some more parishioners. You will join, won't you?"

"Tsk, tsk, Father O'Casey," Breena laughed. "More gossip for the parishioners?"

"Good Lord, I hope so!" Michael prayed looking up past the ceiling. "Dear Father in Heaven, would our little lass understand thy blessings of name dropping?"

Aida brought in a large silver tray holding an urn and two cups filled with freshly made hot chocolate.

"Ahh, ambrosia, food of the gods," Father Michael said inhaling the heavy chocolate aroma. He reached for a cup Aida offered him.

Aida then offered Breena a cup and placed the silver tray on the server next to the fireplace. "Will that be all ma'am?"

"Yes Aida," Breena appreciated. "Thank you very much. I don't think anyone can make a cup of chocolate quite as good as yours."

"I only add a touch of cinnamon and vanilla bean," Aida acknowledged humbly. "I'm glad you like it." She left the parlor and returned to making her bread in the kitchen.

"Mmmm,' Michael savored. "This is the best hot chocolate I've ever tasted. I may have to visit you quite often."

"I'd like the company Father O'Casey," Breena invited. "Please visit us as often as you would like."

"Thank you Breena," Michael winked playfully. "I will enjoy our visits immensely. Even a parish priest enjoys bright company now and then."

"Tell me Father O'Casey, why would you be interested in a simple parishioner?" Breena queried.

"I'm interested in every sheep in my fold," Michael answered taking another sip and enjoying the flavors. "I could tell you I'm desperate for every new sheep. I could tell you I noticed how well dressed you and your families were at mass. That means money for a poor small parish. I could tell you I was charmed by your beauty and all of it would be true."

"Why do I feel there is a small *but* in that statement?" Breena guessed.

"But there is a Colonel Gregory Wagner who is fascinated by your countenance," Michael answered honestly. "The Colonel asked me to find out about you and hopefully obtain an introduction if indeed all that was gossiped about you in the parish was true. You aren't married are you?"

"No I'm not married," Breena laughed. "Tell me about this Colonel who wants an introduction.' Emotionally she was a little flattered. Than the pang of missing Dwayne and not hearing from him resurfaced a twinge of pain once more.

"Colonel Wagner is a man near my age. He is a U.S. army regular. He fought in the Civil War and was promoted from the ranks," Michael informed. "He's never been married. He's a good honorable man and a good Catholic. I can honestly say I've known the man for several years and this is the first time he's shown any interest in any woman in or out of the parish."

"Are you playing matchmaker, Father O'Casey?" Breena joked.

"Have you ever known a good Irishman not to if given an opportunity?" Michael fired back with jest.

"No!" Breena laughed heartily. "I can honestly say I have not ever met such an Irishman."

"Colonel Wagner will be thrilled if I can give him an introduction to you," Michael guffawed. "I might get him to open his wallet a little more for the collection plate."

"I hope I'm worth that much," Breena shot back with the same humor.

"Lord, Breena Hodges! I think I like ya a lot," Michael admired. "You are a true Irish lassie. I'm bragged to tell ya!"

"So Uncle Duffey has said numerous times," Breena boasted.

"Did they?"

"Breena, of all the family, our Irish blood has settled into one stubborn lass!" Breena imitated.

"I know I love ya," Michael gulped nearly choking on a laugh as he was sipping his hot chocolate. "Ya will attend mass every Sunday, won't ya?"

"Yes I will," Breena agreed. "I want a look at the Colonel first before you make introductions."

"Won't take a pig in a poke, eh?" Michael taunted. "No Irish lass in her right mind would. Tis agreed."

"How will I know this Colonel?" Breena asked.

"He'd be the one staring at ya during the mass when he should be contemplating his lustful sins," Michael chuckled. "He is a good looking man for his age. Ya will see lass."

"I think I'll be the judge of good looking," Breena came back teasing. "Would you like some more hot chocolate?"

"Sinful delicious that is," Michael replied holding his cup. "I would love some for this sinful priest."

Breena stood up and poured a second cup. She handed Father O'Casey another serving of hot chocolate.

"Tell me more about ya lass," Michael prodded. "Is it true you have a legal background and work for a Senator in the Capitol?"

"My goodness," Breena sucked in with surprise. "Your gossip vine is quite accurate."

They spent the rest of the afternoon exchanging most of their life stories. The day ended in the evening when Father Michael O'Casey returned to the parish rectory after a large very tasty supper meal prepared by Aida.

Chapter 7

"Thank you for taking the case and working it to conclusion so quickly," Grady told the Pinkerton.

"We weren't working on any major case at the moment," Colter Brody answered. "My two agents and I needed something simple when you wired me. You inquiry was a blessing for us."

"You've done well," Grady observed reading Brody's reports. "Your agents are still watching the two of them?"

"They know where the two are at any given moment," Colter replied sipping at the wonderful imported French brandy. "Where do you get your stock?"

"My chef, Marseille Aumond, obtains it from his family in France," Grady answered automatically still concentrating on the reports in front of him. "Aumond imports the best I'm told."

"They are telling you the truth," Colter laughed enjoying the brandy with another sip. "Do you want us to stay for the fireworks?"

"Most certainly," Grady smiled to the Pinkerton. "We'll need you as foundation when we meet with the families."

"Those two cooked up quite a scheme," Colter implied in conversation. "Blackmail pure and simple. The documentation we have is enough for trial and conviction."

"Yes, I know," Grady said thoughtfully. "We have no intention of prosecuting. We only want to leave a solid example for others not to attempt to blackmail the McGillinen family."

"Blackmail is a plague of the wealthy," Colter Brody remarked lighting a cigar. "The McGillinen's are an extremely wealthy family."

"You've checked?" Grady teased.

"Always want to make sure Pinkerton will get paid," Colter snorted in humor.

"I guess my credit must be good," Grady guffawed. "You accepted the case."

"Your credit and creditability with my good friend, Brian Duffey," Colter replied inhaling the essence of the cigar. "Cuban?"

Grady nodded.

"Only the finest here. I guess I can't blame the little Miss Deborah Wheeler for wanting a part of it," Colter joked. "Her and her Tim Miller would get a substantial grubstake."

"I would have been more inclined to give them the money as a wedding present if they had asked directly," Grady growled. "I don't take kindly to having my son's name dragged through the mud."

"We've taken care of that," Colter said with resolve.

"Yes, you have," Grady grinned wickedly. "Here's to you and the Pinkertons." Grady toasted raising his brandy glass. "The sad part of this story is, that if Dwayne did indeed father a child I know in my heart he would want it, cherish it, and do the honorable thing."

"I'm sure he would," Colter agreed. "From the little I know and heard of the boy, I believe he would."

"Or I might have to kill him," Grady roared with laughter.

Colter laughed with Grady and then asked, "When do you want us to gather the two for the meeting?"

"Dwayne needs to go to Harvard in two weeks," Grady informed. "I want this taken care of well before he leaves. Can you arrange this for next Monday?"

"No problem," Colter replied. "Consider it done."

"I'll send word to Ryan," Grady said thinking out loud. "I know it will be hard to pull Ayden away from the twins for a day, but I'm sure he'll do it for Dwayne."

"I saw the twins. I can't believe how beautiful babies can really be," Colter said in conversation. "There's a double blessing."

"The twins are beautiful and perfect," Grady responded. "They look like their mother, Paige. They have blonde hair and eyes we are certain will be violet like hers. I have to admit that Adam and Abigail are really fine productions. My list of grandchildren keeps growing, but they are my grandchildren."

"I've seen your youngest son Dwayne with the twins. He's real good with them," Colter observed.

"He's good with all the grandchildren," Grady bragged. "Some day he will be a great father."

"All in good time, eh?" Colter grinned.

Grady nodded.

"Thanks for putting me up here," Colter appreciated. "It's like being in a European Castle made of logs. Only the finest is brought in here. I feel honored to be in this house. Not only is it luxurious, it feels like a real home. It is also convenient for me to be your guest and go into town to meet my operatives."

"No one has guessed they are working for you?" Grady asked still in unbelief.

"Pinkerton's are discreet," Colter crowed. "No one has a clue."

Payton Lee

That Saturday afternoon two mounted figures rode up to the ranch house. The big one with a cradleboard on his back dismounted from Chiseler and helped his wife from her mare. They were followed by Old George who had been sent to Geneva's Branch on the mission of bringing them to Grady.

"Careful!" Twiggy reprimanded Ryan when he lifted her off her mare. "I do wish you would let me carry Aurora Blue! You always make me nervous when you jump from Chiseler."

"I didn't jump!" Ryan scowled. "I'd never jar my little baby girl. You know that!"

"I know," Twiggy conceded. "I wish I could carry my own baby once and awhile."

"You get to feed her," Ryan reminded.

"Oh I keep forgetting," Twiggy teased punching Ryan in the shoulder. "That's the one thing you can't do!"

"See?" Ryan teased in return. "You do get to hold my little Aurora!"

"Briefly at best," Twiggy growled. "Let's get in the house. These March winds are fierce! I don't want Aurora to catch the sniffles and I am anxious to see the twins."

"Can you believe it? Twins!" Ryan declared. "That older brother of mine always has to do the one upmanship."

"I don't think your brother intended to put poor Paige through that," Twiggy disagreed. "It is a blessing of Tam Apo. Even Tells the Truth said so."

"It's almost ironic Paige got double of everything for the baby," Ryan mentioned while opening the door to Geneva's Hope.

"Like I said, a blessing of Tam Apo!" Twiggy taunted.

Ryan slipped the cradleboard from his back and started to undo the bindings. Little Aurora Blue was sound asleep from the ride and all nice and snuggled inside her rabbit lined cradleboard. Tied leather flaps over the domed headboard had kept the wind from biting at her angelic face. She was wearing a warm woolen gown and knitted bonnet with matching little mittens that Lucy had made for her as a present.

Aurora Blue gurgled peacefully as her daddy picked her up from the cradleboard.

"Did you bring the moss?" Ryan questioned. "I think Daddy needs to make a change on Aurora Blue's nappies."

Kerry walked into the hall at that moment and gasped. "Ryan changes nappies?"

"The only thing he doesn't do is feed her," Twiggy laughed running to Kerry and giving her a great big hug. "Where are the twins? I do so want to see them."

"They're in the parlor with Paige and Ayden," Kerry answered returning Twiggy's embrace. "Ayden is simply awed with his babies. I'd never believe Ayden would be so doting. He was always so aloof. And Ryan? Changing nappies? Will wonders ever cease?"

"Twiggy!" Ryan growled. "I need the moss!"

"It's in my bag right by your feet," Twiggy replied walking toward the parlor with Kerry. "We'll let Ryan change Aurora Blue before he brings her into the parlor to see her cousins, uncles, and grandparents."

"This family is growing by leaps and bounds," Kerry agreed walking with Twiggy hand in hand. Upon entering the parlor Kerry announced, "There they are! Here are the newest additions to the McGillinen family. Meet Adam and Abigail McGillinen."

The three men were in a corner near the fireplace. Ayden held Adam. Dwayne held Abigail. Braden held Jared. Garrett was in his mobile walker and Little Rain was keeping a close eye on him. She was kept quite busy removing articles from his hands. Little Rain was trying to keep him occupied with his new toy horse. He had just celebrated his first birthday. Bennett was with Eye of Hawk at the Sosoni' camp. Victoria was with Bennett giving a well-deserved break to Amore who had been curled next to Paige.

Paige rose to greet Twiggy. "Dear sister! Come see my babies!" Paige embraced Twiggy and asked, "Where is my pretty little niece, Aurora Blue?"

"As always, she's with her Daddy," Twiggy complained. "I declare Ryan will only let me hold my own baby for small moments at a time."

"The McGillinen men seem to be like that," Paige agreed. "Lucky I had two at one time. I get to hold one of them for a time occasionally."

Ryan walked in with a sweet smelling freshly diapered baby girl. "Let me see those adorable little ones." He walked over to Ayden and peered over his shoulder. "Mighty fine creation. You did really well."

"Thanks brother," Ayden laughed. "This is Adam, my son. You're Aurora Blue has grown in a short time."

"She eats like her daddy," Ryan returned with humor.

"Amen to that," Twiggy added. "Aurora Blue has a healthy appetite."

"Where are Pa and Morning Song?" Ryan queried. "Seems to me those two are always near the grandbabies."

Suddenly everyone's face turned serious.

"What?" Twiggy asked creasing her brow. She sensed the change immediately. "What has happened?"

"They're in the study with Colter Brody, the Pinkerton," Kerry answered.

"Pinkerton?" Ryan roared in surprise. "What the Sam Hill is a Pinkerton doing here. Old George was pretty closed mouth when he told us Pa sent for us. What is going on here?"

The tonal change of her father's voice frightened Aurora Blue. She began crying. Twiggy took her from Ryan and soothed her with a mother's soft and reassuring voice. Aurora snuggled into her mother and tried feeding through her mother's dress.

"It's all right darling," Twiggy soothed. "Mommy will feed you."

Aurora's crying also disturbed Jared who immediately wanted attention.

"Come with me to the library," Kerry suggested to Twiggy. "We'll feed the babies privately in there. The men need to talk with Pa."

"Thank you," Twiggy appreciated following Kerry. "You will tell me what's going on?"

"Of course," Kerry whispered. "You know I will."

At the sudden disturbance, Garrett looked up from Little Rain and his toy horse to see his big Uncle Ryan. "Wyain!" His little voice muttered incoherently. He was only just learning to talk. Little Rain was a bit distracted watching Kerry and Jared. Garrett took advantage of the moment and took off in his walker like a shot. He rammed right into Uncle Ryan's leg."

"Geez!" Ryan almost swore until he looked down to see an eager and happy little face looking up at him hugging his leg. "Wyain!"

"Hey there little guy!" Ryan acknowledged bending down to give Garrett a hug. "How are you doing cowboy?"

Garrett gurgled with delight.

Ryan picked Garrett up and held him high over his head shaking him gently to Garrett's delight.

"You want to trade Twenty Hands for Aurora Blue?" Braden teased. "Kerry won't give me a little girl."

"Not on your life!" Ryan laughed. He enjoyed the fact he had the prettiest little girl first. He had what Braden wanted and it was a prime teaser for the both of them. Ryan actually liked the British Lord, a lot. "My nephew is real smart. He knows which Uncle is the best."

Ayden put Adam in the cradle. Dwayne handed Abigail to Paige.

"Paige, why don't you take Abby and join Kerry and Twiggy," Ayden suggested seriously.

Paige nodded taking her baby girl and spoke quietly, "Veronica, bring Adam with us. Little Rain, you may want to bring Garrett."

"I'll take him," Little Rain offered to Ryan.

Ryan turned the happy little Garrett over to Little Rain.

Garrett didn't want to leave his Uncle Ryan and pouted instantly. Garrett's lower lip trembled slightly and he broke out into a loud cry.

Little Rain ignored Garrett's temper tantrum. She placed him in his walker and pushed him toward the library.

Back in the seriousness of the atmosphere surrounding him, Ryan asked, "What is going on here?"

"Let's go to the study," Braden said solemnly.

"Has someone died?" Ryan grumbled. "What is all this secret stuff about?"

"Nothing secret big brother," Dwayne reassured. "Just a legal matter we are about to take care of."

Ayden led the way to their father's study. He knocked lightly at the study door.

"Yes?" Grady's voice could be heard.

"Ryan's here Pa," Ayden answered.

"Come in," Grady invited. Upon the entrance of his sons and son in law Grady stood tall behind his desk. "Ryan, this is Colter Brody. He's the Pinkerton Brian Duffey employed to find information on Twiggy's family."

"Pleased to meet you," Ryan said offering his hand in greeting.

Colter accepted Ryan's hand and shook it, "I hear you and your wife had a baby girl."

"The prettiest little angel in the valley," Ryan boasted proudly. "She's as pretty as her Mama."

"Aurora Blue has a rival," Ayden charged playfully. "Paige gave us Abby."

"Abigail is the prettiest little angel in your England," Ryan countered. "Aurora Blue will reign here until she has a little sister."

"Sister? Sister?" Braden joined in. "Twiggy will give you another little girl?"

"You should have known how stubborn Kerry is when you married her," Ryan ribbed. "You made your bed, lie in it. Besides, nothing wrong with sons."

"Then how come you only want girls?" Braden questioned raising an eyebrow.

"Boys are too much trouble," Ryan replied quickly. "Besides, the McGillinens have too many boys in the family. We need some more pretty, smart, and stubborn little girls."

"I thought we get that when we marry them," Braden snorted.

"When we marry the right one," Dwayne added ruefully.

Ryan turned to his younger brother. "Why was I called here?"

"I've got a problem," Dwayne admitted.

"We are a family," Morning Song stated. "We have a problem."

"What the Sam Hill did you do now?" Ryan growled at Dwayne.

"Believe it or not big brother, nothing!" Dwayne grumped and plopped down on one of his father's big chairs.

"Dwayne was accused of paternity," Colter Brody said nonchalantly.

Ryan didn't wait to hear the rest. He grabbed Dwayne by the shirt and literally picked him up from the chair. "Can't keep your fly buttoned can you? Well the time to pay has come. Let's get us this little women and get you married."

"I'm not going to marry her!" Dwayne screeched balling his hand in a fist to strike a blow at his big brother.

"The Hell you ain't!" Ryan snarled blocking his brother's swing.

Grady groaned.

Colter Brody chuckled, "Are they always like this?"

"Always," Morning Song answered. They watched for a few minutes as the brother's swore, cursed, and swung at each other. Finally she raised her voice. "Ryan! Put Dwayne down and listen for a change!"

Morning Song's voice quieted Ryan immediately. He loved and respected his stepmother.

"Ryan, Mr. Brody said Dwayne was accused of paternity," Grady went on. "The baby is not Dwayne's. We have proof of that from the Pinkertons. The girl is using this for blackmail."

"Blackmail?" Ryan latched on quickly and paid attention.

"Deborah Wheeler wants $100,000 from me," Dwayne growled dusting off his shirt to remove Ryan's invisible handprints. "It's not my child. She only wants money and is threatening to tell the entire town its mine if I don't pay her."

"Deborah Wheeler?" Ryan gasped and sat down in a leather chair. "That little gal is so pretty she could have any man she wants."

"She wants money. She doesn't want me," Dwayne rebuked angrily. "Mr. Brody here has proof the father is Tim Miller and it was his idea to use me for his grubstake to get away from his overbearing big brother. I understand that actually!"

"What's that supposed to mean?" Ryan snapped jumping up to swing at Dwayne.

"Exactly what you think you big lug!" Dwayne growled blocking Ryan's swing and pulling back for a swing of his own.

"Boys!" Grady roared threateningly with paternal authority. "Stop this right now! Mr. Brody is going to get the wrong impression. We need to take care of this. Dwayne is leaving for Harvard in two weeks. I want this settled Monday. Do you hear me?"

"Yes Pa," both boys said obediently and sat down quietly.

"This is my plan," Grady began and explained what each brother's role was to be.

"So what is this all about Kerry?" Twiggy asked after Aurora Blue was contentedly fed and asleep. " Ryan has been in the study for some time. I haven't been able to hold Aurora Blue this long since she was born. Ryan even takes her out in her cradleboard when he works in the barn or rides the ranch. I only get her back for about ten minutes of feeding time and she's back in the cradleboard on Ryan's back."

"You are teasing," Paige queried. "I thought Ayden and Braden were over doting fathers."

"Trust me," Twiggy giggled. "I am not teasing or exaggerating. This is the longest I've held Aurora Blue since she was born."

"I believe it," Kerry beamed. "I know what a big cuddly bear my overbearing big brother really is. I kind of feel sorry for Dwayne when Ryan finds out. Ryan won't listen to the entire story. Ryan will threaten Dwayne and scold him. The two will fight, and then Pa and Morning Song will set them straight."

"Just what is Ryan going to find out?" Twiggy asked in curiosity. "What is this all about?"

"There is this girl named Deborah Wheeler. She's quite lovely actually. Well she decided she wants one of the handsome McGillinen men to pay her blackmail," Kerry related.

"Blackmail? What would this girl use for blackmail?" Twiggy gasped.

"She's threatening to bring a paternity suit against Dwayne," Paige replied.

"What?" Twiggy choked. "Is Dwayne the father?"

"No," Kerry answered quickly. "Pa hired Colter Brody, a Pinkerton, to find out the truth of the matter."

"Right," Paige added. "It turns out the father is a Tim Miller. It was the father's idea to blackmail our Dwayne. They were rivals during school years so it's a personal vendetta."

"What is a vendetta?" Twiggy questioned furrowing her brow.

"He wants to hurt Dwayne," Kerry explained. "Apparently Tim also wants the money to get away from his overbearing older brother. Hank Miller keeps Tim on a short rope and is tight with the purse strings."

"So he talked this Deborah into blackmailing Dwayne with a paternity legal suit?" Twiggy queried.

"Right," Paige responded. "Almost bloody successful ways to get money except for the fact the McGillinen's are so family powerful."

"So what is going to happen?" Twiggy asked.

"Well Pa has this plan," Kerry replied and shared the entire scheme with Twiggy.

Monday mid morning several carriages, wagons, and riders arrived in Ely. The carriages stopped at the hotel where several women with children and babies took rooms. The wagons continued on to the Crawford Mercantile and the riders seemed to disappear after their horses were tied to the posts in front of the hotel.

Several of the townspeople wondered why all the McGillinens were in town at the same time. All of them at once did not bode well for someone. When they showed up in family force, it meant they were united against a common foe. *Heaven help that person.*

Deborah was unaware of the McGillinen congregation. She was suffering with a bout of morning sickness. Her father had gone to sweep the newspaper office. Tim Miller had just left the ranch to visit Deborah and find out if she had heard anything from the McGillinen family. It had been a month since she dropped the news to Dwayne. She had been careful never to name Dwayne as the father to her parents. Harriet Weiss had spread the gossip itself. When the McGillinens did not respond and the Crawfords had rebuked the paternity to customers that suggested it, most of the gossip had stopped.

When the family showed up in force. The townspeople of Ely were wondering if the McGillinens were there for a confrontation or a wedding.

Tim Miller was getting nervous. He truly did care for Deborah. He was proud as could be that the prettiest girl in Ely was interested in him. He wanted to take her, his baby, and move away to his own life. The problem was, Dwayne McGillinen wasn't responding at all.

"Hey there Tim," Granger Tyler greeted. He was a new hand Hank Miller had hired only three weeks ago and Tim liked Granger. They had become friends. "If you're going into town, I'll come with you. I want to check out a new saddle. Hank is already on his way to Ely."

"Hank never goes into Ely," Tim said in surprise.

"It appears something important caught his attention," Granger answered. "He left early this morning. Talked about some meeting with someone."

Braden entered the newspaper office. "Mr. Wheeler?"

"Yeah?" Wheeler looked up to see Braden. "Ain't you the Brit that McGillinen gal married?"

"Happily and proudly I am," Braden answered.

"Your brother in law got my little girl in the family way," Wheeler snapped. "Don't know what to do about that yet."

"No need to worry," Braden assuaged. "We came into town to take care of this. Would you come with me sir?"

Grady sat in Marshall Ewal's office waiting for Hank Miller to arrive. The two men played a game of chess while they waited. The door finally opened revealing Hank Miller.

"What's this all about McGillinen?" Hank demanded. "What is the meaning of this message to meet you regarding an urgent legal matter?"

"All in good time Miller," Grady replied. "Checkmate!"

"I'll be blamed," Kent groaned. "Guess its time to take care of this matter."

"Let's go Hank," Grady suggested as he rose from the chair in front of Kent Ewal's desk.

"Just where are we going, Grady?" Hank queried.

"We and the family are going to meet at the Wheeler house," Grady informed.

"The Wheeler house?" Hank asked. "What in the Sam Hill do the Wheeler's have to do with a legal case?"

"You really don't have any idea do you?" Grady asked.

"Hell no!" Hank declared. "Would you care to enlighten me?"

"All in good time my friend," Grady chuckled. "All in good time. Come with me."

Deborah had recovered from her morning sickness and her friend coaxed her into coming shopping with her. They were walking down the boarded streets of Ely when Ayden approached them

Ayden dipped his hat to Deborah and her new California friend, Melanie Brighton. "Morning ladies."

"Good morning, Ayden," Deborah replied coolly. "You're little brother didn't happen to come with you?"

"Actually Miss Wheeler, he did," Ayden replied flashing a broad smile. "We all came to pay you a visit. May I accompany you and your pretty friend back to your home?"

"Dwayne is there?" Deborah choked.

"We are all there," Ayden chuckled. "We are all there waiting for you."

Tim and Granger walked toward the mercantile when a large shadow appeared to hover over them. Tim turned around to stare at Ryan McGillinen's broad chest.

"What the hell?" Tim gulped.

"Tsk, tsk, watch that language," Ryan warned. "Come with me little man. We have a meeting to attend."

"Huh?" Tim gulped hard when Ryan's broad hand grabbed his jacket and pulled him up to eye level. "Granger do something!"

"Can't do that," Granger chuckled. "My boss told me to help Ryan get you to the meeting."

"Hank?" Tim breathed out fearfully.

"Nope, Colter Brody is my real boss," Granger laughed. "I work for the Pinkerton Agency in Carson City."

"What?" Tim choked.

"That's right little man," Ryan answered releasing his hold and pushing Tim toward the Wheeler house. "Go ahead little man. We have a meeting to attend."

Tim Wheeler was terrified. He hadn't counted on anything other than the McGillinens releasing money to shut his Deborah up. He hadn't counted on Ryan McGillinen showing up.

"Hello Mrs. Wheeler," Kerry greeted cheerfully when Margaret Wheeler opened the door to Kerry's knock. "May I come in?"

Margaret was always a shy and reclusive woman. She was also timid and nervous. Having Kerry McGillinen at her door frightened her a little. She had heard the town gossip about her daughter and was hopeful her little girl would marry into them, but she was still afraid of the wealthy family. "Of course. What can I do for you?"

"I kind of came ahead of time to warn you to expect my entire family to show up," Kerry answered sweetly. Everyone knew Margaret Wheeler was a shy and nervous woman. The McGillinen family certainly did not want to make her sick or upset her. "We are going to have a little meeting. We need to settle this matter of paternity with your daughter. I hope you understand?"

"Er yes, I mean of course, I mean, well yes," Margaret Wheeler stammered.

"May we have some tea?" Kerry suggested. She hoped preparing for the arrival and preparation of tea might calm the nervous woman.

"Yes, I'll make some right away," Margaret replied. She felt more comfortable knowing tea would be served.

Kerry sat down on the small divan in the small parlor. She hoped there would be enough room for everyone. The men would remain standing and she knew this meeting wouldn't last too long.

The door opened when Margaret brought in the pot of tea for Kerry. "What are you doing home?" Margaret asked her husband when he entered. Then she saw Braden Wessex behind her husband.

The men had no sooner entered than Ayden arrived with Deborah and Melanie who was the other Pinkerton agent.

Grady followed Deborah with Marshall Ewal and Hank Miller.

Dwayne knocked on the door to be let in with Colter Brody.

Ryan appeared behind him with Pinkerton agent Granger and Tim Miller.

Hank looked at Granger with question.

Tim answered the unspoken question. "He's a Pinkerton agent, Hank."

Hank growled at his little brother with menace. "What the blaze is going on here?"

Deborah sank into the chair and tried to control her hysteria. She was terrified. This wasn't supposed to happen. It was supposed to be so easy. Everything was supposed to be easy, Tim told her that. "Tim?" she cried weakly.

"It's all right Debbie," Tim soothed walking over to her. He took her hand. "It's going to be all right."

"Glad to hear that," Grady said firmly. "You see we McGillinen's take family real serious like. Mr. And Mrs. Wheeler, we are certain you've heard the rumors my son Dwayne has fathered the baby growing in your daughter?"

"We have," Roger Wheeler answered. "We've been waiting to see what you would do."

"If that child is my son's, we want to let you know we've come to take it," Grady announced.

"What?" Deborah shrieked. "Take my baby?"

"Not literally," Grady assured quietly. "We want you to know that if you continue in your pursuit of naming our Dwayne father, we will file for custody on its birth."

"You would take my baby?" Deborah choked back tears.

"That's right," Ayden concurred. "If you want to come along you'd have to marry my brother. Do you want to marry Dwayne?"

"No!" Deborah shouted hysterically.

"Then we take the baby," Ryan agreed. "If you insist the baby is McGillinen. We will raise it as a McGillinen."

"Tim!" Deborah shouted in panic. "Do something. This wasn't supposed to happen!"

"What is she talking about Tim," Hank demanded of his little brother. He was totally confused by this meeting.

"What happened, Hank," Dwayne piped in. "Tim is the father of Deborah's baby. They decided they would use the McGillinen name as a bank account to give them a grubstake to leave Ely."

"Is this true, Tim?" Hank asked his brother.

Tim nodded sheepishly.

"Grady McGillinen hired me and my two agents here to find out the truth of the matter when Deborah first approached Dwayne McGillinen claiming to call him the father if he didn't give her $100,000," Colter Brody revealed. "We found out the truth of the black mail scheme. Deborah and Tim were going to use it to buy a spread in California."

"Is this true, Tim?" Hank asked his brother once more.

Tim nodded and held Deborah's hand even tighter. "We didn't expect this to happen. We only thought the McGillinen's would give us the money to keep quiet."

"This is black mail and you can be prosecuted for it," Kent Ewal told the couple.

"We didn't think," Deborah cried. "We thought it would be so easy."

"You realize you've committed a crime?" Kent asked directly.

"We're sorry!" Deborah and Tim answered.

"If you really wanted to get away from me, why didn't you talk to me?" Hank asked sadly. "If you still want that ranch, I'll put up the money for you."

"You will?" Tim asked with shock.

"Of course I will," Hank answered. "We're family just like the McGillinens. I hope you have a boy and call him Hank."

"We will, we will," Deborah cried.

"Tim is the father?" Margaret asked her daughter.

"Yes mother," Deborah answered. "And I love him."

"We'll prepare the wedding for this Saturday," Hank promised. "I'll pay for it."

"I don't get it big brother," Tim said completely surprised. "I thought you hated me."

"I promised Pa to take care of you and the ranch until you decided to become a man," Hank answered. "When you took responsibility for your actions, well I knew the time had come. We are family."

Tim rose and hugged his brother. Hank returned the embrace.

"We'll all stay in town and help with the wedding," Kerry announced. "If the McGillinens are present. Everyone will know Debbie and Tim are the baby's parents and there is no ill will."

"Thank you," Deborah appreciated. "Mother and Father, we want you to come with us. We think it would be better for your health. Besides we'll need all the help we can get when we start the ranch."

The McGillinen family left the Wheeler and Miller family with happy preparations.

The wedding that weekend was beautiful. Grady handed an envelope to Tim Miller at the wedding. It had $10,000 in it. "This is to help you and Deborah out."

Tim and Deborah Miller were even more surprised when Dwayne drove a wagon up to them that was filled with foodstuffs and supplies. "This is my wedding gift to you two. It'll help you get started."

Ryan sent word to Cassidy at Geneva's Branch and he, Lucy, and their baby boy showed up with six magnificent mustangs from the ranch stock. Carrying his Aurora Blue in the cradleboard on his back, Ryan and Twiggy handed the tether ropes to the bride and groom. "Good Fortune and the blessings of Tam Apo."

Ayden handed Tim and Deborah another envelope containing $10,000. "This is from Paige, myself and our children. We wish you well and lots of happiness with your baby. Lord knows how happy and blessed we are with the twins."

The next morning Tim and Deborah Miller left with Roger and Margaret Wheeler, their wedding presents, and hopes to California.

Everyone in the town knew Tim Miller was the father of Deborah's baby and the McGillinen name was clear of any gossip. The people also marveled at the generosity of the McGillinen's toward a couple that would have used them for money.

Ayden explained it the best when he was asked by a townsperson of Ely at the wedding why the McGillinen's were so nice to the couple, "Honesty is its greatest reward."

Chapter 8

"It is really becoming warm, Liberty," Breena commented to the puppy lying at her feet. "I received a post from Dwayne today. Do you want to read it?"

"Yap, yap," Liberty responded wagging her tail.

"I want to read it, but I don't want to read it," Breena lamented. "Do you know I haven't heard from Dwayne McGillinen since the day after Christmas. I'm not sure I want to know what he has to say."

"Yap, yap," Liberty barked excitedly.

"Very well," Breena laughed. "I'll read you his letter." Slowly and carefully Breena opened the sealed envelope. The return address showed Harvard University, Cambridge, and Massachusetts. Even more slowly and with hands trembling she opened the post pulling the letter from its envelope. Breena closed her eyes and allowed her hands to open the letter. "Well Liberty, if you're ready we'll read the post."

Dear Breena,

I can't believe time has passed so quickly. With all the winter storms I never got a chance to see you off. I wanted to wish you well. Hopefully things are all working out for you with the Senator.

"Things are working out very well, Dwayne," Breena sighed. "We've already started summer recess. The Senator and Mrs. Jones have returned to Nevada for the summer holiday. That's how long it has been."

I've completed the first semester at Harvard. I hope you'll be proud of me. I placed well with grades. Not as good as yours if you were here, but I'm trying.

"You've got that right," Breena laughed. "I've always done better in school than you."

I'm staying with Auntie Audrey and Uncle Henry. They are really great. I get to see little Matthew a lot and he's a doll. Of course seeing him makes me homesick for my Bennett, Garrett, and Jared. No one gets to see Aurora Blue very much. That big old bear of a brother, Ryan, won't let anyone hold her. Even Twiggy complains she can't hold her own baby girl. Did you hear about Paige and Ayden? They had twins! Can you believe it? Paige gave Ayden a beautiful baby girl named Abigail and a wonderful son named Adam! From what I understand Auntie Alyson was in Boston with Auntie Audrey when the twins were born. I'm sure Auntie Alyson was disappointed that she wasn't there. But, as Morning Song always said, 'Babies come when they choose, not when we choose.'

"Did you hear that Liberty?" Breena bubbled with delight. "Paige had twins! Isn't that fabulous. I hope they stop to visit before they return to England. I would like to see the twins. I think I'll write a letter of congratulations, send a present, and ask them to visit before they return to England. What do you think Liberty?"

"Yap, yap," Liberty agreed wagging her tail with happiness.

The twins look a lot like Paige. In other words, they are beautiful. Thank heavens they took after their mother and not their father, Ayden. Okay, I'm teasing. Ayden is thrilled with the twins. I'd never believe old stoic big brother Ayden could be so doting and caring. He sure loves Paige.

Just think Breena; both my brothers are married with families. Things have changed in such a short time. Where has yesterday gone? Remember how we used to go to the pond to fish, ride horses and let the summer winds blow thru our hair? Your hair always got messed up bad. We were kids just yesterday.

"Yes Dwayne," Breena sniffed with nostalgic melancholy. "It was just yesterday we were carefree kids and I had a mountain sized crush on you. And your English grammar is still atrocious."

I came pretty close to getting shackled myself.

Breena's hand started to shake when she read that line. Dwayne married?

Do you remember Deborah Wheeler?

"Yes, I remember Deborah very well. She was the prettiest girl in school. I envied her. She captured every boy's eye. That included your eyes," Breena snapped angrily. Breena could imagine Deborah putting full attention to Dwayne and capturing him in matrimony. "Do you love her? Did you want to marry her?"

Liberty noted the change in Breena's voice. She jumped up placing her front paws on Breena's knees. Liberty whimpered.

"I'm alright girl," Breena choked in response petting the sensitive puppy. "I guess I'd better read on to find out what happened."

Debbie got herself in the family way.

"Oh my God," Breena's voice cracked in despair. Dwayne impregnated Debbie Wheeler. Breena had always been afraid that her wonderful night with Dwayne was simply another typical roll in the hay with other women.

Liberty was really concerned with her mistress's voice and started trying to jump up on Breena's lap.

"There's no room up here girl," Breena sobbed in despair. "If Dwayne saw me now he wouldn't be interested anyway. Ever since I arrived in Washington City I've been gaining weight. I'm getting fatter and fatter. It must be Aida's cooking. So you can see, there is no room on my lap." Breena forced herself to continue reading the letter.

Debbie thought she could blackmail me into giving her lots of money by threatening to tell everyone it was my child. It wasn't, but who would believe whom? Pa hired the Pinkerton's and it was proven that Tim Miller and Deborah Wheeler was a couple. It was his child and they cooked up this scheme to get McGillinen money. I tell you I'm still angry about that little plot. Why does a woman use something like the family way to scorch a man? No woman is ever going to get me that way! No Sir! I'm not going to ever let a woman even try that one on me ever again!

"I agree Dwayne," Breena breathed happily. Dwayne wasn't in love with Deborah, but then again, how many women were out there that could attract him. This

was nonsense. She was a grown woman. She needed to get on with her life and over this childhood crush.

    Since I'm in Massachusetts, I hope I might come and visit you in Washington City, or perhaps you might come and visit us? I'd like to see you again, soon.

    Please write back when you have some time.
Love,
Dwayne

    "I'll lose some of this weight and then see if I can visit," Breena giggled. "I don't want you to see the fat Breena."

    Breena took out quill, ink, and paper. First she sent a letter of congratulations to Ayden and Paige. In the letter she invited them to visit Hyacinth House before they returned to England. Later in the day Breena would shop for a present for the twins and would send it off following the post.

    She then wrote a post for Dwayne telling him about Hyacinth House, her job, and Liberty. She wrote about Auntie Alyson and Auntie Audrey refurbishing the house. She wrote about the Senator, his wife, and their numerous parties. Breena wrote Dwayne about her friendship with Father O'Casey, but did not tell Dwayne about Colonel Wagner courting her. She didn't really know why she didn't want Dwayne to know about Colonel Wagner. It was after she sealed the letter for posting did she admit she still couldn't rid herself of that stupid childhood crush she had on Dwayne and didn't want him to know someone was courting her. She wanted Dwayne to believe she was still available. Well, she was available, really. Breena also wrote to Dwayne she thought what Deborah did was perfectly awful and no woman should force paternity on a man to achieve marriage or money.

    Breena rang the bell for Aida. She wanted Aida to give the posts for Jonathan Miland, their liveryman, to take to the postal office. As she waited for Aida, Breena suddenly felt very strange. For the past few weeks Breena had felt flutters in her abdomen but this time there was something strong and strange. "Oh my God!" Breena breathed heavily placing her hands on her abdomen. She felt her abdomen move.

    Aida observed Breena clutching her abdomen. Breena looked frightened. Aida had realized Breena was pregnant for some time now but said nothing since it was not for servants to speak of unless the mistress did. Breena never spoke of it. Aida did not think about the proper etiquette when she thought Breena was in pain and might be having a miscarriage. "What is it Missus Hodges? What be the problem?" Aida asked rushing to Breena's side and placing her hand over Breena's hands. "Is your chile alright?"

    "Child? What child?" Breena gasped in shock. "What are you talking about Aida?"

    "Oh the chile is jest fine," Aida replied with relief. "Your chile is jest restless and movin a little."

    "Aida, what in the Sam Hill are you talking about?" Breena demanded. Those funny feelings were still strong.

    "The baby chile you is growing in your belly," Aida answered casually as if this were everyday knowledge. "The baby chile is gettin bigger and being cramped up in one place is jest movin on to another."

"Are you telling me you think I'm in the family way?" Breena inhaled deeply with shock.

"Missus Hodges, I don't think you be in the family way. I knows you be in the family way," Aida answered with surprise. "Don't you know you gots a chile growin in your belly?"

"I can't be! I just can't be!" Breena wailed. "I don't have a husband!"

"Missus Hodges, your husband must have planted his seed afore he left. Cuz you be with chile," Aida answered. "When was the last time you done have your flow Missus Hodges. You sho ain't had one since you came here. I'd know if you did."

Breena thought for several minutes. She hadn't had her flow since before Christmas. *Dear God, I'm enceinte with Dwayne's child! I just wrote him how terrible it is for a woman to use a child to get a man or his money. I can't tell him. I won't tell him. No I can't be enceinte. I just can't!* "You're wrong, Aida."

"Missus Hodges, you been growing heavy with chile. We've had to let out your waist on dresses and skirts for two months," Aida scolded. "You are with chile and you should start wearing them mother dresses. That corset ain't healthy for a woman carrying a baby."

"I can't be enceinte," Breena denied. She rose quickly and picked up her bag. "I'll go to the doctor immediately. He'll prove to you I'm not with child." Breena walked to the door and grabbed her light coat.

"Then he'd be one stupid doctor," Aida scowled.

"Please have Jonathan take those letters on my desk to the post," Breena barked nervously. "I'm going to Doctor Whitecliff's office. I'll be back soon."

"Okay, you go and prove what is the fact ain't a fact," Aida quipped. "What shall I tell Father O'Casey and that Colonel of yours when they come for lunch."

"Oh dear I forgot," Breena realized and spun around to face Aida, "Just tell them I went to Doctor Whitecliff to check on something. Nothing more! Do you understand?"

"Yas'm I understand," Aida nodded turning toward the kitchen. She would give the posts to Jonathan and then prepare lunch for everyone. Aida was certain that Father O'Casey would wait for Breena to return. It would be his excuse to eat Aida's cooking. The Colonel was too fancy for Aida. He talked of fancy French cooking and fine Chefs.

Breena finished dressing with help from the nurse and was escorted to Doctor Whitecliff's consultation room.

"Well Mrs. Hodges, you are enceinte. I would say you are close to six months along," Dr. Whitecliff told Breena. "I think you will have a healthy baby. I attend your parish and it is sorrowful that Mr. Hodges couldn't live to see his child, but I'm certain he's looking down from Heaven and smiling."

Breena was still in shock. It was true. She was pregnant! She barely heard Dr. Whitecliff refer to her dead husband. *Dead husband? That's right, everyone thinks I'm a widow. They don't know I'm an unwed mother! I'll keep this charade going.* "Thank you for your kind words, Doctor Whitecliff."

"I'll be more than happy to take care of you during your partition," Doctor Whitecliff volunteered. "Give me a call when your time arrives and we'll take you into Providence Hospital. Until then, watch what you eat and get plenty of rest."

"Yes, thank you," Breena responded automatically. Her mind was a jumbled mess. This was a shock. The others would believe it was the child on a non-existent dead husband, but she needed someone to talk to. She needed, yes, Father O'Casey.

Blindly and numb from shock, Breena hailed a cab and gave him the address for Hyacinth House. Breena didn't even remember how she paid the cabby or how and when she got home. Her head was reeling when she knocked on the door.

Father O'Casey answered the door. Aida had been right. Colonel Wagner wouldn't wait for Breena. Father O'Casey loved Aida's cooking and would gladly wait for Breena to return home.

Both men had worried when they heard Breena went to Dr. Whitecliff, but Colonel Wagner couldn't wait too long. He had a meeting to attend too. He told Father O'Casey he would return this evening if the meeting didn't last long.

"Dear Child!" Father O'Casey declared when he saw Breena's pale face and dulled eyes. "You look like you've seen a ghost!"

"In a manner of speaking I have," Breena choked. "Father, I need someone to talk to. I need you to listen."

"I'm here for you," Father O'Casey reassured embracing Breena and walking her into the parlor. He placed her gently on the divan and sat next to her holding her hands. "What is it my child? Did the doctor find something wrong?"

"I don't know if you call it something wrong. Well yes it is wrong, but it isn't really," Breena rattled on making little sense. "It is, but physically no, well yes."

"Breena? I want ya to know lass ya are makin no sense at tall," Michael said in exasperation. "Are ya ill lass?"

"No," Breena answered and her lower lip quivered. Suddenly the words came out in three blunt words. "I am enceinte."

Michael O'Casey sat back in shock. It took him several minutes before he asked, "Is the Colonel the father?"

Tears threatened to spill over in a flood when Breena unbuttoned her coat and placed Father Michael's hand on her abdomen. The baby decided to move briskly at that same moment.

"My God! I'd never guessed you were this far along." Father Michael declared feeling the rapid and strong movements on the large abdomen. "Tis your deceased husband's child. Tis a miracle it tis! When is the child expected?"

"Father, the parish gossip about my being a widow is just that, gossip," Breena said holding in a sob.

"The no good left ya then," Father Michael concluded.

Breena shook her head, "There never was a husband. I'm an old maid. I never married, Ohhhh," Breena's tears began to flood her eyes and slowly ran down her cheeks. "It was only one night, well two, but I was stupid, foolish, I was so stupid."

"Now, now," Father Michael soothed reaching for Breena and pulling her into his strong arms. "The one that is foolish is the man that let you slip through his fingers. I take it the father is alive some where?"

Breena nodded her head against Michael O'Casey black priest frock.

"Don't cry lass. Tell me who the man is and we'll find him and tell him about the baby," Father Michael consoled. Or at least he though he did.

Breena pulled back with a sudden jerk. "No! I can't do that. I can't! I simply can't"

"The father should know lass," Michael contradicted firmly. "A man should know about his seed."

"You can't, swear to me! Swear an oath you won't tell him," Breena cried out with terror.

"Alright lass. I swear. Ya haven't told me who he is anyway," Michael complained raising his hands. "Lass calm down, you're terrified. Tis not good for ya or your child. I'll ask Aida to make you some soothing chamomile tea." Michael rose from the divan to find Aida.

"Father, I am so sinful," Breena sniffed pathetically.

"No one is hearing confession right now and no one is making judgment. We'll work through this," Father Michael promised. "Don't ya worry lass. Ya are with friends."

At that moment Aida came in the parlor from the kitchen wiping flour from her hands with a linen towel. "I thought I heard your voice Missus Hodges. Are you alright?"

"No! No, I'm not all right. I'm with child just like you said," Breena cried pushing her head into the back pillows of the divan. "Why couldn't you have been wrong? Oh God what am I going to do?"

"Ya are going to have some tea for starters," Father Michael stated firmly. "Aida, will you prepare some calming tea for our Breena?"

Aida was next to Breena in a breath rubbing her back lovingly. "It's goin to be jest fine Missus Hodges. We'll have us a fine baby. We'll love our baby and watch our baby grow. Our baby will grow in heaps of love. Ya hear?"

Those words brought Breena out of her hysteria. "Yes, our baby. We will love our baby."

"See lass," Father Michael smiled sitting next to her on the other side of the divan. "Ya are amongst friends. Tis a happy time. Tis a blessing it tis."

"I will make us some tea and send Mattie in with some biscuits," Aida volunteered. "Ya must be hungry by now."

Father Michael held Breena for the time it took Aida to make the tea and Mattie to come in with fresh baked biscuits.

Breena had calmed down and started to think rationally once more. "Maybe it would be a good thing to let people believe I am a widow. I don't mean lie, but simply don't tell the truth. Let them believe as they will."

"Ya can do that, but what about your family? Surely they will want to know who the father is," Father Michael counseled. "Ya can't keep this a secret from them."

"Yes I can, or at least for quite awhile," Breena countered. "My family will know who the father is. You see I've had a crush on him since I was a little girl. They would guess. I can't let that happen. I can't! Not for a while."

"I wish you would let me know why you can't tell me who the father is," Michael grouched. "We'll stand beside ya lass, but ya have to trust me."

"I do trust you, but the father is enrolled in a university seeking a degree," Breena shared quietly. "I grew up with him. What I did was wrong, but I'll accept the responsibility. I can't destroy his life. Not now."

"How do ya think finding out about his child would destroy his life?" Michael queried. He couldn't understand Breena's reluctance to tell him. Instead she would risk her own reputation. Father Michael believed Breena truly loved the man and felt sad such a man wouldn't know such love.

"He was falsely accused of paternity only a short while ago," Breena related. "He swore no woman would get him shackled because of a child she claims is his. Besides he is in college working to be a success."

"Ya really love the lad, don't ya?" Michael teased lovingly touching his finger to her lips.

"I'm simply a foolish girl," Breena answered patting her enlarged tummy. "A foolish girl who is going to take care of her responsibility."

"And what would ya have me tell the Colonel?" Michael asked tucking Breena in the crook of his arm.

"Do we have to tell him?" Breena returned in tease.

"Breena, the Colonel has been officially and properly courting ya for two full months," Father Michael chided. "I think he should be told."

"Please only tell him about the baby," Breena requested quietly. "Let him come to his own conclusions as to my propriety."

"And what of your position with Senator Jones?" Michael asked.

"Congress is in recess for the summer," Breena reminded. "They won't be back in session until late September. Doctor Whitecliff said the baby should deliver in September. I'll ask for a little time sick leave before I return to work. I'm sure that will be fine."

"And what about your family?" Michael pushed. "Don't you think they'll come to visit?"

"Uncle Duffey and Auntie Alyson love Nevada. I doubt I'll see them for several years. We'll write to each other," Breena excused. "Auntie Audrey and Uncle Henry aren't really that close. I'll just send them letters occasionally."

"I don't understand girl, but we'll support ya," Father Michael promised. "We won't lie. We'll let conclusions be drawn. I'll be there with ya when the wee one is born and I'll baptize the child."

"Thank you," Breena said gratefully.

"Since you've settled your mind, settle your stomach and have some tea," Aida admonished coming out from the kitchen. She hadn't meant to eavesdrop but she was worried about her employer. Aida placed butter, bread, cooked chicken, broth, and cooked carrots in front of her mistress. "This is good for you."

Breena had calmed down and found she was quite hungry. She ate the entire plate Aida set for her.

"How far along is she?" Gregory Wagner asked Father Michael O'Casey. His voice was calm and reserved. Never showing any weakness was a sign of a good officer. Gregory was good at that. Yes, he was shocked when Father Michael told him Breena was with child, but he wouldn't reveal any emotions. His thoughts as he sat down were strictly military. This was an obstacle, but only an obstacle in the battle plan. There would be a solution. The solution would reveal itself when he was completely calm. Gregory sat down with a cigar and brandy in his favorite stuffed leather chair.

"Breena is heavy with child. She's kept this a secret for some time," Father Michael answered sipping from the snifter of brandy Colonel Wagner had given him when they entered his parlor. "Breena was enceinte when she arrived in Washington City. She of course didn't realize it for some time. The poor girl never had a mother to instruct her in such matters. Her mother died when she was a child, and as we know there are no other women about her house to inform other than two servant women."

"The two niggers," Colonel Wagner replied. "Low account useless people. Breena should have hired good white Christian people."

"Mattie, Aida, and Abel Thornton are good Christian people," Father Michael corrected. "They aren't Catholic, but they are good Christian people. They go to church every Sunday."

"You know what I mean, they are almost animals, those niggers," Colonel Wagner remarked. "They are like the Indians. Savages all of them."

"I disagree, but this is not the time to discuss that," Michael growled angrily. "Do you wish to cease your courting of our Breena?"

"Heavens no," Gregory refuted. "I've always wanted a child and a wife. We'll raise her child as our own. This is convenient actually. The proper courting time is a year. People will see I have allowed her to have her dead husband's child and that I'll adopt it. I'll continue the proper courting and then propose in Spring of eighty one."

"That is quite honorable of you Gregory," Father Michael extended. If he weren't a priest he would have said propriety be damned. He'd ask Breena to marry him immediately, but Father Michael O'Casey was a man of passions. Apparently the military came from a different cut of humanity.

"I'm fond of Breena," Colonel Wagner stated puffing from his cigar. "She's attractive, of fine family roots, and a proper lady for society. I've never been attracted to a woman before. When I saw Breena in mass and queried different parishioners I knew I had finally found a woman to be my wife. The child is an added benefit. The pregnancy will be awkward, but I'll work around it. This is only a small obstacle in the primary battle plan."

"We'll expect you for brunch on Sunday?" Michael queried. He wasn't certain he believed Gregory Wagner was the best marital choice for Breena, but he had offered to adopt the child and he would be a good husband. Even if the man were a bigot, he would take care of Breena.

"I've been called away for several months," Gregory told Father Michael. "I found out yesterday when Breena couldn't make it for lunch. It seems I have been assigned to President Hayes as bodyguard. I'll be with them when they visit Ohio this summer."

"That's no drinking for ya then," Michael teased. "Mrs. Lucy Hayes is a strong opponent of barley corn."

"It's my duty," Gregory replied firmly. "Please tell Breena I will return as soon as possible to renew my suit."

Chapter 9

"I have to be askin ya," Father Michael addressed Colonel Wagner. "Ya know Breena is with child. Ya tell me ya are fond of her. Ya tell me ya are willin to adopt the child, but ya tell me ya intend to follow the proper courtin schedule? Why man?"

"You of all people should understand how important reputation can be," Gregory answered in surprise. "People might think I defiled Breena. They might gossip that Breena is a wanton woman. Not withstanding people might gossip about my pristine God-fearing reputation. I can't afford that marring my political career. I've worked too hard to get where I am to jeopardize that. Why at this moment I am on the inside of the White House and Presidency itself. I've been selected as one of President Hayes' bodyguards."

"Ya are tellin me ya career is more important than family is what ya are tellin me," Father Michael reprimanded.

"A man's career takes care of his family," Colonel Wagner corrected. "When I do propose marriage I will be in a better position to care for Breena and her child."

"Your entrance into the Washington elite has been through many of Breena's connections. She works for Senator Jones, and she is related to the Astors. She is a wealthy woman of her own right," Father Michael dared to suggest. "It is ya that has escorted Breena Hodges to all those political soirees where ya met those high and mighty Senators, Generals, and all them rich powerful society people."

"I am gratefully aware of Breena's connections," Gregory conceded. "As your friendship has benefited you also. I've noticed more of the cream of society attending your parish. I'm certain the bishop has noticed. A promotion may be in store for you as well."

"I am extremely fond of Breena," Father Michael retorted. "She is like a daughter to me."

"And I intend to wed Breena. I will make her my wife," Gregory replied. "I repeat, a wife will benefit from the husband's career."

"I think it is time for me to return to my parish," Michael groaned. He really wasn't certain Colonel Wagner would be the right husband for Breena. He decided he would somehow find out just who was the baby's father. Michael would let the man know somehow about his child. In the meantime he would circumvent Colonel Wagner's marriage plans, but not interfere. Michael would keep his oath to Breena, not interfere, but unite Breena and her love. "I will let Breena know you will be in service for the next few months. I'm certain Breena will be happy for you and your advancement into the home of the Presidency." With those words, Father Michael O'Casey left Colonel Gregory Wagner's tiny row house.

September 19th, 1880, Breena was roused from her sleep with hard pains banding across her abdomen. Several minutes later Breena managed to pull the bell alerting Mattie she needed assistance. Breena remained in bed feeling these bands twice before a worried and harried looking Mattie knocked on the bedroom door.

"Ma'am?" Mattie queried quietly. "Ma'am did you ring for me?"

"Mattie, come in," Breena cried. "Something's happening."

Mattie was in the room and by Breena's side in a shot. At that moment Breena suffered another labor pain. Mattie watched Breena turn rigid and ashen.

"It hurts!" Breena cried.

"I think your chile be coming," Mattie said quietly denying her own terror. "I'll fetch Mama!" Mattie left Breena walking calmly and then ran down the stairs and out to the cottage so fast she was breathless when she ran into her parent's room. "Mama, Papa, wake up! Wake up!"

Aida stirred and wiped the sleep from her large brown eyes. "Is it Missus Breena's time?"

"I think so Mama," Mattie breathed heavily. "She done told me it hurts."

"Lawsy," Aida shrieked rising from her bed and slipping her dark blue calico dress over her chemise. "It must be the time. Wake up Abel your lazy no account excuse for a man. We's about to have a baby."

The three ran up the stairs to Breena's bedroom. Abel had barely managed to button his pants fly when they walked in.

Breena was in the middle of another contraction. Tears were falling freely. "It hurts."

Aida turned to Abel, "It's time. Go fetch Jonathan and have him ready the carriage. Mattie and I will help Missus Hodges dress and pack. We's will take our Breena to Providence Hospital. They can send for Doc Whitecliff."

Abel obeyed immediately. He had a huge smile on his face. He was always happy to part of the miracle of a birth. He was looking forward to having a baby around the house. If everything worked out with Mattie and Jonathan he might even have his own grandchild. A bigger smile stretched across his lips.

Shortly after her order, Aida helped Breena walk down the stairs to the waiting carriage. Once Abel helped Breena in the cab Aida growled at Jonathan. "You take it gentle and slow. We's don't wanna jar our baby! You hear me you slow witted excuse for a man?"

Jonathan nodded his head in mirth. He enjoyed Aida and her vivacious personality. If everything worked out with him and Mattie, Aida would be his mother in law and he liked that idea. Jonathan was well acquainted with Washington City streets and managed to avoid most every rut and hole. The ride for Breena Hodges was smooth and slow.

Breena wasn't aware of Jonathan's considerations. She was scared and hurting. Breena knew people who loved her surrounded her. She couldn't help but wish Uncle Brian, Auntie Alyson, and her Dwayne were there with here. Gratefully Breena let Aida

walk her up the stairs to Providence Hospital. Breena held her breath for another contraction as Mattie knocked on the heavy doors.

A young nurse opened the doors allowing Aida to walk Breena into the hospital. "What is it?" she asked.

"Our mistress is having her baby," Aida told the nurse.

"Where is the father? He is the one who should be bringing her," the young nurse questioned looking over the women and not finding an adult white male.

"Our mistress be widowed we be told," Aida fibbed. She certainly wouldn't tell anyone the truth of Breena's affair.

"I'll get a chair and the head nurse," the young woman answered.

The young nurse reappeared with a wheeled chair. A matronly woman was behind her. "I've been told you are a widow. This is a blessed miracle to continue your deceased husband's name. Who would be responsible for payment? This is not a charitable hospital."

"Breena Hodges, Hyacinth House," Breena growled menacingly. "I'm quite capable of paying my debt. I'm only here on Doctor Whitecliff's instructions."

"Doctor Whitecliff?" the matron gasped. "We'll send for him at once."

"Yes, do that!" Breena hissed. This labor made her quite cranky and she had little patience.

"Take her to the private room in the east wing," the matron ordered the young nurse. "I'll have our guard send for Doctor Whitecliff."

Abel, Jonathan, Aida, and Mattie attempted to follow Breena.

"Where do you think you are going?" the matron snarled.

"We's be goin with our lady," Abel answered.

"We don't allow colored people here," the matron dismissed haughtily.

The Thorntons and Jonathan were quite used to those words and knew never to argue about it. The end results were never worth it. They walked out the door and returned to the cab.

"Drive us to the parish, Jonathan." Aida commanded. "Well get Father Michael, he'll want to know about Breena and he'll stay with our mistress."

A little bit later Abel was knocking on the rectory door.

A groggy half asleep priest named Michael O'Casey answered the door in a nightshirt and robe. "What?" Michael yawned.

"It be Missus Hodges," Abel replied. "The baby be comin. We done took our mistress to Providence Hospital, but those people won't let us in and be with our mistress."

"I understand," Michael answered waking up immediately. "Give me a minute to dress. Do you have a cab for me?"

"We took our Breena to Providence Hospital. Her carriage be waitin outside," Abel told the parish priest. "We's be waitin for you."

"Right," Father Michael answered. He ran up the stairs to dress. In less time than it ever took him, Father Michael was dressed and out the door with Abel. A little later they were at the door of Providence Hospital. "Go on home, I'll keep you informed." Father Michael entered the hospital and questioned the young nurse regarding Breena Hodges.

The young nurse took Father Michael O'Casey to Breena's room. Breena wasn't very lucid and Father Michael became concerned. "This isn't right. Have you given her something?"

"Laudanum, we give it to all the delivering mothers," the young nurse replied. "She's fine. Doctor Whitecliff will be here shortly."

Hours drifted past. Father Michael left for breakfast and came back to find Doctor Whitecliff. "How is Breena?"

"She's doing well," Doctor Whitecliff replied. "I've examined her and it looks like it may be some time before delivery. You may want to return to your parish. We'll call you when the baby is delivered."

"No, I want to stay with Breena if that's alright," Michael answered quickly.

"Prayers and that eh?" Doctor Whitecliff chuckled. "I'll let the nurses know you may stay with Mrs. Hodges."

"Thank you Doctor Whitecliff," Michael appreciated. He wanted to be near Breena. He did feel almost like her father. Michael returned to Breena's room and pulled a chair next to her bed. He picked up her hand and held it. Every once and awhile Breena would squeeze his hand until it was almost bloodless. Father Michael noted that whenever Breena started to become lucid and the pains became more regular and difficult, the nurse would give Breena more laudanum. Michael began to believe the laudanum was actually inhibiting natural childbirth. Early the next morning when the nurse came to give Breena a dosage he distracted the nurse and told her he would give Breena the laudanum. When he didn't give Breena the laudanum, she became lucid, aware, and ready to deliver the baby.

Doctor Whitecliff was summoned from his sleeping bed in the hospital and two hours later he emerged from Breena's room. "It's a healthy boy, Father O'Casey. Shall we bring him out for you to see him?"

"Yes of course," Father Michael answered happily.

Doctor Whitecliff re-entered Breena's room and came out with a nurse carrying a small bundle. "She did very well. Breena is sleeping. You may see her this afternoon."

The nurse handed Father Michael the little bundle.

"Oh he's a fine lad!" Michael declared. In his arms he held a new life with curly sandy brown hair and light blue eyes that told him they would be a light color blue or gray. "Praise be to God both mother and child are well."

After holding the baby for a few minutes the nurse spoke to the priest, "We need to take the baby to the nursery."

Reluctantly Father Michael placed the newborn boy in the nurse's arms. Father Michael left Providence Hospital to return to Hyacinth House. He was certain the Thorntons must be frantic with worry. He was right. Before he could knock on the door he was surrounded by the three of them and being asked so many questions at once he couldn't begin to respond. He slowly moved and gently pushed the servant family into the house and told them Breena was fine and had given birth to a healthy baby boy.

Several hundreds of miles away Geneva's Hope received a visitor. Tracker asked to see Morning Song and Grady alone. In his hand he carried a decorated pouch.

Tracker sat in one of the over stuffed chairs near Morning Song in Grady's study. Grady took his seat behind his massive desk.

"Needless to say Tracker, we are most interested in your visit and secrecy," Morning Song addressed to Tracker in Sosoni'. "Since my husband's Sosoni' is not that good, perhaps you can speak to us American?"

"It is better I speak to you in American," Tracker complied. "I have been sent by Tells the Truth. Even I do not understand his words, but I have faith in them."

"Is something going to happen?" Grady questioned worriedly. There were always new people coming in and out of Ely. There were always new commanders of the forts. There were always problems with the continued Manifest Destiny. These factors always resulted in problems for the peaceful Sosoni' who lived on Geneva's Hope and Geneva's Branch lands.

"It has happened this day," Tracker replied. "So Tells the Truth has said to us."

Morning Song's eyes opened wide. Her hands fumbled with a kerchief. "Tell us his words."

"Tells the Truth says, the promise has given life to the sacred spirit. He will wear the black frock and serve our people," Tracker repeated. "Those are the words he told me to say. He also told me that it would be many moons before this present can be given to sacred one, but it is his gift to be given. One day the sacred one will hold its contents and be given a vision by Tam Apo. Our people will be blessed with love."

"May we see it?" Grady requested.

Tracker nodded and stood upright to hand the decorated pouch to Grady.

Grady opened the package and pulled out an intricately carved wooden crucifix. His questioning look prompted Tracker to respond quickly.

"This sacred piece was given to our ancestors many moons ago by men wearing black frocks. It was held by Tells the Truths family all these years and handed down with the vision that one day a shaman of the family will see the birth of one who will wear the black frock and this will be returned to him. The receiver of this sacred piece will also have a vision and bless our people," Tracker shared. "Tells the Truth says the time is here."

"Tells the Truth speaks of Catholic priests," Grady related.

"Tells the Truth had called Dwayne the promise," Morning Song remembered. "This makes no sense at all."

"We would have known if Dwayne married or if a child would be born to him," Grady shook his head befuddled. "At least a woman would have let us know if she bore Dwayne a son."

"Tells the Truth also told Tracker to tell us it will be many moons before the present can be given," Morning Song reminded. "Is this why Tells the Truth told you to tell us secretly?"

"Yes," Tracker responded simply.

"Nonetheless, I will write to Dwayne today and try to find out what is going on," Grady stated firmly.

"You must be careful what you write husband," Morning Song warned. "Dwayne is still a bit angry over Deborah Wheeler's accusations. I also have a feeling Dwayne may not know what this is about either."

"I have always trusted your instinct," Grady replied lovingly. "I will be careful what I write to the boy."

"We invite you stay with us this evening and have dinner with us Tracker," Morning Song invited. "Tell us why Tells the Truth did not accompany you with this message."

They rose together to enjoy dinner.

"Tells the Truth told me it was only necessary to give you the message on this occasion," Tracker said quietly. "When the secret is revealed and another message will be delivered, he will come."

"Colonel Wagner," Breena addressed from her bed in Providence Hospital. "I trust your duty was satisfying."

Gregory Wagner entered the room holding a bouquet of roses. He handed them to the nurse in Breena's room. "See to these for Mrs. Hodges," Gregory ordered. He returned his attention to Breena. "I've been allowed to view your son from the nursery. He's a fine looking boy. You've done well, Breena."

"Thank you Colonel Wagner," Breena responded sweetly. In her heart she always felt just the slightest uncomfortable around Gregory Wagner. She felt like he was always judging her for something she did not know or understand.

"Your husband must be smiling in heaven," Gregory added reminding her for reasons of his own he believed the father of her baby was deceased.

Breena forced herself not to respond to that remark and was delighted when Father Michael came through the door holding a bouquet of yellow mums. "Father Michael, look and see who came to visit."

"Father Michael," Gregory acknowledged. "I had just returned from duty as bodyguard to President Hayes when I went to call upon Breena. Her servant informed me Breena was here and had given birth to a son."

Michael frowned. He still hadn't had the opportunity to find out from anyone who the father of Breena's child was. He always wanted to be present when Gregory Wagner was around. Michael believed God wanted it also since he chose this very moment to visit.

After a week in the hospital Breena was going stir crazy. "Doctor Whitecliff, I should like to return to Hyacinth House. I feel I would recover much faster in my own home and with my own people."

"If you feel strong enough," Doctor Whitecliff agreed hesitantly. "Most women choose to rest in the hospital."

"I've had plenty of rest, really!" Breena declared. "If you would give me your costs and have the hospital give me a totaled amount I would pay today and leave." Father Michael had already given Breena her bank drafts, quill and ink. Breena had requested him to do so because Aida, Abel, and Mattie were not allowed in the hospital. Breena found that odd. Negro people did all the cleaning and dirty work. These attitudes were always difficult for Breena to understand.

Later in the afternoon, Breena paid the medical costs and a nurse brought a wheeled chair. Reluctantly Breena sat upon it and her baby was placed in her arms. Father Michael pushed the wheeled chair through the halls and into the elevator.

Waiting outside was Breena's carriage, Abel, Aida, and Mattie. Abel opened the door to the cab when he saw Father Michael emerging with Breena. Aida and Mattie ran

to Breena. As Father Michael carefully brought the wheeled chair to the carriage, Mattie picked up the baby in Breena's arms.

"Lawsy Missus Hodges, this be the prettiest baby I ever done see!" Mattie cried with happiness. "He be so beautiful! Oh there little one."

Father Michael lifted Breena from the chair and into the arms of Jonathan who was waiting for Breena in the carriage. Gently he placed Breena on a soft cushioned seat. "You all right Missus Hodges?" Jonathan asked worriedly.

"I'm fine really I am," Breena smiled comfortingly to the big black face. She reached to touch his brow. "Put those worry wrinkles away. Soon you and Mattie will jump the broom and you will have your own baby. Be happy, Jonathan."

"You done give me permission to marry Mattie?" Jonathan asked excitedly.

"Don't be silly. You don't need my permission. You only need Mattie's permission and Abel and Aida's blessings," Breena chided. "You mean you haven't even asked Mattie yet?"

"I reckon them slave minds be mighty hard to break," Jonathan grinned. "I will ask my Mattie tonight." He left the carriage cab with a large smile.

Father Michael entered the cab and sat next to Breena. Aida entered and took the baby from Mattie's arms. Mattie climbed into the carriage and sat next to Aida who was holding the baby.

"Oh, ah," Aida cooed over the little bundle in her arms. "Lord Jesus done blessed us righteously. He be such a fine chile Missus Hodges."

Breena extended her arms to hold her son. Aida gave up the bundle only a little reluctantly.

"Have ya thought of a name for the lad?" Father Michael queried. "We should be baptizing the lad soon."

"Yes," Breena answered placing her gloved hand over the sleeping infant's lips. She marveled at how much he resembled his father. If any of the McGillinen's happened to see him, they would know he was Dwayne's child. She wouldn't tell anyone. Not for a long time, not until her baby was older and could possibly understand things. Understand things? Even she didn't understand her own feelings and hesitations. "I've decided to name him Dwayne Michael McGillinen."

"Tis his father's name?" Father Michael asked hopefully.

"Yes," Breena smiled and looked up to the handsome middle-aged priest. "And yours!"

"I am honored," Father Michael responded placing his hand upon the baby's blanket. A simple smile spread over his lips. At least he had the name of the father to go by now. If he would be patient he was certain other information would be revealed to him by the grace of his God. Michael was convinced God didn't want Breena to marry Gregory Wagner either. You could call it instinct if you like, but Michael was convinced Breena and the father of her baby needed to be together.

Breena's family settled in to a routine quickly. Little Dwayne was never in need for attention. Everyone in the household doted upon him. To Breena's surprise, Gregory Wagner came to call more often. He would ask to see the boy on his visits. Breena actually was correct in believing Gregory was pleased she had given birth to a boy.

Somehow Breena instinctively knew Gregory was counting on a son and heir. She was convinced Gregory Wagner wouldn't have been the least bit interested in a girl if she had born one. More and more Breena avoided the subject of courtship. She devoted all her thoughts to her little Dwayne. It was also time to return to work, but she knew she couldn't return to work full time and care for her new baby. Senator Jones had returned to the capitol only yesterday. She would go and speak to him about her situation tomorrow.

"No, I won't hear of it," Father Michael objected firmly when Breena told him of her plans to go to the Capitol. "Lass ya have only just given birth two weeks ago. Ya must rest. Such a trip would be too draining."

"But I must speak to Senator Jones. I can't put this in a note," Breena pleaded. She knew Jonathan would not prepare her carriage if Father Michael said no.

"I understand that," Father Michael agreed. "I shall go speak to the Senator on your behalf."

"Would you?" Breena said gratefully. Talking to Senator Jones and telling him of her confinement was not something she had looked forward too. She was fearful she would lose her position and she did enjoy being Senator Jones' legal assistant.

"Of course," Father Michael promised. "I'll see to it today."

True to his word, Father Michael took a cab to the Capitol building and went directly to Senator Jones' office.

"Sir, a Father Michael O'Casey is here to see you," a page announced to the Senator.

"A friend of Breena's. I was wondering why she wasn't at work," Senator Jones acknowledged. "Send him in."

"Thank you for seeing me," Father Michael said.

"You are most welcome here," Senator Jones greeted rising from his chair behind the desk. "Would you care for a refreshment? I'd offer you some liquor but our current First Lady has prohibited any such liquid in the Capitol."

"I would really prefer lemonade," Father Michael replied. "I personally prefer to keep wine as a sacrament."

"Unusual for an Irishman," Senator Jones teased.

"Perhaps," Father Michael agreed. "Actually I'm here to speak to ya about Breena Hodges."

"Dear God, I hope she is alright," Senator Jones gasped with fear. "I was worried when she wasn't at work yesterday."

"Breena is fine," Father Michael assuaged.

"She doesn't want to end employment does she?" Senator Jones asked with dread. Breena was a talented assistant. He didn't want to lose her.

"No, she is asking for a temporary leave of absence," Father Michael explained. "Breena is in confinement."

"Confinement?" Senator Jones asked in surprise.

"Two weeks ago Breena gave birth to a son," Father Michael told the senator. "She needs time to recuperate and take care of the lad."

"Well I'll be! Breena was certainly successful keeping this a secret from us!" Senator Jones declared sitting down for the surprise. "Mrs. Jones will be thrilled. Of

course tell Breena to take as much time as she needs. Perhaps when she's up to it we could send messengers to her from the Capitol. Breena might find it easier to work from her home for awhile."

"That would be wonderful," Father Michael grinned happily. He knew Breena would be pleased.

"How is Colonel Wagner taking this birth of Breena's child? Is he bothered with a deceased man's son?" Senator Jones asked conversationally. "Between you, God, and me, I really don't know if he is the right man for a woman as bright a Breena."

"That is up to our Breena to determine," Father Michael replied sipping his lemonade the page had brought in. "But between ya, God, and me, I agree with ya."

"It seems to me he is more interested in what our Breena is than who are Breena is," Senator Jones stated factually.

"I believe ya are correct," Father Michael agreed.

"I shall make every attempt to keep our Breena occupied with work allowing little time for Colonel Wagner's courtship," Senator Jones smiled mischievously.

"Little Dwayne will keep her occupied for the rest of the time," Father Michael returned wickedly with the same thoughts. "Her confinement will also prevent her from attending those soirees that Colonel Wagner enjoys escorting her to so much."

"There is a new fangled contraption the First Lady introduced to the White House secretary. It's called a typewriter. I would buy one for Breena and send it to her house. Apparently there is a specific way to use it and a typesetter can train her."

"Ach I would be knowing Breena would love that," Father Michael replied. "Breena loves all these new fangled inventions."

"I'll take care of it today," Senator Jones smiled. "Tell Mrs. Hodges that Mrs. Jones and I will call on her this evening. We are anxious to see this little boy."

"There's one more thing we need to discuss," Father Michael added.

"That would be?" Senator Jones queried.

"Breena would like you and Mrs. Jones to be god parents for Dwayne Michael McGillinen. Since ya are not Catholic I need to get approval from the Bishop, but I'm sure it would not be a problem."

"McGillinen? Why does that name sound familiar?" Senator Jones stroked his long beard.

"Breena uses her maiden name," Father Michael explained. He hoped he might get a clue from the Senator as to the real father. "Breena named the lad after his father."

"Perhaps that is where I heard it," Senator Jones said thoughtfully. "No matter. Speaking for myself and Mrs. Jones, we would be delighted and honored to be the boy's god parents."

At the same time Breena received a wire from Ely. Telegraphs were usually harbingers of bad news and Breena treated the wire gingerly. Slowly she opened it and breathed out frantically, "Oh dear. What shall I do?"

"What do that paper say Missus Hodges?" Mattie asked.

"Paige and Ayden are going to stop for a day or two in Washington City for a visit before they depart to Boston and then New York for their return to England."

Chapter 10

In the following month, everything at Hyacinth House was progressing smoothly. A typesetter came to the house twice a week to train Breena on the function of the new typewriter. Breena fell in love with it. The print was very neat and readily legible. The typewriter fascinated Breena. She enjoyed learning to use it and loved typing the legal documents on it.

Breena also enjoyed every waking moment with her son near. While she practiced typing, Breena would talk to Dwayne. Sometimes he would coo in response to her voice. Sometimes he would simply be sleeping.

Liberty took a motherly concern over little Dwayne as if he were one of her pups. Liberty would always sleep near the cradle or would be near to wherever little Dwayne would be.

Everyone in the Hyacinth House noted Liberty's behavior when Gregory Wagner came to visit. She would growl warnings if he got to close to the cradle. Liberty would place her body between Breena and Gregory when Breena was holding little Dwayne and Gregory would visit.

"That dog surely don't like Colonel Wagner," Aida remarked to Abel one day during a visit and they were working in the kitchen.

"Can't say I like the Colonel much neither," Abel agreed. "Liberty be a smart pup alright."

"You really spoil the child," Gregory reprimanded Breena on a visit one day.

"Gregory, you simply cannot spoil a baby," Breena returned quickly. She once again focused on the little baby in her arms returning her smile. "You are so wonderful. Yes, you are. You are so beautiful. Yes, you are."

"Stop that immediately," Gregory grumped.

"Stop what?" Breena asked innocently.

"A boy is not beautiful," Gregory corrected. "You certainly don't want the boy to grow up effeminate do you?"

"Gregory really!" Breena retorted. "Little Dwayne is just a baby. I'm not sending him off to school yet."

"You should start imprinting at birth," Gregory stated firmly. "Your coddling will mar the boy as well."

"What coddling?" Breena demanded to know. She wasn't really happy with Gregory's innuendo on her child rearing. This was her son after all. Little Dwayne was her son and no one else's.

"Discipline should start immediately," Gregory corrected. "You hold the boy too much. He should be left in his cradle. A boy needs to survive on his own without mothering."

"A baby needs mothering!" Breena rumbled angrily. She was about to allow her temper to fly and tell Gregory to leave when there was heard a knock at the door. She rose to answer it.

"Let Abel answer the knock," Gregory ordered placing an arm to block Breena from rising. "You really should treat those colored folk more like the servants they are."

"Gregory!" Breena gasped. "How can you be so cold? Did the war do this to you? Remember the North fought to free the slaves."

"That's not the real reason for the War Between the States and you know it," Gregory corrected.

"Of course I know it," Breena seethed. "All wars are for money, i.e. political power. I was expecting the typesetter. Perhaps you should leave and let me get on with my lessons. The senator is paying a pretty penny for my instructions."

"That's another thing we need to discuss," Gregory complained testily. "You really shouldn't be working at all. A proper mother maintains her home and isn't seen in public without escort."

"Are you saying I'm not a proper mother?" Breena snarled defensively keeping her voice down so as not to frighten little Dwayne.

"Of course not, but wasting your time learning that new fangled machine is incomprehensible," Gregory continued. "It's just a play toy and will never replace quill and ink."

"Oh but it will replace quill and ink," Breena said defiantly. "It is typesetting on a single sheet of paper. The print is clear and easily legible as opposed to handwriting which can be difficult to read on occasion due to penmanship."

"You are truly deluded my darling," Gregory chided.

Breena was about to ask Gregory to leave when Abel brought in a young man wearing a bell boy uniform from the Washington City Hotel.

"Excuse us Missus Hodges," Abel interrupted. "This boy here has a message for you."

"Thank you, Abel," Breena acknowledged and took the folded piece of paper from the boy's hand.

"I'm supposed to wait for a reply," the boy said stoically. The bellboy was trying very hard to be professional and grown up.

"Of course," Breena answered. She returned to her seat on the divan and still holding the now sleeping little Dwayne, opened the note.

"What does it say?" Gregory inquired.

Breena felt like saying it was none of his business but replied sweetly, "It's from my cousins Ayden and Paige. They are in Washington City only for the night and ask if I would join them for dinner."

"Wonderful," Gregory smiled cheerfully. "I finally get to meet some of your family."

"I haven't met any of yours," Breena reminded.

"They don't live here either my darling," Gregory chortled. Gregory never wanted Breena to meet his family. He was ashamed of his sister and brother. They lived in squalor compared to the luxury he wanted. Gregory thought his backwoods family was too beneath him and his Washingtonian friends and society. "Go back boy and tell them we'll be honored to have dinner with them this evening."

"The invitation was for me," Breena stated with surprise at Gregory's audacity in inviting himself.

"For us my darling," Gregory restated. "A proper lady wouldn't go without an escort and since I am courting you, of course I am your escort."

"Gregory, they have twins," Breena warned. "The twins are eight months old and getting into everything. At least that's what Paige told me in her last post."

"I'm certain the twins will be in bed tucked away by their nanny when we arrive for dinner," Gregory suggested. "When is dinner?"

"The note said seven o'clock," Breena replied.

"That's rather early for dinner," Gregory remarked.

"Ayden and Paige want me to dine with them and the twins," Breena chuckled. "I haven't even seen the twins yet. Of course I want time with them."

Gregory shook his head. "It must be a motherly sort of thing inside of women. Of course I understand your need to see her twins. I'll take the boy back to the hotel in my carriage and return promptly at 6:30 to escort you." With those words he placed his hand on the boy's shoulder and led him out of the house.

Tom Bywater, the typesetter, met them at the door.

Breena enjoyed her lesson before she prepared for dinner. "This is going to be an interesting evening," she mumbled smoothing a wrinkle on her deep burgundy velvet suit.

Paige opened the hotel door and greeted Breena with a hug and kiss. "We've missed you!"

"I've missed you," Breena returned. "Where are those twins? You've written so much about Abigail and Adam. I can hardly wait to meet them."

Just then their heads turned toward the sitting room. There had been a loud crash and a baby started crying.

"I'm sorry mum," Veronica excused. "I just took my eye away from Adam a split second and he pulled the cloth on the table. He isn't hurt, mum. He was just frightened by the crash."

Paige walked hurriedly to the crying baby in the circular walker. "Don't worry Veronica," Paige comforted. "We all know what a handful these two are." Paige picked Adam up and consoled the crying baby. Another crash was heard. This time it was accompanied by a hiss and spit sound from a cat. "Poor Amore, I think Abigail is trying to catch her again."

"No! No! Abby!" a stern male voice was heard. "Mustn't pull Amore's tail. She doesn't like that." A second later a tall well built handsome man holding an adorable little blonde haired and violet eyed baby girl presented himself in the parlor. "Breena, so glad you could make it. Who is this?" Ayden queried looking at Colonel Wagner is full dress uniform.

"This Colonel Gregory Wagner, my escort," Breena introduced. "Colonel Wagner, these are my cousins Ayden and Paige. These adorable babies are Abigail and Adam. Oh Paige, they are beautiful. They look just like you!" Breena was careful not to

use their last names. She had been careful never to mention little Dwayne's full Christian name, but in the future she didn't want anyone to associate the name McGillinen.

"Indeed! The children do have a strong resemblance to you," Gregory agreed while bowing formally. "I am most charmed to make your acquaintance." He turned to look at Breena. "My darling, you didn't tell me how beautiful your cousin is."

"Darling?" Ayden whispered in question to Breena who was standing next to him taking Abigail into her arms.

"He's courting me," Breena replied quietly.

"I hope you're not taking him seriously," Ayden whispered. "He's a little old for you, don't you think?" Ayden couldn't help it. His brotherly instincts were still strong. Breena was like family. Ayden knew instinctively Dwayne cared for her. Paige had even talked to him about the fact she believed Dwayne was in love with Breena.

"He's faithful, dependable, and a pristine example of pious virtue," Breena chortled quietly holding Abigail. "If you don't believe me, ask him."

"I think I'm going to be ill," Ayden chuckled. "I think I need to have a long talk with my younger brother when I see him."

"Please don't!" Breena declared fearfully. "He needn't think about me. He's so busy with Harvard. I just received a post from him. Studies are difficult for him. He needs to concentrate."

"Always worried about him aren't you?" Ayden returned lovingly. "At least he writes to you."

"Yes. Yes he does," Breena breathed in relief. "Tell us all about Abigail and Adam before we eat. Tell me everything!"

"First tell me about you," Ayden suggested wearing that gorgeous McGillinen smile. "I want to hear about this paragon of virtue. Need my brother worry?"

"No, not at all," Breena laughed. Abigail started pulling on her hair curls and putting them in her mouth. "Ayden, she's wonderful."

"I think so," Ayden beamed proudly. "We are fond of our children. Family is everything to us. You know that."

Those words cut into Breena's heart. For the first time she felt a little guilty for not telling Dwayne about his son. Christmas was only two months away and she remembered Dwayne's words last Christmas. She remembered making love with Dwayne. That was the night her little Dwayne was created. But things change and people change.

"Did I say something wrong?" Ayden asked worriedly seeing the change in Breena's face.

"No of course not," Breena responded taking little Abigail's hand and kissing it. Another knock at the door announced the hotel's delivery of dinner.

"I hope you don't mind," Paige excused politely addressing the stuffy Colonel. Or at least Paige's impression of him was being quite stuffy like her grandfather and others of her acquaintance. She was so happy Ayden came along and saved her from that life. "We didn't realize Breena would bring an escort. We thought we'd have a simple family meal in the sitting room."

"You haven't written to your cousins about me?" Gregory Wagner questioned Breena.

"Well I uh, well that is no I haven't," Breena stammered.

"I'm happy you allowed me to accompany you this evening," Gregory slithered smoothly. "I appreciate the opportunity to meet your cousins, especially one so lovely as your Paige. You're from England aren't you? I noticed a trace accent from you as well, Ayden."

"That comes from being around Paige so long," Ayden laughed picking up Adam from Paige's arms. He tossed his wife a devilish wink. "I'm American."

"Not any more you're not!" Paige scolded. "You are English tried and true. We're returning home you see. My father and his new wife are already in Boston waiting for us, but we just had to see Breena."

"You have holdings in England?" Gregory queried. This was getting even better. Breena had wealthy relatives in England. That might prove valuable in pushing his political career.

"We have some land," Ayden replied casually. Dunham was really nothing in comparison to size to Geneva's Hope and Geneva's Branch. The responsibility was greater however.

Breena sensed Gregory's interest immediately. She thought she might enjoy playing on it. Gregory may be officially courting her, but marriage to him was not part of her immediate future unless she absolutely had to. "Don't be so humble, Ayden. You see Gregory, Ayden and Paige are titled nobility."

"Where are all your servants?" Gregory questioned watching Paige and Ayden pull children's high chairs up to the table where the hotel staff had placed the foodstuffs. "Surely the nanny will take the children while we eat."

"The nanny eats with us," Ayden replied seriously. "A family that eats together stays together. Our children have and will always eat with us now that they have some teeth and can chew finger foods."

Ayden placed Adam in the child chair next to him. He then took Abigail from Breena and placed her in the child chair set next to Paige. "Come Veronica, take your seat at the table."

The look of shock on Colonel Wagner's face was priceless. Or at least Breena thought when she looked up at him.

"Are you really titled in England?" Gregory pursued. He couldn't believe his good fortune if it were true. He may have to put up with their odd behavior in child rearing but it would be worth it.

"Yes, it is true," Paige answered holding a cup of freshly poured cold milk for Abigail to drink out of. "Ayden is the Marquis of Dunham. That's a good girl, Abby. Drink your milk."

"I must say you two don't behave like some nobility I've met," Gregory offered in conversation.

"That's from being around Ayden so much," Paige repeated returning that devilish look to Ayden.

"Thank you my sweet," Ayden chuckled. "Tell us about you, Colonel Wagner."

Breena groaned inwardly. That was the wrong thing for Ayden to do. Throughout the meal Gregory told his Civil War stories and his rise through the ranks. Breena was bored to tears. She had heard those stories so many times she could repeat them word for word. Sometimes she actually felt sorry for Gregory Wagner. His past

was all he had. His future depended upon being with the right political people. By the end of the meal, several yawns had escaped Breena's lips.

"I think our Abby and Adam are as tired as you are, Breena," Paige noted watching the twins exchange loud yawns. "I'll put them to bed. Help me Veronica please?"

"I'll help," Breena volunteered. She wanted to get away from Gregory and his stories. He had two left. *Dear God, I even know exactly how many stories he tells!* Breena rose quickly from her chair and picked little Adam up before Veronica reached him. Together they walked into the room that was prepared as a nursery by the hotel.

Veronica was already preparing the bath water. Paige opened the trunks and took out two fresh silky nightshirts for the twins. Breena already started to remove Adam's clothing.

"You seem to be an old hand at this," Paige observed. Breena had quickly removed Adam's clothes and was walking the baby to the pan that would be used for his bath. The pan had been placed in the tub. She tested the water with her hand before she placed Adam into it.

Breena realized her faux pas. She had a great deal of experience preparing a baby for his bath and bed. Quickly she recovered. "I guess it must be motherly instinct."

"I wish I would have been born with more," Paige laughed. "Veronica had to train me and that's only because she had many little brothers and sisters."

Paige placed Abby next to Adam in the tub pan. The twins squealed with delight and splashed each other as Veronica soaped them clean.

Once more Breena forgot herself and lifted little Abigail when Veronica had finished cleaning her. She powdered Abigail with talc, fastened a new nappy, and easily slipped the nightshirt and bonnet on the baby with relative ease.

Veronica and Paige stared at each other in surprise.

"That instinct is pretty powerful!" Veronica commented. She finished Adam in the same routine as Breena and gave him to Paige.

There were two rocking chairs in the room. Breena had already taken one and was rocking Abigail in her arms while humming a lullaby.

Paige took the other rocker and followed suit in like manner. In moments both babies were sound asleep and Veronica took them one by one to place them in their cradles.

"I must tell Dwayne when I see him that you are a natural born mother," Paige teased. "Perhaps the two of you needn't wait for your merger until he finishes Harvard."

Breena blushed crimson. She realized how much she had given away and was grateful Paige didn't suspect a thing. "Paige, Dwayne and I aren't betrothed. He writes, but nothing is said about the two of us. I have no idea about how he really feels about me. Besides, Gregory is courting me."

"Dump him! Dump him immediately!" Paige blurted out uncharacteristically. "I shall speak to Dwayne about his leaving you adrift."

"Dump Dwayne?"

"Heavens no! Dump that pompous bore you have escorting you. That leech of a man boring my poor husband to tears in the sitting room," Paige rattled on. "I don't like the man. He's not good enough for you Breena Hodges."

"I'll take that into consideration," Breena chuckled.

"Don't consider it at all," Paige insisted. "Get rid of the leech. He doesn't give a hoot about you. He is interested in your status and wealth. I can spot one of those scoundrels a mile away. I grew up with them about. Remember? Thank God, Ayden came along and saved me from them."

"Paige, I really am tired," Breena excused. She agreed with Paige, but what could she do? She also had to have some resemblance of respectability, especially with little Dwayne. That reminded her. Her breasts were starting to hurt. It was time to feed little Dwayne. She had to get home.

Paige and Breena returned to the sitting room. It was right at the correct moment. Gregory had just finished his last story. Ayden was nodding asleep on and off. If he wasn't tired before dinner he was now. Gregory's stories had nearly put him to sleep.

"Gregory, I'm very tired. I need my coat," Breena requested. She gave Paige and Ayden a hug. "Please keep writing to me and let me know how the twins are doing. They are wonderful. Thank you for sharing them with me." With those words Gregory and Breena left for Gregory's waiting carriage.

"There's something different about Breena," Ayden said thoughtfully to Paige after the couple left. "She's not the little girl from last Christmas."

"She looks more mature, doesn't she?" Paige agreed.

"Yes, like something made her grow up all of a sudden," Ayden observed. "She's fuller as a woman too!"

"Ayden McGillinen!" Paige scowled playfully. "You're not supposed to notice those things! But I noticed it also."

"Do you think that Colonel is fooling around with our Breena?" Ayden suggested angrily. "If he is, I'll have to kill him."

"You would not!" Paige teased.

"No, I wouldn't," Ayden agreed and then cast Paige another wicked smile. "I'd have to write Ryan and let him kill the Colonel."

"Killing him should be Dwayne's assignment. The Colonel may not deserve to die, but his stories do," Paige laughed grabbing her husband's arm. "Let's go to bed!"

"Amen!" Ayden declared taking Paige into his arms. "And Amen!"

"I'm quite disappointed with you my darling," Colonel Wagner addressed Breena once the carriage was on its way to Hyacinth House from the hotel. He took a seat next to Breena instead of across from her this time.

Breena thought it a bit unusual that Gregory was sitting next to her instead of across from her. This did not bode well in her mind and actually she found she was a bit uncomfortable with it. "How did I disappoint you, Gregory?" She wished Father Michael could have come with them. She didn't like being in Gregory's company alone, even if he was a paragon of virtue.

"You never told me you had relatives that were of English nobility," Gregory replied picking up her chin to look at him.

"Is that important?" Breena asked innocently batting her eyelashes.

"Of course that is important," Gregory stated haughtily. "I realize you wouldn't understand the significance of English nobility in modern politics, but it could mean advancement for me, us I mean."

"I'm sorry," Breena apologized lamely. "You see they are just Ayden and Paige to me. They are simply my cousins through marriage to my Uncle."

"Are there any other family ties I should know about? Other nobility, the Astors, such like that?" Gregory queried keeping Breena's chin between his thumb and forefinger.

Breena felt a little naughty. Why not name drop? "Well, there is Lord Wessex. He's married to my cousin, Kerry. Then we have my cousin Ryan, he's married to the daughter of a mercantile owner. Auntie Alyson is a Stuart from the English royal bloodline. As you know Auntie Audrey is married to Henry Astor," Breena answered iniquitously. She took a breath and then dropped the bomb. "My Uncle Grady is married to a Shoshone Indian Princess."

"You are such a tease!" Gregory chuckled. He bent over and kissed Breena's lips. "A tease with a delightful family lineage."

Gregory had never kissed her before. Obviously he was feeling pretty good about Breena's relative connections. His mustache tickled her nose and she sneezed. It was an excuse to prevent Gregory from going further. His kiss was nothing like Dwayne's. When Dwayne Sean McGillinen kissed her, firecrackers were set off. Gregory's kiss was like kissing a wet fish that had hair. "Oh dear, I must be catching a cold. Perhaps you'd better sit away from me."

Fortunately at that moment the carriage arrived at Hyacinth House.

"I'll walk you in," Gregory volunteered.

"That won't be necessary," Breena breathed in relief. Abel was already out the door and opening the carriage. "Abel will see me in. I'm quite tired and you don't need to catch my cold."

"As you wish," Gregory replied. He brushed his lips across her forehead. "I have duties for the week. I shall see you next Thursday."

"That would be fine," Breena replied taking Abel's gloved hand. They hurried into the house.

"I'm so glad to see you," Abel said softly. "My Mattie was worried silly. Little Dwayne wasn't appeased with the sugar tit. Your son be mighty hungry."

"We'll see to it right away," Breena replied. She removed her overcoat and began unbuttoning her shirtwaist. Her breasts were full and hurting. She needed little Dwayne as much as he needed her.

Mattie brought in the squalling baby. Mattie had already prepared him for bed. Once he was fed and asleep, Breena needed only put him in his cradle.

Little Dwayne latched on to his mother's milk and was contented instantly as he fed greedily. His little hands pushed on her breast kneading them as if requesting more milk.

"My sweet little Dwayne," Breena whispered lovingly. "I sometimes wish I could tell your father about you. You are so wonderful."

"Dwayne," Paige said softly to get his attention. He was playing with Adam in the Astor parlor room. It seemed little Adam liked playing with paper if you could keep it out of his mouth.

"Yes?" Dwayne replied. "Gosh, these little young uns of yours are getting cuter every month."

"I thinks so," Paige agreed and then went directly into discussing her mind. "You know we went to visit Breena before we came here."

"Yes. Hey there, Adam. No paper in the mouth! Bad boy!"

"Well, you never asked how she was doing," Paige brought up. "I thought you cared for each other. At least that was the impression I had last Christmas."

"I do care for Breena," Dwayne answered pulling the paper from Adam's mouth once more. "I didn't ask because we send posts to each other every month. I know she's fine. She's getting lessons on the new typewriter machine."

"Then she told you about Colonel Gregory Wagner?" Paige queried hoping for some type of reaction.

Dwayne sat down on his heels. Jealousy showed on his face instantly. "Who is Colonel Gregory Wagner? No she didn't write to me about him."

"Colonel Wagner is officially and properly courting Breena," Paige said nonchalantly. Inwardly she was delighted with Dwayne's reaction. "The Colonel escorted Breena to our hotel for dinner. We met him."

"A dreadful man," Ayden interjected upon his arrival in the parlor holding Abigail. "Breena calls him a paragon of virtue."

"We call him an absolute bore!" Paige added impishly. "I asked Breena if you would mind her courtship. She told me you never asked for her hand."

"I was quite surprised to find out you hadn't staked out your claim," Ayden offered with brotherly affection.

"Breena is a woman, Ayden," Paige chided. "She's not a gold mine."

"I won't argue the point sweet, but nonetheless, Breena is pure gold and if I were you brother, I'd stake out my claim," Ayden suggested solidly leaving no room for misconception. "My personal instinct is that Colonel Wagner is not a man who would make Breena happy as a husband."

Dwayne was dumbfounded. "I asked her to wait for me."

"Maybe you shouldn't make her wait," Paige offered. "You might lose her. Your intentions should be made crystal clear. That is if you have intentions."

"I can't ask her to marry me. I'm not good enough for her," Dwayne complained. "I need to be at least her equal in education."

"While you're waiting for your sheepskin," Ayden retorted. "A wolf is devouring your sheep."

"Maybe I should see her. I should talk to her," Dwayne thought out loud.

"No maybe about it," Paige scolded. "You need to see Breena right away. I couldn't abide that man as any part of our family. He's a leech. He wants Breena for her money, property, and status. I lived with that type my entire life. Don't you think I can recognize one instantly?"

"Breena's smart enough to know that," Dwayne countered trying to reassure his own quaking jealousy.

"Of course she is. But consider this brother, Breena lives in a Hedonistic town of corruption, bribery, and all other loathsome possibility. That Colonel Wagner is probably one of the least of evils," Ayden argued successfully. "Christmas vacation is near. You'd better get your butt over to Washington City and see your woman."

"I'll take care of it," Dwayne vowed to his brother, sister-in-law, and his own self.

Payton Lee

"Well you'd better," Ayden approved. "If you don't, you and Breena could be miserable souls for the rest of your lives. Don't make me get Ryan involved."

"Anyone but Ryan!" Dwayne chuckled. "I'll visit Breena for Christmas vacation."

Chapter 11

The day Christmas vacation started from Harvard University, Dwayne was on a train to Washington City. What he would say to Breena weighed heavily in his mind. He was jealous as could be finding out that some pompous old goat was respectfully courting Breena properly. It wasn't his fault he couldn't court her right. He was in Cambridge, Massachusetts and she was in Washington City. Didn't she understand she was his? He branded her last Christmas. A smile swept across his lips. That branding. What a magnificent Christmas present she had given him. It had been such a wonderful present, Dwayne hadn't even thought about sharing his body with another woman. "No sir, no one is as good as you, Breena!" Dwayne heard himself say.

The conductor looked at him strangely. "Are you talking to me sir?"

"Nope," Dwayne blushed. "Just thinking out loud. I miss my girl!"

"Are you visiting her this holiday?" the conductor asked politely.

"Yep," Dwayne replied. "I'm on my way there now. She lives in Washington City. She works for a senator as a legal assistant. My girl is real smart. Real Smart!"

"I see," the conductor acknowledged. "I'm happy for you." The conductor left the car and continued his business.

Dwayne continued thinking. He couldn't tell her not to see that ass any more. If he did Breena would tell him off. He could just hear her, *'Don't you tell me who I can and cannot see. You don't own me! I am an independent woman.'* Dwayne chuckled and covered his mouth so no one would hear it. Yes, his Breena was a wonderful, smart, independent woman whom he loved. He would be good enough to ask her to marry him. He was giving his all at Harvard. He was also grateful that Ayden and Paige had warned him that a polecat was invading his territory. Breena belonged to him. No man would take her away. No man would take her away and live. All he would have to do is call Ryan if he needed muscle. They fought a lot, but they loved each other and would fight to the death for each other. After the court case Dwayne told Ryan about Breena and Christmas Eve. He told Ryan he loved Breena and she was the reason he was even considering leaving Geneva's Hope to go to Harvard. He wanted to be good enough for her.

Dwayne remembered wondering why Ryan didn't beat him up for defiling Breena. He asked his big brother. Ryan told him that he'd always guessed Dwayne and Breena were special. Somehow, Ryan always knew that Dwayne loved Breena. Since Ryan had married Twiggy he understood. He understood that when you love someone special, sharing your body with that person was *'pretty dang wonderful!'*

Finally the train pulled into the station. After disembarking from the train, carrying his small valise, Dwayne found a cabby quickly and handed him an address. The driver read the address. "Do you know where that is?" Dwayne queried.

"It's a short fifteen minute ride from the station," the cabby answered pointing his finger to a street. "Massachusetts street is right there."

The ride was indeed a short one. The cabby soon pulled up in front of a Greek revival façades house. "Do you need me to wait?"

"Yes," Dwayne replied handing the cabby a large denomination bill. "This should cover it."

"Aye, that it will," the cabby replied quickly stuffing the bill in his coat pocket. That was more than he made for an entire day of taxiing people about.

Dwayne knocked on the door.

Breena had just put little Dwayne down for a nap after feeding and told Abel she would answer the door. She thought it might be Gregory even though he told her he would busy through Christmas. Perhaps it was Father Michael needing Mattie to help with some last minute sewing for the choirboys Christmas robes. She stood breathless when she opened the door and saw Dwayne Sean McGillinen standing there.

"Merry Christmas, Peanut!" Dwayne announced smiling broadly. Breena looked even more beautiful than ever. "Can I come in? It is a bit cold out here."

Breena swallowed hard. Big Dwayne was here. There was the love of her life. There was the father of her son. "Of course. How silly of me. Come in. You've really surprised me," Breena choked out. What would she do? She couldn't let him find out about little Dwayne. It was Christmas. He was here. He came to see her on Christmas. Christmas was their special day. If he found out about little Dwayne he'd hate her. She didn't want to spoil Christmas. No, she couldn't spoil Christmas. This was little Dwayne's first Christmas. The servants! Abel, Aida, Mattie, and Jonathan. She had to warn them not to say anything.

"Breena, you look a little pale," Dwayne observed. "You ain't breathing right either."

"You are not breathing right," Breena automatically corrected. Dear oh dear, she was acting like that lovesick child again.

"Thank God you're alright!" Dwayne laughed and planted a long deep kiss on her lips. "I've missed you. Did you miss me? You're still wearing my pendant."

"I never take it off," Breena answered without thinking. "It means a lot to me and reminds me of that Christmas Day." Dwayne did it to her once again. Her brain turned to jelly. She had switched into physical and lost her mental capabilities. Then cold reality came back.

Dwayne smiled and said, "Thank you for that Christmas present, Peanut."

Mattie came in to ask Breena a question about lunch when she saw Dwayne kissing Breena. "Lawsy!" Mattie screamed. She put her hand to her mouth but kept screaming. Before her was little Dwayne's father. Her heart started racing.

Liberty heard Mattie scream. She ran down the stairs because she smelled a stranger and heard Mattie screaming. Liberty took her role as house protector seriously and ran up to the stranger barking ferociously.

'You don't know the half of your Christmas present', Breena thought.

"What is this little fur ball?" Dwayne chuckled bending down to the yapping spaniel dog.

"That's Liberty. She doesn't like strangers. We don't get many strangers at Hyacinth House," Breena explained to Dwayne. "Excuse me, I have to take care of a problem with Mattie."

"Okay Peanut," Dwayne responded and knelt to look at this barking dog. "It's okay girl. I'm not a stranger. I love your mistress."

Liberty sniffed at Dwayne. Her senses told her this was part of little Dwayne and that he was safe. Her tail started wagging in friendship.

"That be him. That be little Dwayne's Pappy," Mattie gushed out after Breena had dragged her in the kitchen to Aida.

"Watch your tongue or I shall be very angry with you!" Breena warned heatedly. "He mustn't find out about little Dwayne. Do you understand me?"

"Why?" Aida queried. If that be little Dwayne's Pappy and he come here for you. He should find out about his baby boy."

"Dwayne is in college. He has to finish his education. I know it is difficult for you to understand and it is a very long story, but he mustn't find out about little Dwayne," Breena said in one breath. "Mattie, you go upstairs and stay with little Dwayne. Don't let him cry. Aida, you find Abel and Jonathan. Tell them what I told you. If Dwayne finds out about little Dwayne I will be very angry with all of you."

"Yas'm, I sho don't understand, but we all loves yo and would do anything for yo," Aida capitulated. "Does yo want me to make tea and lunch?"

"No, I'll take Dwayne to a hotel, most likely we'll have lunch there," Breena thought out loud. "I have to get him away from Hyacinth House."

Breena returned to the parlor. To her surprise, Liberty was on her back letting Dwayne scratch her tummy. "Which hotel are you staying at, Dwayne?"

"I thought I'd stay with you," Dwayne teased. He had planned on staying at the Washington City Hotel. Paige and Ayden had recommended it highly.

"You can't!" Breena shouted.

"Why not?" Dwayne asked innocently. He loved getting Breena upset. Those childhood pranks would be something he never wanted to give up.

"This isn't a castle like Geneva's Hope in the middle of nowhere. I have neighbors. I have a reputation," Breena choked on the last statement. She had a reputation indeed. She had let everyone believe she was a widow. She had let everyone believe little Dwayne's father had died. Yes, she would get a reputation as a trollop very quickly. She would lose her job and everything she worked for. "The servants would talk."

"I thought you loved me," Dwayne answered with false dejection.

"I do, but I simply can't have you stay here," Breena blurted out without thinking.

"Well, as long as you love me," Dwayne chuckled. "I'll stay at the Washington City Hotel. Ayden and Paige recommended it. I was so anxious to see you, I thought I'd check in later."

"It's Christmas! They might be fully booked," Breena groaned. What would she do if Dwayne had to stay at Hyacinth House? "I'll go with you right now." Breena grabbed her hat, coat, mittens, and muff from the coat tree.

Dwayne helped her on with her coat and his wayward hands caressed her breasts as he helped button her coat. "You're larger than I remember," he whispered seductively.

Breena felt herself flush crimson.

Peeking around the corner, both Aida and Abel looked at the handsome young man in the parlor with Breena.

"Little Dwayne shorely do look like his Pappy," Aida remarked.

"Praise Jesus," Abel agreed holding his wife by her shoulders. "Even Liberty likes the Pappy. See?"

Liberty was wagging her tail at the window. She watched the new man and her mistress enter the cab waiting for them. Once they were gone, Liberty bounded up the stairs to maintain her post by sleeping little Dwayne.

"Yo like little Dwayne's Pappy?" Mattie asked the dog.

"Yap, yap!" Liberty answered with a quiet bark. She knew little Dwayne was sleeping and was always quiet when he was.

"Well, we can't tell no soul about him, but I hope he done come back to stay," Mattie stated hopefully.

Fortunately there were several rooms available at the hotel. The concierge handed Dwayne his key and a bellboy took his valise up to the hotel room.

"I'm famished," Dwayne explained after his stomach made embarrassing rumbling noises. "Can I hope you can be seen with me for lunch?"

"I'd be delighted," Breena answered. She was feeling far more relaxed now. Dwayne had a room and they were away from little Dwayne. He would be waking from his nap in two hours and he would want to eat once more. She had some time to enjoy Dwayne's company. She hated to admit it even to herself, but she loved him deeply.

Lunch went too quickly for them both. They talked of many family things and Christmas.

"I can't believe you came to visit me," Breena said in wonderment.

"I've missed you," Dwayne replied lovingly. "This is the longest time we've been separated even when you went to Wesleyan College. I looked forward to your holidays and summer vacation."

"It has been one whole year," Breena agreed. "But we've posted to each other regularly."

"Yes, I enjoy reading your posts every month. I've kept all of them," Dwayne admitted sheepishly.

"You have?" Breena gasped in surprise. "I've kept all of yours."

"I even reread them several times looking for a mention of Colonel Gregory Wagner," Dwayne said seriously. "Funny you never mentioned he was courting you."

The color in Breena's face faded. "Ayden or Paige?"

"Ayden and Paige," Dwayne replied reaching for her hand and squeezing it. "Breena, I have no intention of telling you not to see this Colonel any more. I know I have no right to do that. I have no right to tell you who to see and who not to see. I am asking you not to see him anymore."

"Father Michael arranged the courtship," Breena attempted in explanation. "I've been allowing the courtship because Father Michael thinks…" Breena caught herself.

She was about to say that Father Michael thinks little Dwayne should have a father. But he had never really said that. Is that what she believed? She certainly shouldn't have even used little Dwayne's name in front of his father. "Well Father Michael thinks I would be respectable if I was courted proper. I am a single woman alone here."

"Ayden calls this a Hedonistic city full of crime, corruption, and bribery," Dwayne shared. "He even told me that your pompous bore was more than likely the lesser of most evils, or was that Paige?"

Breena couldn't stop herself from laughing. "He is really."

"He is what?" Dwayne asked. He found he started laughing with Breena. He loved it when she smiled.

"A pompous bore," Breena snorted. She put a napkin over her mouth she was so embarrassed. People looked at her when she snorted.

"Is that this Father Michael, or your Colonel Wagner?" Dwayne chuckled. It was wonderful to be with Breena.

"Colonel Wagner," Breena guffawed. "Father Michael is a wonderful fun human being. Especially for a Catholic Priest."

"I'd like to meet Father Michael if he's your friend," Dwayne suggested squeezing her hand a little tighter.

Reality slapped Breena in the face once more. She couldn't let Father Michael meet Dwayne. Father Michael would recognize at once that Dwayne was little Dwayne's father. Little Dwayne looked so much like him. "I'm sure we can arrange that sometime in the future. Father Michael is very busy with Christmas Season. How long will you be in Washington City?"

"I promised Auntie Audrey and Uncle Henry I'd be back by Christmas Eve," Dwayne replied wondering what made Breena so serious once more. "I just had to see you and know you are still mine." Just as serious as Breena, Dwayne continued. "I know I can't court you proper like, but Peanut, I'm asking you to wait for me. Promise me you'll not marry anyone. Promise you'll wait for me. It'll only be a few years and then I'll finish Harvard. I'm not even returning to Geneva's Hope for summer holiday and I didn't take summer holiday this year. I want to come to you as your equal."

"Dwayne, I," Breena started to reply. He brought tears to her eyes. He was trying to impress her. That's why he went to college. Maybe she should tell him about little Dwayne. He didn't have to be her equal in education. She loved him.

"Wait for me," Dwayne pleaded.

"I didn't realize it was this important to you," Breena replied placing her hand over his.

"It is!" Dwayne said simply.

No, she couldn't tell Dwayne about his son. He needed to finish his college or he would regret it for the rest of their lives. This was very important to him and she wouldn't muck it up.

Unknown to them, two sets of eyes were watching them during lunch.

Mrs. Suzanne Henderson and her husband Major Henderson had decided to have lunch at the hotel. Like Colonel Wagner, Major Henderson was out for political power and career. He had even married Suzanne soon after her debut. She was the third daughter of a highly prominent social family of Washington City. She brought the right

contacts and social status to his career. Unfortunately he was still behind Colonel Wagner in progress.

"Isn't that Breena Hodges?" Suzanne queried her husband. She was just as social conscience as her husband. She envied Breena's political connections, social status, and independent wealth.

"Yes my dear. I do believe it is," Major Henderson agreed. "I should wonder if Colonel Wagner knows she is about with a very handsome young man. Quite improper I would say."

"I wonder who he is?" Suzanne asked aloud.

"I suppose he could be a cousin," Major Henderson suggested putting another fork of succulent duck in his mouth. After he chewed the piece he again suggested. "You know Breena has a large family through her Uncle's marriage to someone in Nevada. Colonel Wagner told me he and Breena were invited by her cousin the Marquis of Dunham for dinner only two months ago."

"I suppose you're right. They do seem familiar with each other," Suzanne agreed. "Actually fond of each other." Suzanne noted when Dwayne squeezed Breena's hand.

"It's still improper," Major Henderson harrumphed. "If a male cousin is visiting General Wagner should be with her. I know he's not that busy with duty."

"He makes himself busy," Suzanne criticized her husband. "If you kept yourself busier, you might be a Colonel by now."

Dwayne found another cabby and escorted Breena back to her home. The sun was beginning to set as they arrived in front of Hyacinth House. As Breena rose to leave the carriage, Dwayne pulled her into his strong chest and placed his lips upon hers. He pressed her close to his body and his tongue teased and tested her lips until they parted for him. His hands on her back pressed her closer to him as their tongues danced their duet of love. Breathlessly he broke away. If he didn't quit he might take his Breena in the cab. He was hurting bad. Instead he released her just as the carriage door opened. "You're branded Peanut! With my brand!"

Abel offered his hand to Breena and helped her from the carriage. "You're needed in the house urgently Missus Hodges," Abel said nervously.

"Do you need help?" Dwayne asked in concern.

"No, Missus Hodges will take care of it," Abel answered quickly ushering Breena toward the door.

As the door opened Dwayne thought he heard a baby screaming. It had to be something else. For a moment he thought to follow Breena and make certain she was safe. He shrugged his shoulders and decided against it. He tapped the carriage roof and the cabby returned to the hotel.

"Praise Jesus yo be back!" Mattie said in relief.

"Is little Dwayne hurt?" Breena asked in concern. Her son was screaming and bright red with fury.

"No Missus Hodges. Yo done been gone five hours. Little Dwayne woke from his nap three hours ago. Sugar tits ain't never enuff for this hungry boy," Mattie explained in exasperation. "Our baby boy be might hungry. That's all."

Breena ripped off her coat and popped several buttons opening her shirtwaist to feed little Dwayne. His screaming was even scaring her. How could time fly by so quickly? Fortunately as soon as little Dwayne had his nourishment he quieted down. Every once and awhile he would tremble with a sniffle. "I'm sorry pumpkin," Breena apologized. "I promise I'll be a better mommy."

Breena took little Dwayne to bed with her that night. He snuggled into her and Breena felt wonderful. He woke her up twice during the night with his little movements snuggling next to her. Once he made mouthing motions as if feeding and she opened her nightdress so he could. He was such a wonderful baby. He was such a beautiful baby. He was Dwayne's baby.

Because little Dwayne had slept with her, he was fed, bathed, and dressed for the day by the time Mattie took him to the nursery.

Not to anyone's surprise, Dwayne was at the house bright and early. He went into the kitchen and asked Aida for a cup of coffee.

"I done fixed Missus Hodges flat cakes and sausage for breakfast with eggs. Our mistress loves her coffee in the morning and I done made some already," Aida told Dwayne. "Would you like breakfast?"

"As good as this smells," Dwayne answered sincerely. "I would love some."

Breena was dressed in a pale blue striped satin shirtwaist dress when she walked into the kitchen. She wasn't surprised to see Dwayne there either. That is why she selected this dress. It was one of her best. "Good Morning Dwayne."

"Good Morning Peanut!" Dwayne greeted. "You look radiant this morning. Almost as radiant as Christmas Day last year."

Breena blushed at the memory.

A brown spotted dog scrambled down the stairs and leaped into Dwayne's lap.

"I can't believe Liberty took to you," Breena said in surprise. "She doesn't take to strangers very well at all. The only other person she likes outside of the family is Father Michael."

"They say animals are a good judge of character," Dwayne answered scratching Liberty's head. "I've got to meet this Father Michael of yours."

"Some day soon," Breena stated quickly. "Did you come here for Aida's breakfast or another reason?"

"I came here for you, Peanut," Dwayne answered reprovingly. "Would you like to do some Christmas shopping with me? I thought you might help me select something really nice for Auntie Audrey and Eloise."

"I do know the best shops in Washington City," Breena agreed. Then she remembered her promise to little Dwayne and how hungry he was when she returned home last night. "But I must be home before noon today. I have an obligation waiting that I must take care of."

"Anything you say Peanut," Dwayne agreed. She looked so beautiful this morning. "Aida, can I bother you for lunch?"

"It be ready when you gets back," Aida smiled. She liked little Dwayne's pappy. He didn't carry airs at all. Not at all like that Colonel. "Come and eat yo breakfast, everything be ready."

Breena ate quickly. She wanted to spend time with Dwayne but she had to get back to feed little Dwayne. When they had finished breakfast she asked Dwayne sweetly, "Would you mind getting my coat?"

Payton Lee

Dwayne didn't answer but left the room to retrieve it. He was anxious to be with Breena again even if it was just for shopping.

"Not a word, do you understand," Breena reminded Aida. "He mustn't find out about little Dwayne. When we return I'll say I have toiletries to take care of and feed little Dwayne. You and Mattie be prepared."

"Yas'm," Aida complied meekly. She wouldn't argue with her mistress, but she was glad to know little Dwayne's father was around and interested in Breena. "I'll have lunch ready."

Breena and Dwayne spent the morning shopping and Dwayne boldly held her hand or placed his arm around her shoulder several times throughout their shopping trip.

Again Major and Mrs. Henderson observed this.

"He must be a kissing cousin," Suzanne sniped to her husband.

"I think I should mention this to Colonel Wagner when I see him next," Major Henderson suggested. He wanted to pour some grease on Colonel Wagner's cherry pie. He was actually delighted to deflate that pompous windbag.

The next two days were idyllic for Breena and Dwayne. Dwayne showed up the next day with a Christmas tree and they spent the day decorating it. Aida served her famous hot chocolate and delighted in serving Breena and Dwayne her cooking. Liberty even left her post by little Dwayne several times to get attention from big Dwayne. Mattie and Breena worked out a signal when it was time to feed little Dwayne. The baby was kept clean, diapered, and fed. Mattie played with him in the nursery when he was awake. Not once did he cry when big Dwayne was in the house.

The following day Breena was up early helping Aida prepare breakfast for big Dwayne's visit when Aida found the courage to say, "Yo cain't keep that baby up in the nursery all his life when his Pappy visits."

"I know I can't," Breena sighed. "I'll tell Dwayne when he graduates. He needs to achieve his goal."

"How much longer would that be?" Aida questioned.

"Almost three years," Breena told her. "He stays through summer to finish in less than four years."

"His chile would be nearly three years then," Aida calculated. "It gonna be hard to keep a three year old chile quiet when his Pappy visits."

"I'll visit him next time," Breena concluded. She began setting the table.

"Good Morning Peanut!" Dwayne greeted. "I come bearing gifts. Come see!"

"Is that why you're so late this morning?" Breena teased allowing Dwayne to take her hand and pull her in the parlor.

Under the tree were at least thirty presents.

"I bought some the first night I was here, last night when I left, and this morning," Dwayne bubbled. He loved Christmas. "Your tree looked naked without presents, so I fixed it."

Breena ran to the tree like a child. She found several presents with her name on them. Some had Aida, Mattie, Jonathan, Abel, and even Liberty.

"It's not much. Not as wonderful as the Christmas last year, but it shows I'm thinking of you," Dwayne offered humbly. "I'm leaving on the afternoon train. It was the last ticket available. I promised Auntie Audrey."

"I know. I love you for that," Breena cried.

"I'm glad you love me," Dwayne said embracing Breena and holding her closely. "Maybe next year we can make it a better Christmas. Maybe I can get another wonderful Christmas present."

"Maybe I'll come to see you next year," Breena offered. Little Dwayne would be a year old then and wouldn't need her for feeding.

"Promise?" Dwayne asked hopefully.

"I promise," Breena sighed. She was a little disappointed she and Dwayne didn't exchange their special Christmas present. She still felt warm and good all over with the memory.

"Let's eat Aida's wonderful breakfast and then I'll let you take me to the train station," Dwayne said with humor.

Christmas morning Breena attended sunrise mass. Father Michael gave the sermon and Breena was feeling wonderful. She hadn't seen Gregory in a week. She had spent that time with little Dwayne's father. She was blissfully happy around her big Dwayne.

Breena returned home and little Dwayne was awake waiting to eat. Once that was accomplished Aida, Mattie, Jonathan and Abel began to open presents with Breena. Everyone marveled at big Dwayne's generosity. Breena had bought hem bolts of fabric for new dresses. Dwayne had bought them satin and silk fabrics as well as two very expensive sewing kits. He even bought a new fangled sewing machine for Mattie. Breena had told him how talented she was with the needle. Breena bought Abel a store bought suit and Dwayne bought him shiny new leather shoes, two pairs of them. He also bought Abel a new woolen coat and gloves. He bought Jonathan a fox lap robe, new gloves, a new woolen coat and top hat. Dwayne bought Aida a set on new fry pans. She had complained about the old ones she was using. As for Breena, Dwayne bought her a mink wrap, leather gloves, a pair of diamond stud earrings, and several diamond and emerald bracelets.

"Lawsy, that Pappy of little Dwayne is a generous man!" Aida declared. "He must be a rich man for sho!"

"Oh yes, Dwayne McGillinen is quite wealthy," Breena told her servants. "You can be certain he's not interested in my money or status. Not like someone else we know and love."

They heard a knock at the door.

Abel looked out the window and sighed, "Speak of the Devil hisself."

"We must be nice," Breena groaned. "It is Christmas."

Gregory walked in upon Abel opening the door. In his arms were two packages. One package was for Breena and one for little Dwayne. His eyes opened wide when he saw all the presents and wrappings under the tree and around the floor.

Breena rose from her place on the floor and took little Dwayne in her arms. "Merry Christmas Gregory."

"I hope you didn't waste all your money on these," Gregory criticized. "Christmas isn't an excuse for being over indulgent."

"Actually they are all gifts to us from," Breena began to explain.

"That male cousin that came to visit you?" Gregory said with reproof. "Major Henderson took the time to inform me you were seen about unescorted with a male gentleman. Major Henderson assumed the man was a male cousin since he was so familiar with you."

"Then I surmise Major Henderson was correct," Breena said sarcastically.

"Breena, this is nothing to be whimsical about," Gregory reprimanded. "Your reputation is at stake. I will not have you tagged as some cheap trollop."

"Cheap Trollop!" Breena blustered angrily. "If any of my family or friends visit. I have every right to visit with them and do as I wish!"

"Of course you do," Gregory assuaged. "You must let me know and I will accompany you so tongues do not wag. I do keep forgetting your family is extremely wealthy. I hope my presents are acceptable."

Breena didn't say a word. She snuggled little Dwayne and put up with Gregory for the day because it was Christmas. She was relieved when Father Michael came for Christmas dinner. By then, the presents had been put away from Gregory's scrutiny.

Chapter 12

July 2nd, 1881. Breena was at the train station with General Wagner. The new ecclesiastic President James Garfield was impressed with Gregory Wagner's piousness. Even though Gregory Wagner was a Catholic, President Garfield liked the strength of his religious fanaticism.   Breena liked President Garfield enough, but thought he was a bit fanatical.

For the past several months Breena was dragged to every party in Washington including the inauguration. Gregory showed off his prize future wife like a medal. It seemed most every one in Washington who was anyone of importance in Washington City genuinely liked Breena. They actually tried hard to like Gregory Wagner, because if Breena was considering him as a future husband there had to be more to the man than they could see on the surface. He certainly was older than her by many years.

In spring, Gregory had proposed to Breena. She refused his marriage proposal. "I'm not ready to commit yet," Breena excused.

Gregory took it as simply losing a battle but not the war. He needed Breena and he knew it. He took her to eat at the Washington City Hotel every Thursday evening. He wanted all the patrons to see Breena was with him and that cousin had been merely visiting. Breena was grateful when Father Michael came with them.

Gregory made certain to visit every weekend and arrive early Sunday to accompany Breena to mass. He brought her flowers, candy, and little trinkets continually trying to win her favor.

This July General Wagner had insisted she see him off at the train station. He would be accompanying President Garfield to Williams College to address his Alma mater. He told her Robert Lincoln would be there and Robert and his wife had commented how much they enjoyed Breena's company at parties. Robert Lincoln was an important man in current politics and he also wanted President Garfield to see his Breena see them off.

Reluctantly Breena agreed if only to stop Gregory nagging her everywhere she went. It was summer recess but she still went to the capitol to work for a little while. Gregory would track her down and discuss her appearance.

Robert Lincoln noticed Breena and General Wagner approach. He walked toward them and suddenly they heard gunshots and everyone started screaming in panic.

Lying on the ground was President Garfield. A bullet had grazed his arm and one had lodged in his back.

General Wagner, Robert Lincoln, and Breena raced to the President's side. President Garfield was conscious. He rose bravely and asked to be taken back to the White House.

General Wagner and Robert Lincoln accompanied the President. Breena returned home visibly shaken by the assassination attempt. "They've shot the President. They've shot the President," she repeated several times upon her arrival at Hyacinth House.

Abel sent for Doctor Whitecliff and Breena was sedated for several days.

Gregory spent a lot of time at the White House with the President and Mrs. Garfield. He prayed with them and even accompanied the President to the Jersey Shore house he rented for his wife.

On September 19th, 1881. On the day of little Dwayne's first birthday, President Garfield died. Breena attended his funeral with General Wagner who was quite shaken by the President's death. Even Breena opened her heart to his sorrow. Gregory was deeply grief stricken. Breena did not utter one complaint when Gregory asked her to come to the train station this time. He was accompanying President Garfield's body to Cleveland for burial.

The train moved out of eyesight as Breena waved her kerchief to General Wagner who stood somberly next to the coffin on the train. She said out loud, "You do have many faults General Gregory Wagner, but you are a man of loyalty and feelings."

General Wagner remained in Cleveland with Mrs. Garfield for more than a fort night and November found him kept busy by the new, President Chester A. Arthur.

When Breena told Gregory she would be off visiting her Uncle Henry and Auntie Audrey for a time he said nothing more than, "Take Aida with you as escort. Mattie and that Jonathan are married now. It wouldn't be proper for them to accompany you."

Breena agreed, but it was because Mattie needed to stay at home with little Dwayne and care for him. He was only fourteen months old and was walking already. He was getting into everything and was even learning to talk. His first words were, "Mom..me!"

Actually, Breena completely ignored General Wagner's advice and took the train alone. It was a week before Christmas and as promised, she would visit Dwayne. She took little luggage with her. Instead her baggage consisted of numerous presents for the family. She learned Auntie Alyson and Uncle Duffey would be there when they heard she was planning on visiting for Christmas. She was nearly as generous with presents as Dwayne had been last year. This year she even took little Dwayne with her when she shopped for presents. Kerry and Braden decided to visit with Grady and Morning Song as a surprise. The Astor house was filled with children and family. It was the biggest Christmas planned ever, but Breena wouldn't be there Christmas Day. She planned on a quiet Christmas with her Aida, Mattie, Jonathan, Abel, and her son!

Dwayne and Breena were never alone for a moment the entire time she was in Boston. Even when Dwayne tried to take her shopping alone, Kerry or someone went with them. Breena loved the excitement. Dwayne got grumpy. The family was disappointed when Breena took the train back to Washington City Christmas Eve morning, but gave her twice as many presents to take back as she brought with her.

Gregory was waiting for her at the station when she disembarked. "How did you know?"

"I questioned Abel everyday about your return until yesterday when he gave me your wire," Gregory answered taking her arm. "I was told you left with a train car load of presents. You really shouldn't waste your money like that. I also was upset to learn you left without escort. You simply must stop going off like that. It isn't proper."

"I came back with two train car loads of presents," Breena growled. She hated it when Gregory showed his miserly side. "And it is perfectly proper for a mature woman such as myself to travel to Boston to visit my family for the holidays!"

The porter brought up two carts loaded with presents. "This belong to you ma'am?" he asked.

"Yes, those are mine," Breena answered and handed the porter a folded bill so Gregory couldn't see it. "Send these packages to the address on the outside of the bill and keep the rest as your tip."

"How much did you give him?" Gregory inquired. He always seemed to be watching Breena's spending.

"Enough to pay for a wagon to bring the presents from my family to the house," Breena replied testily. "And enough for a small tip."

Gregory always knew when he was pushing Breena to a point where he might lose her. He eased off the subject and laughed, "I always forget how large and wealthy your family is."

Breena allowed Gregory to take her home. Once more he sat next to her instead of across from her. That always made Breena uncomfortable. Whenever he did, he made awkward attempts to kiss her or be slightly promiscuous with her. He was becoming more aggressive and obsessive with her.

"I really have an awful headache from the trip," Breena attempted lying. She felt when she bit her lower lip. The excuse worked.

"Of course my darling," Gregory answered sympathetically. He put his arm around her and kissed her forehead. "When we get home you must lie down a bit."

Breena was grateful when Gregory walked her to the door and kissed her lightly on her forehead. "Lie down my darling. I'll be by tomorrow morning for sunrise mass. We'll celebrate Christmas together. I bought something special for you this year."

Abel opened the door and Breena waved to the carriage. "I'll bet you did. You probably bought a pair of knitting needles and yarn. Last year you gave me a book of the most atrocious poetry I've ever had the misfortune to read. To make matters worse, it was one of your friends who wrote the book. The year before that you bought me a brooch pin for my dress since my décolletage was too low for your tastes." Breena rattled on angrily. "I'll show you!"

"Welcome home Missus Hodges," Abel greeted. He was used to Breena mumbling incoherently when Gregory Wagner had upset her.

A small streak with sandy brown hair ran toward her. A brown fur ball followed the streak. "Mommy!"

"Hello my little man," Breena greeted warmly picking up her son and hugging him with all her might.

"Wibertee, see wibertee," little Dwayne gurgled happily. "Mommy bwing pwesent?"

"Oh yes little Dwayne. Lots and lots of presents," Breena looked at the Christmas tree in the parlor. "Thank you Abel. You and Jonathan did a wonderful job decorating the tree."

"Welcome home Missus Hodges," Mattie greeted warmly. "Our little Dwayne missed his Momma."

"Really did he?" Breena responded hugging her son and kissing him all over. "Mommy missed her baby."

"Everyday he would climb up that big old chair, push the curtains aside, and say, Mommy?" Mattie told her mistress.

"Oooh, Mommy missed you too my pumpkin," Breena cooed.

Two hours later a deliveryman piled a mound of presents under the tree.

"Lawsy, little Dwayne's Pappy out did himself again," Aida gasped at the presents.

"Big Dwayne, Lord and Lady Wessex, Uncle Brian, Auntie Alyson, Uncle Henry, Auntie Audrey, cousin Robert, cousin Eloise, Morning Song, and Uncle Grady," Breena laughed. "The house was full with laughter and children. I got to see all the children again. Bennett, Garrett, Jared, and Matthew. They made me miss my little Dwayne even more."

"We's glad to have you back home," Abel volunteered. "Father Michael said he'll be stopping by once again for Christmas Dinner and to thank you and Mr. Astor for the large donation. He done said he would meet with the architect's right away and start on the church wing."

"We was wondering why this wing is so special to Father Michael," Aida wondered aloud. "He nearly jumped up as high as the heavens itself after he read the post you sent us to give him."

"It's special because then you and all your family and friends can attend our St. Jerome Parish." Breena smiled. "I had Uncle Henry take care of the bank draft when I visited in Boston. The wing is for colored folk to attend. I know you and your family are good Christians. I want you to attend mass with me. Since there is still too much animosity with reparation, Father Michael and I agreed to build a special wing for all of you to attend mass, become Catholics, and receive communion."

Christmas morning Breena woke early to attend mass. She felt a little wicked and decided to be a little devilish. When she dressed she wore a lower than normal décolletage and allowed prominent display of Dwayne's heart pendant. She put on the diamond-studded earrings and diamond emerald bracelets Dwayne had given her last Christmas. She had kept them in the music box Dwayne had given her their first Christmas.

Gregory had arrived earlier and was waiting for her when she came down the stairs. He raised his brows in disapproval. "Where did you get all that jewelry?"

"They were gifts," Breena returned sweetly.

"They are garish and make you look like a kept woman," Gregory criticized. "But if you insist on wearing them please keep your coat on during mass."

"I do insist," Breena stated firmly. "They match my forest green velvet suited dress I'm wearing."

"The décolletage is far too low for mass," Gregory noted. "Please keep your coat on." On the way to Saint Jerome Gregory put his hand on Breena's knee. "I wanted to let you know that our President Chester Arthur was quite impressed with you at dinner last month. He's asked about you several times since then. We are invited back for New Year's Eve. I accepted for us. It's quite an honor don't you agree?"

"Quite an honor," Breena seethed. She hated it when he accepted dinner invitations without asking her first. More and more he was becoming possessive of her. She didn't like it one bit. Every time she was about to send him packing something would happen that made her feel sorry for him. Currently he still hadn't recovered from Garfield's death and funeral. He was beginning to adjust to the new President.

When they arrived for mass and Breena said her prayers she removed her coat to Gregory's consternation. He really became agitated when he notice several male parishioners looked upon Breena with admiration. The women of the parish looked at her with envy. But he said nothing. He couldn't afford to anger her. President Arthur liked Breena and he needed her to further his career. He also needed her money. He had made a bad investment and his funds were slightly lower than usual. Somehow Gregory needed to persuade her to marry him and soon.

On the ride back from Christmas mass Gregory related his irritation with Breena's behavior and dress, "Why do you purposely defy my wishes? Am I so unreasonable in my requests?"

"Sometimes I feel you don't understand who I am as a person, Gregory," Breena replied. "I am not your possession, nor will I ever be. I am a person in my own right and not a shadow of your person. You must understand this if you wish to continue seeing me. If not, then I understand completely."

"Breena, my darling," Gregory sighed heavily. "I care for you deeply and have since I saw you at St. Jerome's mass for the first time. It is because I care for you I worry about your good name."

"Well Gregory, you sometimes you worry for my good name more than you should," Breena warned her suitor. "Perhaps you might start looking at me as an intelligent and quite capable person."

"I do," Gregory countered. "Everyone admires you for your talents and capabilities. I don't want anyone to find something to gossip about and hurt you. Here we are."

The carriage stopped in front of Hyacinth House. Gregory assisted Breena from the carriage and knocked on the door.

Breena realized he was staying and that surprised her. "You aren't returning home to change?"

"No Breena, this Christmas I want to spend every moment with you," Gregory replied following her into the parlor after Abel opened the door. His brows raised in surprise when he entered and saw the presents surrounding the tree.

"Breena, you simply must stop squandering your funds on Christmas like this," Gregory commented.

"I didn't squander anything and don't," Breena retorted. "I brought back all these gifts from my family who is visiting in Boston."

"I apologize once more," Gregory said humbly. "I do keep forgetting how wealthy your family is. I fear I am frugal because I must be. Everything I have I've

worked very hard for. Even now I made a poor investment and have reached a critical level with my funds. I should like to visit with your Uncle Henry Astor. It seems my dire straights are because of an unwise investment."

Breena immediately felt sorry for Gregory once again. He looked sad and pathetic. Never in her life had she wanted for something. Her parents, her uncle, and now her family were old money wealthy. "May I ask how much did you lose?"

"Although it is something you needn't worry about, it was nearly all my savings," Gregory sighed. "I lost nearly $15,000."

Breena nearly cried in sympathy for Gregory. In her personal bank account alone she often carried balances of well over $250,000. Her personal bank account didn't include her property investments and other financial investments Uncle Henry Astor handled for her. It must have hurt him to see her wearing her jewelry. The diamond earrings alone must have cost half of his losses. Even as a child Breena had been sensitive to the feelings of others. What was wrong with her lately? "If you excuse me, I must take care of something."

"Of course my darling," Gregory responded. "I must also take care of some toiletries."

Breena walked to her study and retrieved her bank draft folder. She removed quill and ink and made a draft for Gregory in the amount of $25,000. She was certain Uncle Henry would question the withdrawal when he reviewed her bank account but she felt she had to do it. Gregory was a pompous bore, but he did try to be a good man. That was difficult in Hedonistic Washington City, as Ayden put it. Taking an envelope she wrote Gregory's name upon it and hurriedly returned to the parlor. Before Gregory returned she had been able to place the envelope under the tree.

"Before we open presents, I would like to give you mine," Gregory announced sitting next to Breena on the divan and taking her hand. He pulled out a small velvet box from his waistcoat and handed it to her.

Breena groaned inwardly. She hoped it was not an engagement ring. How many times wouldn't he take no as the answer? When she opened it she found it was not an engagement ring, but a lovely delicate ring. It was an intricately scrolled band that had tiny heart shapes. "Why Gregory, it's lovely," Breena told him sincerely. It must have cost him dearly she thought. Money he really didn't have and she felt very guilty for her behavior.

"I realize you still want more time before you decide to accept my proposal, but I do notice you like fine jewelry. I found this and thought you might like it because it matched the heart pendant you always wear," Gregory shared happily. "I wanted to get you something special this year. Can we call it a promise ring?"

"Yes," Breena replied. Gregory's thoughts were quite touching. He tried so hard for her, but she couldn't love him ever. Her heart belonged to little Dwayne and his father. It wouldn't be fair to marry Gregory. He wasn't a man she particularly liked, but he was a good man.

"Wonderful," Gregory replied happily. "Thank you Breena. Now where is little Dwayne? I bought something special for him this year." Gregory rose and walked to the tree pulling out a large wrapped package. "Someday I want to be little Dwayne's Papa, you know."

Mattie walked in at that moment carrying little Dwayne. Mattie didn't even have time to dress little Dwayne properly. He woke and called for her. When she tried dressing him he fidgeted and started crying, "Mommy! Pwesents!"

"There you are young fellow," Gregory greeted. "This is for you."

Mattie placed little Dwayne next to the package. His little hands started pulling at the paper.

"Pwesents!" little Dwayne repeated.

"Need help?" Gregory offered beginning to tear the paper away. Soon little Dwayne saw his present from Gregory Wagner. It was a beautiful carved almost real looking wooden rocking horse. "I know how much you like to ride Breena, and I know you will want little Dwayne to learn. I thought this might give the little fellow practice and we might ride together in the spring."

"This is quite thoughtful," Breena said quietly. She was truly surprised at the sensitivity Gregory did possess. He might have to dig deep down inside of himself, but he did possess it.

Little Dwayne tried to climb up but failed several times.

Gregory lifted him up and sat him upon the rocking horse. Gregory then placed little Dwayne's hands on the handles and gently rocked the horse for movement.

Liberty watched warily but did not growl at Gregory this time.

Little Dwayne gurgled in delight.

"I do believe he likes it," Gregory said proudly.

"Yes he does," Breena agreed. She loved seeing her little Dwayne happy and the fact Gregory actually did buy a thoughtful present made her feel even happier. Suddenly she was in the Christmas Spirit. "Let's open the rest of the presents. Mattie, would you call Aida, Abel, and Jonathan in? Let Christmas begin!"

Breena passed out the presents but made certain any presents to her from Dwayne remained hidden under the tree. She would open those later. How could she explain the expensive jewelry and personal gifts Dwayne always gave her for Christmas? She also didn't want Gregory to feel bad about his less expensive gift. Although Breena had bought a silk muffler for Gregory prior to Christmas, she offered him the package with the envelope.

Gregory's face turned ashen with surprise when he opened the envelope to find the bank draft. "Breena, I don't know what to say. I know you are wealthy, but this is unbelievable."

"Just accept it as a Christmas gift," Breena said quietly. She had no idea her gesture had spared her from another marriage proposal.

"I shall make every effort to meet your Uncle Henry Astor post haste," Gregory stammered. "This gift will be wisely invested."

"You might be able to meet Uncle Henry in a month or two," Breena told Gregory while handing Mattie another present from under the tree. "When we spoke a few days ago, he told me he was interested in setting up an office here in Washington City."

"To be nearer to your holdings?" Gregory assumed incorrectly.

"Gregory, you should know that I am the poorest member of the family," Breena admitted honestly. It was wrong of Gregory to believe the Astors cared about her paltry wealth when comparing hers to theirs and the McGillinens. "Of all our family my entire holdings wouldn't even dent the Astor holdings. They could buy and sell me a thousand

times over. So you see, I need to be far more frugal than my rich relatives. And I live more simply for it."

"I apologize once again," Gregory offered. "I seem to have a habit of putting my foot in my mouth when it comes to your family."

"Indeed you do," Breena reprimanded. "That shoe leather should taste awful by now, so let's not discuss my family any more and simply enjoy our Christmas."

"I still would be interested to learn why your Uncle is considering opening an investment house in Washington City," Gregory requested.

"Uncle Henry told me that there are two types of people in Washington City business and politics, swindlers and swindlers. Since both have money to invest he offers an honest investment firm," Breena clucked mischievously.

"And your Uncle Henry is positively correct," Gregory agreed with a hearty guffaw. "I look forward to meeting him and being one of his first clients. I promise you Breena, that is where my Christmas money will be invested."

"That would be a wise investment," Breena soothed. She turned her attention to Aida. "Is that Christmas goose I'm smelling?"

"It is," Aida grinned. "Our Christmas lunch should be ready in a few minutes. Are you hungry?"

"I am famished Aida," Breena answered cheerfully. "When you wake early in the morning for sunrise mass and cannot eat until after you have communion and get home only to spend hours upon hours opening *pwesents*. Well one does develop a hearty appetite."

Little Dwayne enjoyed tearing apart the papers for his pwesents, but as a toddler wasn't all that interested in the clothes his mother had bought for him. He liked the wooden train Abel carved for him and the rag doll Mattie sewed for him, but in truth he did love that wooden rocking horse and attempted to climb it once again. This time Breena helped him up.

Breena enjoyed watching her darling son rock on his horse.

"Can I believe even for a day I've actually found something to please you?" Gregory hoped out loud.

"You can believe it," Breena shared. "The way to my heart is through my son."

"You're a fine mother," Gregory offered sincerely.

Breena squeezed his hand affectionately. This is the Gregory Wagner she liked. Unfortunately she didn't see this side of him very often.

Chapter 13

"Whoa!" Father Michael exclaimed as a small body whizzed past his trouser leg and a brown spotted dog trailed him yapping happily.

"Wibertee! Wibertee!" Little Dwayne teased running away from the spaniel dog.

Mattie was behind the two scolding little Dwayne, "Chile, youse come back here. We's gotta get yo cleaned up for your Momma."

Father Michael turned on his heels and his long muscular legs caught up with the little imp in moments. He scooped little Dwayne up.

Little Dwayne planted a kiss on Father Michael's cheek and gave him a big bear hug around his neck, "Fadder Mikewell!"

"Bless yo Father," Mattie sighed in relief retrieving little Dwayne from his arms. She was a very large nine months pregnant and due for partition any day. "I's gots to get this chile cleaned up befo his Mamma comes home from da Capitol."

"You really can't keep this up Mattie," Father Michael said in concern. "Little Michael is a whirlwind and you're going to have Jonathan's baby any day. You simply cannot handle two young children at the same time."

"I's gonna half ta," Mattie replied struggling to hold on to little Dwayne "Jonathan done tole me he wants lots of freeborn chillun."

"Be that as it may, I've brought someone with me and we'll wait to see Breena upon her return," Father Michael said sternly. "I've brought my widowed sister in law from Ireland. Her name is Kate O'Casey."

"Youse kin is welcome in our home," Aida added looking up from the bread dough she was kneading.

"I'm glad to hear that," Father Michael appreciated. "Kate! Kate, come into the kitchen would ya?"

An attractive middle-aged woman with bright green eyes and thick curly red hair walked into the kitchen. "Hallo all."

"Aida, Mattie, and Abel," Father Michael introduced. "This is my deceased brother's wife, Kate."

"We're pleased to meet yo," Aida greeted.

Mattie and Abel followed suit with handshakes.

Payton Lee

"And I am pleased to meet ya," Kate returned with a large smile and sparkling eyes. "Me brother has told me about all of ya in his posts that I feel I know ya all already. Kate took little Dwayne in her arms. "Ach, tis a fine lad ya are little Dwayne."

"Do you have children?" Mattie asked.

"The good Lord gave me three but took two away," Kate sighed sadly. "Me only child came to this country of yours last year. She lives in a place called Maryland. Father Michael here tells me Maryland is not to far from here."

"It isn't," Father Michael stated. "Your lovely daughter lives only an hour or two away. I've visited Mary several times this past year. She will be thrilled to see ya."

"Where's my little Dwayne?" Breena's voiced rang through the house.

"Mommy!" little Dwayne gurgled and began struggling to get out of Kate O'Casey's arms.

"Go run to your Mamma," Kate laughed putting little Dwayne down. She followed the toddler as he ran to his mother.

"Hello my darling," Breena said lovingly while picking up her son. She looked at the woman behind him. "You must be Kate O'Casey. I've been looking forward to your arrival."

"Lawsy, yo been expecting the Father's kin?" Mattie asked with surprise.

"Missus Hodges paid my passage and expenses to come here," Kate replied gratefully. "I can't tell you how wonderful it was to be in second class. The trip was luxurious and beyond my wildest dreams."

"I wanted to make it first class, but your brother in law was afraid you would be uncomfortable with the snobs," Breena chuckled.

"That I would be," Kate agreed smiling broadly. "I can't abide people with airs about them."

"Then you'll feel quite at home here," Breena stated. "None of us can abide people with airs about them. We're all glad you decided to take the position."

"Position?" Mattie queried. "Missus Kate is going to be with us?"

"I wanted it to be a surprise for you Mattie. You are such a dear trying to take care of my little Dwayne with your own child on the way, but I simply can't let you do it anymore," Breena explained. "I've hired Kate to be little Dwayne's governess. Once your baby is born I want you to rest and take care of your own child. You've taken excellent care of mine. When you have rested I want you to concentrate on your dressmaking. Everyone loves the dresses you make for me and I've noticed they have approached you to design clothes for them."

"I done tole them no ma'am," Mattie responded fearfully. She was terrified she would lose her job with Breena Hodges. She loved Breena and wanted to stay with her family. That's why she always told them society ladies from the church she had no time to make them dresses.

"Well I want you to tell them yes," Breena said stubbornly. "You're very talented Mattie and there is no reason you can't earn more money for your family with that talent in your spare time."

"Is you telling me yo is lettin me go?" Mattie gulped shaking with fear.

"Heavens no! We need you at Hyacinth House," Breena reassured. "I'm giving you more time to earn extra money, but you have to promise me to charge those social piranhas a fortune for designing and making dresses for them. I will expect a fair price for myself of course."

"With all that pretty material youse buys for us," Mattie breathed happily. "I's make all yo dresses fo free."

"That is a wonderful price. I won't turn that offer down," Breena replied cheerfully still holding her son. "Kate, let me show you to your room. Father Michael, can you bring Kate's baggage to upstairs?"

"Your servant," Father Michael answered. He returned to the parlor and retrieved Kate's three bags. He followed the voices up the stairs to a room next to the nursery.

"Missus Hodges, this room is fit for royalty it tis," Kate breathed in disbelief. "And ya are telling me I share it with no one. Tis my room alone?"

"For now, yes," Breena replied. She was thrilled Kate was happy with the room. Mattie had stayed here until she and Jonathan were married. Mattie started living next to the livery with Jonathan in a small cottage. Breena spent a sizable sum remodeling the cottage to adjoin the livery. In doing so she added several rooms that would be needed for a growing family with a private life of their own. Little Dwayne was nearly two years old now and when he woke she tended to him until Mattie or Aida would arrive. Actually Breena enjoyed playing a more active role in little Dwayne's toiletries. Breena had agreed with Father Michael that dealing with a newborn and little Dwayne might be too much for Mattie to handle. Breena also wanted Mattie to use her creative talents and possibly rise from a servant position with Mattie's own dress shop. Breena accepted Father Michael's suggestion to bring his sister in law as governess. Breena readily sent the offer of position to Kate O'Casey. When Kate accepted the position, Breena and Father Michael handled the immigration papers through Senator Jones' office and Breena paid for the passage. "I'm happy you like it."

Father Michael put down the luggage. "What's not to like about this blessed and loving household?"

"Nothing!" Kate exclaimed. "I'll say several prayers of thanks in mass to our good Lord for His kindness bringing me here."

"That's me girl," Father Michael acknowledged lovingly.

"I'll help you unpack and get settled," Breena volunteered. "I'll show you the toilette room, the nursery, my room and quarters upstairs if we have guests or other needs."

"I'll be leaving ya two lovely ladies alone then," Father Michael excused. The aroma of Aida's fresh baked bread was intoxicating. He planned on returning to the kitchen for samples.

Breena noted Father Michael's interest in the aroma and giggled playfully, "Of course you're invited for dinner."

"I'll say my blessings at mass for my daily bread today," Father Michael teased. He loved Breena's wit and humor. He walked briskly down the stairs into Aida's kitchen. "Do ya think ya might have a scrap o' fresh baked bread for a poor priest to taste?"

"With or without butter and honey?" Aida taunted. She loved Father Michael as much as Breena.

"With," Father Michael drooled. He watched excitedly while Aida sliced the fresh baked bread, buttered it, and poured a little honey over it. Aida placed the bread on a plate and Father Michael took the serving greedily.

"Did Missus Hodges tell yo she wanted Mattie to sew dresses for the ladies of the parish?" Aida asked Father Michael. She would feel a little more comfortable if that was really her mistress's plan.

"That be God's own truth," Father Michael replied wiping a drip of butter from his mouth. "Breena would like to give Mattie a chance to advance her lot. Mattie does make mighty fine dresses. I still cannot understand how fast she makes them."

"It done take only half the time with that new fandangle sewing machine little Dwayne's Pappy bought Mattie for Christmas past," Aida bragged without thinking. Breena had sworn them to secrecy about big Dwayne's visit.

"Little Dwayne's Pappy gave Mattie a Christmas present," Father Michael choked and struggled to swallow that piece of bread he just bit off. When his breath returned he asked with eyes wide open, "Do you mean to tell me little Dwayne's father was here? When?"

"Did I say that? No I meant that new machine Missus Hodges bought," Aida lied miserably.

"Aida!" Father Michael scolded. "It's a sin to lie!"

"I .. er.. I ..," Aida stuttered.

"Tell me the truth Aida Thornton," Father Michael scowled menacingly. "When was little Dwayne's father here?"

"Lawsy, Missus Breena would done be mad at me fo tellin yo," Aida cried wringing her hands in a towel.

"God will be angrier with you for lying to me," Father Michael threatened harmlessly. "Tell me everything and I won't let Missus Hodges know you told me. You have my promise. When did he come here and does he know about little Dwayne?"

"He's a handsome one. He be kind and a good man. He don't have no airs about him, no suh!" Aida described. "He done just showed up two Christmases ago. He spent time with our Breena, made her laugh and be happy. I's never seen Missus Hodges so happy afore his visit. He done spent money on her! Lord he spent money on her. He done bought us a tree and decorated it real purty like. He's a wonderful man."

"Does he know about little Dwayne?" Father Michael asked impatiently.

"No suh," Aida shook her head with answer. "Missus Hodges managed to keep that little chile a secret alright. Lawsy it be a real shame. Them two is so happy together, but Missus Hodges wouldn't let little Dwayne's Pappy know about his chile."

"Is he coming back?" Father Michael queried hopefully.

"Missus Hodges never done say so. Last Christmas time she done went to him," Aida explained. "She tole us she's going up there this Christmas time. With that man, I wouldn't be one bit surprised if he doesn't just show up anytime. He done loves Missus Hodges. Yo can see it in his eyes. Those eyes sparkle with love."

"We've got to get them together," Father Michael grouched with exasperation. "He should know about his son."

"Praise be to Jesus," Aida agreed crossing her body.

"You're right, Jesus will show us the way," Father Michael grinned mischievously. "I believe that. Can I have another piece of bread?"

Kate was settled in by little Dwayne's second birthday. She had taken complete responsibility for little Dwayne. They even started taking him to mass on Sunday. Gregory didn't complain once. As long as Kate was there to manage the boy he didn't mind and thought it was a good thing to prepare the boy for proper behavior in the future.

Mattie was recovering from the birth of her son, Abraham Lincoln. Jonathan and Mattie wanted to name their son after the President of the United States who gave slaves freedom and opportunity. At least they believed Abraham Lincoln did.

Breena called their son Linc and the nickname took. Except when Father Michael baptized him in the colored wing of the parish, his full name was Abraham Lincoln Masters. Father Michael lost some of his parishioners when he opened St. Jerome to the coloreds, but many like Gregory Wagner supported the move saying the heathen souls needed a chance to be saved.

Two-year-old little Dwayne was fascinated with Mattie's baby. His interest in Linc was loving and he could be found on occasion kissing little Linc's forehead. "Good babwe."

Henry Astor visited Washington many times after the Spring of 1882. By summer he had purchased land on Pennsylvania Avenue and had construction begin on a three story brick building that would house his investment firm. He told Breena he intended to have his new investment firm open by fall of 1883. Henry would stop in at the Capitol near the end of the day and take Breena to dinner whenever he was in town. He admonished Breena for her gift to General Wagner but understood her generosity. In fact he told her that the general had come to him at his hotel and gave him a large portion of the $25,000 to invest. General Wagner did accompany them to dinner on some occasions after that.

Gregory worked harder and applied more time to his career. He would spend longer hours in his offices. The politics of Washington City included conversations about the Indian wars. These wars continued on and off since 1866, right after the Civil War. Indigenous people who had first assisted white settlers were fighting back. Breena and Gregory avoided discussion on the subject. Breena became extremely angry when Gregory referred to the indigenous people as wards of the government.

"They are people with minds, hearts, and souls," Breena would argue. "They are not incapacitated mindless animals. Some animals are smarter than humans and some Shoshone I know are smarter than Washington City politicians."

The disagreement only continued to worsen from there and Gregory never wanted to upset Breena. The truth was, although he was fond of her, Gregory didn't understand her. Women were supposed to be meek and docile. Breena was neither of those. He admired her for that, but he wanted her to be more what he thought a wife should be.

Breena concentrated on her work. She became Senator Jones right hand for handling information exchange, proposals, and bill writing. Breena admitted when she stopped being irritated with Gregory's attitudes, she learned the ins and outs of Washington City policies. Breena began to build her own private network in the proper society. With the right connections Breena was able to persuade Senator Jones and other

Senators in many issues. She wrote bill proposals that hid agendas with flowery words on a weaker issue. Breena learned the intricacies of Washington City politics well.

"You've received a post from Boston, Mum," Kate announced cheerily. Kate was helping little Dwayne make dough sculptures when his mommy arrived home. "I put it upon your desk in the study."

"Thank you Kate." Breena received her monthly letter from Dwayne a little earlier than usual. Dwayne's letters were like clockwork and this disturbed Breena. She put her worries temporarily aside and cuddled her cherished son. "Mommy loves you so much!" Breena repeated every night. Their ritual was to nuzzle noses and then sit on the divan where they would play cat in the cradle. Dinner would be served and Breena allowed little Dwayne to escort her. After dinner they would go to Breena's study where she would read part of a book to him every night. She would let him select the book. When Breena would read to him little Dwayne would point at the pictures he recognized and name them. Later Breena would bring a chalkboard out. She would draw a picture and then write the word. Little Dwayne soon tried to write the words. He was a smart little boy.

Kate came in promptly at 9:00 p.m. "Tis time for your bath and night dress my little prince."

Little Dwayne ran to his loving Kate, "Bubbles? Bubbles?"

"Yes my little prince. Ya'll get the bubblies and duckies," Kate promised scooping up the cherubic bouncing happy child. "I'll call ya for prayers when I've got the lad tucked into bed."

"Thank you Kate," Breena appreciated. She moved quickly to her desk and opened Dwayne's letter.

Dear Peanut,

My letter is a little early because I have disappointing news for us. I know you said you were coming here again for Christmas, but I was determined to spend Christmas with you. I can at least get a little quiet and private time with you in Washington City.

"Yes, you did get a little grumpy last year," Breena chuckled. "It's not so disappointing you're not coming here. I'll visit you in Boston. At least I get to see you every year."

I can't come to Washington City and I won't be in Boston for Christmas. Pa and Morning Song have asked I come home to Geneva's Hope for Christmas.

It appears the uprising of the Comanche and Apache peoples have caused problems in Geneva's Hope and Geneva's Branch with our families living there. Pa needs me to show strength of force with all the brothers and Kerry. Even Ayden and Paige are returning. The Bureau of Indian Affairs agent will be at Geneva's Hope for Christmas. We will wine, dine, patronize and bully our way through maintaining peace with our Shoshone family on our lands.

I hope you understand why I must be there. Uncle Duffey and Aunt Alyson are planning to be there.

"Of course I understand, " Breena sighed. She looked out the window of her study. The deep blue sky with twinkling stars and a bright moon caught her eye. I wish I could be there with you. I'll start checking with my contacts and give you legal assistance from Washington City."

I'll miss you terribly. I'll have to stay in Geneva's Hope through all the holidays. I'll be back and make up my missing time. Visit if you can in the Spring. If you can't, you can be guaranteed I'll expect you to attend my graduation in Summer. If you can't I'll be knocking on your door right after matriculation.

My grades are quite acceptable as of now. I've changed my major and doing better.

Are you still wearing my pendant? I miss you.

Love,
Dwayne

"I love you too!" Breena whispered pressing the paper to her lips. "I miss you more than you can imagine. Of course I wear your pendant." She took paper and quill to write Dwayne back immediately. She wrote she would miss him and would attempt to help matters in Nevada through Senator Jones' office. She sent her love to everyone and would shop and post all the presents this month and the next. Breena wrote she was thrilled to learn he was doing so well and would matriculate in Summer.

"Kate is calling for prayers," Aida announced wiping her wet hands on a towel.

"Aida, would you ask Jonathan to send this post for me first thing in the morning?"

"Of course Missus Hodges," Aida replied taking the envelope and putting it in her apron pocket. "Jonathan will post it at first light. Then he'll take you to the Capitol."

"Thank you Aida," Breena appreciated rising to walk to the stairs. Soon she was next to her son's bed saying prayers with him.

Chapter 14

"Ya are really happy here aren't ya lass?" Father Michael asked his sister in law. They were sitting in the morning room sharing breakfast. Breena was off to work early this morning and little Dwayne had the sniffles so he received a tonic and was sleeping in.

"Missus Hodges is a fine upstanding woman. I admire her immensely and she treats her staff gently," Kate bragged on her employer. "Tis a great boon to work for our lady."

"Our Breena is quite independent," Father Michael agreed. "I admire her as much as ya. Though I think she works too hard."

"A fine mind she has," Kate commented. "Tis a God given talent. A woman should use it."

"Be that as it may Kate, she is pushing her person," Michael complained. "How is little Dwayne Michael McGillinen coming? Are his sniffles better?"

"I was worried yesterday. The lad had a fever," Kate shared with her brother in law. "Thank our Lord the tonic worked. He slept well last night. I checked on him several times. So did Missus Hodges. We talked a bit."

"Did ya now?" Michael responded drinking a cup of hot coffee to wash down the toast and eggs.

"I told her I knew a McGillinen family in Fermanagh. Mary McGillinen told me her husband's brother went to the Americas. He did very well. This Grady McGillinen married, had four children and did very well here. It seemed Grady McGillinen even owns land," Kate O'Casey rattled on. "It turns out Missus Hodges knows Grady McGillinen. She grew up in Nevada where he lives."

Father Michael sat straight up in his chair and paid attention. "Continue Kate."

"I commented to her ladyship that it was strange to have a son with the name McGillinen, my friend's family here, and her ladyship even knew the McGillinen family as a child," Kate told Father Michael in one breath. "Do you think it odd?"

"It explains much. I'd hoped for information and here it is," Father Michael grinned broadly. "Breena told me some time ago little Dwayne's father was her childhood love. She grew up with the McGillinens in Nevada you say?"

"That was the name she told me last night," Kate said. Of course she knew Missus Hodges wasn't a widow like others thought. It didn't matter to Kate anyway. Breena was a wonderful person whom she liked a lot. One mistake created a beautiful child that Breena took very good care of. That's all that mattered to Kate. "Tis a shame it is that the little lad's namesake uncle doesn't come about to visit often. I heard he came two years ago and no one's seen him since."

"I heard that. I kept hoping he would return," Father Michael stated. "That's little Dwayne's Papa, not his Uncle. Our Breena has kept his son a secret from him."

"No!" Kate gasped. "The lad writes to our Breena every month without fail. She's never told him about the lad?"

"Writes every month?" Father Michael inhaled quickly choking on his coffee. "How do you know this?"

"I've taken posts for her," Kate answered perking to full attention. "The lad writes from a place called Harvard in a city called Boston."

"Thank you Lord," Father Michael praised. He rose quickly and started walking out the door.

"Where would ya be going Father?" Kate called out after Michael.

"Don't say a word to Breena. The Archbishop has called me to Boston for a conference and I think I'll visit this time. I want to visit this Harvard," Father Michael called back happily.

Father Michael packed his valise and took the next train scheduled for Boston. He found comfortable quarters in the diocese mansion located near Beacon Hill. After attending the Catholic conferences Father Michael decided to eat at an open-air restaurant he had seen from the diocese grounds. He promised himself he would visit Harvard University tomorrow and ask around for a Dwayne McGillinen. After he seated himself he noticed a young and quite handsome man walking with a beautiful blonde haired and violet-eyed woman. The young man was quite attentive to the beautiful woman. Father Michael kept staring. The young man looked like little Dwayne as a grown man. Could it be he stumbled upon little Dwayne's father?

"Dwayne, that priest at the other table keeps staring at you?" Paige noted. "Have you committed some grievous sin lately?"

"Other than being envious of my brother Ayden for getting his woman and children? No! Nothing!" Dwayne teased. "He is staring at me like I've got two heads. Maybe I should talk to him."

"Invite him over," Paige suggested. "I'd like to know why he is staring at you."

"For you my pet," Dwayne answered adoringly and kissing her gently on the forehead. "I'll invite the priest to share our lunch." He rose and walked over the middle aged and gray haired Catholic Priest. He bowed slightly and commented, "I couldn't help but notice you seem to recognize me. Have I had the pleasure of your acquaintance?"

Father Michael found himself a bit embarrassed. He hadn't realized he was staring so blatantly. "I think I might know ya, tis all that be on me mind."

"I'm Dwayne McGillinen. Pleased to make your acquaintance, Father?"

"Father Michael Patrick O'Casey of St. Jerome parish of Washington City."

"St. Jerome? Do you know Breena Hodges?" Dwayne asked excitedly. "Breena attends mass at that parish regularly. Oh yes, Father Michael. She's mentioned you in her posts."

"Indeed," Father Michael replied brightened hopefully. He had finally found little Dwayne's father. Now he needed to get him to Washington City and introduce him to his

son without breaking his oath to Breena. "She is one of my favorite parishioners. I have dinner at Hyacinth House quite often. Me own deceased brother's wife is recently in her employ."

"How is Breena?" Dwayne questioned eagerly. He had just sent his graduation invitation to her. It was only a month away. Then he and Uncle Henry would have a real surprise for Breena. "Would you join us for lunch?"

"I wouldn't want to impose," Father Michael hesitated. Who was that attractive blonde he was with? How could he not punch the man if he found out Dwayne was courting a woman with Breena and his own son in Washington City.

"Paige asked me to invite you," Dwayne insisted with that big McGillinen smile. "I won't take no for an answer."

Father Michael rose to join them at the table. The name Paige sounded familiar. He remembered Breena mentioning it. Old age must be setting in. He simply couldn't remember who she was. Father Michael was still watching that McGillinen smile. Little Dwayne smiled just like that. This man would be so proud of his son if he only knew.

"Father O'Casey, I would like the honor to introduce Paige McGillinen," Dwayne informed pulling out a chair for the priest.

Father Michael swallowed hard, "Paige McGillinen? Tis your wife then?" Father Michael felt his heart stop a beat. Would he punch the cur? What would he do?

"Heavens no," Paige denied. "Dwayne is adorable but I'm in love with my husband. He's coming over right now with our twins. Look over there!"

A gorgeous blonde haired and violet-eyed four-year-old boy ran to Paige, "Mummy! Mummy, look Papa bought me a book. It has pictures of Boston. See?"

Paige's arm quickly circled the little boy and kissed his forehead. "Yes I see, Adam. What did Papa buy your sister?"

"Papa bought me charcoal pencil and paper so I can draw," Abigail showed proudly. "I'm going to be an artist," she announced proudly to the black-frocked stranger at the table. "Why are you wearing your collar backwards?"

"Why are you wearing a dress?" Adam popped in with question for the stranger.

"Abby! Adam!" Ayden reprimanded sternly. "Mind your manners!"

Father Michael laughed loudly. "Thank you lord for this blessing."

Paige and Ayden looked at each other for the priest's response to their children's questions.

Father Michael gained control of his emotions. He was so relieved Paige was married to Dwayne's older brother. Michael took little Abigail's hand and answered. "I'm a priest. My collar turned backwards tells everyone I'm a Catholic Priest."

"Your dress should do that," Adam added innocently.

"Adam!" Paige scolded. "That isn't a dress."

"The boy is correct. It is a dress in a manner," Father Michael replied with mirth. "You see some Episcopalians wear backward collars. When I wear the dress and the collar everyone knows for certain I am a Catholic priest."

"Oh," Adam accepted and sat down on a chair next to his mother.

Ayden reached across the table extending his hand in friendship to the priest, "I'm Ayden McGillinen. I apologize for the directness of our twins. They are sometimes uncontrollably precocious."

"I adore children. The fact your children are so observant is something to be proud of. They remind me of a special little lad from my parish," Michael responded referring to little Dwayne. He wanted desperately to tell them about him, but he gave Breena an oath. "I'm Father Michael O'Casey of St. Jerome Parish in Washington City."

"Breena has mentioned you in her posts," Paige brightened. "You know our Breena!"

Father Michael then remembered the name of Paige. Breena had told him of their visit and how much she adored their twins. This was wonderful. He was meeting Breena's family, but she referred to Paige as a cousin. He wanted to find out the blood relations of this family to make certain little Dwayne was not a sinful error. "Breena is one of my favorite parishioners. I believe she said you are her cousin."

"We call Breena our cousin," Ayden explained. "Actually she became our cousin when her Uncle Duffey married our Auntie Alyson."

"We were just discussing Breena becoming our sister," Paige announced.

"I beg your pardon?" Father Michael choked.

"We came from our home in England to help Pa with a small problem of our Shoshone family in Nevada. We decided to stay for Dwayne's matriculation from Harvard," Ayden explained. "We simply questioned Dwayne about Breena and he told us this Gregory Wagner we met was no obstacle. Dwayne intends to propose to Breena and be married before fall."

"So we are staying for Dwayne's marriage to Breena," Paige bubbled. "I do so love Breena and soon she will officially be my sister in law."

"I'm so glad we met you," Dwayne added. "Perhaps you would officiate the marriage?"

"I would be honored," Father Michael beamed. He thought he would burst with joy. "Breena has never mentioned your engagement."

"That's because my dimwit brother has never officially proposed," Ayden sniped. "He has this thing about being good enough to ask her. He's always felt inferior to Breena."

"She is smarter than me," Dwayne defended. "She also has a university degree. When I get mine we'll both have one."

"I'm smarter than Ayden," Paige teased smiling adoringly at her husband. "He still proposed to me."

"You may be smarter, but I have to protect you from yourself, Silly Goose," Ayden teased in return.

"And I adore you for it," Paige answered bending toward Ayden and kissing his lips.

"I know Gregory Wagner is no obstacle, but I may need Ayden, Paige, and your help to convince Breena I'm good enough for her," Dwayne said sadly.

"Do ya really love the lass?" Father Michael asked.

"That boy is so lovesick and has been for the past four years," Ayden remarked. "He's nearly impossible to deal with ever since Breena left for Washington City. He's afraid she'll reject him is his problem. Can you help, Father O'Casey?"

"I will do my best and I will pray every night for it," Father Michael replied with delight. He couldn't be happier than if Jesus Christ had came to him personally. "When I

see Breena I'll prepare the way, but I think it best if ya do the proposing. When will ya propose marriage?"

"I've invited Breena for graduation ceremony and she said she'll attend," Dwayne answered quickly. "I hope to ask her then."

A month later Father Michael was grinning like a Cheshire cat when he took Breena to the train station.

"You are exceptionally happy lately," Breena noted to Father Michael. "It's as if you know some happy little secret that no one else in the world knows." Little Dwayne was sitting on her lap. She was smoothing an errant curl on his head. "What do you think little Dwayne? Does Father Michael have some happy little secret we don't know about?"

"Fadder Mikewell gots a secret," little Dwayne agreed. "Miss Kate and Fadder talk happy."

"Indeed?" Breena grinned at the priest. "Little secrets have we?" She looked over to Kate O'Casey who blushed crimson.

"Tis no sin to exchange happy talk," Kate responded gaining control quickly.

Little Dwayne took attention away from the secrets, "Twain! Look Mommy, Twain! You gonna wide Twain?"

"Yes my pumpkin," Breena answered hugging her son. "Mommy is going to visit Boston for a day. I'll return tomorrow afternoon."

"You can stay longer if you like," Father Michael volunteered. "You know Kate, Aida, and Mattie can handle the house."

"I know that, but I'd miss pumpkin," Breena replied kissing the top of little Dwayne's curly head. "I also have work to catch up on at the Capitol before summer recess ends."

"Ya work to hard," Kate grumbled. "Ya need time to make a family."

"I have my family," Breena responded in confusion. "You are all my family and I love you. I don't need anymore. It would be asking too much of our Father in Heaven."

"Ya need a husband, ya do," Kate insisted belligerently.

"You know I don't feel that way towards Gregory," Breena snapped angrily.

"I wasn't referring to that pompous bore," Kate answered too sweetly. "Ya need a real man to be a Daddy to our little Dwayne."

"Father Michael is an excellent male figurehead for little Dwayne," Breena countered.

The conversation ended when the carriage stopped in front of the railway station. Father Michael assisted Breena from the carriage. Jonathan handed Breena's valise to a porter. Little Dwayne hugged his mother and Kate took the boy in her arms.

"Whatever happens in Boston," Father Michael whispered in Breena's ear. "Think deeply about it."

"Whatever do you mean?" Breena asked stepping up to board the train.

"Remember me words, that's all," Father Michael smiled to her. "Be happy my little Breena. Be happy!"

Breena took her seat in the posh first class car and watched out the window as her son held by Kate disappeared into the distance. Breena loved her son more than life itself.

"Breena! Breena Hodges! It is you!" A matronly lady screeched and plopped in the seat next to her.

"Harriet Hampton?" Breena recognized in surprise.

"It's Mrs. Weiss," she bragged. "My husband was here on political business. He's a wealthy industrialist you know." Harriet adjusted her mink stole and flashed her diamond bracelet.

"How is your daughter, Claudia?" Breena questioned in politesse.

"Claudia is happily married to one of my husband's underlings," Harriet responded haughtily. "We already have two grandsons with another on the way. Claudia's husband Orin can't keep his hands off her. Have you married yet my dear?"

"I've been too busy with work," Breena excused. Suddenly she felt judged and condemned for not following the proper female career pursuits.

"That's a shame. Your problem is you are too smart for men. Men don't like women smarter than they you know," Harriet censured. "You always were too smart. It turned all the young men off in Ely. I remember Claudia telling me how you followed Dwayne McGillinen around like a little puppy dog."

Breena felt her body flush with heat. She was getting defensive and she didn't know why. Was Harriet on the mark of accuracy? She had given birth to Dwayne's son because she was a lap dog for the handsome Dwayne McGillinen.

"Did I upset you dear? I'm sorry. Dwayne McGillinen was kind to you, wasn't he?" Harriet said driving the knife deeper into Breena's heart. "Of course he always did enjoy the pretty girls like Deborah Wheeler. I mean Deborah Miller. She married Tim Miller you know? That was several years ago. There are still some people in Ely that wonder if she carried Dwayne's child and the McGillinen's paid Tim Miller to marry her."

"I'm certain you are one of those people," Breena seethed sarcastically. Breena's heart was hurting once again with an old wound. She had actually forgotten about Debbie and had been looking forward to seeing Dwayne again. Breena was actually thinking about telling Dwayne about his son now that he was graduating.

"Why would you think that?" Harriet gasped in false surprise. She placed her hand upon her throat. "I heard he has someone special he sees now and he plans on marriage. I was at the Crawford Mercantile a few weeks ago. Kerry Wessex came in with Lord Wessex and ordered a perfectly lovely wedding gift for her brother Dwayne. I heard her say so."

Breena's heart sank to its lowest level. What was she thinking? Dwayne never proposed to her. There had to be someone else. She hadn't seen him in over a year. It was almost two years. Why didn't he write her and tell her about his fiancé? What could she say? She never told him about Gregory. She held back the mists in her eyes. Of course Gregory was never considered to be a real fiancé. Maybe she should consider his courtship more seriously. She didn't hear anything else Harriet talked about. She only nodded her head and smiled.

Mr. Weiss joined his wife and soon Breena relaxed talking to him. He was an intelligent man with an active interest in politics. They discussed the new American Federation of Labor and its potential affect on the industrial revolution. When the conversation was over, Breena realized Harriet had barely spoken a word and was glaring at her.

When they disembarked from the train Harriet growled, "I told you. A woman simply shouldn't be smarter than a man. That's why you are an old maid."

Breena's ego was incredibly bruised by those hurtful remarks. It especially hurt because Breena believed them to be true.

"Breena?" a voice interrupted her sad thought.

"Uncle Henry," Breena greeted warmly and embraced him needing some small security of affection.

"What is it child?" Uncle Henry asked immediately. He could tell something upset her.

"Henry Astor?" Harriet gasped with surprise. "Mr. Weiss, look it is Henry Astor."

"Her!" Breena growled angrily.

Henry Astor smiled patiently as Harriet Weiss continued with introductions and prattle. "We'll dine sometime," Henry said politely excusing himself. "Right now I must get Breena to the hotel she requested."

"Thank you Uncle Henry," Breena breathed gratefully.

"There will always be condescending people in this world, Breena," Henry advised lovingly. "You simply smile to ignore them."

"I'll remember that," Breena replied wiping a tear.

"Whatever she said to upset mustn't be thought about a moment longer," Henry told his niece. "Are you certain you do not wish to stay with your Auntie Audrey and myself?"

"I'm certain," Breena answered firmly. She was certain now more so than ever. She promised to attend Dwayne's graduation this afternoon and she was proud of him. Since she couldn't bear the sight of him with a fiancé. Instead of spending the night she would slip away on a hired cab and get a ticket back to Washington City right after the ceremony.

Chapter 15

"You should have made her stay with us," Audrey reprimanded her husband Henry. "Where can she possibly be? The ceremony is about to commence and we're all here. She's the star of the graduation and Breena is no where to be found."

"The hotel isn't far from here," Henry commented in worry. "If she doesn't come soon I'll take our carriage and find her. She promised she'd be here. Breena never makes a promise unless she intends to keep it. I hope to God nothing has happened to her."

"Our Dwayne will be most disappointed if she doesn't show," Audrey commented. "All he's been talking about is proposing to his Breena."

Kerry walked up to Henry Astor, "Where is our Breena, Uncle Henry? Dwayne is asking for her."

"There she is," Bennett called out behind his mother. He started running toward her. It had been four years since he had seen her and he was ten now, but he remembered. "Auntie Breena! Auntie Breena!"

Kerry's eyes followed her son's run and saw Breena paying a cabby driver. "Thank Goodness! Dwayne was sick with worry for her."

The other children picked up on Bennett's call. They had never met Auntie Breena or really remembered meeting her, but they all remembered her wonderful birthday and Christmas presents with special letters. Adam, Abigail, Jared, and Garrett followed suit running toward the woman Bennett was running toward. They were all screaming, "Auntie Breena!"

"Run along to your class," Paige ordered addressing Dwayne. "The commencement is about to begin. Don't worry about Breena, she'll be here."

"Are you sure Uncle Henry said he brought her from the station?" Dwayne queried. His brow wrinkled with concern.

"Yes! For the hundredth time, yes!" Ayden scowled. "Breena will be here! We'll be celebrating your engagement together right after the ceremony!"

"Run along to your class," Paige repeated in exasperation. "Or Breena won't have your commencement to celebrate!"

A breathtakingly beautiful young woman with blonde hair and blue eyes suddenly took Dwayne's arm. "There you are Dwayne McGillinen," Blanche Baldwin cooed. "Roderick told me to find you."

"I bet he did," Dwayne grumped sarcastically. Roderick found out how wealthy the McGillinen family was and had been trying to set up his sister with Dwayne for the last semester. He wouldn't listen to Dwayne explaining the only love in his life was Breena.

Roderick would answer, "All I see are posts from your girl. How come I've never seen her? At least my sister Blanche is a living, breathing, flesh, and blood woman. She's awfully beautiful and can have anyone man she wants. You should be proud she set her sights on you."

"Oh you darling you," Blanche cooed. "Come along. Roderick and the class are holding up commencement just for you." She stood on tiptoes and kissed Dwayne's cheek.

"Blanche, cut that out," Dwayne protested. "This is my family! Go tell Roderick I'll be right there."

"You need to find your own family before commencement starts," Paige sniped impatiently. She didn't like this girl one bit. She especially didn't like this girl kissing her brother in law in front of the family. Dwayne belonged to Breena. Paige was about to bop the girl when she felt a hand pull her back.

"Silly Goose, let Dwayne get on to his class," Ayden chided. He knew his beautiful petite wife was about to lay a right hook on the flirtatious Blanche.

Dwayne turned to walk to his class and Blanche grabbed his arm. "I'll walk you to Roderick."

"Grrrrr!" Paige growled. "I'd like to walk her right off a ship's plank in the middle of the ocean."

"Silly Goose! Lord how I love you," Ayden chirped delightfully. "Dwayne can handle this himself. We both know how much he loves Breena. He hasn't as much as looked at another woman."

"Well that she witch has her nerve kissing him like that," Paige scowled pulling at her bodice testily.

Breena looked up and saw a blonde beauty kissing Dwayne. Her heart stuck in her throat. Tears threatened to spill over. That must be his fiancé. The fiancé Harriet Weiss had been talking about. She would have turned tail and ran like a coward right there and then if not for the children who had surrounded her.

"Everyone is waiting for you!" Bennett urged pulling her by her hand to the family.

"Did you bring us anything?" Garrett asked blatantly.

"That's rude," Bennett as the older brother reprimanded.

Breena pulled back. "As a matter of fact I brought presents for all of you. She opened her large bag and began pulling out intricate wooden puzzles. Several were round and a few were square. She gave Garrett the first one and he grabbed it eagerly. "I know how much you love to take things apart little Twenty Hands," Breena laughed. She gave a round one to Abigail and Bennett. She gave a square puzzle to Jared and Adam."

"How do you know everyone by name?" Bennett quizzed. "We haven't seen you in so long."

"It's easy," Breena laughed. The children made her feel much better even though her heart was breaking. "Adam and Abigail haven't changed much since I saw them last. They look like their mother. I would never forget you, Bennett. Garrett looks like his father and Jared looks like his Uncle Ryan. I was there when he was born. Remember?"

"I do!" Jared beamed with pride. "I look like Uncle Ryan!"

"He's Uncle Ryan's favorite for sure," Garrett grouched. He was already taking the puzzle apart.

"So," Jared defended. "You're Grandpa Grady's favorite!"

"He is not," Adam argued. "I am!"

"Children!"

The voice with authority immediately quieted the argument.

"I'm sorry Breena," Kerry apologized. "The children are so excited to see you. Where have you been? We've all been so worried."

"I was delayed," Breena lied. She bit her lip. She hoped no one noticed her affectation. Morning Song would know she was lying, so would Auntie Alyson.

"We're just glad you're here," Braden said stepping forward and taking Breena's arm. "Come along little mother," Braden said to Kerry taking her arm. "We mustn't keep you on your feet too long. It isn't good for baby."

"You're?" Breena asked Kerry.

"Yes, I'm enceinte," Kerry answered with a smile. "I couldn't help it. When I held Ryan and Twiggy's new daughter, Samantha Alyson, I wanted another baby. Braden agreed. I'm only two months along, but we are as happy as can be."

"I'm hoping for my daughter this time," Braden added.

"I wanted a daughter as well, but Braden insists on making boys," Kerry sighed.

"Me?" Braden countered innocently. "I won't hear of it. This is my daughter!"

Kerry was about to give her rebuttal when Morning Song, Grady, Henry, Audrey, Duffey, Alyson, Paige, and Ayden surrounded them.

"Hurry," Alyson urged taking Breena's hand. "The ceremony is about to start."

"Where's Ryan and Twiggy?" Breena asked looking around the sea of McGillinens.

"There still was a little trouble with the Shoshone and military authorities about Geneva's Branch and Twiggy's adopted Shoshone family," Uncle Brian told Breena embracing her warmly. "He didn't want to leave until it was completely settled. He really doesn't like the big Eastern cities very much anyway."

"Don't fret," Alyson bubbled. "You'll get to see Ryan, Twiggy, Aurora Blue, and their new baby girl, Samantha Alyson soon enough."

Breena just nodded her head. She would be leaving right after the commencement and glad she was. She couldn't bear watching her Dwayne with his new gorgeous fiancé. A celebration of his graduation was something she simply couldn't pull off. The reason she was late was because she returned to the rail station with her luggage after taking out the children and Dwayne's present. She bought a ticket back to Washington City right after the commencement ceremony.

The McGillinen family took their seats that Robert and Eloise Astor had saved for them. Robert and Eloise had brought Matthew and their new son Edward with them. Audrey took Edward from his nanny and held him throughout the ceremony. When Dwayne stepped up for his diploma the entire family stood and cheered.

To Breena's surprise it was a degree in Business. He told her he changed majors, but a business degree surprised her. She noted Uncle Henry was cheering the loudest and whistling like a schoolboy. It was uncharacteristic behavior for her stoic business only Uncle. Her blood Uncle Brian was cheering and whistling right along with Uncle Henry. Breena marveled at their behavior.

At the end of the ceremony Breena bent to whisper to Bennett sitting next to her. He had been concentrating on his puzzle. "Please give this to your Uncle Dwayne when

he comes to over to the family." She gave a small brown paper wrapped package to Bennett.

Bennett took it without thinking to ask why. He almost had the sphere puzzle put back together.

When the caps had been thrown in the air and the graduates had retrieved them, the families began to surround their graduate.

Dwayne was surrounded by what seemed to be an army. He was happy and took every kiss and hug from his family. Soon he realized he still didn't see Breena. "Where's Breena?"

"She's right here," Brian Duffey turned to point to her. He was baffled when he couldn't find her. "Where'd she go?"

"She was here," Alyson said in worry.

Everyone looked around and didn't see her anywhere.

"Where on earth did she go?" Grady questioned gruffly. "We are all excited about Dwayne's proposing."

"Auntie Breena left in a cab," Bennett blurted out.

"What?" Dwayne shouted at the boy. "Where did she say she was going?"

"She didn't tell me," Bennett answered his grouchy uncle. "She told me to give you this." He handed the package to his Uncle Dwayne.

"I've got to find her," Dwayne said firmly putting the package in his trouser pocket.

"You can't find her in that cap and gown," Morning Song said calmly. She always was the mind of reason in a family crisis.

Dwayne nearly ripped off the gown and handed it with the cap to his stepmother. "Maybe she returned to the hotel," Dwayne thought aloud.

"It's a place to start," Henry agreed. "We'll take our carriage."

Dwayne was in the cab before Henry could catch up to him. Henry Astor ordered his driver to the hotel Breena was staying at.

"Let's all go to Beacon Hill," Audrey suggested. "We'll wait for them there. We can at least start the celebrations."

Somehow the entire family managed to fit in the other four carriages that were left.

"What do you mean Breena Hodges checked out?" Dwayne screamed at the hotel clerk. He had reached over the desk and grabbed his tie nearly choking the poor clerk. "She just checked in!"

"I am well aware of that sir," the clerk replied sarcastically pulling his tie back from Dwayne's hands. He casually began to retie it. "Miss Hodges checked in with him," pointing to Henry Astor, "went to her room and back downstairs once more only a few minutes later. She checked out paying us for two full days and asked for a cab. We sent her luggage to the rail station. Miss Hodges told us she was returning to Washington City this afternoon and wouldn't be staying the night."

Dwayne left the hotel lobby in a shot back to the carriage.

Henry Astor ran to catch up. Jumping in the cab he chastened Dwayne, "Boy, you have to understand I'm an old man. I simply cannot keep up this pace of yours."

"Sorry Uncle Henry," Dwayne apologized. "I don't understand why Breena left like this. I've got a sick feeling in the pit of my stomach."

"I understand, but son take it easy on me," Henry requested catching his breath.

At the rail station Dwayne told Uncle Henry to stay in the carriage. He came back a few minutes later with an angry and worried face.

"I missed her," Dwayne told his Uncle slamming his fist into the carriage side. "The train for Washington City left a few minutes ago. What am I going to do?"

"Go after her," Uncle Henry said calmly. "When is the next train to Washington City?"

"I don't know," Dwayne answered suddenly full of hope once more.

Henry stepped out of the carriage and put his hand on Dwayne's shoulder. "Come along. We'll find out when the next train leaves and we'll get you a ticket for it."

"All the family is at the house," Dwayne remembered. "Do you think they'll mind?"

"All of us want to see you and Breena together," Henry told his nephew. "We are happy for the two of you. We've waited a long time for this wedding and your graduation. All of them would buy the ticket for you if they were here. I promise you that."

"Thanks," was all Dwayne could say.

Together they walked to the stationmaster and purchased a ticket for the next train to Washington City.

"Did you find my niece?" Brian Duffey questioned as soon as Dwayne entered the room.

"No," Dwayne answered. "She returned to Washington City."

"What in the Sam Hill for?" Alyson stated abruptly. "Breena knew all of us were here and would be giving you a party."

"Only God knows," Dwayne complained. "I didn't even get to see her."

Paige thought a moment and then gasped. Everyone turned to her. "Do you think she saw that little witch kiss you?"

"What little witch?" Kerry queried. "What the Sam Hill did you do Dwayne Sean McGillinen? Were you fooling around?"

"It wasn't me," Dwayne defended. "Blanche grabbed me and kissed me."

"Blanche who?" Grady growled. "You tell us you're going to propose to Breena and someone named Blanche shows up. You'd better have one good explanation boy!"

"He is innocent Father Grady," Paige defended. "That little witch came out of nowhere. Dwayne tried to get rid of her."

"I did!" Dwayne agreed readily and stood next to his defender. "I tried to get rid of her. Roderick Baldwin has been trying to get me hooked up with his sister for a year now. I've made it clear Breena is the only one for me."

"Auntie Breena must have seen her kiss you," Bennett blurted out. "I saw it too when Auntie Breena was walking with me."

"Son of a Bitch!" Dwayne cursed.

"Watch your language! There are children present," Auntie Alyson scolded. "You'd better get your little ass to Washington City right away and explain things to our Breena."

Everyone burst out laughing when Alyson used a curse word. Even Alyson Duffey started laughing. The children didn't even understand what was going on, but they laughed with the adults.

"I've already purchased tickets for this evening's train," Henry announced. "We came back to get a bag packed for Dwayne. I'm afraid our guest of honor won't be at the party very long."

"That's perfectly fine," Kerry spoke for the entire family. "We'll celebrate for you. You go get your woman!"

"Thanks sis," Dwayne appreciated and gave his sister a big kiss on the cheek. He ran up the stairs to his room and quickly packed a valise for his trip.

Uncle Henry drove with Dwayne back to the train station. "It will work out," Henry promised. "I'll tell the family about our surprise tonight."

"You know Uncle Henry, I'm actually afraid," Dwayne confessed. "I had everything planned so well. At the party tonight I would give her the ring and get down on my knees. She couldn't say no, not in front of everyone. Now I'm not sure she'll accept me."

"Believe in yourself boy," Henry advised lovingly. "Just believe in yourself."

The elder man watched his young nephew board the train and whispered a prayer, *'He needs your help, Lord. Please give it to him. He's worked so hard to make this happen. He really loves the girl.'* A bright light flashed across the sky. It was a shooting star. Henry took that as an omen. *'Thank you, Lord.'*

Father Michael was sitting on the divan playing cat and the cradle with little Dwayne when the door opened. His mouth dropped when Breena walked in holding her valise. "Lass what are you doing home. We didn't expect you back for a day or two!"

"I missed pumpkin," Breena said telling a half-truth. She walked over to little Dwayne who jumped up to give her a big welcome hug.

"Saints preserve us!" Kate exclaimed when she walked into the room carrying three crystal glasses of her famous lemonade. "Is something wrong? We didn't expect you home this evening."

"I can come home if I want," Breena replied irritably. "What is wrong with you two?"

"Not a thing," Kate answered quickly. "You told us you would be in Boston a day or two with your family for a special celebration. Did something happen?"

"I was there with for celebration," Breena answered cuddling little Dwayne. "When I saw all the children I simply missed my pumpkin."

"Somehow I think tis more than that," Kate pursued. She and Father Michael knew she was going to Dwayne McGillinen's graduation and he was going to ask her to marry her. Something must have happened. They both knew it had to be something bad. They also knew Breena wouldn't tell them. She was a tight-lipped stubborn woman when it came to her own personal life.

"No," Breena denied. She simply didn't want to discuss her broken heart with anyone. She would wait until everyone was asleep and then she intended to cry her heart out.

"I think I'll be leaving now. Tis getting late," Father Michael excused. "Do ya want to walk me to the door, Kate?"

"I'd like that very much indeed," Kate agreed readily. Once outside the door she whispered. "What do you think happened?"

"I don't know but I think I'm going to make a quick trip up to Boston this weekend and find out," Father Michael told his sister in law. "I know the lad told me he intended to ask her to marry him after the graduation. There wasn't enough time for that to happen."

"Her ladyship tells us nothing, but her eyes show heartbreak," Kate noted. "I hope you can fix whatever happened up there."

"With God's help," Father Michael prayed looking up to the clear starry sky. "With God's help."

Chapter 16

Breena tucked her sleeping son into his bed. "Sweet dreams little Dwayne. Mommy loves her little man." She bent over and kissed his cherubic head.

"He's a good boy," Kate whispered. "He says his prayers so well you know."

"Yes I know," Breena replied touching her son lovingly. "He's my entire world."

"Will ya be going to bed?" Kate queried. "I'll stay awake to help ya."

"No I need to think things through," Breena excused. "I'm going to make a cup of warm milk and think a little in my study."

Breena stared out her window. She spoke to the big silvery moon, "Dwayne, I love you so much. Why didn't you tell me there was someone else? I've held on to this hope foolishly for so long." Tears started to flow and she allowed them. Sobs followed. Breena buried her head into her arms and cried inconsolably.

Dwayne fidgeted on the train. Why was it moving slowly? The normally short eight-hour ride seemed to last an eternity. Half way through the ride he remembered the package Bennett had given him. It was from Breena. He reached into his trouser pockets and pulled it out. Dwayne ripped open the paper like a child. He opened a small box. He smiled broadly and began to laugh waking other passengers. "Sorry," he apologized to the irritated travelers. He brought the laugh down to a chuckle. Inside the box were cufflink studs. They were gold and forged in the shape of a peanut. His initials had been carved on the right side of the shell, DSM. A note was underneath. *'With love from your, Peanut.'* "I love you too, Peanut," Dwayne said softly fingering the studs.

At last the train pulled into the station. It was nearly midnight. Dwayne didn't care. He would find a cab to take him to Hyacinth House and bang down her door if need be. Fortunately many cabbies were always waiting at the train station for a fare. Dwayne gave him the Hyacinth House address. They arrived a little after midnight. Dwayne paid the cabby and told him not to wait. No matter what, he would be spending the night even if he had to camp out on Breena's front porch. Dwayne ran up the stairs and knocked quietly at first. He waited several minutes and when there was no response he banged on the door with his fist calling, "Breena! Breena I know you're in there. Open up!"

Breena stopped crying and wiped her eyes when she first heard the knocking. "Who in the world could that be?" Breena asked no one. "If that is Gregory Wagner I think I'll shoot him. I simply can not bear any man at the moment." Breena was only a few steps away from answering the door when she heard Dwayne's voice and his banging on the door. "Dwayne?" Breena whispered. "It couldn't be!" She opened the door and there he was. He stood in front of her with that McGillinen smile staring her in the face.

"Go away!" Breena hissed and tried to slam the door on Dwayne.

Dwayne moved faster and pushed aside the door stepping into the parlor. "Why did you leave Boston?"

"You dare ask me that?" Breena seethed. "I was happy for your graduation. I wasn't ready to see.. to see.. to see you with your fiancé."

"Fiancé? What the Sam Hill are you talking about?" Dwayne returned angrily. His hands folded over Breena's arms and pulled her into his large muscular frame. "You're the only woman for me."

"That's not what I saw. That beautiful blonde wasn't straightening your cap and gown," Breena huffed. "I met Harriet Hampton Weiss on the train. She told me Kerry and Braden were shopping for your wedding gift."

"And you believed Harriet Hampton Weiss?" Dwayne asked in astonishment. "You believed that gossip? She wouldn't know the truth if her life depended on it."

"Was that blonde a figment of my imagination?" Breena hissed angrily moving her face to avoid Dwayne's descending lips.

"That blonde was the sister of a fellow classmate, Roderick Baldwin," Dwayne told Breena sensually. His lips were desperately seeking hers.

Breena knew if Dwayne's lips found hers she wouldn't think anymore. She wouldn't let herself be hurt anymore. "She wasn't your fiancé?"

"No," Dwayne answered finally finding Breena's lips. "You're the only woman for me. I've branded you, remember?"

"Yes I remember," Breena breathed between Dwayne's onslaughts of kisses. She even forgot about Kerry shopping for her brother's wedding. Breena never could think when Dwayne was kissing her. She felt his hands pressing her on her back. He was pressing her deeper into his frame. Her arms folded around him under his dress coat and felt his muscular frame. It was hard and strong. She could feel every ripple through his linen shirt.

Dwayne groaned.

Breena felt Dwayne's hands start to unbutton her bodice. "No Dwayne, not here. The servants."

"Where is your room?" Dwayne asked laving his tongue across the top of her breasts. He managed to unbutton enough of her bodice to reveal the tops of her creamy white feminine globes. He scooped her up in his arms and headed for the stairs. Dwayne mounted the stairs two at a time never stopping his kisses. In the landing he asked. "Which door?"

Breena pointed to her room. Her lips never left Dwayne's.

Dwayne opened the door while still holding Breena. He was hot and hurting. He had waited nearly four years for this day. He felt his manhood bulging against his trousers. After several years of not sharing his needs with another his desire exploded into critical mass. Once in Breena's room he kicked the door shut and turned the lock. Slowly he let her slide down his frame until she was on her feet. His hands began removing her clothing. This was heaven. This was hell. This was Breena and he would have her.

Breena felt Dwayne's hands finish unbuttoning her bodice. His hands deftly untied the corset laces, her skirt tie, petticoat fasteners, and broderie lace with the same urgency she found driving her. Unthinking she removed Dwayne's coat and unbuttoned his shirt. She fumbled at Dwayne's trouser buttons but managed to open his fly and release the tight constraint on his bulging hot manhood. Breena groaned passionately when she let her hands feel Dwayne's manly jewels. She had missed his lovemaking. She wanted Dwayne. She needed his body.

Dwayne had removed all Breena's clothes leaving them where they fell by the time her hands encased his hard organ. Slowly and carefully he walked her to the bed. A soft gaslight allowed him to see where everything was and where he needed to be. Dwayne gently pushed her onto the bed. He wiggled out of his trousers and silken boxers as he lay next to her. He kissed her mouth, neck, breasts, and navel. Dwayne kicked off his shoes and used his toes to pull off his woolen socks.

Breena breathed heavily allowing Dwayne to kiss her body. His lips were hot brands tingling and teasing her to a heated need only Dwayne could fill. Yes, fill her completely! Her hands floated over his shoulders and back. He felt wonderful. He smelled wonderful. She burned for him.

"Peanut! Oh God Peanut!" Dwayne breathed heavily. He lay upon her flushed body knowing she needed him as much as he needed her. His leg gently pushed her leg aside and mounted his love. There was no time left for any more foreplay. He drove into Breena. She was hot, wet, and needing him. He drove in her again and again and again. He couldn't control himself. He exploded in orgasm and filled her with his seeds.

Breena arched her hips into every one of Dwayne's thrusts. He felt wonderful. She was burning for him and he was soothing her hurt. Her body shook and released a violent orgasm. Dwayne must have felt it because he moaned in ecstasy followed by an expulsion in orgasm of his own.

Dwayne collapsed on Breena. He was breathing heavily. "Forgive me Peanut I couldn't control myself. I needed you so bad."

"Shhh," Breena soothed stroking Dwayne's sweaty hair and perspiring head. "I needed you in the same way." Breena was breathing fast. Her heart was racing. She still wasn't thinking clearly but she didn't care. The day had been a long one and now she was tired. She was very tired. She closed her eyes. The euphoria of lovemaking allowed her to sleep deeply.

Dwayne rolled onto his side. Breena's rhythmic breathing was Dwayne's first clue Breena had fallen asleep. His second was her angelic face with a smile and closed eyes. "I love you Peanut!" he whispered into her hair. Carefully he pulled the coverlet and moved Breena carefully under the covers. He snuggled next to Breena and covered his body. "I'm never letting you go again, Peanut," he vowed. He soon was blissfully asleep next to his Breena.

It was still dark when Breena woke from her sleep. Next to her was Dwayne. Breena thought he looked so angelic while he was sleeping and then it hit her like a hard slap in the face. He looked exactly like little Dwayne. Her son! How could she forget her son? What was she going to do? She had to tell big Dwayne about his child. How could she? What would she say? Would he hate her and toss her aside? Would he deny his parentage? Hundreds of thoughts of dread and fear crossed the synapses of her brain.

She was wide-awake. Breena had to get away from Dwayne. When she was around him she couldn't think and she had to think. Quietly she rose from her bed being careful not to jar the bed or make a sound. She realized she was naked. "Dwayne, what do you do to me?" Silently she walked to her closet and pulled out a white silk nightdress with matching robe and slipped into them. She found her slippers and slid them on her feet. When she turned in the dimly lit room she saw her clothes, petticoats, and broderie strewn across the floor. Mixed in with her personals were Dwayne's clothes and personals. It almost made her laugh. "Dwayne, what do you do to me? How shall I ever explain this to Mattie?"

Breena closed the door behind her as she left her room. She opened the nursery door and peeked inside. Little Dwayne was sound asleep in his bed. His arm was under the pillow his head rested upon. He was sleeping on his right side. "Just like your Daddy," Breena said wistfully. She rested her head on the doorframe and smiled. "I love you, little Dwayne. I love your Daddy. How shall I tell him about you?"

Breena pulled the sash tighter on her robe and walked down the steps. She went to the kitchen and prepared a pot of coffee. She also sliced some bread, spread butter on the slices, and poured a little honey on top. "Mmmm," Breena appreciated. "Now I must think of how to tell you about your son, Dwayne McGillinen." A few minutes later Breena poured herself a cup of delicious hot coffee. She placed it on the table in front of her with her second slice of bread and stared into the pink tinged waking clouds of the dawn.

"Missus Breena?" Aida questioned walking into the house at dawn. "Is yo alright. Yo ain't feelin sick is yo?"

"No Aida," Breena sighed heavily. "Unfortunately I'm feeling pretty darn wonderful."

"What's that supposed to mean?" Aida pursued. "Yo sho like confusin a person early in the mornin."

"Nothing, nothing at all," Breena answered sipping her coffee.

"That be another thing," Aida chuckled. "Yo sho be closed mouth."

After Breena sipped her coffee she took a deep breath and was about to tell Aida that little Dwayne's father was here and sleeping upstairs in her bed when Gregory Wagner walked into the morning room.

"Breena!" Gregory exclaimed in a bit of surprise. "I couldn't sleep last night but I didn't expect to find you awake this early."

"If you didn't expect me to be awake, why are you here so early," Breena gulped. Now what was she going to do? Gregory was here, Dwayne was here, and little Dwayne would be awake soon. Breena felt as if she was about to placed into an iron maiden. Maybe she could get rid of Gregory before either big Dwayne or little Dwayne woke.

"I couldn't sleep as I told you," Gregory repeated. "I thought I would come to Hyacinth House and have some of Aida's filling breakfast while I thought about what I need to say to you."

Upstairs Dwayne's hand reached across the bed fumbling for Breena's soft and inviting breast. His hand dreamily stretched and reached to find nothing. He woke with a start and looked for Breena only to find an empty bed. A wicked smile crossed his lips, "Looks like I have to drag you back to bed Peanut." He flung the coverlet to the side and

swung his legs over the bed. He looked at the floor and saw all the clothes strewn across the wooden parquet. "First I have to find my clothes," he chuckled. After several minutes he had retrieved his trousers, shirt, socks and boots. "That's all I need for now, and that's just in case your servants are about." Dwayne made his way down the stairs. He stopped short when he heard a male voice. "What the Hell?" he silently asked.

"Breena, I've been transferred to a post out West," Gregory announced. "My orders are to report to Fort Bridger in Wyoming before winter."

"Is that good? Or bad?" Breena asked. She wasn't certain what Gregory thought about it or if it was a promotion or demotion.

"It means a promotion to three star General," Gregory bragged. "They need me to guide the wards of Fort Bridger during this beginning peace with the savages."

Breena groaned. She hated it when Gregory was pompous and flaunted his white superior attitudes.

"I won't go without you Breena," Gregory suddenly stated. "It is time you accept my proposal of marriage."

"Like Hell!" Dwayne grumbled quietly. "It's time for me to step in and let that guy know who Breena is going to marry. Wait, I can't go in there pistols cocked. Breena will get angry. I'll play the idiot along for a while. Yes, that's what I'll do." He entered the morning room in a whirl. "Good morning," he said walking with a stride into the room. "I thought I'd bring my Peanut back to bed. Whoops, what's this? I didn't know we had company?"

Breena stiffened and turned bright red. *My God, what is he doing?*

"Who is our guest?" Dwayne questioned already suspecting it was that Gregory Wagner. Why hadn't Breena told him to go away long ago?

"I'm hardly your guest," Gregory snapped angrily. "I was having a conversation with Breena if you don't mind."

"I don't mind at all," Dwayne replied smugly walking to the coffee pot and pouring a cup of coffee. "What's the matter Aida? Your mouth is wide open. You trying to catch flies?"

Irritated but strong in mind Gregory continued, "You will accompany me as my wife, Breena. This courtship has lasted too long. I've been patient and tried to understand many things, but I won't take no for answer."

"And if her answer is no?" Dwayne interrupted.

"I am not discussing this with you," Gregory snarled impatiently. He returned his focus to Breena. "We haven't much time. I suggest we marry next month and this month you can turn over your bank accounts, papers, investments, and properties to my name."

Breena forgot Dwayne was even there. How dare he? This was hers and she wasn't about to give up one coin to a man, any man much less Gregory. "This is not a time to discuss this Gregory," she hissed in warning.

"Oh but I think this is the perfect time to discuss this," Dwayne egged on. This was delightful. The old coot had no idea if he persisted Breena would flail him alive. How dare any man try to take over her independence? Dwayne certainly knew better. This was fun. It was like handing a dead man a shovel for his own grave.

"Shut up!" Breena told Dwayne clenching her teeth. "Shut up!"

"This is something that must be handled quickly," Gregory continued. "As your husband of course I must take charge of all monies and properties."

"Get out!" Breena shouted turning on Gregory. "Get out now!"

"Why are you upset?" Gregory questioned. "Is it because of this twit who decided to irritate you and our conversation. Make the twit leave."

"Gregory," Breena seethed balling her fists. "Get out before I break a pan over your head or cause serious injury to your person."

"What is the matter with you child?" Gregory said patronizingly.

That was the last straw. Breena blew like a cannon in the middle of a battle. Frustration, fear, and anger combined into one major explosion. "In the first place I will not marry you much less leave with you for some God forsaken place like Fort Bridger. I have my life, my career, and my family. Further more, if you think for one minute I would turn my family heritage over to you, well you are quite out of your mind!" Breena shouted angrily. "How dare you assume I would marry you? How dare you assume I would turn over my estate to a pompous, self righteous, bigoted man?

"Hear! Hear!" Dwayne applauded Breena's diatribe.

Breena and Gregory turned their heads and shot angry glares at Dwayne.

Gregory thundered angrily, "Why don't you find your missing peanut and mind your own beeswax!"

Dwayne grinned wickedly. He walked triumphantly behind Breena. His hand moved her hair from the nape of her neck. Dwayne placed his lips upon her soft nape and kissed her gently, "Oh but you see I have my Peanut right here." His hand slid under arm and cupped a breast squeezing it gently.

Gregory watched Dwayne. He was livid with rage. How dare he touch Breena like that? How dare he kiss his intended? Gregory didn't think. He pushed Breena away and raised his fist to slam in the upstart's face.

Dwayne was furious to see Breena manhandled by the general. He saw the fist aiming for his face and blocked the blow with his forearm. He balled his fist and rammed it into the general's abdomen. The general bent in pain and lost his wind. Dwayne followed with an upper cut smashing into Gregory's face. Blood splattered on impact.

Gregory fell on his knees. He choked for air. His hand wiped the blood from his lip.

Breena worried for Gregory. Dwayne was a younger and stronger man. The fight hadn't been fair. She picked up a napkin dipping it in a glass of drinking water and knelt next to Gregory. Gently Breena wiped the blood from his lips.

Gregory suddenly realized Breena was wearing bedclothes. Two and two made four. He rose from the floor grasping her wrists. "If you needed a man all you had to do was ask. I've respected you and made no attempt to force intimacy."

"Gregory you're hurting me," Breena cried struggling to free her wrists.

Gregory released her and hissed, "I see you satisfied your carnal urges with this twit. Good God Breena, you could have had a real man."

Breena stared at Gregory in disbelief at his words. She didn't see Dwayne lunging for Gregory.

Gregory didn't see Dwayne either. Another fist slammed into his face.

"You bastard!" Dwayne shouted putting his fist into Gregory's face. "Don't you use my Breena's name in the same breath as those foul remarks you plebian ass."

"Stop it!" Breena screamed so loudly even her ears hurt. She was trembling. Everything was out of control. She was out of control. "Stop it!"

Payton Lee

A small boy came running into the kitchen and started pulling at Breena's nightdress shouting with a little voice, "Mommy, Mommy, I scared! I scared Mommy!"

Breena looked down to see her son, her child, and her life. "Don't be scared. Everything is fine baby," Breena lied. She bit her lip so hard it started to bleed. The emotions and turmoil caught up to her. She started sobbing and tears flowed down her face.

"Mommy, don't cwy!"

Chapter 17

Breena looked at Dwayne. She saw the confused and questioning look on his face. She looked at Gregory. His face was bloodied and contorted with rage.

Gregory watched little Dwayne run in. It was then it hit him. Breena's son was a duplicate of his father. His father was the man in the room. "Tramp! Liar! Jezebel!" Gregory spat out venomously. "You told all of us the boy's father was dead! You led us to believe you were a widow! Liar!"

The ferocious yapping of a brown spaniel soon joined the melee. Liberty took a protective stance next to little Dwayne and bared her teeth in warning to the two men.

Breena's world began to swirl. Her world was crashing in on her and slamming her from all four corners. Breena was close to hysteria. The only sane thing that mattered in her life was little Dwayne. Her arms wanted to fold around him but she felt her body swaying. Suddenly she saw only blackness.

"Peanut!" Dwayne shouted. He saw her eyes go backwards and her body go limp. He raced to her side and picked her up before she slumped to the floor.

"Sweet Jesus!" Father Michael proclaimed upon entering the kitchen in time to see Dwayne catching Breena. He had heard the shouting from the parlor.

Abel had let Gregory in. When he heard a different voice he peeked into the morning room and saw big Dwayne. He knew there would be trouble. He sent Jonathan to get Father Michael. Fortunately Father Michael was awake and was about to begin sunrise mass. Father Ralph took over for him. When Jonathan was fraught with worry and said there would be trouble at Hyacinth House he didn't ask why. He followed Jonathan and rode bareback on the horse with Jonathan.

Little Dwayne was crying loudly. "Mommy! Mommy!" He grabbed at her nightdress as big Dwayne carried her to the stairs.

Liberty jumped out of the way and stood by little Dwayne growling.

Father Michael scooped up little Dwayne and comforted him. As calmly as he could he told the petrified Aida and Mattie, "Get Doctor Whitecliff right away." He looked for Kate. She had moved to the side allowing Dwayne to pass her and carry Breena up to her room. Father Michael handed little Dwayne to Kate. "Take him to his

room and keep him there. Calm him down. I'll get Aida to take up breakfast for the two of you."

Kate opened her arms and the frightened little boy reached for her. She hugged and soothed little Dwayne with her low loving words and voice.

Liberty stopped barking and growling. She followed little Dwayne and Kate up the stairs to little Dwayne's room.

Gregory was attempting to follow Dwayne's path when Father Michael's hand stayed him. "Let me through Father. Breena is my intended."

"I heard what ya called her just moments ago," Father Michael reprimanded. "Ya don't need to be seeing our Breena until things can be righted. I suggest ya leave now. I'll be in touch with ya later."

"Perhaps we all need time to calm down," Gregory agreed wiping his swollen bloody lips with his sleeve. "What about the boy's father? That's him you know."

"Yes, I do know," Father Michael confessed. "I met him last month. I'll be doing some talking with him first. Ya can be guaranteed of that. Have the army doctor tend to ya in the mean time."

"I'm not giving up Father," Gregory warned. "I've waited more than three years for Breena Hodges. I'm not giving up." He straightened his uniform and walked out of the morning room. Soon he was in his carriage and on his way back to his town home. The army surgeon would go to his house because he was a general.

Dwayne carried Breena to her room and placed her gently on the bed. He undid her sash tie and quickly removed her robe. Without a moment's hesitation he ripped the buttons off the top of her nightgown. Her breathing was raspy and uneven. Dwayne was really frightened.

"That be indecent," Mattie scowled at Dwayne stepping over the scattered clothes. She saw him remove Breena's robe and undo the buttons on Breena's nightdress. "I be here to take care of our Missus Hodges. Yo best gets out of here. Doctor Whitecliff be coming."

"I'm not leaving Breena's side," Dwayne stated angrily.

"Oh yes yo is," Jonathan Masters said behind him. "My Mattie would take care of our mistress Doc Whitecliff don't know yo. Yo be leavin alright." Jonathan was a mountain of a man. He was as big as Ryan if not bigger. Jonathan easily picked Dwayne up by the shirt collar and pulled him out of the room. "Father Michael says he wants a chat with yo. So's a chat is jest what yo's gonna have." Jonathan led Dwayne back downstairs and took him to Breena's study where Father Michael was waiting for him.

Dwayne allowed Jonathan to plop him down into a large chair in the study.

"You can leave us Jonathan," Father Michael reassured. "We'll be fine. Would you have Aida bring us some breakfast after she sees to Kate and little Dwayne."

"Little Dwayne?" Dwayne swallowed the words with surprise and awe. "Father, what the Hell is going on? What the Hell is happening?"

"First ya need to calm down," Father Michael counseled. "Take some deep breaths."

"Peanut," Dwayne cried. "I have to know if Peanut is going to be all right." He allowed his tears to seep from his eyes.

"I presume your Peanut is our Breena?" Father Michael smiled understandingly.

135

Dwayne nodded. He put his head between his knees. "Who was the little boy who called my Peanut, mommy?"

"That little boy is your son, little Dwayne," Father Michael replied bluntly. "I'm certain Breena didn't want you to find out this way, but it is about time you found out."

Dwayne sat straight up. His eyes were wide with shock. "My son?"

"Yes, your son," Father Michael repeated. "Little Dwayne has been Breena's secret from ya and her family. She's kept the love of her entire world to herself."

"Peanut had my son and never told me?" Dwayne gasped. His world started crashing in on him. He was a father. Breena had his son. She never told him. Suddenly he rose from the chair and slammed his fist on the desk. "Why the Bloody Hell didn't she tell me?" he shouted angrily.

"That I don't know and I doubt I'll ever know," Father Michael said quietly to counter Dwayne's fluctuating emotions. "She told me when she found out she was enceinte you were her childhood crush and she couldn't encumber you with a child. You had just started attending a university."

"Why didn't you tell me?" Dwayne accused. "Why didn't you let me know?"

"I didn't even know who the father was until last month," Father Michael grouched in return. "I received little hints every now and then, but it wasn't until a month ago I found out who little Dwayne's father was. It was you! I went looking for you and I found you, remember?"

"Oh yes I remember," Dwayne answered hotly. "I remember you not telling me I was a father."

"I couldn't," Father Michael responded rising from the chair behind the desk. "I swore an oath to Breena."

"You just broke that oath," Dwayne snarled. "You could have broken it sooner."

"I don't think I broke my oath lad," Father Michael corrected. "Ya saw little Dwayne. He looks just like ya. Ya heard him call Breena mommy. Tell the truth lad. Ya know damn well the lad is your son."

"God I'm so confused," Dwayne wept raking his hands through his hair. "I don't know what to think or how to act. I sure don't understand why Peanut didn't tell me."

"That is something only Breena can really tell ya," Father Michael soothed placing his hand on Dwayne's shoulder.

"Do you think Peanut is going to be alright?" Dwayne asked worriedly. "I really love her you know."

"I think I've always known deep down in my heart that little Dwayne's father wouldn't desert Breena or his child," Father Michael consoled.

"God, Peanut didn't tell you I deserted her?" Dwayne choked. "I'd never desert her. If I had known I would have forced her to marry me."

"Maybe that's what she was fighting inside," Father Michael suggested. "No one can force Breena to do anything. Even if she wants to do something, if she's forced she'll fight it."

"Boy isn't that the truth," Dwayne laughed. "Peanut is twice the stubborn of a mule."

Father Michael was relieved Dwayne was calming down. He thought he'd help the lad calm down more. "Why do you call our Breena, Peanut?"

"Oh!" Dwayne brightened. "I've known Peanut since we were kids. She has always been a tough hard shell on the outside, but a delicious soft morsel on the inside just like a peanut."

Aida knocked on the door.

"Come in," Father Michael invited. He had recognized Aida's knock.

Aida carried in a silver tray containing plates filled with hot cakes, fried eggs, sausages, and fresh baked bread. "I'll be back with fresh coffee, butter and jam."

"Is Doctor Whitecliff here yet?" Father Michael questioned.

"My Abel went to fetch him, but he and Abel ain't showed up yet," Aida replied placing the large tray on the desk. "My Mattie be staying with Missus Hodges and I jest gave Kate and little Dwayne their breakfast. Jest like yo said Father Michael."

"How is Peanut?" Dwayne asked Aida quietly. "Is she alright?"

"If yo meanin Peanut to be Missus Hodges, Mattie tells me she be right worried about her," Aida grumbled. "Yo done upset our Missus Hodges. Mattie tells me our Missus Hodges still ain't breathin right! If anything happens to our Missus Hodges yo will pay in damnation yose will!"

"Aida, I'm so sorry!" Dwayne apologized. "I'd cut off my arm and legs if I could take this all away."

"It be too late," Aida scolded. "We is jest gonna pray right now and hope Doc Whitecliff gets here soon." Aida shook her kerchief wrapped head and left the room.

"I want to go see Peanut," Dwayne said to Father Michael as he started to walk toward the door.

"I wouldn't do that lad," Father Michael warned. "I'm pretty sure Jonathan is standing guard. I wouldn't go up against him. Not now I wouldn't"

"I want to at least meet my son," Dwayne requested.

"Eat your breakfast first," Father Michael ordered. "Let little Dwayne eat his breakfast. Both of you need some quiet time and we need to find out from Doctor Whitecliff how our Breena is before we do or think about anything."

Obediently Dwayne sat by the desk. He made two plates and offered one to Father Michael. "If I eat, you eat."

"I'd never turn down Aida's food," Father Michael. "She's too good of a cook."

The two men ate in silence. They were in their own thoughts while sipping hot coffee when they heard a carriage pull up in front of the house.

Father Michael ran to the parlor and opened the door. "Come in Doctor Whitecliff."

"What's happened? Abel is incoherent," Doctor Whitecliff complained. "All I understood was there is an emergency at Hyacinth House and Missus Hodges is ill."

"Breena is upstairs," Father Michael said showing the way with his hand. "Breena has been through an intense emotional trauma. We are very worried about her. She's fainted and not come about."

"How long?" Doctor Whitecliff asked in concern walking faster.

"It's been nearly an hour," Father Michael told the doctor. "She's breathing, but breathing raggedly."

"Who is with her?" Doctor Whitecliff queried while stepping up the stairs with Father Michael.

"Mattie," Father Michael said as he walked through the hall to face Jonathan. "Open the door, Jonathan."

The big black man bent to open the door and allow Doctor Whitecliff in. "Yo goin in Father Michael? He ain't!" Jonathan said holding an arm as a block in front of Dwayne.

"No, Jonathan," Father Michael replied placing his hand on Jonathan's arm to lower it. "I'm going to stay in the study with Dwayne. When Doctor Whitecliff has finished examining Missus Hodges, please send him down to see us."

"Yas suh," Jonathan answered. "I'd do that." He took his position of guard in front of Breena's door once more. He spread his legs and crossed his arms as if in a dare to let Dwayne just try and get past him.

"Where's my son?" Dwayne asked Father Michael in the hall. "I think I should see my son."

"I think you should go downstairs and wait for me," Father Michael ordered.

"Where are you going?" Dwayne inquired in exasperation.

"I'm going to the nursery to check on little Dwayne and see if he has calmed down," Father Michael replied coolly. "Your son is only about three years old. He's still a baby in a manner of speaking."

"Let me go to him," Dwayne pleaded. His head was spinning. This was all so new and shocking to say the least. He had a son almost three years old and he didn't even know about him until this morning. He was happy, sad, angry, thrilled, and excited all bunched up in mixed emotions.

"The boy doesn't even know who you are," Father Michael reminded. "He's upset and probably frightened half to death seeing his mommy faint. Give him some time. I'll check on him. Trust me."

"I have no choice," Dwayne mumbled. These people lived with Breena. They all loved her. They knew all these things about her that he didn't. He had no choice but to trust their decisions. No matter how much he loved Breena, she trusted these people more than him. That hurt deeply.

Father Michael peeked in the nursery. Little Dwayne was playing with his toy train. Father Michael whispered to Kate, "When you feel little Dwayne is ready. Bring him downstairs to meet his Daddy."

Kate nodded in acknowledgment. Instinctively she knew little Dwayne would need to see his mother before he should meet his father.

"Drink this water Missus Hodges," Mattie coaxed. She was so relieved when Breena finally gained consciousness, but frightened because Breena couldn't stop shaking. To make matters worse, Breena started crying and sobbing. "Little Dwayne! I want little Dwayne. Where is my baby?"

"Calm yoself and drink this here water," Mattie insisted. She turned to see Doctor Whitecliff standing in the doorframe. "Praise be to Jesus!" Mattie sighed in relief. She was proud of herself for cleaning the room of the mess there had been there earlier. "Doctor Whitecliff be here for you Missus Hodges. He can help yo and make yo all better."

Doctor Whitecliff placed his bag upon the bed by Breena's feet. He knew Breena was in emotional trauma. Her face was pale and her body shaking as if encased in ice.

Her movements were not coordinated. Her movements were spasmodic. "What happened here Mattie? What upset your Missus Hodges to this state?" He took Breena's trembling hand and felt her pulse. Her pulse was strong but erratic. He needed to sedate Breena.

"My pumpkin," Breena wailed. "I want to see my pumpkin."

"You certainly are not going to see your son in this condition Mrs. Hodges," Doctor Whitecliff warned. "You'd scare the boy half to death. You've already scared ten years of age off your Mattie here."

Doctor Whitecliff's bedside wit helped Breena become a little more cohesive. She quieted somewhat but her shaking continued.

Doctor Whitecliff smiled and reached for his bag. He pulled out two papers and mixed the powders. "I'm going to put this mixture in the water and I want you to drink it Mrs. Hodges. We're going to wait a few minutes and let Mattie here tell me what happened. After you're more relaxed Mattie will fetch your son."

Breena nodded her head and drank the glass of water mixed with the sedation powders.

"Good," Doctor Whitecliff stated noting Breena's color returning and normal breathing return. "Now Mattie, tell me what happened."

"I's don't know for sho. I heard yellin, screamin, and carryin on the likes of never heard in this house afore," Mattie related. "I just knows little Dwayne's Pappy, the general, and Missus Hodges was havin mean and cruel words with each other. It be words I never done heard in this household."

Doctor Whitecliff found a reason for Breena's state, or at least he thought he did. Little Dwayne's father was here. The man was supposed to be dead. Yes, that would upset a woman or a man if a dead spouse suddenly showed up. "I'm not surprised at you fainting upon the sight of your dead husband. That would be enough to send anyone into such a fit."

The sedation was already beginning to take affect. Breena merely nodded. Her mind was already clouding over, but it didn't hurt to think any more. All of life was becoming a foggy blur. Desperately she maintained a thread of reason, "Pumpkin?"

Mattie rose and ran to the nursery. In a moment Kate and Mattie were back with little Dwayne.

"Mommy?" little Dwayne asked when Kate put him gently next to Breena on her bed. He crawled next to her and put his little hand on her head. "Mommy sick?"

Doctor Whitecliff patted the boy's head. "Yes son, mommy is sick but she is going to get better. Remember your sniffles. You took a tonic and felt better?"

Little Dwayne nodded his head.

"Your mommy took some tonic and she is going to be better soon," Doctor Whitecliff promised the little boy.

Dwayne placed his little lips on Breena's forehead and whispered, "Mommy be better soon."

Breena's eyes fluttered maintaining one last lucid moment. "I love you, pumpkin." Her eyes shut and she was sleeping.

Little Dwayne laid his head upon Breena's and said, "I wuv you Mommy. You sweepy now." Without prompting he said, "Now I way me down to sweep. I pway the

Word to keep..." Little Dwayne said his nighttime prayer for his Mommy. For as young as he was, his face was filled with concern and love.

Kate choked back her tears. That little boy was such a good boy. A wonderful loving boy.

Doctor Whitecliff found himself emotionally involved with the obvious love of the little tyke. He waited until little Dwayne had finished his prayers before he told the boy, "Let's let Mommy sleep for awhile. When she wakes up she'll feel better. Alright?"

Little Dwayne shook his head in agreement. He reached out for Kate to pick him up. "Shhh, Mommy sweeping," he told his nanny.

Kate cuddled the little boy and kissed his little face. "Ya are such a good boy." Kate took him from his mother's room and returned to the nursery. She wanted to make sure little Dwayne was up to meeting his father before she brought him downstairs to meet big Dwayne.

Doctor Whitecliff gave Mattie more powders with instructions on how to mix them. The first dose was potent to calm Breena. Each dose afterward would be weaker in potency. "There is enough here for two weeks. I want your Missus Hodges to rest for those two weeks. She is to have no excitement or excessive stimulus. I also think she should stay in bed and rest for at least one of those two weeks. After that I want her to see me before she returns to her normal lifestyle. Is that understood?"

"Yas suh," Mattie acknowledged taking the precious powders and putting them on top a sideboard in the room.

"I'll be back tomorrow to check on Mrs. Hodges," Doctor Whitecliff said closing his bag. "I'll go downstairs to speak with Father O'Casey now."

"I'll stay upstairs with Missus Hodges for a little bit longer," Mattie volunteered.

"Good," Doctor Whitecliff appreciated and left the room for the Hyacinth House study.

Chapter 18

When Father Michael was about to enter the study where Dwayne sat waiting Abel pulled him to the side and whispered in Michael's ear. Father Michael looked at Dwayne and nodded decidedly.

Dwayne was becoming more and more irritated. He wanted to know what was going on, why so many secrets, why the guarded protection of Breena, and why he couldn't even see his own son. All of this shock and news in one day was more than enough to tip his temper. "What now?" Dwayne grumbled when Father Michael entered the study.

"Abel found your valise on the front porch earlier," Father Michael stated factually.

"Aw shit!" Dwayne swore with mild oath. "I forgot I left it there."

"Abel brought it in and prepared a hot bath and your shaving utensils in the toilette room near the morning breakfast room," Father Michael explained. "He thought you might like a hot bath and shave. He is ready to assist you."

"I guess I'm so tense I forget what good people work for Breena," Dwayne said sheepishly.

"The Thorntons, Masters, and me own sister in law Kate are good people," Father Michael agreed. "Abel is right. You look like Hell warmed over and tis no way to greet a son you've never met."

Dwayne palmed his growing stubble. "I think you may be right."

Doctor Whitecliff walked into the study carrying his black bag. "Well Father Michael, Breena will be all right. She simply needs plenty of rest."

"Can I see her?" Dwayne asked pleadingly.

Doctor Whitecliff turned to look at the stranger. "As her husband, Mr. Hodges, you have that right."

"Husband? Mr. Hodges?" Dwayne questioned furrowing his brow. Behind the doctor Father Michael moved his hand in a motion recognized as don't say anything.

"Unfortunately I believe you are the cause of Mrs. Hodges vapors attack," Doctor Whitecliff commented. "Imagine son, a woman sees her dead husband walk in out of nowhere. It would send any human into the vapors."

Dwayne looked at Father Michael with a genuine look of perplexity. *What the hell was going on here?*

"I will allow you to see your wife at the moment because she is resting," Doctor Whitecliff continued. "I have given her heavy sedation. Son, this is one of the worst cases of vapors I have ever seen."

"Thank you," Dwayne responded without any more questions. He was just happy he could finally see Breena.

"Your son looks like you. It's amazing," Doctor Whitecliff observed. "Well I must be off. I left two patients waiting in the consultation room to tend Breena. Call me if there are changes. I left sedation prescriptions with Mattie." On those words the Doctor left Hyacinth House.

Father Michael saw him to the door and signaled Abel to retrieve Dwayne. Michael then walked into the toilette room where Dwayne had entered the tub for a hot bath.

"Do you want to tell me what this dead husband returning is all about?" Dwayne questioned. He used the soft cloth and soaped his body. It was then he realized how tense he really was.

"When Breena first arrived in Washington City it was difficult for most people to digest a simple fact that a single woman had come here to seek a career," Father Michael began to explain. "The parishioners created a story of Breena being a widow. When Breena found out she was carrying your child we decided it would be best if we continued to let people believe in a dead husband."

"You've been part of this deceit?" Dwayne chided. "I thought priest's never lied."

"Tis true," Father Michael chuckled. "I never lied. I did not divulge the truth."

"Why didn't you make Breena tell me?" Dwayne asked angrily splashing the water with a closed fist. "I have a son, a three year old son and I never knew about him. That's wrong Father. That is really *really* wrong!"

"Don't use that tone with me!" Father Michael retorted hotly. "I never knew who little Dwayne's father was. How was I to know you weren't a drunken wife beating scoundrel that Breena ran away from? Breena never told me her reasons for not telling you. For all I knew you would deny your son and cause Breena pain. I didn't even have a clue that you were a good and decent man until a last year and I've been trying to find out who you were ever since."

"Instead I've been punished," Dwayne grumbled. "I've been denied my own son."

"Better you than Breena," Father Michael said stubbornly. "She's a good pious loving mother."

"And I've never been given the chance to be a good father," Dwayne pouted.

"Well, ya have your chance now," Father Michael scolded. "Don't muck it up."

Dwayne finished washing and rose from the tub. Father Michael handed him a towel.

Father Michael remained silent and waited patiently as Dwayne shaved, combed his hair, and dressed in fresh clothing.

Dwayne smiled when he put the peanut shaped cuff studs in his shirt and showed Father Michael. "Breena gave me these for graduation. She loves me. I know it."

"Maybe that is the reason she never told ya about little Dwayne," Father Michael said thoughtfully. "Perhaps Breena loves ya too much. That can be dangerous son. Ya need to tread carefully."

"I will," Dwayne vowed. "You have my promise. Can we see her?"

"Let's go," Father Michael said putting his hand on Dwayne's shoulder. "Tis almost lunch time. We can meet little Dwayne shortly."

Jonathan had left his guard position at the door. Mattie had left Breena sleeping in the room and the two of them went to check on their son, Linc who was being cared for by Aida, his grandmother.

Once in Breena's room Dwayne ran to Breena's side. He didn't know why, but he felt he was at fault for her current condition. In his heart it didn't matter what he did or did not do. He felt personally responsible for Breena's condition. He only knew he loved her and had loved her since they were children. He planted his body next to hers. She was indeed sleeping restfully and soundly. Her breathing was regular once more. Color was returning to her face.

Dwayne pushed an errant curl to the side and kissed her cheek. "Breena, why didn't you tell me about my son?" he whispered sadly. "Why couldn't you love and trust me as I love and trust you?"

"She can't hear you son," Father Michael warned. "Breena is sedated."

"I know," Dwayne stated. "I have this need to tell her things right now whether she can hear me or not." He took her hand and kissed it over and over again. "I didn't mean to upset you. Lord Breena, I love you with all my heart. I want and need you. I want and need your son, my son, our son!"

"You talk to her while I check to see if little Dwayne is ready to meet you," Father Michael stated smiling. He liked Dwayne and knew he loved Breena. This was a couple that belonged together. He left the room to talk to Kate in the nursery in the room next door.

"Father Michael?" Kate asked squinting to see the dark shadow entering through the door.

"Tis I," Father Michael answered. "I came to check on little Dwayne and see if he is ready to meet his daddy."

"I think so," Kate observed as objectively as possible. She turned to watch little Dwayne playing catch ball with Liberty. "He's calmed down a lot since he spoke to his mother."

"Good. Tis almost noon time meal," Father Michael said. "Bring the boy down to the formal dining room. I'll force Dwayne from Breena's side and bring him downstairs. Tis time they meet each other. They've been too long not knowing each other."

"I agree," Kate returned solemnly. "Little Dwayne, come with Kate. We're going to be eating soon."

Little Dwayne looked to Kate and cast her that charming McGillinen grin. "Come Wiberty, we eat!" He stood up and walked toward the door spotting Father Michael. "Hewwo Fadder Mikewell. Did you see Mommy?"

"Yes I did," Michael answered the boy. "Ya Mommy is still sleeping. I'll meet ya downstairs in a bit. There's someone I want ya to meet."

"Yes swir," little Dwayne answered respectfully taking Kate's hand.

Father Michael left the room to retrieve Dwayne. He walked in to Breena's room to see Dwayne kissing Breena softly on the lips and whispering loving words to her. "Tis time to meet your son," Father Michael announced. "He'll be waiting for ya in the formal dining room."

When Dwayne entered the dining room he saw Kate in conversation with a little sandy haired boy. The boy looked up at him with curious eyes. Dwayne marveled at how much little Dwayne looked like him right down to the mystical gray eyes. "Hi!" was all he could choke out.

Little Dwayne looked at big Dwayne carefully. His little brow furrowed.

Dwayne stepped up to be next to little Dwayne and then knelt beside his son.

Little Dwayne's brow furrowed deeper and then his lower lip pushed out. No one noticed his little hand form into a fist until it slammed right into big Dwayne's lower lip.

"Whooooaaaa!" big Dwayne gasped in surprise. He lost his balance with the blow and nearly fell backwards.

Father Michael's eyes widened in panic and wondered what big Dwayne would do. He'd never once witnessed little Dwayne showing such temper or violence.

Kate gasped is shock. She never imagined little Dwayne was capable of such action let alone thought.

Both Father Michael and Kate watched big Dwayne. Both were ready to pounce and protect little Dwayne if they were needed. Instead both were more surprised when big Dwayne returned to his original position and started laughing.

"That's some arm you have there," Dwayne laughed. "There is no doubt to anyone in the world you're my son. You have your Uncle Ryan's blood running about in there too!"

Little Dwayne looked at the man curiously and then folded his arms across his little breast in defiance. "You make my mommy cwy."

Dwayne stopped chuckling immediately. He became stone serious. "Son, I never meant to make your Mommy cry. I'd never purposely make your Mommy cry. You see I love your Mommy like you love your Mommy. Little Dwayne, I'm your Daddy."

Little Dwayne wrinkled his face in question and turned to Kate, "What Daddy?"

Big Dwayne gently took little Dwayne's shoulders and told him, "You have your Mommy who loves you. Mommy has Daddy who loves you. Understand?"

Little Dwayne took that defiant stance once more. "No!"

"I guess I'll have to show you what a Daddy is and how he loves you," Dwayne grinned hopefully. He showed little Dwayne that McGillinen charming smile. "Will you let me show you what a Daddy is?"

Little Dwayne recognized the smile. He had seen his own in the mirror many times. He remembered his mommy showing him his smile in the mirror and telling him his father had the same charming smile. He always thought his mother meant Father Michael. Suddenly he understood what the strange man meant when he said daddy. "Show me Daddy."

Big Dwayne rose to his full height and scooped little Dwayne up and put him on his shoulders. "How about some food. I smell Aida's wonderful cooking. Don't you?"

"Hungwy," little Dwayne gurgled in delight. This man was nice and fun. Father Michael used to put him on his shoulders before he got too big. He liked being up high above the other adults. Somehow this man seemed to know that. The man even hopped

a little to make it feel like a horsey ride. Yes, little Dwayne liked this man and knew he would have fun.

Big Dwayne carried little Dwayne to the table and put him on a regular chair.

"We have a child chair for him," Kate suggested tentatively.

"Naw, he's a big boy that needs to sit next to his Daddy," big Dwayne countered. "He needs a little more height." Dwayne looked around and spotted what he needed. "Ah, there's what we need." He pulled out the two large books that were lying on a sideboard. Breena must have been studying them. They were law books. Dwayne picked little Dwayne up and put the books underneath him. "There you go. You eat with the big boys now."

Little Dwayne beamed with pride when big Dwayne pushed the chair into the table.

Big Dwayne took the chair next to little Dwayne.

Throughout the meal big Dwayne was there for his son. When lunch was served, big Dwayne cut up the meat into smaller pieces, mashed the vegetables, and buttered little Dwayne's rolls. He talked to Dwayne like a big person asking him about his favorite toy and favorite story. Big Dwayne learned that little Dwayne had his own pony and Jonathan had been giving him riding lessons since he was a year old.

Kate confirmed little Dwayne's equestrian experience and added he was a talented horseman for his young age. "You're very good with children. How do you know so much about them and know about caring for them?"

"Well, Grady and Morning Song McGillinen now have fourteen grandchildren counting little Dwayne and one on the way," Dwayne shared with Kate. He wiped little Dwayne's mouth with a napkin. The butter had dripped down little Dwayne's chin when he ate a biscuit. "I've been around all of them since they were born. I guess some of the parenting rubs off. One of the most caring is my big brother Ryan. He carries his babies in a cradleboard, dresses them, puts them to bed, and even changes their nappies. He adores his two little girls."

Kate was amazed.

After noon meal big Dwayne asked little Dwayne if he would like to show his daddy his equestrian skills.

Little Dwayne was delighted and scooted off the books without help. He ran to find Jonathan and ask him to saddle his pony, Wabbit.

"Wabbit?" Dwayne chuckled.

"Rabbit," Kate corrected. "His pony has unusually long ears for a pony and Missus Hodges bought him for little Dwayne last Easter. Little Dwayne has trouble pronouncing his l's and r's."

Father Michael showed Big Dwayne where the livery and stables were. Little Dwayne was already there with Jonathan.

Big Dwayne watched with immense pride as his son helped saddle his own pony. Obviously Jonathan had done an excellent job in training little Dwayne.

"Which horse can I use?" Dwayne asked Jonathan and looking at the magnificent horseflesh in the stables.

"That Morgan over there know da city," Jonathan offered pointing to one of the stalls. "I feel yo know horses, but out in the country. Yo don't ride in da city much does yo?"

"You're right," Dwayne readily agreed. He pulled a western saddle from the livery and walked to the Morgan. "Breena bought this didn't she?"

"Missus Hodges don't cotton to ridin side saddle like'n ladies about here. Nor like ridin English Saddles," Jonathan smiled broadly showing his bright white teeth. "Missus Hodges like that saddle with her skirt pants. She always tell us she be more comfortable."

"Breena can ride like the wind on a saddle like this," Dwayne bragged. "She really knows her horseflesh too."

"Fo Sho! Missus Hodges knows almost as much as I does," Jonathan teased big Dwayne. Jonathan helped little Dwayne on his pony and then pulled an English saddle to put on his favorite horse, an Irish Thoroughbred stallion.

"He's beautiful," Dwayne commented to Jonathan about the horse.

"Fastest piece of horseflesh east of the Mississippi," Jonathan bragged. "Missus Hodges lets me take him to Washington City's open lands for good runs. This stallion can run faster than a wind storm."

"What's his name?" Dwayne asked mounting the Morgan.

"Twister," Jonathan shared. "Sort of fits don't it?"

"How did Breena get Twister?" Dwayne wondered in question to Jonathan.

"A visitor friend of Senator Jones took a liking to Missus Hodges a couple of years back. He admired her knowledge of horses. Thry rode together many times during his visit," Jonathan related the story for Dwayne. "When he went back to Ireland, he sent Twister to Missus Breena as a present. He told her to call the horse any name she wanted. When I done told her how fast this horse was, she called him Twister."

"That's my Breena," Dwayne clucked. "Yep, that's my Breena. Are you ready to show me Washington City, little Dwayne?"

"Uh huh," little Dwayne answered nudging his pony to a slow gait.

"Do you know where a wireless office is?" Dwayne asked Jonathan.

"Yas suh," Jonathan responded. "I'll show yo." He placed Twister in the lead and Rabbit followed behind, as was the standard practice for rides in the city. Twister led, Rabbit in the middle, and Breena's horse, Lavender in the rear.

Dwayne was truly amazed at how well little Dwayne set a horse. He kept thinking of how proud Ryan would be of little Dwayne. Ryan had put Aurora Blue on her first pony when she was one. Twiggy was beside herself with worry, but Aurora took to the pony like ducks take to water. At least that is what Ryan said.

"Here be the wireless office," Jonathan announced reining Twister. He jumped off the Thoroughbred and took Rabbit's reins, and Lavender's reins. "I's waits for yo here Massah," Jonathan offered.

"Thanks Jonathan," big Dwayne appreciated. He walked to Rabbit and lifted little Dwayne from his saddle. Big Dwayne put his son on his shoulders once again. "I need to send a few wires. I'll be back."

"Yas suh," Jonathan acknowledged.

"Yes sir," the man behind the counter greeted cheerfully. "May I help you?"

"I'd like to send a wireless to Ryan McGillinen of Ely, Nevada at Geneva's Branch and Brian Duffey and Henry Astor at Beacon Hill, Massachusetts."

"Henry Astor?" the man croaked. "Doesn't he have one of them new fangled telephones that Bell created?"

"Yes, but I want them to get a wire," Dwayne explained readjusting his son on his shoulders. "I really don't want to talk to them about this on one of them telephone things."

"Of course, I understand," the man stated condescendingly. "What are your messages?"

Dwayne was already scribing the first telegram. *"Ryan, bring Twiggy and the girls. Blue and Sam have to meet their cousin, my little Dwayne. Hurry. I need your help."* Dwayne handed the paper to the clerk and then scribed the second note. *"Uncle Duffey and Uncle Henry. Come to Washington City right away. I need your help. Come alone. Very important! Come alone! There is a real bombshell Breena has for us. We have to talk. Hurry. I'll expect you on the 6:00 p.m. train tomorrow. Hurry and Urgent, Dwayne."*

Dwayne paid the clerk the fees and walked outside to Jonathan.

"Where to now suh?" Jonathan asked.

"We're going to visit Pennsylvania Avenue and the new building Uncle Henry built," Dwayne announced. "I want to show little Dwayne where his Daddy is going to work."

"Yo's staying then?" Jonathan asked.

Dwayne put little Dwayne on his pony. "I plan on staying a long time and being a good Daddy," Dwayne said to his son and then added for Jonathan's sake, " and a good husband."

Chapter 19

Dwayne led the way to the Pennsylvania office building. After he dismounted Lavender, he picked little Dwayne from his pony. Big Dwayne tied Lavender and Rabbit to the post by the boarded walk. "Tie Twister to the post and come in with us Jonathan," Dwayne invited. He held little Dwayne in his arms. To other's it might seem unimaginable, but big Dwayne loved his son. It was instant love and an automatic bonding. He was proud of his son. Big Dwayne repressed his feelings of resentment that Breena had kept his son a secret. He was angry that she had not shared him. Little Dwayne was a wonderful boy.

"Yo think dat be right with the white folk?" Jonathan questioned in reservation.

Dwayne felt Jonathan's reluctance and understood. He replied strongly, "Those white folk better not mind. I'm their boss. If they run up against me they'll be sacked."

Jonathan trusted Dwayne and followed him into the building.

"Afternoon Rogers," Dwayne greeted a gray haired clerk studying a blueprint.

"Mr. McGillinen," David Rogers recognized. "We didn't expect you for a month or two."

"I've had a change of plans," Dwayne grinned and readjusted little Dwayne in his arms. "I came to take care of family business."

"I didn't know you had a son," David commented. "The lad looks exactly like you."

"Yes he does," Dwayne boasted.

Little Dwayne noticed the smile on his father's face and said, "Daddy!" he gave big Dwayne a hug.

Big Dwayne felt his heart melt. If he could give the world to his son at that moment he would. "I want to show little Dwayne his Daddy's office."

"It isn't finished yet," Rogers answered apologetically. "We only have your desk, chair, and files. The gas lamps aren't in. The decorating hasn't started."

"Actually that's good," Dwayne responded. "I want my wife to decorate my office."

"Is she with you?" Rogers queried looking past Dwayne, little Dwayne, and Jonathan.

"Not yet," Dwayne grinned mischievously. "But she'll be here in awhile."

"Very well sir," Rogers acknowledged. "This way." Rogers led the trio up the well-polished intricately carved stairway.

"This look like some great hall," Jonathan commented walking gingerly on the polished white marble floors. Paintings on the wall were hung with gilded frames. There

were paintings of the Astors, the Presidents of America, and noted statesmen. Jonathan was impressed.

"Where is Mattie?" Breena asked Kate. She had woken up to Kate's ministrations. Kate was brushing Breena's hair while she slept.

"Mattie is downstairs taking care of Linc and helping Aida make supper," Kate answered still brushing Breena's hair.

"Who is taking care of little Dwayne? Is he napping?" Breena asked immediately. Breena had slept off the first sedation and she was awake and alert. Her first thought was concern for her son.

"He's off with his Daddy," Kate replied without thinking.

"What?" Breena screeched. She attempted to jump from bed. "Where did big Dwayne go? Where did he take my son? How could you let him just walk off with my little Dwayne? He doesn't know my son. He doesn't know anything."

"Actually he's very good with little Dwayne," Kate corrected pushing Breena back into bed. "Little Dwayne's Daddy didn't even bat an eye when little Dwayne popped him on the lip."

"What?" Breena groaned. How could Dwayne take care of her son?

"Tis a funny story," Kate teased. "Lie back quietly and I'll tell ya. Doctor Whitecliff left instructions that you mustn't excite yourself. If you wait a minute, I'll tell Mattie you are ready to eat. You are hungry aren't you?"

"I'm starved," Breena answered. "Kate, you haven't answered me. How could you let big Dwayne leave with my son? What if they don't come back?"

"I've never heard such nonsense from you. Don't you fret," Kate reassured. "Jonathan is with them."

After Breena had eaten supper Kate gave her more sedation. Although Breena was lucid, Kate noticed her hands were still shaking. Breena was about to fall asleep when a little toddler ran into her room and jumped on her bed.

"Mommy, Mommy!" little Dwayne squealed in delight. "Look Daddy bought me twain." In his hands was an ornately carved steam locomotive. "We go widing and we go to big building."

"Pumpkin!" Breena greeted sleepily. She forced herself to stay awake and looked at little Dwayne's train. "It's beautiful. Did you ride Rabbit?"

"Uh huh," little Dwayne answered snuggling into his mother. "You better?"

"Yes pumpkin," Breena answered with a large yawn. "Mommy better." Her eyes fluttered and she was once more sleeping.

"Let's eat supper son and let your Mommy sleep," Dwayne said at the doorframe. He walked to the bed. He kissed Breena's forehead taking a moment to tuck the covers around her. Then Dwayne lifted little Dwayne into his arms. "Shhh, let Mommy sleep so she gets better."

Once again big Dwayne impressed Kate with his understanding of childcare. Dwayne took charge of little Dwayne from the beginning of the meal to the end. He carried little Dwayne upstairs and prepared his night bath. Dwayne selected his nightdress, bathed him, powdered him, combed his hair, listened to his prayers and tucked him into bed. To Kate's surprise he began telling little Dwayne the story of Little

Bear and the red wolf. It was a story he made up as he went and included little Dwayne as the hero with Little Bear, Shoshone chief. Little Dwayne was sleeping contentedly half way through the story.

Dwayne went downstairs for a sip of brandy. It had been a long day and he needed to think about tomorrow. He would meet Uncle Henry and Uncle Duffey tomorrow. They had to help him convince Breena to marry him right away. Still, the Doctor warned him not to upset Breena in any way for two weeks. Upset her? Hell! She kept his son from him!

"Massah," Abel interrupted Dwayne's deep thoughts. "Yo received these wires whilst yo was ridin." He handed him two telegrams.

Dwayne ripped open the first one. *Fortunate I was in Ely. We will be in Washington City in two weeks. I understand your urgency. Will be there for you. Ryan.*

Dwayne smiled, "Thanks brother." Dwayne ripped open the second wire. *Will be on the 6:00 train tomorrow. Worried sick about you and Breena.*

"What do you mean you're leaving for Washington City?" Audrey questioned demandingly. "What did that wire say? Why are you so closed mouth for Heaven's sake?"

"I want to know the truth Brian Duffey!" Alyson demanded placing her hands on her hips. "Something is going on and why would the two of you leave not taking us and not telling us what the Sam Hill is going on!"

"Maybe it's because even we don't know," Brian replied quietly.

"Dwayne's wire requested Brian and I leave immediately," Henry confirmed. "That's all he said. We don't know what it is, but he asked that we come alone."

"This isn't like Dwayne at all," Kerry noted. "He loves being the family darling and center of attention. I'm really worried."

"You need to worry about our little girl and that's all," Braden said lovingly and patted Kerry's belly. "If Dwayne wants only the older and wiser men, there must be a reason. I'm perfectly comfortable with that. We'll wait here quietly until Henry and Brian send for us. Understood my sweets?"

"Not a bit," Kerry sniped.

"I agree with Kerry," Paige concurred. "I have a feeling about this. Dwayne is going to need all of us. I've always felt something wasn't quite right. I think we should all go together. A united front sort of thing."

"We will stay here Silly Goose," Ayden countered. "If Dwayne wanted a united front sort of thing, he'd ask. I agree with your instincts and Kerry's statement on Dwayne normally loving to be the center of family attention, but he wants only Henry and Brian. We'll support him. Understood?"

"Very well," Paige complied belligerently.

"I don't understand why he didn't ask for me. I'm his Pa," Grady asked in confusion. "He should want me with him if he's got trouble."

"I think it is quite clear husband," Morning Song explained. "The trouble is with Breena. Why else would he ask for the help of the older men that influenced her life? If he were in trouble he would want you. This must concern Breena."

"I hate it when you are so danged smart," Grady grumped.

"The McGillinen men supply brawn," Morning Song teased. "The McGillinen women supply the beauty and brains."

Everyone chuckled.

"If that isn't the truth," Braden laughed. "Our women are just too smart."

"I think this all settled then," Brian stated firmly. "Henry and I leave on the early afternoon train."

"Good," Henry responded. "Let's all get some sleep. The children are already tucked away."

"I've prepared your bed and bath," Abel announced interrupting Dwayne's musings. "Jonathan told us you be stayin.'"

Dwayne looked up at the older man. "Yes, I will be staying." He rose to follow Abel up the stairs to the guest room near Breena's room. When he entered he was impressed with Abel's skills. Dwayne's silken pants were laid neatly upon the down turned bed covers. A robe was folded neatly next to the pants.

Abel assisted Dwayne in disrobing and dressing in the prepared nightclothes. A towel and soap bar was now in Abel's hands along with Dwayne's leather cased shaving kit.

"This way Massah," Abel said leading the way to the toilette room Dwayne had used for preparing little Dwayne for bed. Once again Abel showed his prowess in being a man's gentleman.

When Dwayne was shaved and redressed after his bath he excused Abel, "You may go now. It's late and we've all had a long day."

"Yas suh," Abel bowed politely and disappeared.

Dwayne knew Abel would be returning to his small cottage and be with Aida his wife for the night. Quietly Dwayne opened the nursery door and checked on little Dwayne. His son was sleeping soundly. Dwayne swelled with pride. He had been around all his brother's children and his sister's children, but his son was wonderful. He looked cherubic lying there. There was no doubt in his mind his son was the best of the McGillinen family. Dwayne shut the door quietly and his eyes wandered to Breena's closed door.

Silently Dwayne opened Breena's door. In the subtle gaslight she looked angelic. Her hair was brushed and flowed on the pillow like rippled streams. God, she looks beautiful. What the hell am I thinking? Sleeping in a guest room? That's my Breena! Dwayne walked into the room with resolve. He started removing his robe.

"Who is it?" Breena asked sleepily. The sedation was still controlling her body.

"Dwayne," he replied softly.

"What are you doing in here?" Breena said in a semi lucid state. "It isn't proper."

"Proper is a husband sleeping with his wife," Dwayne chuckled removing his silken trousers. "Albeit a dead husband you've cooked up, but a husband none the less." He lifted the covers and slipped under them. Before Breena could utter another word his lips were upon hers and his hand swiftly unbuttoning her nightdress.

Dwayne had done it again. Breena didn't have a chance. Once Dwayne started kissing her coupled, with the sedation, she was lost in sensations. Those same wonderful sensations Dwayne always gave to her when he made love to her.

Dwayne concentrated on his love making with the same passion he applied to living. Once he opened Breena's nightdress his hand roamed her body freely. He focused on every nuance of silky warmth and curve of her body. His tongue laved Breena's throat, down her collarbone until he reached her cleavage. His hand cupped her breast and laved tiny little circles around her teat until his mouth encircled his treasure and he began to suckle this wonderful delicacy. "Now I know why you're larger," Dwayne chuckled. "You suckled my son."

Breena responded to the sensation and arched her back to allow Dwayne full access to her breasts. She was breathing rapidly and groaning with her growing needs. The needs only Dwayne fulfilled.

Dwayne dipped his hand into her feminine warmth. She was wet. Her groaning response signaled to him that she was ready for him. He was more than ready for her. Dwayne mounted his Breena, his filly. His knee moved her leg to the side opening her body to his. He drove into her.

Breena responded by arching her body fully into every thrust. Her arms encircled Dwayne's body and her fingers dug into his back. "Oh my God!" Breena breathed when her body reacted in orgasm.

Dwayne felt Breena's orgasm allowing him to seek his own. He expelled his seeds in pulsating force into her cone of womanhood. It was his agony and his ecstasy. Rasping he laid his sweaty head on Breena's neck and whispered into her ear. "See what you do to me Breena?"

Breena still under control of the sedation and floating blissfully in her sensations answered, "Mmm."

Dwayne rolled over and laughed. "My new goal in life is to make love to you and not have you fall asleep. I want you to tell me at least once in my life that I am a magnificent lover. That's all I ask."

Breena didn't answer. Instead she snuggled into Dwayne's body.

"Okay, close enough," Dwayne chuckled enclosing her even closer. He placed his chin on the crown of her head and stroked her long hair.

Dwayne woke before the sunrise and dressed in his pajama pants and robe. When he walked out he heard little Dwayne. Opening the nursery door he found little Dwayne was dreaming and talking in his sleep. Dwayne walked to his bed and tucked the covers around the little boy.

Little Dwayne's eyes opened. His voice still scratchy from sleep asked, "Daddy?"

"Yes it's me son, Daddy," Dwayne answered bending over to kiss little Dwayne's forehead.

Little Dwayne put his hands on his father's head to hold it and told big Dwayne, "I wike you. You pway with me. You pway with me wike Mommy and Mrs. Kate."

"That's what Daddy's are for," big Dwayne reassured.

"Do you wuv Mommy?" little Dwayne asked.

"Yes I do. I love Mommy very much," big Dwayne told his son.

"I hungwy," little Dwayne said.

"Me too," big Dwayne chuckled and lifted little Dwayne from his bed. "How about you and I fix us some breakfast? Maybe we'll even make Mommy some eggs and bacon?"

"Oh boy," little Dwayne gurgled happily.

Dwayne carried his son downstairs and into the kitchen. He opened the gaslights for a brighter light. The two went through the cupboards and the icebox to find everything they needed.

Little Dwayne was helpful because he knew where some of the things were and told his Daddy. Especially where the fresh sweet, butter, and jam were kept is one of the things little Dwayne showed his Daddy.

Big Dwayne started the iron stove and pulled out the big iron frying pan. "You know son, it's a good thing your Grandma and Grandpa taught me and your Uncles how to cook. I can't wait until you meet them."

"Gwandma? Gwandpa?" little Dwayne repeated. All these words were new to him. His face reflected confusion.

"Don't fret little Dwayne," big Dwayne assuaged. "You're going to learn about all this family and loving soon enough. You are a McGillinen and you will be raised as one." He concentrated once more on the eggs in the pan-frying with the bacon. "Mmmm, this smells good."

"Praise Holy Jesus!" Aida screeched when she walked into her kitchen moments later. Big and little Dwayne were sitting in the morning breakfast room eating their faire. "What yo men done to my kitchen?"

A mischievous smile crossed Dwayne's lips. Aida was a female version of Cho Ling, Ryan's cook. Obviously she didn't ever want anyone in her kitchen. "Little Dwayne and I woke up early and we were hungry. I made a little breakfast. I'll clean the mess up."

"No yo taint!" Aida grumped. "Yo stays outta my kitchen. Yo hears me!" Aida reprimanded. "Jest look at this mess yo done made. It take me all mornin to clean this up." For the next half hour Aida grumbled as she cleaned the kitchen and dishes. "What nerve yo got wakin that chile up so early in the morning. Mrs. Kate will give yo a piece of her mind on that. Fixin that boy bacon and eggs fried together. Yo's gonna make that boy sick. Mrs. Kate don't let little Dwayne eat two pieces of bread, butter, and jam. It be bad for his constitution. What yo doin to that boy? Mrs. Kate gonna rail yo a good one."

An hour later Aida had cleaned up the kitchen to her requirements and began cooking the rest of the family breakfast.

"Call the constable!" Kate shouted from the hallway and ran into the kitchen. "Little Dwayne is gone. He's stolen! Call the Constable. Do you think his Daddy took him?"

"I knowed his Daddy took him," Aida replied calmly. "They be over there after they made a mess of my kitchen."

Kate placed her hand over her rapidly beating heart. She walked into the morning breakfast room and scolded big Dwayne. "Don't you ever give me a fright like that again."

"I didn't mean too," big Dwayne answered sheepishly.

Kate looked at the dishes on the table. "Dear God in Heaven, what have you been feeding that boy?"

" A good breakfast," Dwayne replied defensively. "A growing boy needs a good breakfast."

"And did your mother let you eat this when you were little Dwayne's age?" Kate reprimanded. "I don't think she did. Think about it."

"Aww geez," big Dwayne groaned. "The boy was hungry."

"We'll be lucky if he doesn't get an upset stomach," Kate scolded. "Come with me little Dwayne. I'll give you a tonic."

"No!" little Dwayne answered stubbornly. "I no want tonic."

"The boy is fine," Dwayne argued. "Leave him alone. If he gets a tummy ache we'll give him tonic. My Pa always said, '*if it ain't broke don't fix it.*'"

Little Dwayne jumped from his seat and ran into Dwayne's arms for protection.

"How dare you come in here and interfere?" Kate bellowed.

"I dare because I'm the boy's Daddy," Dwayne stated firmly. "Remember? Breena may have decided not to inform me about my son, but get this straight. I am little Dwayne's Daddy and I know about him now. I have every intention of taking part and having a say in my son's upbringing."

"That's the way it should be," Father Michael's voice came through the shadowed hall. "Kate, ya know very well a good Daddy takes part in his son's life."

"I have to admit I like the man," Kate grinned. "A man that won't back down and takes responsibility for his children."

"All we have to do is convince Breena of that," Dwayne injected. "I still don't understand why she never told me."

"Ya needs to ask her, but not yet," Father Michael said. "Doctor Whitecliff gave explicit instructions not to upset Breena in any way. Breena has the worst case of vapors he's seen in a long time. She can't be upset in any way."

"It can wait," Dwayne conceded. "Right now I want to get to know my son better."

"Do I smell a breakfast cooking?" Father Michael questioned jokingly. "Ya wouldn't happen to have an extra plate for a starving priest, would ya Aida?"

"There be always an extra plate for yo, Father," Aida returned humorously. "It wouldn't be Christian to let a priest die of hunger."

"Bless ya," Father Michael said taking a place at the breakfast table in the morning room.

Breena woke up with a clear head. Her hands were still shaking and she still felt weak. Feeling a big strange she looked under the covers and found her nightdress unbuttoned to the hem. A strange warm remembrance filled her memory. "You did it to me again didn't you, Dwayne McGillinen?" Or did she dream it? Her head was foggy. The sedation medicine clouded her thinking. Was she only hoping Dwayne made love to her? Maybe of all this, Gregory and Dwayne, the fight was all a bad dream.

Mattie walked into the room. "I done prepared yo bath Missus Hodges. You be ready?"

"Yes Mattie," Breena answered weakly. She managed to button a few of her buttons before Mattie came in. That small effort had exhausted her. She still attempted to stand but failed.

"Yo be as weak as a new born kitten," Mattie clucked walking to her side and helping Breena to stand. "Yo gonna make it to the toilette?"

"I think so," Breena whimpered. She felt a little better and stronger with every step. What was holding her back seemed to be her foggy mind. The body was sluggish for the sedation. By the time Breena was in the hot tub bath she was feeling much better.

"I be right back Missus Hodges," Mattie informed Breena once she was confident Breena would be safe left alone for a few minutes. Mattie walked briskly down the stairs and into the kitchen. "Missus Hodges be doing toilette and I think she be hungry soon enough. If you make her a breakfast tray, I'll be back down for it. Right now I want to get back next to her. She be as weak as a new born kitten, Ma."

Big Dwayne heard Mattie. "I'll go upstairs and take care of Peanut."

"Yo will not! That be indecent," Mattie admonished. She turned around and went right back upstairs.

"I guess that told me," big Dwayne chuckled. He turned to little Dwayne and Father Michael. "Any one want to play train?"

Little Dwayne had been watching Father Michael eat and perked up. "I want to pway. I be the engine!"

"I'm the caboose," big Dwayne claimed position.

"I guess I'm the passenger car," Father Michael said despondently.

"You can be the mail car if you like?" big Dwayne suggested.

"Don't the mail cars get robbed?" Father Michael queried playfully.

"Oh boy," little Dwayne gurgled. " I be fast so them wobbers don't get you Fadder Mikewell. Whooo Hooo, Choo! Choo!" Little Dwayne shuffled his feet and moved his arms through the kitchen and hall.

Big Dwayne followed little Dwayne pulling a pretend cord. "Toot! Toot!"

Father Michael left the table and fell in line between little Dwayne and big Dwayne. "Chug-a-chug, Chug-a-chug."

Aida and Abel watched the small parade and laughed.

"That be some sight," Abel chuckled. "Massah sho do bring happiness into this house in a big way. I never done see the chile this happy."

"The Massah be jest one big kid hisself," Aida noted smiling as broadly as her husband. "The chile always be happy and a good boy, but now he got hisself a nice daddy to make him happier."

"Praise the Lord and Amen," Abel agreed.

Chapter 20

"I get yo back to bed," Mattie told her mistress after Breena's bath and toilette. Mattie had helped Breena walk back to the bedroom. She could tell Breena was a little stronger. "Then I's brush yo hair."

"Let me sit at the vanity," Breena suggested. "I'd really like to sit up for awhile. I felt like I've slept away two days of my life."

"Actually yo has," Mattie agreed helping Breena to sit down at the vanity chair. "Doc says yo need to sleep. Look at yo hands Missus Hodges. They still be a shakin."

Breena did look at her hands. They were still trembling. "Where is Gregory and Mr. McGillinen?" She knew all of this was real. She only had hoped it was a bad dream. Right after the words came out of her mouth a small boy ran into the room followed by a yapping spaniel. The little boy hugged her legs.

"Mommy, Mommy," little Dwayne greeted. "Feewing better?"

"Yes my little pumpkin," Breena answered. She felt better having her son near by.

"Glad to hear it," big Dwayne announced carrying a large silver tray filled with aromas of fresh bread, sweet butter, eggs, bacon, and juice. "I hope you're hungry. Aida made enough food to feed an army."

Breena looked at the tray Dwayne placed on the sideboard near her bed. "What? No griddle cakes?"

"I'll run downstairs and ask Aida to make some," Dwayne teased back.

Little Dwayne ran to his father and jumped on his lap. "Daddy gonna take me fishing."

Breena raised her eyebrow. "Is that so?"

Before Dwayne could respond Mattie butted in, "Yo need to take yoself outta this room. It be indecent coming into our mistress's room and she taint properly dressed."

"I'm her husband, remember," Dwayne teased.

"No yo ain't," Mattie scolded. "Other peoples outside dis house may think so, but yo know it taint the truth and so does we." Mattie returned to brushing Breena's hair. "Yo get yoself outta here. Yo be dead, remember?"

Those words made Breena feel very guilty and ashamed. She hadn't lied, but let everyone believe lies.

Those words also hurt big Dwayne. It brought back those angry feelings again that Breena had denied him his son. "Come on little Dwayne. We need to go to the mercantile and buy us some fishing rods."

"Playing the Daddy up right are we?" Breena seethed watching Dwayne once again take her son away from her. She shouldn't resent his fatherliness, but she did. She was guilty and defensive. Being nasty was a defense. "All of a sudden you take care of my son?"

"Some one didn't have the right to keep him from me," Dwayne snapped back. He didn't mean for it to come out like that.

Mattie caught the terseness of the words and scolded, "Yo get outta here right now. Doc done said not to let our Missus Hodges get upset."

Dwayne scooped little Dwayne in his arms and left the room. He was ready to go head to head with Breena, but Mattie reminded him not to upset little Dwayne's mommy. He would settle this soon enough and not when he was angry. At this moment he had a son to play with and learn about.

Breena's hand started trembling visibly once more.

"Yo take this tonic right now," Mattie ordered pouring the powders in the hot coffee. Mattie had no idea the heated liquid made the powders more potent. Breena barely finished a third of her breakfast and she was sleeping soundly once again.

"Jonathan, bring Linc and come fishing with us," Dwayne offered. "First we are going to walk to the mercantile and buy us rods and tackle."

"Yassuh," Jonathan beamed. He used to run off at dusk to the river and catch fish with his friends. It was dangerous and if the overseer caught them they would get whipped but he and his friends loved to fish. Today, Jonathan could fish with this new Massah and he was free.

Little Dwayne walked proudly into the store with his Daddy. The clerk greeted Dwayne warmly and showed him several rods and reels. Dwayne talked to the clerk for sometime and little Dwayne listened to every word intently. Dwayne picked out three fly rods and four rods with reels. He also picked out several hand made flies for speck fishing in the parks pond after he talked to the clerk to find out what was biting and what it was biting. Dwayne also bought three wicker creels. The clerk put everything in a big bag. Dwayne couldn't carry the rods, bag, and hold little Dwayne's hand so he put little Dwayne on his shoulders and walked back to the house. A buoyant Jonathan greeted them. "Linc and me be ready. Mattie ain't' to happy bout it since he only be a toddler."

"We'll have to be very careful," Dwayne acknowledged. "I have a feeling our woman are scrutinizing us under a microscope."

"Huh?"

"We'll be careful," Dwayne chuckled. "You have the horses ready?"

"Yassuh. Aida done packed us a nice big lunch basket," Jonathan said happily. "I sho like to fish."

"We're going to the park pond," Dwayne related. "The mercantile clerk told me that is the best speck fishing right now."

"Yassuh," Jonathan bubbled like a child. "Sho would be nice to bring Aida fresh fish for supper."

"We will," Dwayne announced cheerfully. "Let's go." He picked little Dwayne up and put him on Rabbit. He mounted Lavender and Jonathan easily mounted Twister holding his son Linc.

Aida and Abel were watching out the kitchen window.

"Yassuh, that little Dwayne's Daddy be one great big kid hisself," Aida giggled.

"Looks like that he be rubbin off on Jonathan," Abel observed. "I don't recall that big ole nigger ever lookin that happy before neither."

Dwayne rented a boat. The man in the park didn't look pleased when the large black man and the little boy with him climbed into the boat. Dwayne noticed the man's uneasiness and handed him a much larger bill. "This should take care of your uneasiness."

The man looked at the bill and looked at Dwayne. He nodded, "Yes sir, just leave the boat on the shore when you're done. I'll collect it later."

Dwayne shook his head. It never ceased to amaze him what money could do. There didn't even have to be a bloody civil war. All one had to do was buy it. If everyone were rich there would be no war. War was only a battle for wealth. At least that is what he thought. "I intend to stay rich so I can live the way I choose," Dwayne said to himself.

Jonathan, Dwayne, and their sons spent the day fishing. Both Linc and little Dwayne enjoyed themselves completely with their fathers. Both boys had their father's complete attention. Both boys were taught how to cast that day. Little Dwayne was the proudest when he caught the first fish.

Jonathan put the fish on a line and put it back into the water explaining to little Dwayne the cool water will keep the fish alive a little longer because fish spoil so quickly.

Dwayne told his son how proud he was bringing home supper. Aida was going to be thrilled to have fresh fish to fry and Mommy would be proud of her little man.

They rowed back to eat Aida's super lunch of fried chicken, biscuits, fried potatoes, black-eyed peas, and apple pie. There was also a canteen of fresh milk and juice.

"Aida really knows how to pack a lunch," Dwayne admired. "I can't wait until Mommy feels better and we can take her on a picnic. You'd like that wouldn't you little Dwayne?"

Little Dwayne grinned from cheek to cheek. The butter still dripping down the side of his mouth onto his jacket.

Big Dwayne chuckled and wiped the offending drips. "I'm going to have to buy you some more practical clothes like Linc's." Dwayne pointed to little Linc's white handspun linen shirt and his cotton trousers. "Your Mommy sissified you too much."

The men returned to the pond and caught a whole string of fish by afternoon.

"We'd best be getting back," Dwayne announced. "I have some people to meet at the train."

"Does yo need me?" Jonathan asked. He really liked Dwayne McGillinen.

"Yes I will need your help and Breena's carriage," Dwayne answered. "I'm picking up Breena's Uncles Brian and Henry."

"Yo done sent for them?" Jonathan asked holding his sleeping son securely and mounting Twister.

"Peanut needs all the loving support she can get right now," Dwayne shared. "I didn't mean to make her sick. You know that don't you?"

"I sho do. I knows yo loves Missus Hodges and yo boy," Jonathan answered.

"I also need their help to get Peanut better so we can get married," Dwayne added. He helped little Dwayne get on his pony, Rabbit. "I've got my son to take care of too!"

"Is yo still angry that Missus Hodges didn't tell yo?" Jonathan asked on the return ride to Hyacinth House.

"Does it show that much?" Dwayne replied keeping an eye on Little Dwayne. He didn't take a nap that day and he was up early. He knew the boy was ready to fall asleep.

"Yassuh, it does," Jonathan returned. "None of us understood, but we let our love for her make us forget. I hopes yo forgets about it."

"I'll try, but it hurts that Peanut couldn't trust me and I missed out on a lot of little Dwayne's life," Dwayne grumped.

"But yo is in the here and now," Jonathan said wisely. "Enjoy this special time. The Good Lord sends us good and bad. We live with it all the time."

"That is hard for me to understand, Jonathan," Dwayne admitted. "It seems my life has always been charmed. This has been the only rock through my window."

"I prays to the Lord that's the only rock yo would ever see," Jonathan teased.

"Yeah, well I hope you don't have to see any more rocks either," Dwayne responded. "I'll do my best to see that our little family never sees any rocks through the windows."

"Wealth sho do make that the truth," Jonathan agreed.

"Did anyone ever tell you that you are a wise man?" Dwayne laughed.

"No suh," Jonathan replied seriously.

"Well you are," Dwayne told the big man.

By the time they returned to Hyacinth House little Dwayne could hardly keep his eyes open. Mattie had run outside to greet them and took her sleeping Linc into the cottage and lay him down for the night. Dwayne picked up little Dwayne. His son promptly fell asleep in his arms.

"Take care of the horses for me please, Jonathan," Dwayne requested. He carried his sleeping son into the house and up to the nursery. Kate followed him closely. Dwayne laid his son gently on the bed and removed his shoes, socks, pants, jacket, and shirt. Gently he put a clean nightshirt on little Dwayne that Kate had pulled out for him. Then Dwayne tucked his son into bed. "I think he'll sleep through the night. He's plumb tuckered out."

"I can't imagine why," Kate said sarcastically. "His father wakes him up before sunrise, takes him out all day. He doesn't have a nap. Why on earth would the boy be tuckered out?"

"All right Kate," Dwayne defended. "You've chastised me enough. How is Peanut?"

"Mrs. Hodges is resting comfortably," Kate answered glibly. She liked Dwayne McGillinen and loved giving him a run for his money. "She woke up this afternoon and ate lunch. Mattie gave her more tonic and she's resting again."

"Is Peanut still shaking?" Dwayne inquired.

"It's a little better," Kate shared. "Missus Hodges has a delicate constitution. Why do you call Mrs. Hodges, Peanut?"

"Hard shell on the outside," Dwayne answered without thinking. "Soft and delectable on the inside."

Kate smiled on that remark. She rose from little Dwayne's beside and announced. "I'll be staying up here checking on Mrs. Hodges and little Dwayne. Would you let Mattie and Aida know?"

"I'll be happy to do that," Dwayne volunteered. He bent over to kiss his sleeping son and went to the guest room Abel had put his valise in. He changed and left to meet the 6:00 p.m. train. Jonathan was ready and waiting to take him to the train station.

Henry Astor and Brian Duffey disembarked from the train. They looked around. Brian recognized the big black man standing nearly a foot taller than the rest of the crowd. "Jonathan!" He waved to the man.

Behind Jonathan Dwayne appeared. "Uncle Henry! Uncle Brian!"

The men greeted each other with handshakes and embrace.

"What is this all about?" Brian asked Dwayne. "Your wire was none to informative."

"I'll tell you in the carriage," Dwayne answered. "Thanks for coming."

The men remained silent until Jonathan clucked to the horses and carriage began to move.

"Tell us what this is about Dwayne," Henry ordered with fatherly tone.

"Peanut is ill," Dwayne sighed.

"Who the hell is Peanut?" Brian growled. "What does that have to do with Breena?"

"Dwayne calls Breena his Peanut," Henry explained to Brian.

"Good God, what's wrong with Breena?" Brian inhaled.

"The doctor diagnosed the vapors. A very serious case," Dwayne told his uncle. "The doctor gave her powders and orders for her to remain kept sedated and calm for two weeks."

"My little Breena is just like her mother was," Brian stated wringing his hands with worry. "My little Breena is very delicate. She has a delicate constitution."

"Is that why when we were kids you drove her to school and picked her up in your buggy every day?" Dwayne asked.

"Yes, I have always been concerned for her. She's not like your sister Kerry or sister in law, Twiggy. She's like fine porcelain."

"Why didn't you ever tell us kids?" Dwayne asked. "You never told Breena why you were so over protective. That's why she would meet me in her secret place."

"Meet you?" Brian growled. "In her secret place?"

"Every time you would leave town on business Breena would meet me at Schell Pond. We would spend the day riding, fishing, or just hiking," Dwayne told Brian Duffey. "We never knew she was, well you know, delicate. She sure didn't act like it."

"You met my baby behind my back? You risked her life when I was gone?" Brian roared angrily.

160

"Brian, for Pete's sake! They were kids. Breena is grown up," Henry reminded his friend logically. "If she was diagnosed with vapors what upset her so badly?"

"I think it was Gregory Wagner and me in the same room. I kind of lead him on to put his foot in his mouth," Dwayne confessed. "He took his jealousy a little too far with his mouth and I had to punch him."

"Who is Gregory Wagner?" Brian asked with exasperation. Nothing was making sense to him and his little girl was ill.

"General Gregory Wagner has been pursuing Breena for almost four years," Henry explained nonchalantly.

"Why didn't I know about this?" Brian growled angrily. Some man was courting his Breena and he didn't even know about it.

"It's not my fault Breena didn't tell you," Henry answered stoically. "I thought she wrote you about him. General Wagner is quite a boring pompous personality. The poor soul can't get it through his thick head he never had a chance with someone as bright and independent as Breena."

"I'm happy to hear that! Yes I am indeed," Brian sniped heatedly.

"Continue Dwayne before my friend here gets apoplexy," Henry chuckled.

"I popped the General when little Dwayne came in," Dwayne related. "Then the General said some pretty nasty things. I had to pop the General again and little Dwayne became really frightened. That upset Breena."

"Little Dwayne?" Henry questioned furrowing his brow.

"My son," Dwayne said and waited for the explosion.

"When the Sam Hill did you have a son? What the Sam Hill was your son doing in my Breena's House?" Brian roared.

"Breena had my son," Dwayne said quietly. "Little Dwayne lives with his Mommy."

Henry pulled Brian back before his fist hit Dwayne in the face. "Calm down old boy. We need to hear this entire story. We can't do that if Dwayne is knocked out can we?"

Brian sat back and spoke hissing through his teeth, "When did Breena have your son and why wasn't I or even your family told?"

"Peanut didn't even tell me for God's Sake," Dwayne snapped back angrily. "Little Dwayne is nearly three years old and Peanut never bothered to tell me. I'm the boy's father and she never told me."

"When did you take my baby?" Brian snarled. He was furious at Dwayne for participating in sexual activity without benefit of marriage. He besmirched his little girl.

"It was Christmas Eve 1879," Dwayne returned regretfully. "Breena gave me a special Christmas Present. She gave herself to me. I've always loved her. I loved her since she was a kid."

"You couldn't wait for marriage? You couldn't ask her for marriage?" Brian accused hotly.

"I did ask her to marry me, well sort of," Dwayne excused.

"What the Bloody Hell do you mean by sort of?" Brian snapped. "Either you did or you didn't."

"Peanut told me she was off to her job in Washington when I asked her to wait for me," Dwayne barked back. "I was off to college to prove myself to her. We wrote to each other every month all these years. She could have told me!"

"You knew about Gregory Wagner and his pursuit," Henry wondered out loud. "Why didn't you propose to Breena?"

"I did! I asked her to wait for me," Dwayne replied. "I came here to Washington City as soon as Paige warned me about the man. Breena hadn't written about him ever. I thought he was out of her life and she would wait for me."

"You thought she would wait for you," Henry said thoughtfully. "You've never really proposed to her have you?"

Dwayne looked at his Uncle Henry with a new understanding, "No, I never have really."

"You aren't about to do it now," Brian warned. "We will follow the doctor's advice. Breena will remain calm with no excitement for the next two weeks."

"I'm not about to upset her in any way," Dwayne defended. "I'm first getting to know my son. I'm kind of spending this time with him."

The carriage pulled up to Hyacinth House. Brian leaped from the carriage and ran to the door. Without invitation or knocking he ran into the house and up the stairs to Breena's room. Brian pulled a chair next to her bed and there he stayed until Breena stirred.

"Hi Princess," Brian addressed softly.

"Uncle Brian?" Breena questioned wiping her eyes in disbelief. "Is that you? You haven't called me Princess since I was a little girl."

"Maybe I should have," Brian stated quietly.

"What are you doing here?" Breena asked lovingly.

"Dwayne sent for me and your Uncle Henry," Brian replied. "He thought you might like us both to be here for you."

"He was right," Breena whimpered. "I do need you Uncle Brian. I need to tell you many things."

"Not now Princess," Brian replied knowing she wanted to tell him about her son. "Tomorrow when you're a bit stronger."

"I love you, Uncle Brian," Breena whispered guessing Uncle Brian had already had been told about little Dwayne. She was happy he wasn't angry at her.

"I love you too, Princess."

Chapter 21

Mattie brought up Breena and Uncle Brian's dinner. "Massah Astor and big Dwayne want to know if they can come up to see yo."

"Not now Mattie," Breena sighed heavily. "I'm not just not up to it. Not yet."

Mattie nodded with acceptance and left the two alone.

"Uncle Brian there is something I must tell you," Breena said taking the tray her Uncle placed upon her knees.

"If you mean to tell me about your son, Dwayne already told me," Brian said sitting down with a tray on his knees. "Eat your supper before it gets cold."

"Yes Uncle Brian," Breena replied meekly. "You're not angry at me? You don't hate me?"

"In God's Green Earth why would I be angry with you?" Brian questioned putting a piece of meat in his mouth. "Mmmm this is good. I'd forgotten what a good cook Aida is."

"I gave birth to a child out of wedlock," Breena squeaked out. She put a piece of potato in her mouth and began to chew slowly.

"You gave birth to your son. A son I heard you love and care for," Brian answered smiling. "I can't wait to meet him. He's sleeping I understand. You made me a Grandfather sort of. I'm happy and I love you."

"But I never told you," Breena whimpered.

"Now that does upset me. I don't understand why you couldn't trust me or anyone," Brian responded quietly. "When you are better I do expect an explanation. Eat your supper. It's getting cold."

"Yes sir," Breena obeyed.

"Dinner is delicious as always Aida," Dwayne complimented. "Has little Dwayne eaten yet?"

"Yo tuckered out that boy," Aida chided. "Little Dwayne and Linc still be sleepin. Those two jest might skip their supper."

Brian came downstairs carrying the trays. "You can send Mattie up to take care of Breena's toilette and tonic powders. We've finished eating. Abel, you can prepare the guest room for me. I'll be staying here."

"Massah big Dwayne be stayin there," Abel tried to explain.

"No problem," Brian said calmly. "Take his things and put them in one of the rooms on the third floor. Better yet, Dwayne find a hotel room to stay in. The neighbors here are nosey. It isn't proper for you to stay here anyway."

"Sho be the truth. We had everybody's servants coming over the past two days a borrowin and returnin sugar, milk, molasses, or flour. Anything so's they can hear somethin and take it back to their nosey masters."

"You see!" Brian declared.

"Brian is right," Henry Astor concurred. "This is a volatile situation and it would be best for everyone if you and I stayed in a hotel, Dwayne."

"I want to sleep with my Peanut," Dwayne protested.

"What?" Brian roared angrily.

"I mean sleep near my Peanut," Dwayne corrected quickly. Now was not the time to admit he slept with Breena whenever he could. Premarital sex was something you simply did not discuss in any company. "I'm just as worried about her as you are. I'm going to marry her. She is going to be my wife."

"Until my Princess is your wife you can sleep in a hotel," Brian ordered.

"We'll be staying at Washington City Hotel," Henry announced. "I keep a suite there since I started a building for my new office here."

An hour later Dwayne kissed his sleeping son and peeked through the door at Breena who was also sleeping, he left for Washington City Hotel with Uncle Henry.

"That's a fine looking boy you created," Uncle Henry commented in the cab.

"You should see him awake," Dwayne bragged. "He's real smart like his Mommy. He sets a horse like a real equestrian. I took him fishing today and he caught the first fish."

"Sounds like a great lad," Henry said honestly. "I can't wait to meet him. Are you ready to tell me your plans about Breena."

"I wish I could," Dwayne replied raking his hair. "Problem is, I'm not sure what to do next. I sure don't know what to say and…"

"And you're still upset with Breena for not telling you about your son," Henry observed astutely.

"I can't seem to get through that. I don't understand why she never told me," Dwayne complained.

"It seems to me you should put that on the shelf until later and start devising a plan to get Breena to marry you," Uncle Henry suggested. "I have this feeling getting that woman to accept your proposal isn't going to be easy."

"I've sent for Ryan," Dwayne confessed. "He's a brute but he remains calm about things. I've always been able to confide in him."

"Ah yes, Ryan. He calmly breaks peoples necks," Henry teased.

"You're joshing, right?" Dwayne asked in concern.

"Of course I am," Henry replied with a chuckle. "It's going to be fine. It will all work out. We need to start working on a plan."

"All I know is I love Peanut and now I have a son that I love to pieces," Dwayne stated. "I want them both forever."

"Then we'll work on that," Henry promised. "We need to let the entire family know about this. That is going to be the first step."

Payton Lee

Brian was sitting in the parlor reading the morning paper when he heard a knock at the door. As usual Abel appeared in the hall to walk to the door. "Never mind Abel, I will answer the knocker," Brian volunteered rising from the divan. He opened the door to a man not much younger than he was and dressed in a General's uniform.

"Who are you?" demanded the uniformed stranger.

"I might ask the same of you since you are the one knocking at my door," Brian retorted.

"Your door?" Gregory asked rudely. "I've come to call on Breena Hodges. She is the mistress of this house and I am her intended."

"You are Gregory Wagner," Brian recognized. "I thought you were a bit younger."

"May I come in," Gregory asked impatiently.

"No you may not," Brian bit irritably. He did not like this pompous uniformed army mule one bit. "Breena is ill, under sedation, and doctor's care. She is not to have visitors for at least two weeks."

"And you are the doctor?" Gregory sniped.

Brian squared his shoulders and prepared for battle, " I am Breena's Uncle. I am Brian Duffey, esquire, attorney at law. I am here from Boston to take her care. Now go away." With those words barely emitted from his lips he slammed the door in the General's face. "What Breena ever saw in that ass is beyond me," Brian muttered returning to his paper and cigar.

Gregory never had a door slammed in his face before and it didn't sit well, but he remembered Breena talked about her Uncle Brian a lot. It was obvious to Gregory that Breena loved her uncle very much so he wasn't about to create a scene with the man. Instead he returned to his carriage. When he returned to his rented town house he wrote a brief note, addressed it to Breena and had his orderly take it to Hyacinth House with instructions to present it Brian Duffey. He didn't like Breena's uncle one bit, but he knew he had to use politesse with her uncle.

Shortly after Brian had finished breakfast he was informed that Mattie had given Breena her toilette and she had eaten a substantial breakfast. Once more Breena was given her sedation powders and was sleeping. Little Dwayne was awake, dressed and downstairs with Kate when Uncle Henry and big Dwayne came to the house.

"Daddy," little Dwayne screamed in delight. He jumped from his chair and ran to his father as he entered through the kitchen door. Leaping into his father's open arms he squealed happily, "Take me fishing? Pwease?"

Big Dwayne cuddled his son and grinned, "How about if today we take a train and visit your cousins in Boston? Would you like that?"

"Twain?" little Dwayne gurgled in joy. "You take me on twain?"

"Are you quite serious?" Kate gasped. "You want to take this child to Boston?"

"We are quite serious, Kate," Henry Astor confirmed. "Little Dwayne has been a secret long enough from our family. We just happen to have nearly the entire family in Boston for Dwayne's graduation, and hopefully his wedding to Breena. This little surprise should no longer be a secret." Henry addressed Brian when he walked into the middle of the conversation. "You agree don't you Brian?"

"I do," Brian concurred. "Alyson will be thrilled and so will the rest of the family. He is quite a boy."

"Will you join us?" Henry invited.

"No," Brian rejected. "I wish to stay with Breena. I'm worried about her and someone needs to stay here. Just this morning I sent that General Wagner packing. He is enough to upset me, let alone my Breena."

"He was here?" Dwayne growled. "That man needs to learn the word, No!"

"I sent him packing," Brian bragged. "So you see, I will stay here to guard Breena."

"Well you two men are not taking little Dwayne to Boston without me," Kate said firmly. "He needs to have a governess with him on a trip away from home."

"I'd appreciate that," big Dwayne said gratefully to Kate's surprise. "We'll only be gone for the night. Can you pack the things he'll need?"

"When are you leaving?" Kate queried.

"We'll take the nine o'clock train and arrive in Boston approximately six this evening," Henry related. "Do you think you can be ready in an hour?"

"Of course," Kate responded. "I'll pack what we need immediately."

"Daddy?" little Dwayne asked big Dwayne. "Can Wiberty come on the twain?"

"I'm afraid Liberty has to stay home with Uncle Brian and take care of Mommy while we are in Boston," Dwayne explained to his son.

"Oh," little Dwayne answered. "Can we bwing Winc?"

"I'm afraid we can't this time," Dwayne chuckled. He loved how caring his son was even for such a young age. "But you will have your cousins to play with."

"Cuz ins?" little Dwayne tried to repeat.

"Yes and some of them are about your age," Dwayne explained. "There is Abby, Adam, Jared, Garrett, and Bennett. They all will love to play with you."

Little Dwayne's eyes opened wide with wonder. All those names and they were playmates.

About noon Breena woke from her sleep. Brian Duffey was at her side.

"Uncle Brian?" Breena recognized the man on the chair next to her bed with an open law book. "You don't have to sit with me."

"I'm reading and you are keeping me company," Brian teased leaning over and giving Breena a kiss on her cheek. "I'm quite worried for you."

"I'll be better soon. I promise," Breena vowed. "I don't know why I collapsed in the first place."

"According to the doctor it was the shock of seeing your dead husband come to life in your kitchen," Brian guffawed. "Of course we know Dwayne was never deceased don't we?"

"You know everything?" Breena inhaled with guilt written on her face.

"No Princess. I don't know everything. I only know what Father O'Casey shared with me and apparently he came in on the frolic," Brian responded seriously. "Do you want to tell me what really happened?"

"No," Breena replied biting her lip. "Well at least not all of it."

"Then tell me what you will," Brian encouraged.

"Dwayne came to find out why I left the graduation," Breena started.

"That I know. I was there when he left to find you," Brian stated.

"He arrived late and I let him spend the night at Hyacinth House," Breena explained. "In the morning Gregory Wagner came to demand I marry him because he is being sent to a place out West and he wanted to take me along as his wife."

"Which you refused of course," Brian chuckled.

"Of course," Breena smiled. "I have no intention of becoming his possession here or anywhere else. I would not give up my life for any man!"

"When did Dwayne come into this picture?" Brian questioned.

"I was eating breakfast when Gregory arrived. I thought Dwayne was still upstairs sleeping. He wasn't. Dwayne walked into the kitchen. He purposely antagonized Gregory and horrible words were said," Breena related.

"Antagonizing the General isn't too hard," Brian guffawed. "I did the same to him this morning. He's quite pompous you know."

"I know, but sometimes there is a sweet side to him. Well at least a vulnerable side," Breena shared.

"I knew there had to be something deep down inside him for you to allow the General the time of day," Brian observed. "Continue."

"Things were horrible. Gregory said horrible things and Dwayne punched him," Breena recounted. "The two were physically fighting when my pumpkin came in. He was scared. The men frightened him. Everything was out of control and when I saw my pumpkin and saw Dwayne's face. The shock. The surprise. He recognized little Dwayne as his son. I felt guilty. I felt horrible. Then Gregory said horrible things to me in front of pumpkin. I don't remember anything after that. It's as if my entire world came crashing down on me."

"It's fine now," Brian reassured. "The time was long overdue for us to find out about little Dwayne. We all love the boy. Why didn't you let any of us know?"

"I had my reasons Uncle Duffey," Breena sighed. "I had my reasons. Where is pumpkin? He usually comes into to see me every morning or lunch."

"Little Dwayne went off with his Daddy to visit Boston," Brian told his niece without thinking of the effect it would have on her.

"Noooo!" Breena screamed. She leaped from her bed and frantically pulled clothes from her closet. "How could you let anyone take my son away from me?" Breena shrieked hysterically.

"Breena, calm down," Brian croaked fearfully reaching for Breena to bring her back to bed. "Your Uncle Henry went with them. They simply want little Dwayne to meet the family."

"Pumpkin is my family!" Breena sobbed. "How could you let my baby go with two men that don't even know my pumpkin?"

"Breena for God's sake," Brian scolded grabbing Breena by her shoulders. "Kate went with them. They will only be gone for a night. Our family has a right to know about little Dwayne."

Once again the emotional trauma was too much for Breena. She fainted. Her screaming had brought Aida, Mattie, and Abel up the stairs and into her room.

"Abel, bring Doctor Whitecliff back here," Brian ordered placing the unconscious Breena in her bed. "Mattie, bring me some cool cloths."

Several hours later Doctor Whitecliff came downstairs to meet with Brian Duffey. "Brandy?" Brian offered.

"Yes, thank you," Doctor Whitecliff accepted taking the offered snifter.

"How is my niece?" Brian asked.

"Mrs. Hodges had a severe set back," Doctor Whitecliff diagnosed. "I left instructions for calm and quiet. Did her deceased husband appear again?"

"No he didn't," Brian excused. He knew seeing Dwayne was not the reason for Breena's vapors. Emotional strain, argument, and revelations were the true reasons for her nervous disorder. "Breena's Uncle Henry Astor, Kate, and little Dwayne's Daddy decided to take little Dwayne to meet his family. Our family happens to be currently assembled in Boston. Apparently having her son away from her for the night was something she did not want to handle. Of course we had no idea the trip would upset her."

"Her dead husband suddenly showing up and taking her son?" Doctor Whitecliff questioned raising a brow. "And you didn't think that would upset her?"

"No we didn't," Brian defended.

"I suggest that Breena be kept isolated from everyone excluding her servants and you," Doctor Whitecliff ordered. "I suggest you keep her son near her and do not allow her husband to remove him from these premises for at least two to three weeks. Mrs. Hodges does need some time to recover properly. I have her heavily sedated once more."

"We will of course be more careful," Brian apologized genuinely. The last thing he wanted to do was upset Breena. He was really worried about her. He vowed he would keep Breena calm. He would not allow Dwayne to come near Breena and he would keep little Dwayne near. Although he regretted his agreement to the trip when he saw how upset Breena became, he was happy little Dwayne would meet his family. It still made no sense to him why Breena kept this child a secret from everyone especially him.

The train was late arriving in Boston and by the time the carriage pulled up in front of the Astor home, little Dwayne was sleeping soundly in his father's arms.

Dwayne had Henry retrieve a light flannel blanket from under the carriage seat to wrap little Dwayne in so he wouldn't catch a chill. Dwayne carried little Dwayne up the steps to the Astor mansion and was greeted at the door by Thomas.

Henry was the first in the house and instructed Thomas to add four plates to the dinner table. Henry also instructed Thomas to notify the staff that they should prepare a room for Kate O'Casey near Dwayne's room. He also told Thomas that Dwayne McGillinen would be staying the night with his son. That news raised a brow on Thomas' face. He knew all the family quite well and this was news.

"May I take the boy for you?" Thomas offered reaching for the sleeping little Dwayne.

"No, that's very kind of you Thomas but I'm sure he'll be hungry," Dwayne appreciated. "I'm going to take him to the dinner table and wake him."

"Of course sir," Thomas bowed. "Mr. Astor has instructed our staff to prepare more plates at dinner. The family is seating themselves at this moment."

"Thank you," Dwayne acknowledged He looked for Kate and found she was behind him. "Mrs. O'Casey, please follow me to the dining room."

Payton Lee

As Dwayne, little Dwayne, and Kate entered the dining room one of the servants had just whispered into Audrey's ear that his lordship had returned with three guests.

The dining room previously filled with family chatter suddenly became silent. All stared at Dwayne holding a blanketed bundle in his arms.

Little Dwayne woke and stretched revealing his small arms. He focused on his father's face and then reached to put both hands on his father's chin, "Daddy? Are we there?" He peeked from the blanket and saw all the faces in the room. They were all pretty and everyone was seated at a large mahogany table covered with a white linen cloth. The dishes and glasses sparkled with gold. The flatware was polished silver and reflected the gas light in the room.

Everyone's mouth dropped when the bundle revealed a clone of Dwayne McGillinen and the child called him, *'Daddy'*.

Morning Song was the first to speak, "Come Dwayne, sit my grandson down next to me. Where is Breena?"

Dwayne swallowed hard. Of course Morning Song would know it was his and Breena's son.

"Breena is ill," Dwayne replied taking little Dwayne to his grandmother. "Dwayne, this is your grandmother."

"Gwandma?" little Dwayne repeated in question. "You pwetty."

"Thank you little Dwayne," Morning Song greeted. She moved her chair to allow a servant to put a chair for little Dwayne between her and Grady.

"I'm your grandfather," Grady introduced and shook the little boy's hand. "I can't believe the resemblance. You look just like your daddy twenty five years ago."

"Hewwo," little Dwayne answered.

Grady looked at big Dwayne. "I think after dinner you have a lot of explaining to do."

"Yes sir," Dwayne replied meekly. He was glad the secret was out, but he dreaded trying to explain it to his father.

Kerry finally got her voice back, "Yes big brother. You have a lot of explaining to do."

Braden put his arm lovingly around his wife's shoulder. "Don't be upset my sweet. You know I worry for you. I worry especially when you're in this delicate condition. I'm sure Dwayne has a good explanation. If Dwayne doesn't he knows Ryan will kill him."

Kerry burst out laughing, "My darling Braden. You certainly know how to make a tense situation seem frivolous."

"Ah, I hope not frivolous. I'm looking forward to this conversation, " Braden smirked.

Ayden was holding Paige's hand. He had squeezed all the blood from it until Paige wiggled her hand free and whispered, "Ayden, he's Breena's child. You know it! How could she keep this from us? I thought she loved us?"

"My question is, did Dwayne know?" Ayden whispered back. "If he did, then Ryan won't have to kill him. I'll wail the tar out of him."

"I guess we'll have to wait for the answers after dinner," Paige replied. "Little Dwayne is adorable. I want him to meet Abigail and Adam. You go with the family to the study after dinner. I will take little Dwayne to meet his cousins. But then you must tell me everything."

"Have I ever not told you everything?" Ayden feigned shock.

Paige put her finger to her cheek and tapped it several times, "Well there was the time you nearly lost your life in a fire, there was.."

"Alright my sweet, I promise to tell you everything," Ayden croaked in embarrassment.

The rest of the dinner was quiet with small talk. Grady cut little Dwayne's meat and Morning Song took care of serving and preparing the rest of the meal for little Dwayne.

Little Dwayne was such a well-mannered boy at the dinner table big Dwayne beamed with pride. Breena had done an excellent job of rearing his son.

"How old are you little Dwayne?" Paige inquired during the main course.

"I thwee," he replied. "I wode the twain with Daddy."

"You're a very handsome young man," Kerry offered.

"I wook wike my Daddy," little Dwayne responded wiping a drip of milk from his chin with his napkin.

"And your Daddy is handsome," Alyson agreed. She knew this was Breena and Dwayne's child. He had his father's looks and his mother's manners and intelligence. She would flail Brian alive if he knew about this. She turned to big Dwayne. "Where is Brian?"

"Uncwe Bwian is staying with Mommy," little Dwayne replied for his father. "My Mommy is sick."

"Oh my poor darling," Audrey empathized. She was amazed at little Dwayne's understanding and comprehension. "What is wrong with Mommy?"

"Mommy has wapors," little Dwayne answered nonchalantly eating his mashed carrots.

All the family picked up their napkins and hid their chuckles under them. This little boy was wonderfully precocious. He may not know what vapors were, but he knew enough to repeat the diagnosis.

Little Dwayne looked up to see everyone staring at him with a napkin over their lips. "Gwandma, did I say something wong? I bad?"

Morning Song put down her napkin, "Of course not. We were simply thinking at the same time what a wonderful little boy you are. Your manners are impeccable."

Dwayne cocked his head and then looked at his father, "What's im pek able?"

"It means you are perfect and good," Dwayne beamed.

"May I take this impeccable boy to meet his cousins?" Paige offered rising from her chair and walking to little Dwayne.

"I don't know," big Dwayne started to say.

"Of course," Kate interrupted. "I'll join you. I would love to meet all the children and the family has things to talk about."

"How true," Grady stated.

"Let us adjourn in my study," Henry Astor suggested.

Chapter 22

Henry and Dwayne led the way to the study. Everyone followed on their heels. Before Thomas could close the door every McGillinen and family member was surrounding Dwayne and asking a question.

Normally Henry was a quiet man but this was chaos. He stood behind his desk and shouted, "Enough!" When the room was once more quiet, Henry stated quietly, "Dwayne, take the chair in front of my desk. Tell us all the story from the beginning as you know it."

Dwayne walked obediently and silently to the chair. He felt like he was on trial. This wasn't fair. He had to give Uncle Henry credit for his quiet resolve to see this matter attended. It was a way he could tell everyone what had happened, or at least what he knew of it.

"Go on boy!" Grady grumped impatiently.

"It began eighteen years ago when Brian Duffey moved into Ely with his niece. That scrawny little girl stole my heart right there and then," Dwayne chuckled. "She had an overprotective uncle that drove her to distraction. When he left town on business, Breena would sneak off to the little pond outside of town near their home. I found her there the first time and she shared her secrets with me. I'd know when Duffey would be out of town and I'd sneak to meet her there. I taught her fishing, tracking, berry picking, and kissing."

"You little devil," Braden guffawed. "Sly dog! Stealing kisses from a child behind her guardian's back."

"Hey your lordship, I was a child then too!" Dwayne retorted. "I knew I loved her and wanted to marry her after our first kiss. There was just one problem."

"She is a hell of a lot smarter than you," Ayden snorted. "We all knew that a long time ago. Get to the meat of it!"

"When did you get Breena with child, Dwayne?" Kerry questioned.

"Christmas Eve 1879, the day after little Jared and Aurora Blue were born," Dwayne confessed. "We were both sort of taken in by the miracle and it being Christmas and all it sort of happened. Breena and I couldn't sleep. We got to talking. One thing led to another and Breena asked what someone like me could possibly want for Christmas. I told her I wanted her for Christmas."

Alyson rose and began pacing. "I should wail your backside royally for that bit of lustful animal dwelling in you. How dare you take advantage of an innocent like Breena?"

"An innocent that adores the ground you walk on," Kerry seethed. "An innocent that had a crush on you since childhood. Imagine! The day after my little Jared was born."

"Christmas! The time of our blessed Lord," Alyson hissed. "I should wail you right now!"

"Don't think I haven't thought about doing it to myself a thousand times since I found out," Dwayne said somberly.

"I'll be happy to oblige your thoughts little brother," Ayden grinned devilishly. "Care to step outside for some fresh air?"

"Stop it," Grady objected. "When did you find out about your son?"

"The day after matriculation at Harvard. The day I went to Washington City to find Breena," Dwayne related. "She wasn't prepared to hide him from me this time. Maybe she even wanted me to find out, but I don't think she wanted it to happen the way it did."

"Are you asking us to believe she kept your son a secret for three years?" Kerry demanded angrily.

"No, I am telling you Breena kept it a secret from me for four years," Dwayne snapped angrily. "Four years! F-O-U-R years. I'm still angry about it!"

"Why the Bloody Hell would Breena keep it a secret from you?" Braden inquired. "Was she afraid of you? Did you ever threaten her?"

"How the Bloody Hell should I know why she kept it a secret," Dwayne roared heatedly. "I'd never threaten Breena or frighten her. I want to marry her. Why the Bloody Hell do you think I went to Harvard? I wanted to be smart and good enough for her to accept me so I could ask her to marry me."

"How did you find out about your son," Grady asked Dwayne in a calmer tone. He was trying to get the tempers cooled so logic and truth would prevail.

"The train came in very late. Breena and I talked together into the early morning hours. When I woke up I looked for her," Dwayne began to relate the story.

"You slept with her again?" Ayden snarled.

"Yes I did!" Dwayne growled.

The women gasped in shock. Ayden lunged toward Dwayne to be stopped by Braden. "Let Ryan do it! He's on his way."

Henry stood and raised his hand once more. "Enough! Let Dwayne tell the story. I believe it is a bit late to discuss morality in this situation."

"The Bloody Hell it is!" Ayden howled. "I think I need to take my little brother out for some fresh air."

"Ayden," Henry said quietly. "If you do not control your temper I will have to ask you to leave this family discussion."

"I thought living with the Brits would calm you," Dwayne sneered. "Instead you're almost as bad as Ryan."

Braden leaned over toward Dwayne menacingly, "They don't call us the Bloody Brits for nothing."

"I'd remove your own mote before you poke at mine," Dwayne defended. "You didn't morally wait for marriage vows either!"

"I intended to marry Kerry all the time. I didn't use her for a plaything. I am in love with my wife and our child wasn't born out of wedlock!" Braden responded angrily.

"My child wouldn't have been born out of wedlock if I'd known about it!" Dwayne hollered with a red face. He stood up from his chair and was about to start swinging at Braden and Ayden.

"Stop it!" Henry screamed with crimson face. "Stop it immediately. I will not tolerate such behavior in my home."

"Of course Uncle Henry," Kerry reassured quietly taking her husband's arm and gently pulling him beside her.

Ayden plopped huffily in his assigned chair.

Alyson remained seated crimson faced and livid.

Morning Song sitting on the divan with Grady took his hand and squeezed gently. She quietly stated, "I believe you were going to tell us how you found out about your son."

"I went downstairs to find Breena and I heard voices. I heard a man proposing to Breena. I figured it was General Wagner. It was," Dwayne explained. "I knew Breena would be upset if I went in swinging so I casually went in and sort of led the general on."

"Continue," Grady encouraged.

"Well, I sort of let the general hang himself with Breena. She got angry and he said some nasty things. I had to punch him for that. We got in a fight. Breena got hysterical and then little Dwayne ran into the room crying and grabbing onto his mommy. I looked at the boy and I knew he was mine. I was in shock. It was then Breena collapsed. I took her upstairs to her room. I spent the rest of that day learning about my son from the servants and his governess."

"Who the Bloody Hell is the General?" Braden queried.

"He is a pompous bore using Breena's intelligence, money, and social standing to advance his career," Ayden explained. "He's been courting Breena for four years. I thought you got rid of him little brother."

"I thought I did. I thought I got everything right with Breena. I thought she would wait for me," Dwayne sighed. "But there he was."

"Breena is interested in him?" Kerry gasped. The idea of a man using a woman like that was horrifying to her. It took her months to even understand Paige's weird ideas about mergers and such.

"No Kerry," Dwayne assured. "Breena told me she feels sorry for him. She told me that several times in my letters after I confronted her about it two years ago. I was furious when I found him still trying to make her marry him."

"Then you sent for Henry and Duffey?" Grady asked.

"Right away," Dwayne replied. "When I found out how ill Breena had become over the upset I knew she would need her Uncle Brian. I needed Uncle Henry for logic and a cool head."

"I'm sorry you couldn't trust me for that son," Grady stated sadly. "I wish you would have had more faith in me."

"Pa, I was in complete shock. You're my Pa. I needed someone from outside the immediate family with a cool logical head. He could help me look inside," Dwayne explained.

"It was a wise choice," Morning Song supported. "Your Pa would see you as his son and the boy as his grandson. Duffey was needed for Breena. Uncle Henry could help you adjust to this surprise."

"What are you going to do now?" Grady queried.

"I have to wait until Breena is stronger and well. I am going to marry her," Dwayne answered decisively.

"Is she willing to marry you?" Alyson barked. "It seems to me that something kept her from telling you, me, her beloved Uncle, and all of us about little Dwayne. Whatever that is may prevent her from accepting your proposal. There had to be a strong reason for her not telling anyone!"

"Alyson is correct," Morning Song agreed. "Something prevented her from telling anyone about the baby. It would be a powerful reason."

"We women are in complete agreement," Kerry followed suit. "What could it possibly be that kept her from telling anyone." There was silence and then Kerry gasped, "Oh my! Dear Lord, could it be Deborah? Didn't that happen just after Breena left and before you did?"

"Who would have told her?" Alyson asked. "Brian and I didn't hear of it until we returned to Ely."

Dwayne turned crimson. "I did."

"Breena must have thought you used her like you used Deborah," Braden said stoically. "That was a stupid thing to do."

"Wait a minute!" Dwayne roared. "I never used any woman and I love Breena. I wrote Breena about it because Deborah upset me. Breena and I have always shared our feelings with each other. I told Breena I was furious to be used by a woman like that. Deborah knew damn well the baby wasn't mine."

"That really showed how much you loved her," Ayden chortled. "You can be a real idiot at times."

"Would you care to step outside for some fresh air big brother?" Dwayne threatened.

"Oh stop it!" Alyson snarled. "We have some family planning to do. We have to find out exactly why Breena didn't tell us and we can't go by assumptions. I'm going to Washington City with you tomorrow."

"We'll all be following thereafter," Kerry announced. "It will take Paige and I some time to get the children packed. We will get to the bottom of this and we will see you married, Dwayne Sean McGillinen."

"I'll return with Dwayne and set arrangements at hotels," Henry volunteered. "Heaven help the bureaucrats. The McGillinens are about to invade."

"And this city thought the Boston Tea Party was a frolic," Braden chuckled.

"We'll all come in a few days," Ayden agreed. "We may disagree with your improprieties, but we do support you in your quest."

"This meeting is resolved," Grady declared. "We'll meet again in Washington City with hopefully more information. In the meantime, I want to get acquainted with my new grandson."

"Here, Here," Braden agreed. "He's a cute little one. I think he and Jared will get along smashingly."

"Ayden?" Dwayne called for his brother.

"Yes," Ayden turned.

"You said Ryan is on his way," Dwayne queried.

"I received a wire yesterday from a whistle stop. You probably have one waiting in Washington City," Ayden replied. "He told me he was arriving in Washington City in seven days."

"You want that fresh air now?" Dwayne smiled half-heartedly. He was thrilled to learn his big brother was on the way.

"I'll let Ryan put some fresh air in your lungs," Ayden snorted. "I'm off to Paige and let her know what was discussed here. I want to meet my new nephew also."

"Let's go," Dwayne grinned happily. "He's a great boy."

The travelers were woken early and left for the railway station before dawn. Little Dwayne was allowed to fall back to sleep in his father's arms. Dwayne loved holding his son and truly regretted being denied the pleasure from Breena. That is one thing he really wanted to find out. He wanted to find out the reason Breena never told him about her pregnancy or little Dwayne. He hoped Breena was better so he could ask her.

"Have they returned?" Breena asked wearily. She was heavily sedated by Doctor's orders. "Where's my pumpkin?"

"Jonathan has gone to the station," Mattie reassured. They'll be back any minute.

"Good," Breena breathed heavily. "I want my pumpkin."

A small figure ran past Mattie's skirts. "Mommy! Mommy! Mommy I have cuz ins!" little Dwayne bubbled happily. He jumped on her bed and scrambled to be near. "I have Jawed, Abby, Adam, Gawwett, and Bennett." Suddenly little Dwayne became silent. He touched his mother and cried, "Mommy, you is still sick!"

"Mommy is better now that you are here pumpkin," Breena said weakly.

Mattie came up from behind quickly, "Don't you fret none. Your Mommy is jest fine. She gonna be jest fine."

"Mommy?" little Dwayne queried touching his mother's face. "You gonna be fine?"

"Yes. Oh yes my love," Breena whispered using all her strength to embrace little Dwayne. "Mommy is sleepy. Mommy is sleepy." Breena slipped into sleep.

Little Dwayne lay his head next to his mother's and patted her head. "I make you fine."

"What the Bloody Hell do you mean I can't come in?" Dwayne growled angrily.

"It's doctor's orders Dwayne," Brian attempted to explain. "Breena had a relapse. She is restricted to all outside visitors. Especially you!"

"What?" Dwayne questioned in disbelief.

"Come with me," Henry ordered. "We'll work this out." He realized nothing would be accomplished with more arguments. This called for clear and calm thinking.

"I'm coming tomorrow for little Dwayne," Dwayne turned to tell Brian Duffey.

"I'm sorry I can't allow that either," Duffey stated firmly. "Doctor Whitecliff prohibits you from coming near and little Dwayne from leaving while Breena recovers."

"Like Hell!" Dwayne roared. "Breena kept my son from me long enough. She's not going to keep him away any longer."

"Hush!" Henry warned. "The neighbors will hear you. You're making a scene. That does neither you or Breena any good at all."

Dwayne listened to his uncle but stomped to the waiting carriage. He sulked as the carriage made its way through the streets of Washington City. He spotted a sign on one of the buildings and called for Jonathan to stop.

"What are you planning?" Henry asked worriedly.

"I'm sorry Uncle Henry. I won't be kept from my son!" Dwayne replied leaping from the stopped carriage. "Don't worry I won't make a scene, but I won't be kept from my son. Not anymore! Go to the hotel. I'll meet you there soon."

Henry shook his head. He hoped the hotheaded Dwayne wouldn't do something foolish.

Dwayne walked briskly toward the building with the sign. Ready, Miles, and Linden. When he entered the offices he asked, "Is James Linden available?"

"The elder or younger?" the young woman asked.

"I prefer the younger. Both preferably," Dwayne requested politely.

"Your name sir?"

"Please tell James Linden the younger Dwayne McGillinen is here to see him," Dwayne replied using his well-known charm for the benefit of the young woman. Breena would be furious with him, but he was furious with her at the moment.

The young woman rose from her desk and entered another office to the left. She returned with both the elder and younger.

"Dwayne, you old devil! What brings you here," James Linden the younger greeted offering his handshake. "This is my father."

"Mr. Linden," Dwayne acknowledged and offered his hand.

"My son told me a great deal about you," Mr. Linden shared. "You dropped from law and his classes and went into business I understand. What brings you to visit us in Washington City."

"I'd like to hire your services actually," Dwayne told the men. "I have a small legal problem I need your help with. Frankly I wasn't sure what to do and I saw your sign on the building. I was hoping I could take advantage of our college friendship, Jim."

"Of course," Jim smiled broadly. "Come into my office. I'm first setting up since matriculation." Once in his office Jim Linden offered Dwayne a chair, brandy, and cigar. "What can I do for you?"

"I need your help in a child custody matter," Dwayne said bluntly.

Jim and his father sat down immediately. "Child custody?"

"I recently found out I'm a father and the mother is trying to keep my son away from me," Dwayne explained briefly. He went on to explain the entire story.

"I think we can handle the problem," Mr. Linden suggested. "With strict privacy and keeping things under the rug so to speak."

"What do you have in mind father?" Jim asked.

"We'll simply do a brief, a writ requesting visitation," Mr. Linden explained. "We'll have one of our clerks deliver it to this Breena Hodges uncle. You say he is an attorney?"

"Yes, a very good one," Dwayne advised.

"Even more of a challenge," Mr. Linden laughed. "I'll have it prepared by tomorrow ten o'clock. Where can I reach you?"

"My Uncle Henry is opening up an investment firm here," Dwayne replied writing down the address. "I'll be there tomorrow. I'll be handling this branch."

The elder Linden looked at the address. "Henry Astor is your uncle?"

Dwayne nodded. "Is that a problem?"

"No. I don't understand why you didn't engage one of your uncle's high priced lawyers?" Mr. Linden asked.

"My uncle's attorneys are strictly contracts and investment," Dwayne answered factually. "I need a real family lawyer like you and Jim there."

"We're honored," Jim teased. "You will still get a big high priced bill."

"That's all right with me," Dwayne replied. "Send that clerk to Hyacinth House tomorrow. Discreetly of course." After finishing his brandy Dwayne returned to Washington City Hotel and joined his uncle for supper. He told his uncle what he had done.

Henry shook his head. "I hope you know what you're doing. I would have advised a little patience."

"I'm fresh out of patience," Dwayne growled. "No one is going to keep my son from me. No one."

Chapter 23

A legal clerk appeared at Hyacinth House precisely at 10 o'clock in the morning.

Abel answered the door and was informed by the clerk he had a delivery for a Breena Hodges or a Brian Duffey. He called Duffey from Breena's room. "There's a man downstairs to see yo suh."

"Who is it?" Duffey asked quietly so as not to disturb Breena. She was sleeping again and little Dwayne was in his room with Kate O'Casey.

"I don't rightly knows suh," Abel admitted. "But he looks impotant."

Duffey went to the door. "I'm Brian Duffey, may I help you?"

"I came to serve you this writ," the young clerk informed. "Please sign here for receipt."

Duffey went to the study with the young clerk behind him. He signed the document recognizing it as a legal writ. Handing the receipt back to the clerk, Duffey let Abel escort the clerk from the house. Duffey opened the paper and began spitting and cursing. He was furious that Dwayne McGillinen would do this. Alyson followed her husband from Breena's room and placed her hands upon Duffey's face. "What is it Brian?"

"Your nephew just issued a writ for visitation rights," Brian bellowed angrily. "That boy is demanding to see his son. He won't wait a little while for Breena to get better."

"Brian, I love you. I love Breena. I love Dwayne," Alyson said quietly. "I'm just as upset as you are, but I can't help but feel a little pride for Dwayne. He loves his son and is willing to fight to see him. That is a good man. He is also doing it quietly and legally which is your repertoire."

Duffey smiled at his wife. "You are right. This is a good move. Try to make me see reason and both sides by using my own field."

"So what are you going to do?" Alyson whispered softly.

"I guess I'll speak to Breena when she wakes up and tell her that Dwayne will be taking little Dwayne on Saturday and Sunday afternoon, but he will not be allowed to take little Dwayne longer than a day," Duffey shared with Alyson. "I guess I'm proud of the boy like you are. He is taking responsibility for his son."

The next weekend Dwayne was at Hyacinth House at 8:00 in the morning. He planned on breakfast for little Dwayne and a trip to the rail station. "Uncle Ryan is

coming today!" Dwayne cheerfully announced to his son when little Dwayne ran to his arms.

"I missed you," little Dwayne said innocently. "You been away?"

"I've been busy at my new office," Dwayne fibbed. "You remember seeing Daddy's office?" Little Dwayne was too young to understand grown up troubles. Dwayne didn't want to confuse his son. He was just happy the visitation writ worked. "Daddy can only see you on Saturday and Sunday. I'm pretty busy during the week."

"Uh huh," little Dwayne replied cheerfully. "We go to twain?"

"After we eat breakfast with Uncle Henry at the hotel," Dwayne laughed taking his son's hand and walking toward the carriage. *You did a fine job Breena. A really fine job!* He thought to himself.

A large man dressed in a fringed buckskin jacket, jeans, cowboy boots, and a Stetson emerged from the train. He turned to lift a little girl in pigtails from the train. On his back was an elaborately decorated cradleboard with a baby cuddled inside of it. Behind the little girl was a beautiful petite woman dressed in the current traveling fashion of the day.

Dwayne handed little Dwayne to Henry Astor and ran toward his brother, Ryan. He chuckled when he saw all the horrified faces of the passengers and family waiting for them. They were staring at the strangely dressed mountain of a man.

Twiggy took Aurora's hand when she saw Dwayne running toward them. "Ryan, your brother." She pointed out.

Ryan opened his arms and gave Dwayne a big bear hug.

"Uncle Dwayne," Aurora giggled. "You dress funny."

"Not as funny as you, brat," Dwayne teased and stood aside to look at his niece in button shoes, travel dress and stockings. He tweaked her nose and pulled her pigtails.

"Mama made me wear these," Aurora Blue huffed. "And the shoes hurt."

"Blue," Ryan corrected. "Mama knows what's best."

"Greetings Dwayne," Twiggy said lovingly and gave Dwayne a hug. "I can't wait to find out what brought your Ryan into this big city."

"He did," Dwayne replied taking little Dwayne from Henry and into his arms. "Twiggy, Ryan, Blue, and little Sam I'd like you to meet your cousin little Dwayne. My son."

"How do you do," little Dwayne said politely. "Daddy, more cuz ins?"

Ryan's mouth opened wide. "Son?"

Twiggy giggled, "No denying he's your son. He looks just like you! I believe we understand your urgency. When did you find out you became a father?"

"Less than three weeks ago," Dwayne answered. "Let's not talk here."

"You've got a lot to tell me," Ryan warned menacingly.

"Ryan, can you remove the cradleboard. You're scaring the locals as it is," Dwayne teased light heartedly. As gruff as his brother was, his friend was here.

"I warned him," Twiggy concurred. "Would you let me carry my baby?"

"Temporarily," Ryan grinned. "You know I take care of my daughters."

"We all know," Twiggy smiled. She adored her big bear of a husband. No woman would be able to find a man that took care of his children like Ryan McGillinen.

Reluctantly Ryan removed the cradleboard and handed it to a porter. The porter placed it immediately upon a luggage carrier as if it were infected. Ryan clucked and picked up Aurora after Twiggy took possession of Samantha Alyson McGillinen. The porter then retrieved the baggage and followed the troupe to a waiting cabby. Henry hired a large cab for the family.

"Pa, my feet hurt!" Aurora Blue complained.

"When we get to the hotel you may change," Twiggy conceded. "Then you may put on your jeans and boots."

"She's just like Kerry," Dwayne remembered. "A real tom boy."

"Even prettier and a better rider," Ryan bragged.

"You got what you've always wanted haven't you?" Dwayne queried holding little Dwayne in his arms. "A good loving wife and a Kerry reborn."

"He intends to make both our daughters into a Kerry reborn," Twiggy laughed. "He's already telling our little Samantha how to set a horse and he straps on her cradleboard everyday to take her and Blue for a ride."

"How is Blue Pool?" Dwayne remembered to ask. He liked Twiggy's adoptive father.

"Blue Pool adores his granddaughters," Twiggy shared happily. "The two girls visit him everyday with their Pa. I think the girls have made Blue Pool feel younger. He teaches them Sosoni' words, medicines, and ways."

"And how are Cassidy and Lucy?" Dwayne inquired.

"Cassidy and Lucy just had another son before Sam was born," Ryan answered. "Colt has a little brother named Ryan."

"He didn't name him after you?" Dwayne teased.

"No," Ryan answered. "Lucy did. Lucy likes me a lot."

The cab stopped at Washington Hotel. "The rest of the family is already here," Dwayne announced. "We're waiting for you."

"We are about to have this meeting so I can find out about your *son*," Ryan emphasized.

Dwayne didn't respond but signed Ryan and his family in. He led the way to a suite prepared for the Ryan McGillinen family. Kerry saw her brother and greeted him. Ryan picked her up and gave her a big hug and kiss.

"Watch it you big oaf!" Braden reprimanded. He was always near to Kerry when they were away from Geneva's Hope. "Kerry is in the family way."

"Not surprising for you, lust beast," Ryan taunted.

Braden gritted his teeth. He hated Ryan's taunts. Especially when Ryan was right. Braden lusted for his Kerry all the time. He loved his wife deeply and completely.

Paige heard Kerry and came out to greet Ryan. Everyone was expecting his arrival. Behind her were Abigail and Adam. Bennett, Garrett, and Jared suddenly appeared.

Aurora Blue shouted in glee, "Jared!" She really loved her cousin who looked just like her father. They were born on the same day and they had a special blood bond between them that was like brother and sister, not just cousin.

Jared looked at her strangely, "What happened to you Blue? You look funny, like one of them porcelain dolls Uncle Ayden sends you."

Aurora took a swing at Jared. He ducked and she missed him. "Oooh!" she said stomping her foot.

"You gotta practice your swing," Jared teased. "Come on let's play. Hey there's little Dwayne. Wanna play?"

"What? Play with him?" Aurora complained. "He's a sissified city folk."

"He is not," Garrett corrected. "He's a cousin. He's a McGillinen."

Aurora eyed Dwayne carefully and then looked at her Uncle Dwayne. "All right then. Come and play with us. First I have to change. My shoes hurt."

The children ran into Ryan's suite followed by their mothers and nannies.

Ayden had appeared from his room and embraced Ryan. "Pa is waiting in his suite for us."

"Good," Ryan said following Ayden. "I want to hear about Dwayne's son!"

Morning Song opened the door and greeted her adopted sons. When they were in the room with Grady she quietly slipped out the door and went to find her grandchildren. There were so many grandchildren it was unusual to have all of them in one place at one time. That was excluding her children's children. They were always together in the camp.

Ryan didn't waste a moment. "Want to tell me about your son?"

"I just found out about him," Dwayne began to explain.

"Where's his mother?" Ryan demanded.

"She's sick," Dwayne replied.

"Who is his mother?" Ryan questioned.

"Breena," Dwayne answered.

"You didn't tell me you married Breena," Ryan said angrily. "Why wouldn't you tell me?"

"We're not married," Dwayne replied. Before he could say another word he was on his knees gasping for breath. He didn't even see the fist that slammed into his abdomen.

"That's for not keeping your fly buttoned," Ryan chuckled. "You know I'm funny about procreation without marriage. I haven't changed. Now you want to tell me how you and Breena made a son and you didn't know about it until recently?"

"Yeah, if you wait until I can breathe again," Dwayne wheezed.

Ayden and Braden started laughing. They couldn't help themselves. Ryan was Ryan and always would be Ryan. He was a man of determination, high morals, and a hit first ask questions later kind of guy.

Grady held his chuckle and asked Ryan seriously, "Are you done now?"

"Hell Pa," Ryan snorted. "I've just begun. I can't wait to hear this story. Then we are going to find a preacher and get these two married legal like."

"It's not that simple," Dwayne added gasping for air and finding a chair to sit on.

"You used to take worse than that," Ryan guffawed. "This city life has sissified you. Tell big brother why it ain't simple for you and Breena to get hitched."

"Ryan, little Dwayne is three years old. She kept him a secret from me until almost three weeks ago," Dwayne explained reasonably catching his breath. "Breena is also ill."

"What's wrong," Ryan asked worriedly. He feared something awful had happened to Breena living in this city, and he liked her. He always hoped she and

Dwayne would get together. He loved to tease Dwayne about Breena's crush, but he only did it privately.

"She has the vapors," Ayden answered. He told Ryan the entire story.

Dwayne sat through it hugging his ribs and adding a few facts here and there.

Ryan sat down in a plush hotel chair and asked, "Well Pa, what are we gonna do about this?"

"We're going to think this out," Grady replied. "And we are going to help Dwayne get his girl and his son."

"Thanks Pa," Dwayne said gratefully. "Are you sure you didn't get stronger, Ryan?"

The brothers and Braden sat in Grady's suite. Each one was trying to come up with a working plan. Nothing seemed right. Finally the women and children swarmed into Grady's suite. All of them were hoping for a spot on Grandpa's lap. To Dwayne's delight, even little Dwayne seemed to be overcoming his initial shyness and was part of the fray.

After dinner Dwayne kissed his sister and sister in laws. He told the family he must take little Dwayne back to Hyacinth House before dark. Everyone knew the visitation rights and explanation was not necessary. Everyone understood and could see the heartbreak in Dwayne's eyes. Ryan went with Dwayne.

Paige took Twiggy's hand.

"Dwayne looks so sad," Twiggy sighed.

"He is," Paige agreed holding Twiggy's hand. "He loves his son and he loves Breena. It breaks our heart to see this. Two people love each other so much and fight just as hard to keep themselves apart. It doesn't make any sense at all."

"Why didn't Breena tell Dwayne about little Dwayne," Twiggy asked her sisters in law.

"No one knows except Breena," Kerry complained.

"Why hasn't anyone asked her?" Twiggy asked logically.

"She's sick and kept locked away in Hyacinth House," Morning Song replied. "No one is allowed to see her except Alyson."

"Nonsense!" Twiggy declared. "If Alyson can see her. So can we. We'll all go visit Alyson tomorrow."

"I think it would be better if we brought Alyson here and got her on our side first," Kerry suggested.

"I agree," Paige concurred.

"So do I," Morning Song seconded.

"Very well," Twiggy brightened. "Tomorrow we'll retrieve Alyson and we women will get this solved once and for all."

"What would men do without the aide and assistance of we women," Paige clucked.

"Why fall apart and be useless flotsam," Kerry laughed. "We all know that."

"One for all," Twiggy giggled.

"And all for one," Kerry finished.

The next morning Dwayne went to retrieve little Dwayne for the afternoon. He was given a note by Kerry to give to Alyson. He handed the note to Alyson when he

stepped inside the parlor to wait for little Dwayne. Kate had taken him to mass and was returning home momentarily.

"I'll be accompanying you to Washington City Hotel," Alyson announced. She left to retrieve her parasol and handbag.

Little Dwayne returned with Kate when Alyson reappeared in the parlor.

In the carriage Dwayne gained the courage to ask his aunt, "Is Uncle Brian terribly cross with me?"

"Only a little," Alyson answered adjusting little Dwayne's dress coat. "That was a low blow to use legalities against us. He was disappointed that you didn't have a bit more patience. Don't worry. He'll get over it. Right now we are only concerned for Breena's health."

"Is she getting any better?" Dwayne asked. Worry covered his face. He really did love Breena. He felt terrible when he found out her relapse was caused by his taking little Dwayne to meet the family in Boston. He truly regretted that error. It seemed all he did were the wrong things lately.

"Yes," Alyson comforted. "Finally we can give her less potent doses. Her shaking has finally stopped and she appears to be gaining strength. We hope to have her sitting up this coming week."

"When will I be able to see her?" Dwayne pleaded. "I love her."

"You are also still angry with her," Alyson chided. "You must be more patient. Give her time to get well."

"What I need is to talk to her," Dwayne requested. "I'm all mixed up. Talking to Breena always straightens me out."

"Breena needs to get clear too. She's all mixed up," Alyson told her nephew. "Can you get her straightened?"

"Yes," Dwayne replied firmly. "But I have see and talk to her to do it."

"In time Dwayne," Alyson comforted. "Right now you know Brian won't let anyone other than Henry or myself see Breena."

"I know," Dwayne pouted. "Duffey has over protected Breena since she came to live with him."

"Before that actually," Alyson said cheekily trying to cheer Dwayne.

At the hotel Dwayne found his brothers, the children, his father, Lord Braden Wessex, and Uncle Henry waiting for him in the lobby.

"We are going shopping," Grady announced. "Just us men."

"What are we shopping for?" Dwayne asked.

"Our women told us to get out and about and shop for toys," Braden answered. "We are to shop for men's toys, boy's toys, and young lady's toys."

"I imagine our women wouldn't mind a surprise bauble or two," Ayden added.

"Isn't this a bit strange?" Dwayne cocked a brow. "Don't the women usually want to shop?"

"Of course, that's the beauty of it," Braden grinned. "Our women want to stay in the hotel for tea together and chat women talk. We get to go out and play. We get to spend money on toys for us. Kerry explained it all to me."

"Pa, let's get me a toy," Aurora said bending her head back to look up at her tall father.

"Toy?" little Dwayne asked his father. "Bwue get toy?"

"And me and Abby," Adam stated.

"Papa said Jared and Bennett too!" Garrett replied stamping his foot. "I want another puzzle like Auntie Breena bought me. Don't tell her but I broke the one she gave me."

"That's cuz you are stupid," Jared teased.

"Am not," Garrett defended. "The puzzle was hard. Auntie Breena gave you an easy one."

"Did not!" Jared denied and raised his fist to strike Garrett.

Braden stepped in between the boys and separated them by holding Garrett in one hand and Jared in the other. "Boys!"

Bennett stifled a laugh.

"Good God! History repeats. There is Ayden and Ryan all over again," Grady chuckled. "Let's leave right now and get these children some toys."

Alyson left the men and walked directly to Kerry's suites. They were the largest because she had the most children. Everyone was waiting for her.

"Alyson!" Audrey greeted.

"When did you get here?" Alyson said happily hugging her sister.

"I took the night train to arrive this morning," Audrey said kissing her sister on the cheek. "I admit I spoiled myself by using our private car."

"I thought little Matthew was ill," Alyson stated.

"You don't think I'd leave Eloise until I knew Matthew was all right did you?" Audrey replied quickly. "Before you ask, my new granddaughter Margaret is quite healthy. She didn't catch Matthew's cold and Edward is quite healthy."

"Come sit down and have some tea," Kerry invited pouring a cup for her Aunt. "As I remember you take two lumps of sugar, no cream, but a touch of lemon?"

"It hasn't been that long," Alyson chirped.

"It seems like it has with you being locked up with Breena," Kerry answered smiling. "How is Breena doing? Is she starting to recover?"

"Yes thank heavens," Alyson answered sipping her tea. "She is starting to get her color back and most importantly she is finally stopped shaking. We walk her a little bit every day. I'm not certain I agree with the doctor keeping her so heavily medicated. If you don't use your muscles they weaken."

"I agree," Kerry concurred. "I don't believe in that type of remedy at all. But you know Uncle Brian."

"Yes I do," Alyson grinned. "Quite personally."

"What we need to do is talk to Breena," Twiggy volunteered in information. "She simply must marry Dwayne. There are no ifs ands or buts about it."

"That's for sure," Paige giggled. "If she doesn't marry our Dwayne, your Ryan will kill him or at least pulverize him."

"That's enough Paige," Kerry laughed heartily. "We do need to get really serious."

"I know," Paige replied somberly. "Little Dwayne is absolutely adorable. He's a real McGillinen and belongs permanently in this family and sets of cousins."

"Blue thinks he's a sissy and wants to bring him home to Geneva's Branch to teach him to be a real rancher," Twiggy smirked. "That means my little Blue likes him."

"Jared thinks he's wonderful. I think it's because someone is younger than him other than Sam," Kerry shared. "Bennett and Garrett think of him as a cute little brother, much like Adam."

"So you see Auntie Alyson," Paige stated firmly. "We as the women of the McGillinen family must take charge and make this marriage and family happen."

"I couldn't agree more," Alyson concurred. "Do any of you have a plan?"

"We've been planning all morning," Kerry grinned mischievously. "We've been waiting for you to help our plans work."

"Count me in," Alyson smiled. "No one wants to see this happen more than me."

"Then you will help us with Breena?" Audrey queried.

"As much as I can," Alyson agreed. "Where is Morning Song?"

"She's rocking Samantha," Twiggy explained. "Once I fed Sam this morning Ryan started packing her up in the cradleboard to take with him. Morning Song retrieved her and scolded him for taking Sam from her Grandmother. Morning Song also reminded him that he can't feed Sam and would have to come back to the hotel. He wouldn't like that too much since he'd have to leave Blue with Grady."

"I see," Alyson laughed. "That's how you managed to keep Sam today."

The women laughed and teased about their husbands for a little while. Then they began in earnest discussing numerous plans and ideas to bring Dwayne and Breena together. By the time the men returned they had eaten lunch and had come up with a plan. Alyson required a week or two to accomplish everything, but little by little they would find out just why Breena kept little Dwayne a secret and why she fell apart when Dwayne found out.

That evening Alyson took Breena's dinner to her. Little Dwayne had come home with her and was with his mother. They were drawing on the chalkboard. Unknown to Breena, Alyson had taken the powders Mattie gave her for Breena's sedation and threw away half of it. Alyson didn't agree with the doctor and was determined to wean Breena from the sedation and bring her mind to a clear state once again. Alyson felt once that was accomplished, she could begin probing Breena's reason and thinking regarding little Dwayne.

Chapter 24

Two and a half weeks later Breena had been weaned from the sedation powders. She was strong once more and color had returned to her face. Breena was once more lucid and followed normal hours of family life.

Alyson had tried on several occasions to persuade Breena to confide in her about her feelings for Dwayne and why she never told him he was a father. "That girl is as tight mouthed as mute with his lips sewn together," Alyson complained to the McGillinen women on one of her visits to Washington City Hotel.

"We'll visit this Sunday," Kerry announced. "We will all accompany Dwayne when he collects his son. We will stay and have tea with Breena."

"Do you think you can get Uncle Brian to agree to our visit?" Twiggy queried her aunt.

"Yes, I believe so," Alyson allowed. "Doctor Whitecliff has given Breena a clean bill of health. He even said she could return to work in two weeks if she wished. Brian shouldn't have a problem with your visit."

"He still won't let Dwayne see her?" Morning Song asked.

"No," Alyson complained. "My husband is as stubborn as a mule when it concerns Dwayne talking to Breena."

"I take it he doesn't allow that General Wagner to see Breena either?" Paige asked.

"In Wagner's case Brian is even worse," Alyson chuckled. "Every weekend the man has the door slammed on his face."

"And he still keeps coming back?" Audrey gasped.

"A man and his money are rarely parted," Paige quipped.

"I do believe Brian is overprotective, but Breena is using his protectiveness to her advantage," Alyson offered.

"She really doesn't want to face up to the men does she?" Twiggy guessed correctly.

"I believe you are correct," Alyson agreed. "I believe she is a bit ashamed of herself and it is up to us to let her know we love her and the birth of little Dwayne out of wedlock means nothing to us other than we have another McGillinen that we love."

"This will all happen," Kerry promised. "We'll make certain things are set right and those two will be married. How can two people who love each other so much fight each other emotionally the way they do?"

"I hope we find the answer," Paige sighed. "I would like to return home to England before winter. I won't leave until those two are properly merged."

"Married!" Kerry corrected. "Lord will Ayden ever get that right in your head?"

"It's not my head he concentrates on," Paige giggled.

The women burst out laughing.

That Sunday Breena was sitting in the parlor wearing a comfortable soft green day dress. She was primping little Dwayne for his father to collect him. He had returned from attending mass with Kate. Able was watching for the carriage and when it arrived he would walk little Dwayne to his father.

This Sunday when they heard the carriage Abel looked out and said, "I think yo be havin visitors Missus Hodges."

"I don't want to see big Dwayne yet," Breena said softly so she wouldn't upset little Dwayne. "I'm not prepared to see him."

"It ain't big Dwayne I is referin too," Abel chuckled. "It looks like yo would be havin a social. There be yo Auntie Audrey and four other women coming from different carriages. Lord!"

"What is it Abel?" Breena asked with concern.

"There be seven children and they be surrounding big Dwayne," Abel described for Breena.

Little Dwayne ran to the big window. "Mommy, my cuz ins!"

Breena walked to the window and pulled the draperies aside.

Dwayne spotted her immediately and waved.

Breena backed away and instructed, "Abel, you'd best take little Dwayne to his Daddy. I'll go in the kitchen and ask Aida to prepare for my sister in laws and aunts."

"Lord! That be yo family?" Abel clucked. "With their men kissing them and those young'uns yo family is the size of an army!"

"A total of nineteen to be exact not counting little Dwayne's Daddy," Breena disputed. "That's not exactly an army. You'd best take little Dwayne right now."

Abel took little Dwayne to the door and the little boy pulled away from Abel running to his father's arms. His cousins soon surrounded him. Little Dwayne's uncles walked their respective wives to Hyacinth House.

Breena chuckled as neighbor curtains were raised. It seemed everyone in the neighborhood was a little curious about this small Sunday morning invasion. Bravely she walked to the door and greeted each one of her sister in laws and her aunts. Each one of her brother in laws placed a kiss on her cheek, as did her uncle and Grady. Dwayne remained with little Dwayne and the children. His heart sank a little seeing Breena and not being able to touch her.

Brian appeared shortly thereafter and escorted everyone into the dining room. There was more room there and Aida could serve tea and biscuits.

"What a lovely house," Twiggy admired for Breena's sake. "We were told you, Auntie Alyson, and Auntie Audrey refurbished to match your childhood memories."

"Later we would love a tour," Paige added. She sat demurely in a chair after Abel pulled one out for her. One by one, either Abel or Brian seated the McGillinen women.

Another knock at the door announced the arrival of Father O'Casey. His masses had finished and he came over to visit Breena as he did every Sunday for lunch and these past weeks to check on her health.

"Would you mind an old priest visiting with all you lovely young ladies?" Michael requested cheerfully. "Ya have no idea how happy it would make me to cast these old eyes on such young loveliness. Especially you Mrs. Duffey."

"You can tell you're Irish," Alyson chortled. "Full of Blarney!"

"We would greatly appreciate your presence," Audrey stated quietly. "I think your presence is most fortuitous."

"Really?" Michael cocked a brow.

"Actually yes," Kerry chimed. "You see most of us present including Breena are devout Catholics and quite frankly the questions we will put forth will require truthful answers."

"Ergot, your presence will assist in truthful answers," Paige finished.

Breena showed a sudden nervousness. When her sister in laws first appeared she was under the impression they were here to visit and nothing more. Auntie Alyson had hinted they wanted to visit her for over a week. Breena realized now they had a specific purpose in mind and she dreaded the confrontation. She had been able to avoid her reality for nearly two months. It was time to pay her dues.

"I feel like I walked into the Spanish Inquisition," Father Michael chuckled. He too understood the women's purpose. Father Michael sat back in his chair. He wanted to hear Breena's answers.

"Breena may feel like she is in the middle of it," Twiggy proclaimed and then took Breena's hand. "But we want you to know these questions are only because we love you, Dwayne, and little Dwayne."

Breena gulped hard.

"We'll get directly to the point," Kerry directed as selected spokesperson for the group. "Why didn't you tell Dwayne about little Dwayne?"

"Or any of us?" Audrey threw in. "I could have been with you. We live so close. It's only a train ride away and Uncle Henry visited you quite often."

Breena hedged, "I had my reasons."

"Oh fiddle faddle!" Paige declared. "That is a very poor explanation if I ever heard one. We have reasons, and reasons! We are asking you to give us this reason!"

"That's right Breena," Morning Song added. "No more excuses. Only reasons!"

"You wouldn't understand," Breena evaded.

"Stop it right now," Kerry retorted. "This is your family. This is little Dwayne's family. We demand to know why you didn't tell Dwayne or any of us!"

"I don't feel well," Breena attempted in excuse putting her fingers to her temples.

"If you feign illness you are only prolonging the inevitable," Kerry tsked. "We aren't going away until this is settled."

Brian walked in with a tray of teacups and looked at Breena. He saw she was holding her temple and she looked to him with pleading eyes. "What is it Princess? Are you ill? Should I take you to your room?"

Alyson stood up and walked to Brian. Using her arm as a guide she ordered, "Leave right now Brian. There is nothing wrong with Breena. Not a thing. Go away!"

Brian looked to Father Casey.

"Breena is fine," Michael assured. "Don't worry."

Alyson gently pushed Brian out of the room. "Get the biscuits."

"All Right! All right!" Breena responded. "When I found out I was with child I had received a letter from Dwayne telling me about Deborah. Wheeler."

"I knew it! I knew it," Kerry shrieked. "Somehow I knew that was behind most of this. Didn't Dwayne tell you it was all a hoax? It was to get money out of us so she could marry the real father Tim Miller."

"Dwayne explained all that," Breena sighed. "He also wrote he would never again let a woman use a child to get money from him or leg shackle him."

"Breena, you don't need money," Audrey stated the obvious. "Dwayne is aware of this. He wouldn't think for a moment you would try to use his baby for money."

"But he would think I used little Dwayne to leg shackle him," Breena pouted.

"Of all the nonsense," Kerry chided. "You and he have had a special relationships since you were children! He bought you that pendant you wear. He's stayed in touch with you, idolizes you, worships you, and he even went to college for you. How in the Bloody Hell could you believe he would think you were using his own flesh and blood, his son for marriage?"

"The idiot has wanted to marry you since he was sixteen," Twiggy elaborated. "Ryan told me Dwayne has loved you since that first kiss and my husband would know that."

"That's our childhood," Breena argued. "We are adults and he wrote to me that he would never allow a woman to leg shackle him because of some baby."

"Breena dear," Alyson interrupted. "This isn't some baby. This is Dwayne's son."

"Would he believe me?" Breena questioned nervously. "He didn't believe Deborah Wheeler."

"Of course he didn't believe Deborah Wheeler," Kerry growled. "Tim Miller was the child's father. It wasn't Dwayne's child at all. Dwayne knows little Dwayne is his son."

"Everyone can easily see little Dwayne is his son," Morning Song chirped with agreement. "Can't you see how much he loves his son?"

"And how much he regrets not being able to be a part of his son growing up?" Paige added.

"I think we shouldn't dwell on what might have been," Father Michael added wisely. "I believe we should concentrate right now on what is."

"Father O'Casey is right," Alyson concurred rising to be at Breena's side. She placed her hands upon Breena's shoulder. "The time has come to speak to Dwayne. The two of you must come to grips with the reality of parenting. Little Dwayne deserves both parents."

"But what if Dwayne thinks I am a terrible woman for having a child out of wedlock?" Breena whimpered. "What if he hates me and doesn't want me to be the mother of his child?"

"Damn it!" Paige blurted out. "The man loves you! Are you so blind?"

"Sorry Father," Audrey blushed and apologized for her niece's outburst. "Bloody Hell Breena, it is Dwayne's child!"

"I couldn't have said it better me self," Father Michael grinned wickedly. "Damn it Breena, talk to the lad. Face each other. Face your fear and let Dwayne McGillinen face his."

Brian Duffey came into the dining room with the biscuits. He quietly placed them in the middle of the table in the middle of the sudden silence. He clucked, "Such language coming from such refined women." With that barb Duffey quickly left the room. Even he knew it was about time for Breena to face up to her motherhood and Dwayne McGillinen. He had protected her until she was well. The time had come.

"I'm too scared," Breena choked.

"Breena," Kerry uttered derisively. "I've known you for as long as Dwayne has. I have never known you to back down from anything ever. You have a strong will and a strong mind. Those two things are what Dwayne loves most about you. If he's disappointed with you it is because this isn't you at all. You aren't behaving like the Breena he loves. Frankly you are confusing him and us. This isn't the real you Breena. What has Washington City done to you?"

"Maybe you and Dwayne should come and stay with us at Geneva's Branch until the two of you find each other again," Twiggy suggested. "It seems both the people we know and love are acting rather strangely."

"That's kind of you Twiggy," Breena said quietly with deep appreciation. "All of you are correct. It is about time I stop being such a coward. I used little Dwayne as my excuse for being such a coward. You see all those years I watched the other girls with Dwayne, the pretty girls. He would laugh and tease. He would dance with them. He would eat with them at socials and picnics. He always had his pick of the prettiest girls. I couldn't imagine he would ever be interested in me even though we would spend quiet times fishing, reading, or just walking in the woods. I thought he was just being nice to me."

"If he was simply being nice to you how could you possibly produce a child?" Paige inquired.

"Men use women for physical relief. It isn't necessarily an act of love," Breena stated factually. "I'm aware of this and that night we... I mean when... I mean... Sorry Father. The night we created little Dwayne was love for me but how could I believe it was the same for Dwayne?"

"Forgive me Father for being so blunt but I feel I must," Kerry stated firmly. "I know for a fact that Dwayne always used Dutch rubber protection. I heard my brother's talking about it many times. The brothers usually used the women from the Alley district of Ely. Dwayne was led astray often by girls with loose morals and greedy ideas, he always protected against procreation. Always! The very fact he didn't with you prove how much he loves and trusted you. It sort of reminds me of my Braden. There was no doubt in his mind from the first time we made love that he wanted to marry me."

Morning Song raised her hand to cover her laughter. Kerry was blunt, to the point, honest, and factual. Morning Song appreciated that. So did the other women and even Father Michael nodded his head in approval.

Breena bowed her head. She was ever so grateful for Kerry in being so blunt and even use her own marriage to Braden as an example. "I'm still frightened, but I will speak to Dwayne. You are all right. I must face Dwayne."

"That is marvelous!" Alyson cheered clapping her hands.

"Let's enjoy our tea and biscuits and now indulge in some women talk," Paige cheered.

"Oh I do love women talk," Father Michael teased. "I learn so much I might be able to have an interesting sermon next Sunday."

A baby crying disturbed the chatter for a moment.

"Sam wants to join in," Twiggy beamed.

"May I hold her?" Breena asked. "I haven't met her as yet."

"That's correct," Twiggy bubbled. "Sam, meet your Auntie Breena." Twiggy handed the little bundle in her arms to Breena.

"Oooh, oh yes little one," Breena cooed. "Hello Samantha Alyson McGillinen. You are so pretty. Yes you are."

"Enjoy holding her while you can," Paige teased. "When her Daddy is around no one but him can hold her."

"Is he still like that even after Aurora Blue?" Breena queried holding and coddling little Samantha.

"Worse," the women chimed in unison.

While Breena was holding little Samantha, Father Michael O'Casey pushed the meeting issue. "When will you meet with little Dwayne's father?"

"Perhaps next Sunday," Breena said hesitantly.

"Why not tomorrow?" Kerry asked.

"He is setting up an office with Uncle Henry," Breena excused weakly. "He is going to be busy during the week. Uncle Henry needs him in the new offices."

"Breena, you have run out of excuses," Father O'Casey reprimanded. "You need to face your fears. The sooner. The better!"

"I agree!" all the women chimed in once more.

"Please," Breena pleaded. "I want a little time to think about what and how I am going to say things. This Friday. Is that all right? We'll have a quiet dinner here."

"That's settled then," Audrey urged. She didn't want to force Breena and finally a date had been approved.

The McGillinen women spent the rest of the day with Breena. They toured the house and chatted. It was a wonderful and comfortable day for Breena after all.

At dusk the carriages pulled up in front of Hyacinth House. Ryan was the first one to leap from the carriage and nearly ran to the house. Before he knocked Abel had opened the door and Ryan took advantage. He swooped Twiggy and Samantha up in his arms and carried them out to his carriage. He was kissing Twiggy and Samantha. "Lord I missed you two."

Kerry followed and was surrounded by her sons. Braden lifted her to the carriage and disappeared into it behind her.

Ayden greeted Paige with a kiss and her twins started talking at the same time. Both wanted to tell her about their wonderful day with their father.

Dwayne emerged from Henry Astor's carriage holding little Dwayne. Henry followed him. Audrey walked to her husband as Dwayne put little Dwayne down upon the walkway.

Breena stood near the doorframe where both big and little Dwayne could see her.

Little Dwayne seemed reluctant to leave his father. Big Dwayne knelt next to him, whispered into little Dwayne's ear and gave him a kiss. He had hoped Breena would come out to retrieve their son and was disappointed she didn't. Instead she simply stood at the doorframe and watched her two men.

After his father had whispered to him, little Dwayne nodded and ran to his Mommy. "I wuv you! Daddy wuvs you."

Breena picked up her son and carried him back into the house. She wanted to run into Dwayne's arms and tell him how much she loved him, but was too afraid of the moment. She was emotional and hopeful again. When she spoke with Dwayne she wanted to be completely calm and level headed.

Dwayne sighed heavily and walked back to the carriage. Inside Uncle Henry and Auntie Audrey were waiting. His aunt had an unusually broad smile.

"I have news for you!"

Dwayne sat down on the bench opposite Auntie Audrey in the carriage. "What news? Did everyone have a nice chat?"

"More than a nice chat," Audrey paused allowing a dramatic moment. "Breena has agreed to meet with you for dinner at Hyacinth House this coming Friday."

Dwayne's heart started pounding so hard he hoped his shirt would stay buttoned. "Breena really did?"

Auntie Audrey crossed her chest and heart, "I swear it is true."

"It's about time!" Henry Astor declared. "The two of you need to talk about your future. Your permanent future."

Dwayne leaned back against the carriage walls. Was he dreaming?

Chapter 24

Mattie brought in another outfit for Breena to try on. "Lawsy, yo be as nervous as a cat." This was the fourth outfit Mattie had brought into Breena for tonight's dinner with Dwayne McGillinen. None of them were acceptable for her mistress. Mattie chuckled to her self. It wasn't a point of the outfits were unacceptable. It was her mistress was distressed and taking it out on the clothes.

"Yes, that's better," Breena accepted taking the green brocade evening dress. The décolletage was low but not too low so she wouldn't appear seductive. The flounce around the décolletage was feminine but discreet. The shirtwaist accented her feminine figure. The draped flounces of the skirt also added femininity but still presented a matronly appearance. She didn't admit to herself that green was Dwayne's favorite color. He had told her many times he liked the color green on her. "Look at my hair! It's horrible, it's a mess!"

"That be because yo done changed yo clothes so much," Mattie chided. "Cain't keep yo hair nice when yo be takin clothes on and off."

"Can you fix it before dinner?"

"Missus Hodges, it done be more than two hours befo dinner. I gots plenty of time to take care of yo hair."

"Two hours?" Breena said sitting down on the vanity chair. "I don't think I can survive the wait. You're right Mattie, I am nervous and scared. I've practiced my speech for Dwayne over and over and over again, but I know when I see him I'll forget everything. He does that to me."

"Forgets everythin?" Mattie laughed helping Breena put on the chosen attire. "Yo must be powerful in love with that man if he makes yo forgets everythin."

"Yes, I fear that is my problem," Breena finally confessed. "I love little Dwayne's father to distraction. I've been so afraid if he knew about little Dwayne he'd never speak to me again and I unfortunately do love him with all that I am. That is why little Dwayne is so special to me. His is Dwayne's son."

"It's plain to me he loves his son as much as yo do," Mattie noted buttoning Breena's shirtwaist. "I thinks he loves the boy extra special because yo is his Mama."

Breena turned to look at Mattie and squeezed her hand. "Do you really think so?"

"I does!" Mattie reassured. "I really does. You and little Dwayne's Daddy might tell each other that tonight at dinner."

"Are you certain this dress looks good on me?"

"Missus Hodges, I be absolutely sure! Would yo quit fussin about this? Yo man loves yo and not yo clothes."

"Dinner? What about dinner? Is Aida making everything I requested? Does she know how? The dinner is totally different from what we normally eat," Breena worried fidgeting on the bench as Mattie started to brush her hair. "Should I wear diamonds, the gifts Dwayne sent me? Would I be presumptuous?"

"I thinks yo looks real pretty in diamonds," Mattie commented. "I thinks yo should wear them pretty gifts little Dwayne's Daddy done give yo."

Dwayne was fairing little better than Breena. He was nearly driving Ryan crazy just being near him. "Tell me Ryan, do I look acceptable?"

"Little brother, if you ask me that one more time I'm liable to mess your prissy suit up pretty bad. And quit playing with that tie or I'll hang you with the ugly thing," Ryan threatened. "By the way I bought this box of chocolates for you to take to Breena."

"I don't think Breena likes chocolates," Dwayne stated with uncertainty. "At least I've never seen her eat any."

"All women like chocolates, it's a feminine thing," Ryan scolded. "You don't know nothing do you? Twiggy loves chocolates. Breena will love chocolates. All men bring women something special when courting."

"You didn't bring Twiggy anything special," Dwayne countered defiantly.

"Oh yes he did," Twiggy laughed entering the room carrying Samantha. "The first night we were together on our way to Bright Moon's camp my Ryan brought me chocolate cake. It still is the special treat that takes you right to my heart, and thank you for my box of chocolates sweet husband."

"You bought Twiggy a box of chocolates as well as Breena?" Dwayne teased.

"Of course I did. I love my wife and she loves chocolate!"

"Did you get the rings from the jewelers?" Twiggy queried her nervous brother in law. "If you did can I see them? If you didn't you'd better get them right now. The shop closes in a few minutes."

"Right here!" Dwayne beamed pulling out the velvet box. He opened it to show his sister in law a set of rings. The first ring was a huge diamond in the pear shape cut and faceted to sparkle in even the lowest of lights. It was a simple setting of just the one and half carat diamond on a gold band. The box also contained to simple gold wedding bands. Dwayne pulled out the smaller gold wedding band to show Twiggy the engraving of a small peanut and the words, for *my cherished wife*. "I'm going to have it engraved with our names and wedding date after we are married."

"First you have to make sure she marries you," Ryan cautioned. "I still say Breena deserves better than you but you can't account for tastes. Besides, you have a son and he needs to be raised as a McGillinen. That is your responsibility."

"I have every intention of meeting my obligations, cheerfully!"

"Good!" Ryan warned menacingly. "Now shut up! You're making Twiggy and Samantha nervous."

As Mattie was placing the diamond earring stud in Breena's earlobe Brian Duffey knocked for entrance into her room.

"Enter!"

Payton Lee

"Hello Princess," Duffey greeted and placed a gentle loving kiss on Breena's cheek. He took her arms and looked at her with adoration. "You look every bit the Princess this evening."

"Thank you Uncle Duffey. I have to admit I am nervous."

"You needn't be. It's time this was discussed between you and Dwayne," Duffey suggested. "The reason I came in was to let you know that your Auntie Alyson and I are taking little Dwayne to Washington City Hotel with us for the evening. Since your dinner with Dwayne will be late we don't want to keep him out late and we've decided to take a room for the night at the hotel with the family."

"You won't join us for dinner?" Breena choked in surprise.

"No Princess. You and Dwayne need time and privacy to work this out," Duffey stated firmly. "You take as much time as it takes. Discuss this completely and work it out. You have a son you need to think about. You must decide not only your future, but little Dwayne's future and happiness as well." Duffey said nothing more. He turned and left the room leaving Breena. Duffey collected his wife and great nephew. Soon they were in the carriage and on their way to be with the McGillinen family as Breena and Dwayne worked out their future.

Breena's heart skipped a beat when the knocker in the parlor announced the presence of Dwayne McGillinen. She didn't know that Dwayne's hand was sweating profusely in nervousness of his own. Both had prepared speeches for each other and both realized their brains would be useless when they were with each other. Both were fighting to at least be lucid in conversation.

Abel answered the door and Dwayne entered. He saw Breena and his knees started to buckle. She was beautiful. On her neck was the pendent he gave her four Christmases ago, the diamond choker, and stud earrings. She was wearing a green brocade dress. He loved the color green on her and she knew it. He had told her many times. Could he hope she wore it for him? Awkwardly he handed her a bouquet of roses and a box of chocolates.

Breena smiled broadly. Dwayne was wearing a new linen suit, starched shirt with high collar and tie. He still wore his favorite cowboy boots. Even in the city you couldn't take the country out of Dwayne. When he handed the flowers and bouquet of roses she couldn't help but chuckle. He was so awkward doing it. "Thank you very much. That is most sweet of you."

"You like chocolates?" Dwayne asked skeptically. "I didn't think you did but Ryan said all women like chocolates."

"I eat them on occasion," Breena laughed. "Did Ryan tell you to bring me roses?"

Dwayne bowed his head sheepishly. "No, Ayden told me to give them to you."

"I didn't think you'd be the type to do this. At least you never did before," Breena teased. "You didn't have to do this, but it is a nice gesture."

"I'm a give Peanut diamonds kind of guy," Dwayne grinned. "Diamonds for you are more my style."

"I'm wearing them."

"I know." Dwayne breathed sensually. "You give them their beauty." He walked over to her and bent down to kiss her lips.

Quickly Breena stepped aside. If she allowed Dwayne to kiss her she wouldn't be able to think or say what she needed to say. "Not yet, Dwayne. There is so much between us."

"I'm sorry."

"Dinner is served," Breena informed. "We'll eat and discuss things over dinner."

"Whatever you say, Peanut." Dwayne replied offering his arm to escort her to the formal dining room. He pulled out her chair and she allowed him to seat her. The temptation was too great, he brushed his lips across the nape of her neck and she shivered.

Abel brought in the first course. It was beef vegetable soup, Dwayne's favorite.

"Peanut, I'm not going to waste time with small talk. I will be to the point. I want an honest and truthful answer. Why didn't you ever tell me about being enceinte with my child and the birth of my son?"

"I've been asked that so many times. I'm not certain of the answer myself."

"Kerry railed me for a letter telling you about Deborah Wheeler. She told me it was my stupid fault. I made you believe that I wouldn't marry you if you were in the family way." He leaned over his bowl of soup and squeezed Breena's hand. "Peanut, can you forgive me? I only told you about Deborah because I felt I could tell you anything. If this is what prevented me about knowing about you and my son, I could only beg your forgiveness and hate myself for it."

"Dwayne, as I've said I've come to realize I'm not certain why I didn't tell you. I can only explain my emotions. I have adored you since childhood. When you told me about Deborah I had no idea I was with child. I sent a letter back to you in agreement. It is wrong of a woman to use a child against a man. When we made love on Christmas I took that chance and I would face the responsibility for it."

A tear threatened to spill from Dwayne's eyes. He applied more pressure on her hand. "When we made love on Christmas that is what it was, love. I risked the same chance and should have faced the same responsibility."

"I am like a schoolgirl when I'm around you," Breena confessed. "I was so afraid if you found out about little Dwayne you would hate me and I'd never see or hear from you again and that thought terrified me. I can't stop my feelings for you."

"Does it matter that when I'm around you I'm a tongue tied school kid myself? When I'm around you I get terrified that I'll say or do something stupid and you won't want to see me anymore. I've always felt inferior to you. That's why I decided to go to college and hope you could accept me as an equal."

"You really went to college to impress me?" Breena beamed.

Seeing the light in her eyes was the indication for Dwayne to push forward on his quest. "Yes I really went to college to impress you. I even volunteered to be the manager of Uncle Henry's new investment office here in Washington City so we could get married and stay here. I knew you wouldn't want to leave your home and life here. I would give up Geneva's Hope for you."

"But why?" Breena asked not believing she was hearing. She was wondering if she should pinch herself to see if she was dreaming.

"I love you! I loved you since our first kiss when I was sixteen and you were fourteen. Remember we kissed at the pond? I promised myself then I would work hard to make you proud of me and then we would get married."

Abel came in and removed the soup bowls. He noticed only a little of the soup had been touched. Behind him Aida brought in the main course. Steak, boiled potatoes, carrots, and fresh baked bread was placed before the two at the table. Aida left swiftly after serving.

Breena couldn't believe what she had heard. A whisper barely left her lips, "Why didn't you ever tell me you loved me? Why didn't you ask me to marry you?"

Dwayne had taken a sip of wine to calm his nerves and nearly choked. "I told you I loved you in every letter. I told you after we made love. I did ask you to marry me Christmas day."

"Dwayne, you never asked to marry me Christmas Day. You merely asked me to wait for you until you returned from college. That is hardly a marriage proposal. I don't recall you ever telling me you loved me, ever! As for your letters you never said I love you."

"Peanut, I signed every letter *Love Dwayne*. Didn't I"

"That is a grammatical closing, Dwayne. It does not necessarily imply the emotion," Breena corrected.

"Damn it! There you go again correcting me. This time I won't stand for it. When I sign *Love Dwayne*, I mean **LOVE!** Maybe you don't remember my telling you how much I loved you after we made love because you always fall asleep right after we do! As for marriage proposals, well the heart locket is a betrothal gift and asking you to wait for me means wait to marry me," Dwayne replied with full force and a determination in will Breena had never seen in him before.

"Dwayne, keep your voice lowered," Breena giggled. "The servants."

"Damn the servants!" Dwayne bellowed. "If I haven't done this right before I will damn well do it right this time. Peanut, I love you with all that I am. I love you with my heart, body, mind, and soul. *I love you.* *I LOVE YOU.* I'll shout it from the highest mountain." Dwayne pulled a box from his pocket. He dropped on one knee and gently took Breena's hand. He slipped the diamond engagement ring on her finger and stated in great emotion, "Peanut, will you marry me? Please say yes. Please be my wife and mother of all my children."

Breena couldn't breathe. She was so happy. She couldn't remember being this happy in her life. She loved Dwayne McGillinen nearly all her life and never hoped he could love her in the same way. Today she found out he loved her. Today she found out he wanted to marry her. Today he asked her to be his wife. She giggled nervously. He had been as afraid of her as she had been of him. They were both silly children.

"Peanut," Dwayne warned. "Don't laugh at me!"

"My darling," Breena expelled breathing at last. "I would be honored to marry you and be the mother of our children. It seems we are even a bit ahead in that schedule."

Dwayne jumped up pulling Breena to his strong muscular frame. "You mean it? You will marry me?"

"How could I turn down such a proposal? Especially to a man who would give up Geneva's Hope to live with me in Hyacinth House?" Breena answered with questions of love, hope, and joy. "How could I turn down the proposal of my son's father?"

"Our son!" Dwayne corrected.

"Oh dear, such an equal," Breena breathed seductively. "Now you are correcting me."

Their eyes locked and their lips met. Dwayne's grip on Breena tightened. He pulled her into his body as if to encase her form into him forever. His lips danced on hers. He laved her neck and returned to a deep and passionate delving probe into her mouth. "Peanut, you have made me a very happy man. You could make me happier by telling me you love me. You've never said you love me."

"I haven't?" Breena asked dreamily into a near swoon.

"Uh Uh!" Dwayne replied returning to his onslaught of passionate kissing. "You do love me don't you?"

"Uh huh," Breena murmured. "So very much."

The two were interrupted when Linc waddled into the room. It was then Breena and Dwayne realized Mattie, Jonathan, Kate O'Casey, Aida, and Abel had been eavesdropping.

Mattie apologized quickly, "We all be sorry Missus Hodges. We just be a prayin yo and yo man would jump the broom. We all like little Dwayne's Daddy and yo two belongs together. We forgots to keep an eye on our little Linc."

"That's perfectly all right," Dwayne forgave. "I have witnesses to Peanut's acceptance. She can't back out on me. "

Boldly Aida asked, "When yo two gonna jump the broom?"

"Tomorrow morning," Dwayne answered without thought. It had been his plan all along. "We'll go to St. Jerome's tomorrow morning and have Father O'Casey marry us."

"We can't!" Breena choked in surprise. "What about the family? The license?"

"Our family, including your Uncle Brian, knows our plans. That's why Auntie Alyson and Uncle Brian are spending the night in my hotel suite," Dwayne informed his future bride. "I have the license and our wedding bands. The only thing that would have stopped this was if you said no. Then my family planned on coming here tomorrow and knocking some sense into that stubborn but intelligent brain of yours."

"Dwayne, this is so sudden, so fast."

"So right and long overdue," Dwayne corrected once more cheerfully.

"Will I get used to you correcting me?" Breena laughed hugging Dwayne.

"We'll have a lifetime to find out," Dwayne answered touching his lips upon her brow.

"Jonathan, can you take me to the rectory? I must tell Michael!" Kate oozed in happiness.

"Yas'm, I be more than happy too!" Jonathan grinned. "Wants to go for a ride?" Jonathan asked reaching for his son.

"Now that's all taken care of," Aida ordered. "You two might eat this special supper."

"I did notice it is all my favorite foods," Dwayne teased Aida. "Peanut didn't happen to tell you they were so you could impress me?"

"Jest eat!" Aida grinned sheepishly. "My Abel and I be mighty tired and we jest might needs to get to bed early tonight."

Breena and Dwayne understood Aida's meaning and smiled. He pulled out Breena's chair and seated her. "I am hungry. Can I expect apple pie for desert?"

Payton Lee

"I think you might expect it," Breena concurred.

Dwayne ate his dinner and desert but couldn't stop staring at Breena. At last she would be his legally married wife. Everything was at last perfect. Everything was as he wished it to be. He even had a son to boot.

After the meal they walked to the parlor. Breena offered Dwayne a brandy and she poured herself a glass of sherry.

"If Auntie Alyson and Uncle Brian are using your hotel suite, where will you sleep tonight," Breena asked in simple conversation.

"With you," Dwayne clucked wickedly.

Breena choked on her sherry and spat out nearly half of it. "What will my people think? The family? The neighbors?"

"I'm your returned dead husband to them," Dwayne reminded mischievously. "My family knows I plan on spending the night here. Ryan thought it would take me all night to convince an intelligent woman like you to marry a stupid man like me. I think they even have bets going as to how long it will take me to persuade you."

"Who do you think will win?" Breena snickered. She actually liked the idea of once more spending the night in Dwayne's arms. It suddenly struck her that from now on she would spend almost every one of her nights in his arms. The thought made her quite happy and at that moment didn't care what people may think.

"I think Paige or Uncle Henry," Dwayne mused. "They were the only two that had faith in both of us."

Chapter 25

Breena sipped at her sherry and sat down on the divan next to Dwayne. "For this to work it will take faith in each other."

Dwayne took the glass from her hand. He placed both glasses on the table. Previously he had removed his jacket and tie. He had already unbuttoned the top to his starchy shirt. Turning he drew Breena into his arms and began his invasion on her being. Dwayne started with teasing little kisses on her lips. His hands dipped into her décolletage and toyed with his cherished toys that belonged only to his Peanut.

Breena opened her mouth to his kisses. While his hands roamed, Breena's hands finished unbuttoning his shirt. Her hands meandered slowly across his bare back. She inhaled his scent deeply and relished the aroma. He smelled of leather and sandalwood. Breena felt Dwayne's muscles tense at her touch that gave her much pleasure. She was affecting him as he affected her. His hand burned her wherever he touched. Breena felt her heart pounding and her breathing erratic.

Dwayne savored Breena's breasts as he laved her cleavage with his tongue. His hands unbuttoned the top of her shirtwaist allowing access to her breasts. He pulled down her shirtwaist and tugged at the corset and chemise. At least he freed the captive toys. His mouth descended quickly upon the hardened nipples and suckled.

Breena arched her back allowing Dwayne full access to her. A charge flashed through her body sending heated electricity bolts. She loved the physical feelings Dwayne aroused in her. He would bring her to physical orgasm many times before he would lead her into euphoria. She felt her skirt rising and Dwayne's hand seeking the slit of her broderie where her quim was hidden.

Dwayne found her quim and inserted an investigative finger. His Peanut was hot and wet. He felt his male organ swell even more. It was time to bless each other with conjugal benefits. He wished to take Breena in the bedroom, not in the parlor where servants would find things. Never allowing his lips to leave some point on Breena's body he lifted her in his arms and carried her to the hall, up the stairs, and then into the bedroom. Once in her room he kicked the door shut. Dwayne let Breena slide slowly down his chest. His hands moved quickly removing Breena's gown, broderie, corset, and chemise.

Breena was on fire. She needed Dwayne immediately. Her hands fumbled at his trousers and unbuttoned the fly. Dwayne wiggled and moaned telling her to take his

pants off. Breena gasped when his organ swelled to full length once it was freed. Her hand cupped him and he groaned.

Dwayne backed Breena into the bed. In a flash they were lying upon it and Dwayne mounted her. He felt her wet warmth as he inserted his swelled organ. The greeting of her quim swelled him more. He needed release. Slowly and gently he started needed machinations.

Breena felt him inside her. Dwayne gave her relief at last for her burning desires. She arched her full body into his thrust with synchrony. The pleasure of their lovemaking enfolded her and she felt her body vibrate. A quiet roar of pleasure emitted from her mouth.

Breena's orgasm enveloped Dwayne. He felt her contractions and he released in pulsating ecstasy. "Oh God!" Dwayne howled in his own orgasm. "Oh God! Peanut, what you do to me." His breathing was ragged and heart pounding like civil war drums entering the battlefield. Dwayne slowly lay down next to Breena keeping his elbow on the mattress so he could look down on his Peanut and peruse her womanly loveliness. He watched as her eyes fluttered closed and then open again. "Peanut! Don't you dare fall asleep. I love you! Tell me you love me."

"I love you Dwayne," Breena yawned.

"Why do you always fall asleep after I make love to you?" Dwayne sulked. "Am I such a bore?"

"Hardly!" Breena declared still floating in her euphoric world. "Don't you realize you are so wonderful I'm exhausted?"

"Really?"

"Yes really you big dolt!" Breena giggled followed with another yawn. Her eyes fluttered once more.

Dwayne chuckled and pulled the quilt up over the two of them. He recognized Breena's soft and even breathing. Once more she was asleep. He lay watching Breena for quite some time. Dwayne pulled her into his body. She fit just perfectly. His hands brushed aside errant curls from her forehead. He tucked and re-tucked the quilt around her. His lips brushed her cheeks, her lips, her brow, and her hand that wore his ring. At last Peanut was his and would be his forever. Those thoughts finally comforted him enough to let his body fall into slumber. *Peanut was his forever.*

A soft knocking woke Dwayne up with a start. He looked around and was happy to find Breena was still sound asleep in his arms. He heard the knocking once more. "Who is it?"

"It be me Massah," Mattie replied quietly. "I brought yo and Missus Hodges yo morning meal. Yo needs to wake up and eats so yo can go to the parish today. Father Michael will be waitin fo yo."

"Come in Mattie," Dwayne replied. He whispered quietly to Breena. "Peanut. Peanut. Wake up Peanut."

"Dwayne?" Breena mumbled. "What are you doing here?" Then she woke up with a start.

Dwayne pulled the quilt to cover her exposure when she sat up suddenly. "I'm going to live here. We're getting married today. Remember?" Dwayne chuckled. "That food smells wonderful Mattie. I surely appreciate you and Aida. I want you to know that."

"Thanks," Mattie responded placing the large tray in front of them.

Breena suddenly cupped her hand over her mouth. She ran from the bed stark naked into the toilette room.

"What the Bloody Hell?" Dwayne shouted. He was concerned. Dear God he hoped Breena wasn't going to become ill again. Not on their wedding day. A bit more modest he threw off the covers and grabbed his trousers from the floor. He literally jumped into them and ran to the toilette room. His arms were immediately around Breena. She was kneeling over the water closet retching phlegm. "Peanut? Peanut what's wrong? Do I make you sick?" Dwayne asked worriedly. He found a soft towel and reaching to the sink soaked it with cool water. Gently he applied the wet cloth to Breena's forehead.

Breena turned to face Dwayne. She realized she was naked and started to giggle.

Mattie appeared with Breena's robe and offered it to her mistress.

Still giggling Breena took the robe and dressed. After tying the sash she sat back on her heels. "In a manner of speaking, you do make me sick."

Dwayne's face dropped. His worry turned to complete defeat. His mouth dropped down.

Breena took her hand and gently closed his mouth. "Yesterday morning I went to visit Doctor Whitecliff. He confirmed my suspicions."

Dwayne grabbed Breena and enclosed her in his arms. His chin buried itself in her shoulder. "It doesn't matter. We are together. I don't want to hear it. Just know I love you and we are together. We can get through anything together."

Breena pushed Dwayne away playfully. She was feeling quite devilish at the moment and teased, "You mean to tell me that once again you do not want to know that you are the father of our expected child?"

Dwayne fell on his bottom. His mouth hung open. "Huh?"

"Since I went through symptoms I ignored when carrying little Dwayne, I thought it best to ask Doctor Whitecliff when some of those symptoms began occurring again," Breena taunted. She really was enjoying the look on Dwayne's face. "Yesterday he confirmed that once again I was in the family way."

Dwayne sat there dumbfounded.

"Dammit Dwayne!" Breena growled. "Would you at least say something? Anything?"

"This is wonderful! This is great! This is magnificent!" Dwayne guffawed. "I was wondering how I would approach the subject of a sibling for little Dwayne. You've supplied me with a baby I can watch grow in you. I can be here when the baby is born. Oh this is too wonderful for words. I can't wait to tell everyone!" Dwayne was silent for a minute and then a wide sunbeam streaked across his countenance. "Hey! I'm really damn good. One night with me and we have a baby! How's that for male prowess!"

"You! You egotistical, self centered, pompous…" was as far as Breena got before Dwayne was upon her lips kissing her passionately.

"A fruitful pompous ass," Dwayne finished between kisses. He untied her sash and put his large hand over her abdomen.

"Dwayne, it's too early to tell," Breena informed lovingly.

"Not to me it isn't," Dwayne replied. "It's not to early to tell baby how much Daddy loves little baby! I intend to tell my baby that at least three or four times a day." He leaned over and kissed Breena's belly. "Love you baby!"

"Dwayne, you are being silly," Breena laughed. "Besides, you're stubble tickles."

"You're right! I need to shave and get dressed," Dwayne stated rising to his full height and pulling Breena up to him. "We are getting married today!"

"How about if we eat first," Breena suggested.

"Are you all right about it?" Dwayne asked with concern.

"This is a simple bout," Breena replied. "Now that it's cleared. I'm starved!"

Mattie had remained nearby. "I'll clean up this mess and yo room later. Right now go ahead and eats. I'll prepare yo bath Missus Hodges."

"Did I ever tell you I believe in water conservation?" Dwayne asked deviously.

"What brought that up from no where?" Breena queried in retort.

"I thought we could share the bath," Dwayne offered. "We'll all wash together. You, me, and baby."

"You really are happy about the baby?"

"Delighted! Thrilled!"

Several hours later Dwayne emerged from the carriage and assisted Breena. Father Michael had been expecting them and greeted them when they arrived. "Tis the happiest of news I hear. The two of ya are finally together and ya are making an honest man of little Dwayne's father."

"It is about time isn't it?" Dwayne glowed radiantly. "At last my Peanut is going to be Mrs. Dwayne McGillinen."

"That does make ya happy lad?"

Kate emerged from the carriage. Father O'Casey assisted her. Jonathan tied the horse team to the post and walked up to the couple.

"Beyond words of description!" Dwayne declared happily. "Let's get on with this. I don't want a minute wasted. Kate and Jonathan here are going to be our witnesses if that's alright with the church."

"Two fine Catholic witnesses is very alright with the church," Father Michael agreed. "Didn't ya want any family present?"

"It would take to long to let them know and get here," Dwayne fussed. "I don't want to waste a minute."

Breena stood back and her mouth dropped open. "You told me the family knew about us marrying."

"Peanut, I told you they expected me to convince you to marry me," Dwayne corrected. "They knew I had everything I needed to persuade you. Now that I have your attention I'm not going to waste time letting the family know. We should have been married long ago. Get in the Church!"

"I beg you pardon!" Breena pouted. "Don't order me about like that!"

"Okay I won't," Dwayne answered. His eyes twinkled in absolute joy. He picked Breena up and carried her into the parish. When they were in front of the altar he slid Breena down and held onto her firmly. "You promised me. Let's get married."

Breena shook her head. Somehow Dwayne's caveman tactics delighted her. Today she felt wonderful, special, and she would be Mrs. Dwayne McGillinen. A childhood fantasy had turned into reality.

The marriage ceremony was simple. They exchanged vows and Father Michael O'Casey pronounced them husband and wife. Father Michael was thrilled to officiate at this wedding. He knew this couple was meant to be and would bring happiness to each other and the little parts of the world they touched. He even guessed the Catholic Church might someday benefit. He would be surprised that twenty years later he would be right. Father Michael enjoyed watching the two seal their vows with a kiss that revealed the true love for each other.

"Father, please come to Washington City Hotel with us to celebrate," Dwayne invited. "I want to celebrate this day with my wife and let the family know that at last we are together forever."

"How could a man turn down such an invitation," Father O'Casey replied. "Give me a moment to change my garments." Michael disappeared into the rectory extension of the parish and returned wearing his frock and hat. "Let's go. I'm hoping there be a bit o beer to celebrate."

"You usually don't drink Father O'Casey," Kate reprimanded.

"Usually no. Today yes. Tis a day for celebration."

"You can let go of me now," Breena teased Dwayne. While they waited for Father O'Casey he had kept his arm securely around her body with his hand encircling her waist.

"Not on your life Peanut," Dwayne returned. "I've waited a long time for this and I'm not about to let you further away from me than my arm's length. Especially with the baby."

"Baby?" Father O'Casey quizzed picking up on the words. "Tell me Mrs. McGillinen. Would that husband ya have put ya in the family way again?"

Breena blushed.

"I have!" Dwayne crowed.

"Tis a good Catholic ya are," Father Michael replied in a jocular manner entering the cab.

At the hotel Dwayne opened the carriage door and jumped to the ground before Jonathan had a chance to stop the horses. He opened the door and reaching for Breena lifted her carefully and placed her gently on the walkway. He helped Kate and Father O'Casey. "Jonathan, go back to Hyacinth House and bring, Aida, Abel, Mattie, and Linc. I want all of us to celebrate our wedding day."

"Yassuh," Jonathan responded tipping his hat. "I be right back Massah."

Father Michael and Kate led the way into the hotel lobby.

"Which McGillinen room do you want to go to first?" Kate quipped. She was enjoying watching the newlywed couple entwine each other as they walked into the hotel.

Dwayne looked up. He had been concentrating on Breena. "I think my room. We should announce our marriage to Auntie Alyson and Uncle Duffey first."

"You do that and I'll find the rest of the family," Michael decreed. He headed for the hotel roster to check room numbers. "Come with me Kate. You can help make the announcements."

By the time Dwayne and Breena neared the door to Dwayne's room, Kate and Father Michael were already knocking on Grady and Ryan's door. Ayden and Uncle Henry's door would be next.

Duffey answered the door. He was enjoying his favorite rolled cigars and looked quite handsome in a quilted red smoking jacket. "Breena! Do we have news?"

"Yes Uncle Duffey," Breena replied radiating her happiness. "I have two cannon balls to drop upon you."

"Good News I hope," Duffey responded clearing his throat.

Dwayne walked into the room bringing Breena with him. His arms surrounded her and he bent to kiss her on the nape of her neck as she was trying to remove her bonnet. "We're finally married."

"Married!" Duffey stuttered. "When the Sam Hill did you marry?"

"Father Michael married us this morning," Dwayne beamed pulling Breena into his frame. "May I introduce Mrs. Dwayne McGillinen?"

Alyson was hurt she wasn't invited but at this point it didn't matter. The children were married. "Oh I am so happy for you!" She jumped from her chair to walk briskly by Breena's side and gave her a peck on the cheek. "Isn't that wonderful Brian? Our children are at last married and we have another grandson officially in the family."

"You should have told us," Brian reprimanded sternly. "We should have been there. What is your other cannon ball?"

Breena took several breaths. If her uncle were upset about the wedding, what would he do about the new baby? She hesitated.

"Well?" Brian tapped his foot nervously.

"Dwayne and I are going to have another baby," Breena blurted out

With that news Alyson placed her hand over her heart and found a chair to sit down upon. To everyone's surprise Brian didn't roar angrily. He found Alyson and sat next to her. He found himself gasping for breath in shock.

"Isn't that wonderful?" Dwayne gloated. "Be fruitful and multiply." It never occurred to Dwayne that Breena's pregnancy could be anything but wonderful. He was floating in happiness. He had his Peanut, a son, and an expected baby.

Before Brian or Alyson could recover Paige and Ayden, Morning Song and Grady, Abigail and Adam, and Father Michael surrounded Dwayne and Breena. Soon afterward came Kerry and Braden with their brood of children. Audrey and Uncle Henry who had taken little Dwayne to breakfast with Twiggy, Ryan, Blue and Sam followed them. Little Dwayne and Blue had become inseparable. Everyone was kissing, hugging, and congratulating the newly weds.

Dwayne knelt on one knee and talked to little Dwayne. "Hi son, guess what? Daddy is coming to live with you. We can see each other every day."

Little Dwayne cocked his head to the right and then the left. With a furrowed brow he asked, "Did your work get done?"

Everyone chuckled.

"Yes son, Daddy finally got his work done!" Dwayne lifted his son and embraced him. "We have another surprise for you."

Everyone in the room heard that and stopped talking. They looked at Dwayne.

"How would you like a brother or sister?"

"What's bwother? Sister?"

"Well, that's like Jared or Blue but live in the same place with Mommy and Daddy," Dwayne explained.

The family started looking at each other with bewilderment.

"I wike Bwue! I want a Bwue!" little Dwayne exclaimed excitedly.

"A sister it is! Did you hear that Peanut?" Dwayne grinned happily. "I think I want a daughter so it's unanimous."

"What the blue blazes is going on?" Grady queried.

Morning Song walked to Breena. She placed her hand first on Breena's neck. Then she placed her hand on Breena's belly and laughed. "Our Breena is with child and it is a daughter."

"Hear that Kerry?" Braden whispered to his wife and put his large hand over her swelling belly. "This time we'll both have beautiful daughters."

Chapter 26

"And that is the story of Cougar's Paw learning to be wise from the spotted owl," Dwayne finished. He tucked the covers around his sleeping son and kissed him gently on the cheek. He turned to leave the nursery when he saw Breena leaning against the doorframe. "How long have been there?"

"About half way through your yarn. That's some story," Breena whispered.

"Morning Song used to tell it to us when it was time for bed. We all loved her stories."

"You're a wonderful father," Breena said quietly leaning into Dwayne's hard chest as they walked to the bedroom.

"You should have had faith in me, Breena," Dwayne spoke softly into Breena's hair.

"Will you forgive me for not telling you about little Dwayne?"

Dwayne shut the door behind them. "There is nothing to forgive. You gave me a fine son and now we'll have a beautiful daughter." He led Breena to the bed. "You must forgive me."

"Forgive you?"

"Obviously you never had enough faith in me. It is my hope you now have more faith in your husband." Dwayne gently pushed Breena down on the mattress and placed his lips over hers. He covered her mouth and opened her mouth to the onslaught of his wondering tongue.

Breena's body was instantly on fire. "Husband, I have a lot of faith in you," She moaned between breaths and kisses. "Maybe we can work out a forgiveness program."

"Like forever?" Dwayne breathed hotly. He lifted her nightdress and palmed her still flat belly. "At least I'll be here for our daughter. I can't wait to see you growing fat with my child."

"I'm not sure I'm looking forward to that," Breena retorted and swatted at Dwayne's amorous hands.

"Ah, remember the forever part?" Dwayne teased.

"And you would find a fat woman attractive?" Breena responded once more revealing her insecurity.

"Only as long her name was Mrs. Breena McGillinen." Dwayne began concentrating on his seduction of his wife.

"We're all ready for Sunday mass," Braden announced holding onto Garrett and Jared. "The carriages are outside waiting for us."

"We're missing Ryan," Twiggy noticed. "He and Blue haven't returned from changing Sam."

A loud knock on the door turned all heads.

"Who could that be?" Breena commented. She walked to the door and opened it to find General Gregory Wagner standing at the doorway.

Gregory lunged for Breena and grabbed her wrists. Gregory pulled Breena to him and held up a gun, pointing directly at Dwayne. "Keep away from us. I've had all I'm going to take from you. Breena is coming with me. You were dead and you're going to stay that way."

"Gregory," Breena pleaded. Her breath seemed to choke in her throat.

"Let my wife go," Dwayne said deceptively calm.

Kate had taken little Dwayne into the hall where she was buttoning his shoe. When she heard Gregory's voice she peeked into the parlor. Kate assessed the situation immediately and quickly took little Dwayne upstairs to the nursery with Garrett and Jared. The Wessex boys had followed them into the kitchen hoping for a treat of Aida's cookies and they wanted to see Linc. Fortunately Liberty followed little Dwayne and the boys upstairs.

"Let my wife go," Dwayne said more firmly.

Braden placed his hand on Dwayne's shoulder to prevent him from charging at the General.

"You were a dead man and Breena Hodges is mine. I courted her for four years. She's mine," Gregory hissed waving the colt threateningly at Dwayne. "Then you sashay in here like nothing happened and think you can just go back to the way things were. Well you can't!"

Breena choked out, "Gregory, Dwayne is my husband."

"Your dead husband. For four years I've waited patiently for you. The time has come to leave. You will leave as my wife!"

Braden stepped in front of Kerry and pushed Twiggy behind him. "You don't want to hurt any one General. Put the gun down and we'll talk."

"Just because I don't want to hurt anyone doesn't mean I won't make this husband permanently dead," Gregory growled.

Dwayne stepped forward again.

"No Gregory!" Breena shouted as Gregory cocked the colt aiming at Dwayne. "I'll come with you."

"Where's the boy? I know you won't come without the boy," Gregory demanded to know.

"He's not here. He's with his grandfather waiting for us at St. Jerome's," Breena lied.

"Peanut, don't!" Dwayne pleaded taking a step closer to Gregory.

"One more step and you will be dead," Gregory threatened.

Braden pulled Dwayne back once more.

"If you take my Peanut I will hunt you down," Dwayne snarled with deadly intent.

"It won't matter when Breena is my wife," Gregory laughed. "You can make all the claims you want, but she will be my wife."

"You don't understand," Braden attempted in explanation. "If you force Breena to marry you she would be a bigamist. That's against the law."

"Her husband is dead. Just because he turns up doesn't make him her husband," Gregory chortled.

"In that case you should know that in the eyes of the church, they were remarried yesterday by Father O'Casey in St. Jerome's Parish," Braden offered quietly still shielding his wife and sister in law.

"Is that true Breena?" Gregory asked.

"Yes Gregory," Breena replied. "We were married yesterday."

"Why? Why did you turn me down and marry this .. this .. child?"

"Gregory, I love Dwayne. I'm fond of you, but I could not love you in the way you need a wife to love you," Breena choked out. She was frightened. Her answer may cause him to go crazy or release her.

"I can make you happy, Breena," Gregory pleaded. "Give me a chance."

"She's my wife," Dwayne repeated.

"I can remedy that," Gregory growled angrily. Once more he raised the colt to point directly at Dwayne's heart.

Dwayne stood deathly still in defiance and he stared directly into Gregory Wagner's eyes. Dwayne didn't want to give away his brother, Ryan.

Ryan was directly behind Gregory Wagner. With one swift movement he grabbed Gregory's hand and broke the wrist that held the gun.

Gregory's gun fell harmlessly to the floor.

Dwayne moved quickly to collect it and ran to Breena. He held her in his arms and kissed her several times. "Are you alright? Did he hurt you? Did he hurt baby?"

Breena collapsed into Dwayne's strong arms. "I'm fine. Really. Just hold me."

Dwayne folded her into his massive chest and rested his chin on her head. "I'll hold you as long as you want me." He kissed Breena's hair and rocked her gently.

Gregory Wagner was on his knees holding his broken wrist.

"You came along just in time," Braden chuckled for Ryan. He walked up to Gregory Wagner and offered him a hand up with his good hand.

Twiggy pushed Braden aside and spoke to her big strong husband, "Just where are Blue and Sam?"

"Blue is watching Sam in the cradleboard on the lawn. When I saw this man holding Breena and saw a flash of a gun I thought there might be trouble. I didn't want to take a chance of Blue or Sam getting hurt," Ryan said sheepishly to his obviously upset wife.

"Of course you were right," Twiggy appreciated. She stood on her tiptoes and managed to place a kiss on Ryan's cheek when he bent down a little talking to her. "Take care of this uniformed idiot. I'll get Blue and Sam."

"Where are Jared and Garrett?" Kerry asked with concern.

Aida came from the corner of the hall, "They be jest fine. Missus Kate took all the boys upstairs when she done saw General Wagner threaten Missus Breena."

"Thank heavens," Kerry breathed out in relief. "Braden, you help Ryan take care of this little mess and I'll go upstairs with the boys."

Braden helped General Wagner to his feet and threatened solemnly, "I don't think we'll press charges if you go away and never come back. I think you have learned painfully that when you threaten anyone in our family you will face of all of us. A good General knows a defeat when he sees one."

"If I were you I'd get that wrist checked out," Ryan added cheerfully. "It could just be that it got broken in your fall. Could be that if you don't get it fixed you may never be able to shoot that colt again."

Dwayne handed the colt to Braden. "He lost his gun when he fell."

Braden put the colt in Wagner's left hand. "This would be a good time to leave and never return."

Gregory grunted as he headed for the door, "I did love you Breena."

Breena looked up from Dwayne's chest and replied, "I'm sorry."

"So am I," Gregory answered and walked out the door and out of Breena's life.

Breena shivered slightly in Dwayne's arms. "I'm so sorry."

"You have nothing to apologize for," Dwayne whispered soothingly.

"He could have killed you and it's all my fault," Breena whimpered. "In truth maybe I did lead Gregory on. I shouldn't have allowed him to ever accompany me. In my heart I've always wanted you, but kept him on the side for appearance sake. Not to mention perhaps keep him around to make me feel wanted by someone. Oh my darling, he could have killed you because of my pride."

"You've done nothing to lead him on. After four years and several marriage turndowns, any normal man would have receded into the shadows and sought greener pastures," Dwayne soothed rocking Breena gently in his arms.

Breena looked up into Dwayne's soft gray eyes. "If that's a fact then I'm anything but a normal woman. I've waited for you since I was a child."

"Not the same my Peanut," Dwayne chuckled and hugged Breena even closer. "I've been stupid not to get my ring on your finger sooner. And besides, we've created babies together in our wait."

"It's about time you made our Dwayne an honest man," Ryan remarked. "If he doesn't take care of you proper you let me know and I'll straighten up his thinking."

Twiggy walked in holding Sam's cradleboard and Blue walking in behind her mother.

"Where's Dwayne?" Blue asked her father. "Aren't we going to church?"

"Dwayne's upstairs," Ryan told his daughter. "Why don't you collect all the boys and get them down here. We were held up and if we don't shake a leg we'll be late."

Blue was a streak when she ran up the stairs and brought everyone with her. Little Dwayne was holding her hand when he asked his mother, "I ride with Bwue to mass? I want Bwue. She tell me all about Bwue Pool and camp."

Breena gave Dwayne a pained look. After all they had just been through she was reluctant to let little Dwayne go anywhere without her.

Dwayne grinned and answered little Dwayne, "Yes, you can go in Uncle Ryan's carriage to mass. Uncle Ryan will take good care of you."

Little Dwayne cocked his head and looked up at his tall handsome father. "You be my Daddy? All time? You go away at night?"

Dwayne released Breena and knelt down on one knee to look his son in the eye. He gently took little Dwayne's arms and replied, "Wild horses couldn't pull me away from you and your Mommy. I'll be here every night to tuck you in and hear your

prayers. Your Mommy and I will watch you grow up into a man. You have my promise."

"You wuv Mommy?"

"I love Mommy with my life."

Epilogue

"Wake up," Dwayne whispered into Breena's hair. "Wake up, Peanut."

Breena yawned and stretched her arms out against the soft mattress. "Dwayne? What are you doing still at home?" She turned her head to look at her husband and saw he was fully clothed.

"Kate is getting little Dwayne ready and Mattie fed Katherine for you." Dwayne sat on the side of the bed and pulled Breena up into his arms. "You'd better get ready before I waste more time ravishing you."

"I'm quite satisfied with last night," Breena replied sensually. She bolted from his arms and ran into her dressing room shutting the door behind her.

Dwayne heard her giggling and chuckled. He left the bedroom to walk to the nursery.

Mattie had changed Katherine and dressed her in a warm woolen outfit. She was just tying a woolen cap on Katherine's head when Dwayne walked in.

Dwayne took a woolen blanket from the dressing table and picked up his three-month-old daughter. "Good morning, Princess. Do you have a smile for Daddy?"

Katherine's eyes focused on the face and the familiar voice. She began kicking her legs in delight and gurgled happily in response.

"That's my little girl," Dwayne boasted proudly. He couldn't remember being happier in his life the day little Katherine was born. He was there for her birth and everyday since. He admitted to himself he loved being a father. "We're going for a carriage ride today. You, me, mommy, and your brother."

"Yo still ain't told us where we is going," Mattie mumbled.

"It's a secret surprise," Dwayne bubbled. He wrapped Katherine in the woolen blanket. "You just make sure Linc is ready to go with us."

"My Jonathan done got the carriage ready jest like yo asked," Mattie answered walking toward the stairs to get little Linc from his grandmother.

"Good," Dwayne acknowledged kissing Katherine on her cheeks."

Kate walked in holding little Dwayne's hand. He was fully dressed for an outing and so was Kate.

"Where we going, Daddy?" Dwayne squealed while running to his father's side.

"It's a surprise, son."

"Katty coming too?" Dwayne asked.

"Yes, we're all going together," Dwayne told his son. "Let's go downstairs and wait for Mommy. She was a sleepy head this morning."

An hour later Breena walked down the stairs. In the parlor everyone was waiting for her. She looked about to see Mattie and Lincoln dressed for an outing. "Where are we going?"

Dwayne didn't reply. Instead he asked, "Did you eat breakfast? We left a tray for you in your room. We'll be riding until about lunch time."

"Yes," Breena replied taking her cape from Abel. "Dwayne Sean McGillinen! Where are we going? You've been up to something this entire week."

"Indeed I have!" Dwayne opened the front door. "Let's get going."

"Where are we going?" Breena insisted stamping her foot irritably.

"For a ride in the country," Dwayne chuckled.

"On a Friday?"

"For the weekend!"

"Dwayne, you're up to something."

"Indeed I am," Dwayne chuckled cuddling his baby daughter closer in his arms.

Breena remained silent as the carriage made its way through the streets of Washington City. When the carriage headed toward the bridge to Virginia she questioned once more, "Dwayne, what is going on?"

"Remember I told you I had a surprise visit from attorneys on Monday?"

"Yes."

"Well, those were attorneys from Cecil Mann's estate. It seems Everett Mann's mother died two years ago and his father died last year. You remember about Everett Mann?"

"Yes, he died in a duel that happened in Russia," Breena answered. "Why on earth did they come to your office?"

"Uncle Henry sent them after they talked to him. It seems Cecil Mann's estate would be given to his silent partner, or holder of the partnership since he had no living relatives to inherit."

"I still don't understand?"

"Well Peanut, grandfather Stuart was that silent partner and in his will he left that partnership to my mother. She willed the partnership to be equally divided with all of her living children," Dwayne went on to explain. "Uncle Henry has been working with me, Ayden, Ryan, and Kerry. We've split the Mann estate fairly equally."

"Alright, we are on our way to Virginia. What does Mann's estate have to do with us?"

"Peanut, remember when you were a little girl in Ely? Remember you said your dream was to grow up and have a magnificent horse ranch?" Dwayne said playing with Katherine's finger.

"Yes, I remember my childhood dream."

"Well Peanut, your dream is about to happen because that is exactly what our share of Mann's estate is. We inherited his Virginia Horse Ranch, the Lady M Ranch."

"What?" Breena gasped.

"We get lots of ponies and horses," little Dwayne interjected. "Daddy told me."

Breena turned her attention to little Dwayne. "When did Daddy tell you this?"

"Last night," little Dwayne replied innocently. "He told me all about our ranch after prayers and he tucked me in."

They road in silence once again until Dwayne picked Katherine up and declared, "Look Katherine! Look and see your new home!"

Breena strained to look and her mouth dropped. "My God! It's a palace! It must be as big as Geneva's Hope!"

"Actually it's bigger!" Dwayne laughed. "Wait till you see the stables!"

"Look at your new home Mattie and Linc. Do you like it?"

"But what about my position in Washington?" Breena asked.

"You know very well that your senator is going to retire after this term," Dwayne reminded his wife. "I know you could find work, but now I want you to have your dreams come true."

"They already have, my love," Breena said hugging her husband.

"Mine too!" Dwayne agreed kissing his Peanut and then his daughter. "Mine too!"

Payton Lee

The McGillinen Family Series:

"Geneva's Hope" Book one – The love story of Braden and Kerry Wessex.

"Geneva's Branch" Book two The love story of Ryan and Twiggy McGillinen.

"Geneva's Return" Book three The love story of Ayden and Paige McGillinen.

"Geneva's Promise" Book four The love story of Dwayne and Breena McGillinen.

"Geneva's Force" Book five The story of Aurora Blue McGillinen, daughter of Ryan and Twiggy McGillinen. It is her love story. Brock Hampton raised in the Orient meets and falls in love with Blue. It is the story of spirituality and power in the forces of love.

"Geneva's Legacy" This will be book six. It is the story of Grady and Ashley McGillinen. Who are the parents of Ayden, Ryan, Dwayne, and Kerry McGillinen. It is the story of a dream, a ranch, and family built with devotion and love.

Also read Payton Lee's other Historical Romance Novels.
"Smitten", " Bear River Spirit" ,"Conquer my Heart", "Firedrake of Cumberland", "Five Star Affair", "The Outsider", and coming soon **"Novo Arkhangel'sk".**